Joss Kingsnorth was born and [illegible] Dorset, and trained as a painter at Bournemouth College of Art. She has taught at various schools in England and Switzerland, but gave up painting to become a writer when she won the South West Arts Short Story Prize. THE JOURNEY IN is Joss Kingsnorth's first novel. She now lives in Devon.

The Journey In

Joss Kingsnorth

First published in 1994
by HEADLINE BOOK PUBLISHING

First published in paperback in 1994
by HEADLINE BOOK PUBLISHING

A HEADLINE REVIEW paperback

10 9 8 7 6 5 4 3 2 1

ISBN 0 7472 4560 6

Printed and bound in Great Britain by
Cox & Wyman Ltd, Reading, Berks

HEADLINE BOOK PUBLISHING
A division of Hodder Headline PLC
338 Euston Road
London NW1 3BH

To Jessica and Willow

'Many women artists in our own day are journeying inward, away from inherited statement to an inner truth, as Gwen John did, to the point where all posture and surface appeal is bleached away . . . to the deadening pull toward passivity is added the pressure of politics which would drag the artist in another direction until her soul lies dismembered.'

Germain Greer – *The Obstacle Race*

PART ONE

CHAPTER ONE

It couldn't have happened at a worse time and it couldn't have happened in a worse place. Shocking and disillusioning experiences of this kind are best made in private. It was a Damascus road in reverse; sight restored instead of sight lost, with the proviso that not all revelations are either miraculous or welcome.

After a discovery like this there was not much hope that she would be able to join in the general approbation as she would normally have done; she didn't know what was wrong except that something was, and the truth of it was so conspicuous and so shocking that her first thought was that it must be apparent to everyone in the room.

As always, she was quite prepared to allow that her husband's paintings were stylish, cryptic and sophisticated. These new additions were certainly no worse than any of his preceding work, indeed they were already being lavishly praised as achieving new heights.

She had never before doubted his brilliance, his near genius, but now that she had penetrated the facade she would never again take him seriously. All she could see now was an embarrassing and meretricious display of the spurious, a parade of the utterly bogus, devoid of any meaning or emotion whatever and, almost worst of all dull. Dull, dull, dull.

But who was she to criticise? This was not the first shocking discovery she had recently made; the glaring imperfections of her own painting were already all too fresh in her mind. Why else had she done no work for weeks? Now this new and merciless clarity of vision that could X-ray through the trickiest layers of paint had turned on Robert's celebrated canvases and revealed them as so much hocus pocus.

If only the bombshell had hit her at any time other than at this much-heralded opening of her husband's new exhibition. Their agent, Eustace, had worked hard to ensure that the event was even more high-powered than usual, firstly because there was so much riding on it and secondly because of the current (but temporary,

Eustace said), uncertainty in the market, which Eustace believed in meeting head on.

As it happened, most of the work had already been sold so although Robert would still worry about reviews they could not be said to be crucial to his present success, only his future reputation.

The vast paintings, lit by strategically placed spots, loomed vertiginously overhead. There was no doubt that on first sight they were massively impressive, not for their size alone but because of a certain dark and brooding presence. Critics were disarmed by Robert's way with pellucid veils of paint, much had been written about the wizardry of his technique. The great soft-edged squares and rectangles of grey seemed to hang ambiguously either on the surface of or just in front of a kind of subfusc gloom; each had somewhere on its edge the appearance of the smallest rend or tear, like an unravelling; this had become something of a trademark. Variations on this theme had occupied Robert for the past six years. They were grouped under titles such as 'Disjunction', 'Scission' or 'Fracture', usually with 'I', 'II' or 'III' after them in Roman numerals, for there were endless possibilities just in the titles. Critics had been known to write pages on the subject of these illusory tears and what they imagined to be the philosophy underlying them.

In his overwrought introduction to the glossy new catalogue, Kurt Sagar claimed that they stood as symbols of Robert's compassion for Modern Man's predicament and increasing dissolution of mind and spirit.

To Hester they were simply monuments to Robert's infinite capacity for detachment: cool, cerebral, even she now saw, with a potential for a kind of passionless cruelty, if anything that exciting could be attributed to them. The harshness of this inner comment shocked her, leaving her stunned at the level of betrayal it implied. Poor Robert. The merest breath of such a comprehensive critique, coming from her, would blow him away, for was it not her role to support and encourage her husband, not annihilate him? Making a colossal effort she endeavoured to smother these treacherous thoughts.

She had once enjoyed these social occasions but for some time now they had lost their charm. This evening it was more of a strain than usual. She was becoming gradually less aware of the crowd that surrounded her. Dozens of voices were blending into a hollow rushing like the sound of the sea inside a cave. She had a horrible feeling that she was about to faint, which was something she had hardly ever done.

Alice's face seemed to swim up from nowhere. From the past perhaps.

She spoke with an effort. 'Alice! You came!'

For the past half hour Alice had been making her way valiantly around the exhibition, exchanging conversation with whoever took her fancy. She was not a shy woman. Nevertheless this would have to be absolutely the last time she attended one of these junkets, even for Hester's sake. It was getting to be too much, quite apart from the fact that it 'as not a good time to leave the shop, though she had no complaints about Paul as a perfectly adequate stand-in. These events had changed out of all recognition since the early, more innocent, days and now seemed to be little more than publicity stunts for the press.

She grabbed a glass from a passing flunkey and, having at last found the chair that had been specially placed for her on Hester's orders, sat gratefully while juggling with stick and glass. Her handbag was slung bandolier fashion across her chest. Un-chic but convenient. Bloody hip! She was only forty-five and hobbling about like a centenarian, whilst hip troubie didn't seem to afflict other people until they were at least in their seventies.

The sparkling white wine that passed for champagne was losing its fizz but she drank it all the same. Probably they reserved the real stuff for the VIPs. Alcohol was bad for her of course, as was almost everything she enjoyed, but lately she had allowed herself a few indulgences, making the most of one of the infrequent periods when she was almost free from pain. Almost. She looked about for Hester.

She caught sight of her friend at last through the press of scented bodies, her view half obsc ured by a red-faced man in a well-filled suit talking to Melanie Sofford, which might well account for his apoplectic complexion. Melanie of the multi-coloured knitted hat and dirty lace petticoat, whose art consisted of framed sanitary towels arranged in rows. Probably invited by Hester, certainly not by Eustace or Robert.

As always, the first thing one noticed about Hester was her striking profile, like a Sioux warrior, with the single thick braid that hung, black and shiny as liquorice, down her back. In her ears were the usual slightly barbaric looking earrings, probably bought in Mexico or some other exotic place. These and a single silver ring the size of a knuckle duster were her only adornments. Always spare of frame she seemed thinner, almost gaunt. But that was only to be expected, Alice supposed, after her recent illness.

It occurred to he that there was something odd about Hester's immobility. A tenseness in her posture that suggested someone bracing themself against attack.

She was standing in front of one of Robert's paintings as if she had never clapped eyes on it before instead of having watched it take shape from the very beginning, as she most certainly had. She gave the impression that she was alone with the giant canvas, blind to the crowd and deaf to the emollient drizzle of superlatives that charged the air. Also, Alice noticed, she was as white as the walls of the gallery.

She launched herself back into the crowd in Hester's direction. Hester turned to her.

'Alice! You came!'

Alice kissed her. 'As you see, still just about mobile. Loyal as a Labrador, that's me.' Her voice had just a trace of a Devon burr. At close quarters she scrutinised Hester again. 'And you look bloody awful. Let's get out of this mob and find some fresh air, if such a thing exists between these hallowed walls.'

As they made their way towards the office which was situated at the back of the gallery, Hester saw Robert across the room. His head turned in her direction momentarily, sending her a slightly puzzled, interrogative glance. His need for her was evident in that one small gesture. At any other time she would have sent him an answering signal of reassurance, a look, a smile; but her guilt over her damning reaction to his exhibition, coupled with the feeling that she was about to be rather ill, prevented her. His dependence at a moment like this triggered a sudden acute stab of irritation.

At the door of the office Alice waylaid a young waiter and sent him off for a glass of water.

'And bloody quick!' she ordered.

In the cramped space of the office Alice thrust Hester into the only available chair and, disrespectfully heaving aside a pile of shiny new catalogues, hitched her bottom on to the corner of the desk. The tray bearer returned promptly with a glass of iced tonic.

Alice put it into Hester's hand. 'Typical. You can't even get the real stuff in these high-class joints. Drink it anyway, sweetie.'

Hester drank, then lowered her head. The mist of unconsciousness receded. She would not after all make a fool of herself. She took a deep breath.

'I'm sure you'll tell me to mind my own bloody business,' Alice said drily, 'but don't you think it's a bit soon to be hawking around the circuit like this?'

'I'm not hawking round the circuit. It's just that this evening happens to be very important to Robert. Anyway, I had no reason to think that I wouldn't be all right.'

'What's Robert's opinion?'

'It's what he's been working towards for the past three years. Four nearly.'

'Not this, you fool!' Alice waved a plump arm in the direction of the gallery. 'I mean the pregnancy. The miscarriage.'

Hester let out a gruff laugh.

'Don't!' she said. 'He was madly embarrassed, it goes without saying. And relieved as hell when it all went wrong.'

'Yes, I suppose he would be.' Alice made an attempt to conceal an edge of malice. The two women had known each other since they had been at art school, Hester a painter and Alice a printmaker. Alice had been attracted to Hester's boldness and the aura of drama that surrounded her. Hester liked Alice's humour in the face of her frequently unsuccessful love affairs, her ability to pounce on the nub of any issue and the way she spoke her mind. But Hester's marriage to Robert was one topic on which Alice kept her own counsel. Hester was quite aware of Alice's antipathy to her husband and it was a subject, the only one, over which they both felt the necessity to tread warily.

'Another infant at this stage in our careers,' Hester said, 'Can you imagine it? Amy will be twenty-one this year, for heaven's sake! And can you really see me making feeds and washing nappies with one hand and painting with the other? I did it once, but now . . .!'

'Washing nappies indeed! Yes, perhaps you are just a bit out of touch.' Alice threaded her fingers through rows of ethnic beads. The finger joints were lumpy. 'So you're not too disappointed about the baby?'

'Disappointed? God, no! It was one of those accidents. One tends to get a bit careless eventually and think it can't happen at our age.'

'You know what they say about these so-called accidents,' Alice said.

'I'm not broody, for heaven's sake!'

'No?'

'No. Anyway, never mind that. How are you? Have you been given a date for the op yet?'

Alice shook her head. 'It's like waiting for Godot, only more painful.'

'Is it very bad?'

'Touch wood, it's letting up a bit lately. On the scale of one to ten, it's about three at the moment which is why I decided to come up.'

'I'm so glad you did. What d'you think of it?'

Alice was cagey.

'They're very clever, of course. They always are. And very . . . well . . . big, aren't they?'

'And, how would you put it . . . meaningful?' Hester insisted.

'Good heavens! Don't ask me. Ask Kurt Sagar. He's the expert and he thinks highly of them.'

'Balls, Alice. Since when have you ever listened to what experts say.'

Alice's round face looked mischievous, an effect somehow enhanced by her halo of blonde frizzy hair.

Hester glanced through the open door into the gallery beyond.

'I feel like the small boy,' she said, 'in the story about the Emperor's new clothes. Nothing seems to make sense. I can't go into it now. I'm still feeling a bit shattered by it.'

'Look, my girl. You should think very seriously about taking a Sabbatical. A holiday is what you need. You've been working too hard. First your mother's death, then the miscarriage, and still you go on flogging yourself as if nothing had happened. For God's sake, come back with me to Coombe Ferrers and let me spoil you for a bit.'

'It should be the other way round, if anything.'

'I'm obviously managing better than you are by the look of things. Why don't you come?'

'It just doesn't seem possible at the moment.'

'Surely Robert doesn't need you now the exhibition is up and running. He must know you're desperately in need of a break.'

In the gallery Robert was standing next to Eustace and Gozo. They were with the chairman of a Japanese insurance firm and his advisers. Robert was hunched in characteristic pose with one arm across his chest supporting an elbow, chin balanced between finger and thumb. A listening attitude. A protective attitude.

He was as always elegantly dressed. Navy blue polo-necked cashmere under a loosely tailored Armani suit. His hair had once been an undistinguished dark blond but now a few streaks of silvery grey made him appear altogether more dignified. His head was narrow, his features refined, with eyes always half shielded by well-defined eyelids which lent him an appearance of inscrutability.

Not unusually Eustace was holding forth. Robert was nodding cogitatively and both Eustace and Gozo and the others in the group turned to him, waiting for his views as people tended to do. There was a restrained gravitas about Robert that had the effect of endowing his least pronouncement with a weight that it did not always or necessarily deserve.

As if aware of being watched he looked up, then detached himself and came over. He stood in the office doorway, shaking hands formally with Alice. He was not one for demonstrative kissing. Besides, Alice thought, after all these years he almost certainly sensed her antipathy towards him.

'I was trying to persuade Hester to take a break,' she said. 'But brick walls make better listeners. How about it, sweetie? Are you coming back with me or not?'

'It's an excellent idea,' Robert said.

Hester shook her head. 'Alice, I haven't the energy.'

'Well, that's something new. Have it your own way, you stubborn woman. Now listen, Robert, congratulations. Your show seems to have drawn the crowds. And I see most of it is already spoken for.'

He inclined his head. 'Thank you, Alice. Unfortunately, large crowds are more indicative of the fact that there are fewer rival attractions than usual. However, as you say, most of the work is in fact sold.'

Pedantic so and so, Alice thought, watching him. There he was, a study in introspection, chin in hand, doing his condescending act. Both he and Hester had strong hands, beautiful in their way, characterised by the crackle of immoveable paint in the fine creases and their worn-down nails, and, in Robert's case, by the sepia stains of nicotine between his fingers. Alice was struck afresh by the penetrating quality of the pale eyes and by a sort of defensive blankness that seemed set on giving nothing away. She speculated again on this apparently unlikely partnership. She was quite prepared to accept that there was something about Robert that evoked a powerful response in Hester; perhaps it was the sheer intensity of his need, albeit skilfully concealed from the world at large, of a woman of Hester's strength and courage. His undoubted fineness of mind and his commitment to his art would also weigh heavily in his favour. Yes, it had to make sense. Many marriages she knew of, and which were to all appearances perfectly sound, were built on flimsier foundations than those.

Hester was a warm-blooded woman whose friendship was not

easily won but, once given, was constant as the sea, so perhaps she continued to stick to Robert out of loyalty, or habit. She might even still love him. The uncharitable might point out that a parting of the ways would be tempting Providence and bring about a fatal disruption in their two brilliantly successful careers.

'Now, about Alice's offer, Hester,' he was saying, 'you should think about it. We'll discuss it later.' Then, dismissing the subject, 'By the way, Eustace wants you to meet the Hirschs if Alice can spare you for a moment.'

Neither woman mentioned Hester's momentary faintness. Robert appeared to attribute their withdrawal to the office to Alice's hip problems.

'That's settled then,' Alice said. 'As soon as this shindig's over, you're coming back with me.'

Images of the little estuary town of Coombe Ferrers fell into Hester's mind, filling her with a distant and impossible longing, for it had ceased to be a part of her life, although it was no more than ninety miles from Bristol where she and Robert now lived. It was scarcely ten miles from where she herself had lived from the age of thirteen, and where her mother had continued to live until eighteen months ago. She had always promised herself that she would spend more time with her mother but somehow or other her career had turned out to be too demanding. In any case, Inez had been an energetic sixty-five year old and could have been assumed to have many years to go. Plenty of time. Yet Hester's last visit had been to attend her mother's funeral. It had coincided with the opening of her own one-woman show.

'Hester.' Robert controlled his irritation. It was gravely exacerbated by nicotine deprivation, for no smoking was allowed in the gallery. 'Are you coming?'

Alice elected to stay where she was.

'You'll be talking business. I'll see you later.'

Hester, unable to shake off her troubled mood completely, went to join Eustace and Gozo.

'Ahhh!' Eustace roared in greeting. His huge presence and expansive gestures overwhelmed like a giant comber. 'We thought we'd lost you.'

He stabbed an unlit cigar in the direction of the tall American financier and his wife who stood a few yards away in conversation with Eustace's partner, Bruno Davidson, and the art critic Kurt Sagar.

'Hirsch *is* the First New World and Union Bank,' Eustace said in a stage whisper, his eyes round as poached eggs. 'You know all about his collection, of course. Long Island. I have hopes. There's something in the wind, wouldn't you say, Robert, dear boy?'

Gozo spoke in Hester's ear. 'Hirsch hopes to emulate Chase Manhattan as patron of the arts. It's called the human face of capitalism, you know. And *did* you know that Eustace gave them a *private* private view last night? Hirsch and his art adviser both. Apparently the Citibank Advisory Service put them on to our Robert. What d'you think of that, then?' He gave a subdued, high-pitched giggle. He reminded Hester of a faintly malevolent pixie with his tilted eyes and his twenties-style hair slicked back with gel. He had come to Eustace from a job as a courier with a travel firm whence for some forgotten reason had come his nickname. His real name was Peter Barnes and he was an organisational whizz kid. He and Eustace had been lovers from the start.

Hester shrugged. 'Don't count chickens, Gozo.'

She watched Eustace in action. Eustace Tench: partner in the Cork Street gallery, Lombards, in which Robert's exhibition was being held. He had acted as agent for both Robert and herself practically since they left college. He was as usual of slightly rumpled appearance in one of his greenish or brownish corduroy suits. His shirts were invariably pink or lime or some other excruciating colour accompanied by a bow tie, sometimes terracotta, sometimes electric blue, perhaps emerald. She couldn't imagine where he could possibly buy them. His thinning strands of sandy hair were as a rule pasted to his pink scalp but they frequently came unstuck so that stray filaments drifted about his head like questing antennae. In a sober world of grey-suited dealers and gallery owners he was known as an eccentric, a character. Yet Hester knew that anyone put off or misled by his appearance, his brash manner and naive remarks would be making a grave error of judgement. Eustace was a shrewd businessman and handled 'his' artists' affairs with an unerring flair and Midas touch.

For some time she and Robert had been the two shining stars in his firmament. He had seen to it that their success was no flash in the pan. As he intended, it had built steadily over the years assiduously nurtured and guided by his light hand, which he insisted never meddled in matters of artistic integrity, but concentrated on the how, where and to whom 'the product' was presented.

Eustace had no illusions about the world he inhabited. He was absolutely dedicated to making money in what he thought of as one of the most exciting and dangerous markets in the world. One of his favourite quotations was Behrman on Duveen:

> 'Early in his life Duveen noticed that Europe had plenty of art and America had plenty of money and his entire, astonishing career was the product of that simple observation.'

Not far away from where Hester stood, Eustace's partner Bruno Davidson was making heavy weather of entertaining Waldo and Betty Hirsch, not to speak of Kurt Sagar. He was not an extrovert like Eustace and endured these gatherings as a necessary part of his work. He was well aware that in spite of his more sober appearance (he was one of the grey-suited breed of dealer), he was less shrewd and more sentimental, than his partner, his attitude to painters and painting one of nostalgic romanticism. On the whole he preferred to deal with artists who were recently and safely dead and it was to handle those who were not, as well as for purely fiscal reasons, that he'd first brought in Eustace. It had proved to be one of the best moves he'd ever made. Eustace was also willing to employ strategies that to Bruno seemed ruthless, though he was perfectly willing to admit that in these precarious days they were probably very necessary.

Right at this moment Bruno was feeling anxious as well as slightly depressed. It seemed to him as if the boom in the art market was finally over, yet Eustace was absolutely set on moving to larger premises. The rents would be cheaper since the new premises were not in the West End but suppose that in itself was a mistake?

'The Los Angeles Fair was uneven to say the least,' Waldo Hirsch was saying in his deep resonant voice. 'You can't rely on the Californian collectors. The top end is . . .' He rocked a great hand which was deeply tanned and garnished with gold. 'They're saying that even Schnabel isn't fetching what he was.'

'Ah,' Bruno said. He had run out of responses and was having trouble keeping a glazed look out of his eyes.

'However, Schnabel is indubitably a painter to watch,' Sagar broke in, 'Even in a recession. And I hear the Baselitz exhibition was a complete sellout.'

Nervously Bruno put a hand to his sculptured mass of silvery hair and gazed at Hirsch's tie which was about on his own eyelevel, though he wasn't a short man. The tie was the only item of the American's apparel that to an English eye was in questionable taste. It was not unlike an early Malevitch before that artist had seen the light (or rather white, since his subsequent paintings were notable for a complete absence of colour). Malevitch had, according to Eustace, something to say about neckties in relation to paintings but Bruno couldn't remember quite . . .

'You Brits are doing just great considering,' Hirsch was saying. 'This is a fine show. We're very impressed. Isn't that so, Betty?'

Betty Hirsch smiled her dazzling smile. '*What* an artist!' she exclaimed.

'And incidentally we think the new gallery is a great idea. Cork Street was all very well in the days of easel paintings, but we must move with the times.' He spoke as if he had yet to convince Bruno of the advantages of the scheme. Not far from the truth, Bruno thought. He still had grave reservations about 'corporate art' and frequently yearned for the fifties when he had first started Lombards.

'We're pretty well sure that Gibb is our man, in fact. Isn't that so, Betty?'

Betty smiled. 'Oh, yes. I should say.'

'Now where . . . ?' Hirsch glanced above the sea of heads without even craning his neck. 'Ah! There they are.' Bruno awaited the relief column with thankfulness. When Eustace arrived with Robert, Hester and Gozo in tow he felt marginally less as if he were standing in the shadow of a pair of tower blocks, for both the Hirschs were built on the scale of Wagnerian gods. Waldo gave the impression that he had recently been riding the range or living wild in some mountain redoubt, and this would not have been too far from the truth. He was an extremely physical man. Alert, dynamic and endowed with a pile-driving energy. However, there were no rough edges to the Waldo Hirsch creation. His skin was smooth, his nails manicured and no hair on his dark head was out of place. Bruno thought it extraordinary how perfectly husband and wife made a matching pair, for Betty was Waldo's equal in height, grooming and graciousness. American royalty. Her dress and the cape depending from one shoulder appeared to be cut in one swooping piece. Her few items of jewellery were of a size that would have felled a smaller woman. She possessed enormous amounts of corn-coloured hair that was swept away from her face in graceful curves that defied the laws of gravity.

Eustace was making much of the introductions. Hirsch continued to shake Robert's hand while he spoke.

'Very glad to meet you at last. We think the work is most impressive. Betty and I are *very* optimistic of getting to know you better.' He inclined his head towards Hester. 'And your charming wife, it goes without saying.'

Bruno saw Hester's smile fade rapidly at being addressed as a mere adjunct of Robert. The fact that it must happen infrequently these days would make it no less infuriating. Bruno admired Hester. She was more approachable than her husband in spite of her severe Red Indian looks. He respected Robert Gibb but found him remote in a way that Hester was not. He kissed Hester on both cheeks and thought how unusually pale she looked.

Betty spoke. 'We adore the show. We've been admirers of your work for so long. We decided last night that we simply must have "Disjunction I". Has Mr Tench told you?'

Robert inclined his head.

'Yes, he has, Mrs Hirsch.'

'For goodness' sake call me Betty,' she insisted with a tinkling laugh. 'We are also very fond of your wife's work, aren't we, Waldo?' She glanced from Robert to her husband, barely taking in Hester on the way. As if, Bruno thought, Robert owned a precocious chimp. He heard Hester give a low growl.

'We most certainly are,' Waldo agreed, maintaining eye contact with Hester rather longer than was strictly necessary. 'And we're looking forward to your next show.'

'Now that will be really exciting,' Betty said speaking with what appeared to be completely unfeigned enthusiasm.

The exchanges between husband and wife were like a stately game of tennis, Bruno thought, and one had to believe in their absolute sincerity. He saw that Hester did not appear to be listening. She could be prickly on occasion but just at the moment he was more inclined to the view that she was not as fully recovered from her indisposition as was generally believed.

Eustace was not to remain uninvolved for long.

'So tell us, Waldo. Is "Disjunction I" to go in your superb gallery?'

'It surely is.' He turned to Betty and grinned. 'We've been arguing where exactly to place it, haven't we, Bee?'

Betty made a flirtatious moue at her husband.

Waldo raised an arm to indicate Robert's paintings that loomed at them from all sides.

'Now these paintings . . . what I see in them is this. Society is at risk from subversive ideas, the fabric begins to tear. There you are! The predicament of Modern Man as Kurt here so rightly said.'

Sagar looked embarrassed. It was not quite what he had written.

Standing behind Hester and breathing in her ear, Gozo said, 'When a man that rich says that's what it means . . . that's what it means, right?'

Robert cleared his throat. 'One has to be careful,' he said gravely, 'not to confuse the painter's purely aesthetic preoccupations with tendential didactics. It was never my intention to take the stance of a moralist . . .'

'Couldn't have put it better myself,' Gozo murmured, but Hester wasn't listening.

'The painting as metaphor,' Sagar interposed in his precise voice. 'And the painter's archetypal dilemma.'

'Absolutely,' Waldo said enthusiastically. 'Robert's too darned clever to proselytise . . .'

'"Cut off your tongue!"' Eustace boomed without warning.

'Excuse me?' Waldo stared.

'Matisse,' Eustace explained. 'He said that to be a real painter one must first cut off one's tongue. A lot in that, you know.'

'Goodness. How absolutely *wise*,' Betty said. 'And what an artist *he* was!' She sipped her drink and moved closer to Hester. 'And may one ask when we shall have the privilege of seeing more of your work, Hester? I may call you Hester, mayn't I?'

'I'm not actually working at the moment,' Hester said curtly. Eustace broke in before Hester had a chance to commit further indiscretions.

'Don't be put off by Hester's nonsense. She likes a joke, you know. As a matter of fact,' he continued in a confidential tone. 'She's what they call a workaholic.'

Bruno did not miss Hester's almost imperceptible flinch and wondered why she should be upset that Eustace had called attention to such a positive quality as her commitment to her work.

Eustace flung an arm round Hester's shoulders, took a huge step backwards and with his other arm decoyed a laden tray of glasses in their direction. In doing so he collided with the assistant editor of *Painting Now* who had been standing directly behind him awaiting an opportunity to join in the discussion.

Caroline Childs' professional motives for wanting to join them were perfectly legitimate, but there was another, more compelling, reason. It was so overwhelming that she didn't even notice that Eustace's not inconsiderable weight had come to bear for a moment on her foot. For all she really wanted to do was to breathe the same air as the man she worshipped, until now from afar. Just to be near Robert Gibb was, at least for the present, enough.

Eustace appeared to be apologising.

'Good Lord. Miss Childs, isn't it?'

Caroline held out a hand which was on the end of an armful of bracelets. 'Caroline', she said. '*Painting Now*'. Her gaze swivelled round the group and came to rest inexorably on Robert.

Eustace thumped his temple with the flat of his hand.

'Of course! The interview,' he said. 'Nearly forgot. Next week, isn't it?' He turned to the waiter who had been hovering. 'Now everyone! More drinkies!'

When the drinks had been sorted out, Eustace returned to his original topic.

'I was just saying, Miss Childs . . . Caroline . . . that Hester's definition of not working would exhaust most of us. "A case of ideas coming in swarms, then off she goes like a steam engine." Van Gogh.'

'Van Gogh?' Waldo said, pronouncing it 'Van Go'.

'Quote from his letters,' Bruno said quietly. 'I don't know how Eustace remembers them all.'

'I get you,' Waldo said. 'Right. Van Gogh.'

'What an artist *he* was,' Betty remarked. 'And what prices! You know, I suppose that we put in a bid for "Sunflowers"?' She shook her great head of hair regretfully. 'Past history now, of course.'

Caroline was standing next to Robert.

'We were hoping to get the interview in the same issue as the review of this show,' she said. 'You'll be happy if we record it in your studio?'

'Absolutely. Indeed yes,' Robert said vaguely. He was gazing over the white-gold stubble on her neat head to where Waldo was bending to speak to Hester. The fact that Mrs Hirsch was smilingly aware of her husband's attention to another woman was not lost on Caroline.

Alice looked at her watch. Soon she must leave and catch the train that left Paddington for the West Country just after ten. It would be at least two in the morning before she finally fell into bed. She had been offered hospitality for the night, courtesy of Eustace Tench, but she found she could no longer deal with unfamiliar beds; besides she couldn't afford too long an absence from her crafts shop.

This evening, unexpectedly, she had enjoyed herself. She had met a well-born sculptor who looked like a tramp, an ex-hippy turned West End dealer, Melanie Sofford of sanitary towel fame and Caroline Childs the fidgety, anorexic-looking assistant editor of *Painting Now* who, on learning that Alice had been at art college with Hester and Robert and indeed was an old friend, had tried to pump her about their marriage.

During the evening she had overheard innumerable references to recession and the volatile state of the art market. All the same, these things were relative: there was more cash on show here tonight than she would ever see. Besides the lovely linseed-oily smell of new paintings, great whiffs and tides of expensive scent assailed her nostrils and all round her were designer clothes, good leather and a small fortune in gold and jewellery. Serious money.

She took a lingering sip of fizzy wine. Money. Odd that Hester who had never cared a fig for the stuff had landed amongst it in spite of herself. Even her clothes could hardly be called flashy; cotton trousers, albeit rather nattily cut, and a matching jacket the colour of the sea on a dullish day, were frankly casual in view of the occasion. Nevertheless, in Alice's opinion she made most of the other females present look like high-class hookers.

Hester came to see her off.

'I'll see about a taxi,' she said.

'No you won't. It's already arranged,' Alice said.

They stood at the door of the gallery looking out.

'You will come to Coombe Ferrers, won't you?'

'Yes, Alice,' Hester said. 'I've been thinking about it and decided that I would very much like to.'

'Good. That's settled then,' Alice said. 'Ah, here's my taxi.'

Robert took off his jacket and arranged it on the hanger, fastidiously brushing specks of dust from the shoulders.

'I think it went quite well, don't you,' he said. He opened a section of the wall-sized wardrobe and hung the jacket inside. 'The Hirschs seemed fairly forthcoming. Did you take in what Eustace was saying about them at dinner. You didn't appear to be listening, are you still feeling a bit rough?'

Hester nodded. 'Hm.' She was sitting cross legged on the king-sized bed wearing only bra and knickers, undoing her heavy plait. The hair burst from its confinement in ink-black undulations. Immediately she looked more vulnerable; indeed at the moment she felt both vulnerable and tired. Such weariness was infuriating and quite unaccustomed, at least unaccustomed until just a few months ago.

'You were saying about the Hirschs,' she said, moved, in spite of how she was feeling, by his need for a response from her. 'I gather Eustace thinks they have something in mind for you?'

'They're considered to be among the top American collectors. Eustace has been astute getting them interested. By the way, I know you weren't feeling too good tonight but I think you rather lost an opportunity when they asked about your work.' Relief that the evening had gone well was making him more loquacious than usual.

'Hm,' Hester said again. 'Perhaps.' She brushed out her hair, her face hidden by the dark curtain.

They were in the guest room at the top of Eustace's house. From its windows oblique views of Chelsea were to be had. They'd had a late dinner, little of which Hester had been able to eat, and were intending to travel back to Bristol the following day.

Eustace's house had once been an Edwardian gentleman's residence but it had been practically gutted, so that rather than rooms there were now spaces. The only doors remaining in the house were those of the bathrooms and guest rooms. In fact the place somewhat resembled a rather superior gallery; even Eustace's own room was on open display. His gigantic bed was raised on a low dais, a trendy designer had been employed to surround it with poles from which depended swags of fabric in white, royal blue and gold. Eustace frequently received visitors while laying on it. Gozo, when he wasn't sharing Eustace's bed, had opted for the privacy of one of the guest rooms.

The one Hester and Robert now occupied had been done out in Pompeiian red, but it didn't feel right: something jarred. To Hester it looked like dried blood and made her feel more depressed than ever.

Robert tugged at his jersey. 'Anyway, thank God for the Hirschs, I say. If it wasn't for them,' he said as he emerged from the expensive cashmere, 'we could well be in a serious position the way prices are falling.'

'Your prices aren't falling.' Hester gathered her hair in a great bunch over her shoulder.

'Doesn't invalidate my point. The market is so bloody volatile. Eustace had to work damned hard to clinch the Hirsch connection.' He paused while he removed his trousers and hung them with his jacket. Standing in his Calvin Klein underpants he glanced across at Hester as she slowly began to replait her hair, moving as if she had lead weights attached to her wrists. Robert experienced a moment of acute anxiety. The possibility of Hester continuing to be ill had occurred to him briefly several times of late but he immediately smothered the thought. It made him feel breathless, gave him butterflies in the stomach and immediately increased his heart rate. There was something else too, perhaps connected with Hester's illness, perhaps not; the encouraging comment he had come to expect of her at the launch of a new exhibition had not been forthcoming, at least not to the extent he would have hoped for. He touched on the subject again, like a tongue probing a tender tooth.

'So you think it was a success, the show?' He approached the bed and put his hands on her shoulders but Hester slid out from under them. Robert watched her as she took off her bra and knickers and, unselfconscious in her nudity, began to search in her overnight bag for a nightdress. She had always been slim, wide shouldered and narrow hipped but she had lately lost weight, he could see that. All the same, her body was unmistakably womanly and he momentarily but sincerely wished that he could desire her as he had once done.

She had avoided his touch because deep down she knew that it was insincere. She found her nightdress and pulled it over her head. 'You don't need me to tell you,' she said. 'You saw for yourself that people loved it.' She leaned over the bed and kissed him on the cheek. 'Congratulations, darling.'

This was not the answer he craved but it would have to do. Hester got into the huge bed. Robert took off his underclothes and tucked them into the bottom of his suitcase. He shrugged into the short cotton robe he wore at night and tied it at the waist.

'I think you'd be wise to take Alice up on her offer,' he said. 'A short break will make all the difference.' He couldn't bring himself to visualise her having anything longer than a few days away; firstly because if any important offer came through from the Hirschs in the near future he would most certainly need Hester near and secondly because he had disliked and been suspicious of Alice ever since the day when she had ridiculed a comment he'd made during a lecture when they were students. The fact that everyone else had joined in the laughter, even Hester, had been something he'd never forgotten or quite forgiven though he couldn't even recollect now what he had said that had caused such mirth.

'When you come back perhaps you'll feel more like work,' he added. 'Incidentally I don't think it was a very good idea to advertise the fact that you're not doing any. Fortunately Eustace intercepted so I don't think anyone heard or, if they did, that they took it seriously.' He spoke with a shade more tartness than he intended for this, as he well knew, was a sensitive subject. All the same he couldn't leave it alone . 'You realise that Eustace is going to want to see something any day now . . .'

'Leave it, Robert,' Hester said, turning so that her back was towards him. 'I don't want to talk about it. There's nothing to say.'

'Better to talk to me about it than Eustace, surely? It's been weeks now. Weeks when you've been in your studio but produced damn-all. Just listened to the radio all day as far as I can tell.'

Hester sat up abruptly. 'Robert, please!' she cried. 'This has been your day and it's been a great success. Don't . . .' She paused to take a breath. 'Just don't push your luck, that's all. Leave me out of it. I've tried to explain it to you before and failed, obviously because it's something I don't understand myself. I promise that when I do I'll tell you. I just need time to think.'

Robert looked searchingly into her face in an attempt to satisfy himself that she was holding nothing back.

'Of course,' he said, not altogether happy at what he saw. He turned out the light. Time to think! As if she hadn't had enough already. A cloud the size of a man's hand had appeared on his bright horizon, just when he thought he was moving into the uplands of a more general esteem and recognition.

He lay in the dark, his hands behind his head, uncomfortable with the necessity of sharing a bed with Hester when he was not in the mood for sex. At home they slept in single beds, had done for many years.

It was late but he could not sleep. He was more deeply disturbed about Hester than he was prepared to admit. From the time even before they had both left college armed with good degrees in Fine Art, he had needed her. Her toughness of spirit never faltered in face of situations that at best caused him anxiety and at worst, blind panic. Since they had been together it had never been necessary to face such situations, she had been there, taking over the responsibility that had once been his mother's prerogative.

With her motive power propelling him he had been able to cruise triumphantly through life, receiving his due in respect and recognition. At first prestigious posts in the best art colleges, his work shown in London, Cologne, Milan, New York and Tokyo; his opinions sought after and appearances on Arena and the South Bank show. Hester's success as a painter had run virtually parallel with his own though her name was not as generally well known. But then he was bound to admit that she had a grave handicap. She was a woman.

Her recent behaviour troubled him profoundly just because it was so different from the norm. True, the pregnancy had been a shock; it had certainly shocked him, but she had begun to behave almost as if she'd *wanted* the child! He couldn't imagine how such a mistake could have been made since they were so careful on the rare occasions when they made love. He had been deeply embarrassed by the whole thing, he said it made them seem like a pair of improvident adolescents and refused to tell Eustace the truth about either the pregnancy or the miscarriage. Since it happened he had successfully and thankfully put the episode out of his mind. He couldn't think why Hester wouldn't do the same. She seemed almost unaware of the more immediate causes for anxiety, for the recession was biting deep. If he failed now it would wash him away as it already had a number of other artists known to him, and their dealer-agents too if it came to that; by the time of the next boom his reputation, like theirs, could be non-existent. They had talked about the price of his work but what he really cared about, what in fact possessed him like a demon, was the absolute necessity of preserving his own artistic reputation and his continued survival as an eminently creative being.

Next to him Hester too was awake. She listened to London's faint hum, the occasional boat on the river and thought about the discovery she had made earlier that evening; that she could no longer perceive either her own or Robert's painting as she once had. That Eustace, the Hirschs, Sagar or the world in general still seemed to value it meant less than nothing. Now that she had diagnosed the sickness, how could she possibly ignore it and go on as if nothing had happened? Why didn't Robert see it? Had he deliberately blinded himself to the fundamental defects in his own work, and hers? And why could she not tell him about it? But then how do you tell an artist, particularly if he happens to be your husband, that his work is no bloody good? That it has no soul. It would be as good as saying that *he* had no soul. For it was a truth she could hardly bear to face about herself. When she had first known him it seemed to her, fiercely in love with him as she was, that he could do no wrong. Even his reserve and singlemindedness were admirable. He was an artist, as she was, and must be allowed his idiosyncrasies. They talked about art and about life with a fervour just about equal on both sides. She'd worn beads and a skirt to her ankles; his only concession to the hippy movement had been a sleeveless sheepskin jerkin. There had been good sex then even though she had usually been the one to initiate it. They'd had no money and been very, very happy.

Paul caught sight of Alice almost at once as there were few passengers alighting at Exeter's St David's station at that time of night. She regarded steps in all their forms as a curse and a misery and for once was glad to use the lift.

'How did it go?' he asked as they emerged on the other platform.

'Sweetie, it's another world,' she said.

'Jealous?'

Alice struggled into the passenger seat of the old Renault and Paul slammed the door. When he was sitting beside her she said, 'I always think I'm going to be, you know, but when I looked at Hester this time I knew I wasn't.'

'Trouble?' Paul started the engine and Alice leaned her head thankfully on the headrest.

'I don't know. Perhaps.' To herself she thought that certainly there was and more than Hester was admitting to.

'I've asked her down here to stay.'

'You'll enjoy that.' Paul accelerated out of the station yard and into the darkened countryside heading for Coombe Ferrers. It was quite possible, Paul thought, that Alice would enjoy a visit from her high-flying friend, but he wasn't sure that he liked the idea of importing trouble: it could be catching.

CHAPTER TWO

The cloud hung in the sky, a pearl-coloured mountain, a yeasty pillar against pure cerulean blue. Its lower edge trailed skirts of rain, a dirty apricot over the distant hills. The middle distance was occupied by jumbled blocks of grey, faded pinks and an assortment of whites that represented the town of Tidemouth on the other side of the river. Beneath it was its own reversed reflection and that of the cloud, infiltrated by dabs and slashes of blue like an irregular patchwork.

Hester stopped short, gazing at the cloud. She could have been in a trance. Alice was absurdly glad that the scenery was coming up to scratch. An open fishing boat chugged down the river, a fisherman standing nonchalantly at the stern, steering one-handedly. His companion, sitting in the bow, waved to Alice.

She turned away, pretending not to have noticed.

'Reg Gammon,' she said. 'God help me.'

Hester was not really listening. She dragged her eyes away from the spectacle of the cloud, the town and the river.

'You have a lot of friends here, don't you?' she said.

'Coombe Ferrers is what is known as a close-knit community,' Alice replied with a trace of irony. 'We tend to rub along on a system of mutual barter and the power of the grapevine. Of course you can't exactly have what you might call a private life but they wouldn't let you starve either.'

Alice had a curious bubbling laugh that was normally extremely infectious but Hester couldn't quite bring herself to join in.

'And Alice, how's the gallery going? Are you actually making a living?'

'Gallery is really too grand a word for my outfit. I call it a shop. It's ticking over, just about.'

'I'm sorry you had to give up the idea of converting the old Cider Press. It would have made a stunning gallery.'

'Yes, well, one has to be realistic. With this bloody hip I can't even walk up the hill to it without a lot of grief. I've been offered various kinds of help but a venture like that would have depended utterly on me being able-bodied at the very least.'

'But you do have friends around you. I can't say I have friends like that. Everyone I know, I know professionally, all connected with painting, or dealing or buying. It isn't always safe to confide in anyone.'

'It isn't always safe to confide in anyone round here either,' Alice said briskly. 'But then I fancy that I haven't so much to lose.'

She took a glance at Hester's strong profile as they picked their way along the flotsam-strewn high-tide line of Coombe Ferrers' narrow strand. Hester caught the sharp, evocative scent of seaweed and salt water.

'I'm not sure that I have anything to lose at the moment,' she said. 'To tell you the truth I feel totally bankrupt.'

'I presume you don't mean financially? It seemed to me that you and Robert are doing rather better than most in that way.'

'In spite of all Robert's jitters, yes we are. No, I wasn't talking about money.'

'Physically and mentally then. Are you surprised? Look what you've had to cope with in the last eighteen months. Inez dying so unexpectedly, then the miscarriage . . .'

Hester stopped and stared fixedly at an empty crab shell at her feet. She stooped and picked it up, turning it over in strong exploratory fingers.

'Do you realise,' she said. 'That I haven't so much as touched a piece of charcoal or a paintbrush for months.'

'This bad patch has been going on for some time, then?'

Hester nodded. 'I'm not even sure if it's connected with the events in my life or not.'

Alice moved towards a great tree trunk, laid low by some long-past storm, carried down river and finally beached and silvered on the narrow strip of sand and pebbles. She arranged herself on it tugging her kaleidoscope-knitted garments about her. She patted the place beside her.

'Sit,' she commanded.

Hester lowered her narrow flanks on to the tree trunk and swung her knees up to her chin, folding her arms round her legs. Her oversize jersey could hardly disguise how much weight she'd lost, Alice thought, noting the prominent knucklebones in her friend's wrists. In spite of everything there was no trace of grey in the thick plait that lay on Hester's shoulder or in the escaped strands that blew across her brooding features.

For several minutes they remained without speaking, watching the activity on the river. A cormorant stood on a post in the water with wings outstretched, a man painted a boat, the small ferryboat chugged from Coombe Ferrers to Tidemouth.

'Do you want to talk about it?' Alice said at last.

'I'm not sure that I can. I don't even know what's wrong myself except that I don't seem able to paint.'

'At the risk of seeming platitudinous, I think that what you need is time.'

'No!' Hester said abruptly, almost violently. Then, 'I didn't mean no I don't need time. I meant that I just can't visualise *ever* being able to paint again.'

'Ever! Now darling, isn't that an absolutely infallible sign that you desperately need a break?'

'Listen, Alice,' Hester said, 'It first happened when I was in my studio and then again the other night at Lombards. It was like seeing everything for the first time and seeing it clearly. I had already come to the conclusion that my own work was a sham, second hand and in-bred. Now I see Robert's in just the same way. Alice, it's terrifying, what's wrong with me?' Her voice shook perilously.

Alice thought quickly. The outburst was almost certainly Hester's exhaustion speaking. A miscarriage at any age is no joke but at forty-two it must have been a deeply disturbing experience, especially for a forty-two-year old who refused to make allowances for any kind of physical or mental distress. Certainly this, or something even deeper, had drained the life out of a woman who was usually so vital and physically strong. She knew Hester well enough after all these years to have realised that sooner or later would come a day of reckoning. The question was, was this it? Or was it merely a wobbly moment?

'I know I'm not in touch these days,' she said carefully. 'But I'm not aware of any dissatisfied noises about your stuff emanating from London or New York, even given the jumpy state of affairs.'

'That makes it almost worse. There is even a waiting list of would-be buyers, would you believe.'

'And you feel you can't deliver?'

Hester nodded, bending her head in detailed examination of the crab shell.

'Tell me, Hester. Has Melanie been unsettling you with her talk of a separate, feminist art. I spoke to her at the private view and I must say she's very persuasive.'

'No. I like Melanie and respect what she is trying to do but I think she's a missionary at heart. I never imagined for a moment that I wouldn't carry straight on with my work after Inez died but when I stood in my studio and looked again at what I'd been doing I could have wept. Never in a million years could I go on producing stuff like that. Never!'

'What does Robert think about all this?'

'I haven't mentioned it to Robert.'

'Why on earth not?'

'Because . . .'

Alice waited.

'The trouble is,' Hester said, 'That he still thinks my work is fine as it is. And he's quite happy with the way his own work is developing. As far as I know it's only me who sees both as deficient in quite fundamental ways. It's horrible.'

'From what I saw at the private view, the world and his wife, or to put it another way, the world and her husband seem absolutely delighted with you both.'

Hester gave a short laugh. 'Oh, you know, private views!' She turned disquieting eyes on Alice. 'Yes, I suppose the word is that his latest stuff is the best he's done. You saw it. What do *you* think?'

'Yes, I'm sure it is.' Alice said, disguising her lack of enthusiasm. 'It looked perfectly fine to me.'

The white cloud had bubbled up, spread itself and dragged its drenching skirts out to sea. A crack of celadon green had opened up beneath it and a laser of sunlight pointed up a far hill. There was a cool early April feel to the air.

'There is this,' Alice went on. 'Folks don't normally care to spend thousands on work they consider to be rubbish.'

'That's a false argument. Of course they don't. The important thing is that if they are truly of the opinion that it's good, then I don't trust their judgement. All it means is that they've grown accustomed to the second rate . . .'

'But you never knowingly produced the second rate.'

'Good heavens, no! Until recently I shared their valuation. Now I don't.'

'Uncompromising as ever, I see!' Alice said. 'All the same I think you're being far too hard on yourself. So you've outgrown that stage. What the hell! Painters do it all the time, you don't need me to tell you that. Look at Passmore's celebrated change of direction.'

'Presumably he knew what he would do next, had some idea where he was going. I see nothing ahead but a total blank and there's absolutely nothing I can do about it. Nothing!'

'I think that for the time being, doing nothing is a great idea.'

'I feel just about as eviscerated as this damned shell.' Hester made as if to hurl the crab shell into the water but she had grasped it so violently that it had crumbled to fragments in her palm.

'Surely you don't doubt that you're a bloody good painter?' Alice tilted her head in Hester's direction.

'Oh, I know my stuff, my credentials are quite legit. I've served my apprenticeship, all that . . .' She brushed the crumbs of shell impatiently from her hands. 'But what's the point when it's simply become a mechanical recycling of ideas. I feel as if even my emotions were second-hand. Until now . . .'

'And now?'

'Now, all I feel is numb. Sometimes I want to howl and howl. And yet I can't.' Abruptly she left her perch on the tree trunk and stood with her hands in the pockets of her trousers gazing across the river. She turned and gave a wry smile. 'I'm not the crying type, you know.'

'I know that.' Alice pushed herself awkwardly to her feet, aware that while she had been sitting still a painful stiffness had seized her joints. Hester disciplined herself to wait and not to help. Alice resented help if she thought she could manage on her own.

'Alice, I'm sorry,' Hester said remorsefully. 'I'd no business to keep you hanging about in the cold listening to my nonsense. You must be frozen. Let's go back and make some tea or get drunk or something . . .'

'It's not that cold. I adore the early spring. And don't dismiss how you feel as nonsense. By the way if you *were* the crying type you've come to the right place. There are plenty of wide open spaces round here where you can howl with impunity.'

They walked back through the Sunday streets of Coombe Ferrers. Apart from a spell away while she was a student, another as an art teacher and a short disastrous stab at marriage to a Neanderthal sculptor, Alice had always lived in Coombe Ferrers. She was well aware that she was not in the same artistic league as Robert and Hester but her ability as a printmaker was well known locally. She belonged to the Devon Guild of Craftsmen and her work sold reasonably well. She had never been ambitious for more universal recognition and she liked living where she did, although she was sure that it seemed shamefully unenterprising she had never been able to hit on any other place that suited her better. Her only criticism was that lately she had found its steep side streets, alleys and flights of steps tempted her to stick to the High Street and waterfront. However, she was not yet prepared to call that an inconvenience.

The town was not quite a mirror image of the one on the opposite bank. Tidemouth had continued to grow over the years, to add small engineering outfits to its port facilities, to acquire council estates on its outskirts and to cater in a modest way for summer visitors. On the seaward side children played on the red sands and pebble beaches, fished for shrimps in rock pools and were taken for cream teas in one of the innumerable tea shops, for Tidemouth still possessed a distinctly old-fashioned atmosphere.

Coombe Ferrers had once been a centre for boat building, the export of wool and Haytor granite and the import of guano for fertiliser but since the building of a bridge further upstream in 1922 the deep-water channel had shifted to the further bank. As a result Coombe Ferrers had ceased to grow, making do with fishing, boat trips and the production of lobster pots from the withys that were grown further up the river. It had one remaining boatyard and that dealt mostly with repair work.

In spite of its age and its character the charms of Coombe Ferrers were a moderately well-kept secret. This was partly accounted for by the fact that the main road by-passed it, thrusting on to the popular tourist traps to the east and the west, and partly because it had no beach to speak of, merely the pebbly strand on which Hester and Alice had walked, and that was completely covered at high tide. The town had also fortunately escaped the attention of those who would have sanitised its appearance, straightened its angles and replaced its ancient windows. The houses of its early merchants were scaled down versions of altogether larger and grander dwellings, but for all that they did not seem to have sacrificed anything in the way of rich detailing. The general impression was one of an extraordinary wealth of decorative cornices and bargeboards, lacy Regency balconies and verandahs and multi-paned windows full of eighteenth-century gothic arcuation. The houses were arranged haphazardly and linked by a maze of alleyways and flights of steps so that, seen from the river, they gave the appearance of being stacked one on the other. Most, having been built at right angles to the street, were approached through a walled garden or courtyard. The secret and private nature this gave them was offset by the fact that the gates were seldom shut or locked, some indeed had rights of way leading to even more secluded dwellings beyond.

To reach Alice's house the two women entered a steep and narrow lane that led from the High Street and climbed for a short distance between the walls of houses and gardens. Like so many others it turned its side to the alley and looked out over the roofs of the waterside buildings to the south and west, being approached through a wooden gate in a high wall. Some country mason had lavished great skill even on this, furnishing it with a gothic arch, two semi-circular steps, a bowl shaped concavity to house the bell pull and a decorative iron grille through which it was possible to obtain glimpses of the garden beyond.

In the crevices of the wall, as if nature was not to be outdone by a simple Devon craftsman, grew miniature ferns and the coin shaped leaves of pennywort.

It was years since Hester had seen Alice's house. Their contact had been through infrequent letters, Alice's occasional trips to Bristol, where Hester now lived and, of course Alice's faithful support when private views rolled around.

'I can't get over the way everything burgeons here,' Hester said. 'Even at this time of year every crack and cranny seems to be growing something. And not just any old weed. Some of them look quite exotic.'

'You know Devon,' Alice joked, lapsing into the soft Devonshire burr. 'Debn glorious Debn, raining six days out of sebn.'

'It can't be just the rain. It rains in Bristol, for God's sake. I'd forgotten how everything just . . . proliferates here.'

'It's about time you got reacquainted with your roots, my girl.'

'I'm not sure if, strictly speaking, I have any roots. We always seemed to be on the move, Inez and I.'

Alice pushed open the unlocked gate and they went into the garden where, in spite of the recent sharp weather there was an abundance of narcissi and primroses. Young leaves were already on the point of unfolding on the vine which trailed its branches over the cast iron supports of the glazed verandah. In turn the vine provided a convenient framework for the nodding purple flowers of an early clematis. At their feet a patch of green-white hellebores were in bloom.

The stone-flagged verandah ran the length of the small white house and sheltered the french windows of both the sitting room and the study. Above were three pairs of pointed gothic windows and a smaller arched dormer nestled among the roof slates.

At the end of the verandah the two women entered the kitchen through a side door. Alice ran her hands through her fuzz of blondish hair.

'I think you'm right after all, me 'andsome. 'Tis bloody perishing. Look, I'll sling some more wood on the sitting-room fire, brew up a nice cosy fug and we'll sit and drink our tea like two old crones.'

'Suits me. I'll put the kettle on.'

When the kettle boiled Hester took the tray into the other room where Alice had coaxed the fire into glowing life.

Alice poured the tea from a handmade pottery pot into handmade pottery cups.

'How civilised you are,' Hester said. 'My studio always seems to be littered with discarded mugs of half-drunk coffee. When we run out of mugs we ransack the studios and pile them all into the dishwasher. Amy says we live like squatters in our own house. I'm always saying I'll do something about it but there never seems to be time.'

'You strike me as being like rather well-heeled gypsies.'

'I'm a great disappointment to Robert's mother. I'm sure she visualised a nice, domesticated wife for her son. I don't think she quite realises that a guy who doesn't turn up for regularly cooked meals would drive such a female nuts. And if all his shirts are in the wash he goes out and buys a new one.'

'It's all right for some! Have a biscuit. These ginger ones are scrumptious.' Alice passed the plate.

'I thought you were on a diet.'

'I am. Haven't you noticed that I'm not actually eating any?'

'Oh God, Alice. What a bore.'

Outside a flurry of rain pattered on to the glass roof of the verandah and a brisk breeze agitated the branches of the vine. Like the entire house, Alice's sitting room was a scaled-down version of something much grander. It had painted panelling, a classically decorated fireplace and cornices of vine leaves in deep relief. There were two sets of french windows with wooden shutters and beyond them wedges of oyster grey, cream, azure and jade were all that they could see of roofs, clouds, sky and an oblique view of the sea. Alice's furniture was idiosyncratic, being either antiques of some value left to her by her parents or throw outs from skips and jumble sales which she had rescued, mended and painted with designs of leaves and birds. No shelf or table top was without its piece of sculpture, driftwood or interesting pot; some of Alice's own etchings hung on the walls but they were outnumbered by the work of other artists. Prints, wooden reliefs, enamels and paintings covered the walls and spread through the hall and up the stairs.

Above the fireplace hung one of Hester's paintings which Alice had insisted on buying. That was before her work commanded huge sums of money. Hester glanced at it, recalling with something like nostalgia the circumstances in which it had been painted. Before they had both landed teaching jobs she and Robert had been living in a cold and inconvenient flat, sacrificing both comfort and decent food in order to paint, taking what paid work was necessary to keep body and soul together, painting at night and in the early morning. Partners in survival.

Alice caught the direction of her gaze. 'Bloody good, isn't it?' she said. 'Absolutely crackles with energy.'

'Not much finesse,' Hester said ruefully.

'Bugger finesse.'

It was semi abstract, done at a time when her influences had been the Cornish painters, her references the natural world; rocks, trees, sky and sea, the paint itself. The painting had been started while she'd been staying on the Dorset coast and been excited by the twisted strata of the cliffs at Lulworth. Done at a time when the most of her contemporaries favoured minimal or conceptual art. Robert had by this time already begun to produce a variety of highly intellectual abstraction and he had chided her, though gently, for her preoccupation with what he called a typically Anglo Saxon romanticism, not because her work was representational, for it wasn't, but for its lyrical involvement with shape and colour.

Hester drank her tea from the handmade cup. It had a blue rim and little dashes on the side like birds, or were they vestigial flowers? She had not missed the note of regret in Alice's words.

Alice said. 'How is Amy's course going?'

'She loved her term in Egypt but to tell you the truth I think it's unsettled her a bit.'

'It's never ceased to amaze me that she decided to read Modern Arabic instead of doing a Fine Art degree. She was so talented. Does she never do any drawing now?'

'She brought back a fairly respectable sketch book from Egypt. Otherwise not, I believe. I'm afraid her reasons for *not* doing Fine Art were more pressing than her reasons to read Arabic: teenage rebellion had far more to do with her decision than commonsense. Anything rather than do as her parents had done. I've never been happy about it but she has to make her own choices, right or wrong.'

Hester helped herself to another ginger biscuit.

'Will you need to take in PGs again this summer?'

'I already have one. Paul. He's an artist. Not your sort. He does watercolour views for the tourists in the summer.'

'Well, just so long as he pays the rent . . . What will you do about the Cider Press now that it's not to be a gallery? I must say I did rather fancy helping to found up-market exhibition space in the area. It could do with more.'

'Even if I'd remained perfectly able-bodied it could have turned out to be an expensive mistake. We planned it when the market was a lot more buoyant than it is now. It's the same old story when it comes to the arts. Not enough funding.'

'What will you do?'

'Admit defeat and sell, I expect.'

'A pity, since it's been in your family for so long.'

Alice's family was of old Devonshire stock and had always been keen entrepreneurs. Her great grandfather and grandfather had run a prosperous cider business from the old Cider Press up the hill above the town, diversifying into import and export. In her father's day the cider factory was no longer profitable and he had closed it and transferred his export interests to the now more flourishing port of Tidemouth. Unlike his forebears he was not an astute businessman and had worried himself into an early grave where he was soon followed by Alice's mother. They left Alice the house and the, by now, semi-derelict Cider Press.

Alice smiled. 'When I have the energy I'll dig out an old photograph I have of my great grandpapa standing by the old place complete with bowler hat and horse and cart loaded with cider apples.' She poured more tea. 'And since you sunk money into the hairbrained scheme it's only right that you should get it back. It's bloody good of you to be so patient.'

'How far had the conversion work gone?'

'Why don't you go up there and take a look?'

'We could finish the work and then put it on the market.'

'Then I could only sell it as a gallery. It would limit the number of possible buyers. No, I want to get shot of it, pronto. One of the glorious might-have-beens, I'm afraid.'

A log fell, sending up sparks and scented smoke. A woodlouse scuttled in panic and Hester took it on her finger and went across to the window. She opened it a crack and put the creature outside. It was still raining.

Alice watched her friend's expression, cheekbones and nose emphasized by the cast shadows. She read there a level of tension that Hester's words had only hinted at, either because she was not fully aware of her own malaise or because her way of life had compelled her to stifle inconvenient emotions.

Alice could recollect as if it were months ago instead of years, the day, almost the hour, when Hester had first told her about the new student who had just turned up on the degree course from another art college. Hester had been overcome by the personality of Robert Gibb, which had seemed so much more mature than those of their fellow students. His intense yet austere manner somehow made him seem to have more to his character than the average art student. Until then Hester had revelled in the camaraderie, the espirit de corps, the affairs, quarrels and even the tragedies of student life, though she nevertheless worked like a demon in feverish spasms of brilliance. Robert's results were produced by a dedicated persistence that Hester admired. It was an attraction of opposites if anything ever was. They both emerged as highly successful products of the system. Alice herself had obtained a respectable degree with which she was content. Soon after that Hester and Robert married and Alice found herself teaching art at a school in Exeter.

Another clatter of rain against the windows made the fireside more desirable. A shadow hurtled past and the back door slammed. A moment elapsed and then a young man appeared in the doorway, interrupting their conversation. His shoulder-length blond hair was darkened by rain, coils of it were plastered to his shining face. He wore a small gold ring in one ear and his grin displayed magnificent white teeth.

'Hi,' he said. 'Your antique admirer has sent you a couple of mackerel. I've put them on the draining board. He said that as you had a visitor you might be glad of them.' Paul spoke with a trace of a London accent.

'Bloody Reg. Anyway, thank you, darling. Hester, this is my lodger, Paul.'

'Hello, Hester.' The grin deepened. He actually had dimples.

'Glad to meet you.' His handshake was firm and damp with rain.

'I won't be eating here tonight, all right?' he said to Alice.

'No need to make yourself scarce on Hester's account, sweetie.'

'No, of course not,' Hester said,

'I'm going out with a few of the guys.'

'All right, dear. We'll see you later. Don't get in with that boozy bunch of rascals down at The Cutter, will you? We don't want you coming home completely pissed. You know you're no good at their game.'

'No ma'am.' He saluted. 'The guys will keep an eye on me.'

'That's no comfort. Are you very wet?'

'I hung my oilskins in the outhouse, okay?'

His footsteps could be heard retreating upstairs to his room. He whistled as he went.

Hester looked meaningfully at Alice. 'O, brave new world,' she said, 'that has such creatures etcetera. And you obviously spoil him rotten.'

Alice chuckled. 'Yes, he *is* rather a dish, isn't he?'

'You never let on that your lodger was an Adonis! Does he live here all the year round? I shouldn't think there's much for him in the winter.'

'There isn't. In the winter he works in a wine bar in the West End. Come March or April he comes to Devon ready for the tourist season. If the weather's good he makes more money than I do.'

'Well, he hasn't your overheads.'

'And I haven't his bare-faced cheek.'

'Isn't he any good?'

'I didn't say that. In fact you might say he's overqualified for what he does.' Alice reached for her stick. 'Oh well, I suppose I better go and see about those mackerel.'

She rose, after some preliminary juggling with stick and bag which held such essentials as reading glasses, keys and pills. Hester collected the cups and picked up the tray, putting it next to the mackerel on the draining board.

'You sound as if you don't appreciate Reg or his present,' she remarked.

'Reg is an appalling old layabout who spends most of his time in The Cutter. The rest he spends ogling me. For some reason he has a fixation on me and I wish to God he hadn't. In a place like this you can't get away from him. One of the disadvantages.'

'So there isn't a current lover who could see him off?'

Alice's career had been distinguished by a steady succession of difficult and ultimately hopeless love affairs, mostly with married men, of which her placid existence as the owner of 'The Anchorage Gallery' in the High Street gave little indication.

'You're joking. Crippled old hag like me!'

'Come off it, Alice. I know you too well!'

Alice just smiled, took a clean drying-up cloth out of the drawer and set about drying the cups that Hester had washed.

Much later Hester lay awake in the white attic with its latticed dormer. Alice had already gone to bed. She heard Paul return. Other sounds seemed oddly exotic; the chug of the motor boat on the river, the plaintive piping of a curlew, the sleepy mewing of gulls.

Because of these gentle surroundings and the ostensible purpose of her visit, she made a conscious effort to relax, only to discover that she was more aware than ever of being wound up like a spring. Her shoulders ached and her jaw felt like a steel trap. She pressed her hands across her stomach and sensed its emptiness. As a woman and now as an artist she was barren, unproductive.

She had firmly resisted the temptation to go into detail to Alice about Inez and about the baby. It was all too fresh and too difficult. Her artist's visual memory had seen to it that her mother's face (though surely not her mother, more an effigy on a tomb) was superimposed over the shambles of her own miscarriage. The blood and the pathetic greyish mess was all that would ever be of a child whose existence would, in any case, have been an inconvenience to say the least.

Her mother had lain in the undertaker's chapel which was behind the offices of Hearn and Shapter. It was done up with concealed lighting and chrysanthemums in ostentatious vases. Her mother would have made some joke about not being seen dead in such surroundings!

She had blamed herself bitterly for having postponed paying her mother the attention she deserved until it was too late. Then she had been careless enough to allow a child to be conceived and lost it as if by an act of will, banished to oblivion. The shock of the double loss had been like walking into a wall. No further progress was possible. Robert had made an effort to understand and she had tried to explain but she was beginning to wonder if perhaps this prolonged reaction was hysterical. At first Robert had held the view that she would, in due course, get over both events but recently he'd shown signs of impatience; she had never expected him to sympathise much over the miscarriage, the normal mess and disorder of Amy's babyhood had been quite enough for him, and her associated feelings of guilt over both it and Inez he only partially understood. Poor Robert. She had not been an easy person to live with in the past few months but she had never before endured such an abject and crippling loss of hope.

She wept. The dark cloud that she had held at bay descended. She mourned not only a mother who had died before her time but a child who had never had a time. Perhaps in its embryonic and dreaming state it had dimly grasped the folly of its inauspicious intrusion on lives that had no room for it. She had as good as killed it, she who could hardly bear to swat a fly. Yet she continued to feel its haunting presence on the very edges of her awareness. As if it had some undelivered message to impart.

She moved in a world dominated by male values. Was Melanie Sofford right when she accused her of negating her femaleness in order to survive in that male world?

She slept at last and dreamed that she was presiding over a gallery, selling tickets to a dim, shuffling line of grey people. It was an exhibition of her own paintings but they were all blank, some of them had even turned their blank faces to the wall.

Alice also found sleep difficult. She had taken two co-proxamols but her hip was still troubling her, while her brain trawled up niggling anxieties. The necessity of selling the Cider Press, part of the estate left to her by her parents, felt like an admission of failure, but what else could she do? Business rates were escalating and there now seemed no hope of running the Cider Press as a gallery to attract the very best talent. Unless she sold it there was no hope of repaying Hester the money she'd sunk in it for its renovation. And it looked as if Hester was going to need that money.

Alice pondered the reasons for Hester's present inability to work. She felt that Hester had come to the end of a road along which, surrounded as she was by the male art establishment, she had unconsciously and fatally been losing faith in the very personal vision that had once driven her. It had been infuriating and deeply disappointing to watch. She had always admired Hester for her tough individuality and her contempt for authority, any authority. Alice hoped that she would be able to persuade her friend to stay away from the whole bloody rat pack long enough to rediscover the true sources of her imagination.

CHAPTER THREE

Robert and Eustace were for the moment Lombard's sole occupants. The polished floor glowed aseptically in the light from the glazed panels in the ceiling and from the reflection cast by the spots. Empty, the room appeared larger than on the night of the opening. Robert's paintings dominated the space, but their presence was neither warm nor comforting.

'*Rather* thrilling, don't you think?' Eustace's pop eyes gleamed with apostolic fire. 'I took the liberty of promising more or less that we would hotfoot it New Yorkwards in the not-too-distant future.' He looked questioningly at Robert, his eyebrows twitching like spiny deep-sea creatures. But whether or not Robert himself found the prospect thrilling would have been difficult to say. He simply nodded thoughtfully, standing in his usual attitude with one arm across his chest supporting an elbow.

As Bruno wasn't anywhere about to disapprove, both men were smoking, Eustace had his usual Havana and a curl of smoke twisted upwards from the cigarette clamped like a fixture in Robert's tar-stained fingers.

Eustace was quite accustomed to Robert's reserve. He ploughed on imperturbably.

'It's as I was saying the other night. Waldo, in the shape of the First New World and Union Bank, is looking to re-jig the corporate image, d'you see. Money no object as far as I can gather. We shall in effect, dear boy, be able to name our price.' He held out his arms, cigar aloft, as if to measure the length of a very large gold bar. 'The general scheme is for a prestige installation in the foyer of their brand new SoHo headquarters, New York, you know. And if I say foyer you can forget lobbies and atriums. Think *cathedral*! They say they want the best, dear boy, and think a Brit will give the whole thing that extra cachet, d'you see?'

'So they *were* hoping to keep the cost down,' Robert said drily.

'Not at all! Damn it all, Hirsch already knows the price of a first-rate Gibb!'

'Still more reasonable than a Schnabel or a Hockney.'

'Not for much longer. You're practically up there with Freud, Bacon and Hodgkin as it is. I told our financier friend that you were just the man. He need look no further. Your work is absolutely right. Perfect. It has that *desperate* look, just right for a bank.'

Robert glanced at Eustace sharply. He was never absolutely sure if he was being sarcastic or complimentary but by now he was so used to his mentor's manner, the innocence of his expression, that he gave him the benefit of the doubt. Besides, Eustace was indefatigable in the promotion of both his own and Hester's work. He closed his eyes momentarily against Eustace's vermilion shirt and khaki bow tie.

'I take it that this is a formal offer,' Robert said. 'I mean we are supposed to be taking it seriously.' He dragged on the last of his cigarette and put it out between finger and thumb, refraining in time from throwing the stub on the floor. Eustace had a tendency for over optimism but if he was right this could be the breakthrough he'd always hoped for; all the same he would keep a rein on his reactions until he was one hundred percent sure. But he couldn't control the stirrings of a deep sense of relief. If his work was being commissioned by the First New World and Union Bank it meant he was still considered to be at the top. His reputation, unlike some others, was still secure.

'You say serious? A dead cert. As soon as you've had a chance to cast your eye over the site.' Eustace was now striding about the gallery in his excitement, brandishing the stump of his cigar at Robert's canvases; he slid to a halt before 'Scission', his nose an inch from the paint.

' "Magic and poetry", dear boy,' he roared. ' "Magic and poetry". Sickert.'

'And *he* suggested we went over. To New York, I mean.'

'You don't mind do you, old thing? Crossing the Herring Pond again? Waldo thought soon, you know. These Yanks, they're *so* impulsive, aren't they?' He turned away from 'Scission' and brushed back a strand of hair that had become separated from his scalp; he peered at Robert with eyebrows aloft. Robert fanned out the fingers on which his chin was resting in a gesture of assent.

Eustace said. 'Just leave the arrangements to me. I'll ring our friend tout de suite.' He wagged his head in mock appeasement as if it had been Robert's impatience that was driving him. 'You artists! "Create like God, command like kings, work like slaves!" Brancusi.'

He raced towards the door of his office at a speed decidedly unsafe for a man of his size on a polished floor. Then he stopped and came hurtling back.

'Forgot to ask,' he said, although he had done no such thing. 'How remiss. About that darling wife of yours.' He was out of breath. 'Far be it from me to pry, dear boy, but has she started on . . .' He raised spiky brows.

'Working, d'you mean?'

'Ah, yes. "The mysterious and continual struggle." Bacon.'

'She's due back from Devon next week.'

'And quite recovered from her little indisposition by then, we hope. She never said what it was exactly . . .'

'No. She rang. She sounds much better already. Absolutely.' Robert parried his agent's probing. They had so far refrained from telling Eustace the truth about Hester's illness; Eustace would doubtless bang on about it ad infinitum so it was best that he should, on this subject at least, be kept in the dark. Besides it was just too embarrassing to admit that one had made a balls up of basic procreant potential.

'Good, good, good. Tell her I'm avid to know what she has in store for us. Avid.'

'I'll tell her that.'

'And the divine Amy? Still following the Pharaohs? *What* a pity she didn't follow in the footsteps of her parents instead.'

Robert frowned. The situation between Amy and himself could currently be described as a sort of armed affection with the two of them locked into a cycle of contention and misunderstanding; wilful on Amy's part he had no doubt. 'I thought it was a mistake but there you are. I was hoping that she would have emerged from the state of adolescent pigheadedness before now; as it is she's made her choice and will have to make a go of it.'

'Absolutely. A pity she couldn't have come to your opening.'

Robert gave a short dry laugh. 'She'd sooner be seen dead! She says museums are mausoleums of fashionable taste and that galleries are the playground of the rich and bored. You know the sort of quasi-political spite-speak students go in for.'

'By heart, my boy,' Eustace grinned, exposing dentures of unlikely whiteness. 'Just the process of growing up.'

'Nevertheless it can be extremely boring when it's presented as original thought.'

'Oh, absolutely.' Eustace moved towards the office again with the air of one who has spent just enough time on the social niceties. 'Now, I'm going to press you for just one more minute of your precious time before you rush off. More business, I fear, dear boy.' He ushered Robert into the office.

'Did you hear about the Marcos Old Masters?' he said conversationally. 'Fifteen million they're saying! But you're not really interested in money, are you, laddie? However, I'd like you to cast your eye over a few boring figures if you will . . .'

The street door opened and Gozo came in. He was accompanied by Amanda who acted as a highly decorative gallery attendant and typist. Gozo turned his hand to everything else. Besides being Eustace's lover, he wrote letters, was in charge of publicity, supervised the hanging, entertained buyers in Eustace or Bruno's absence and took care of such details as paying the rent. At around twenty-five pounds a square foot it had proved a very powerful incentive for the planned move to cheaper premises.

Suitable premises had been found in Camden in the shape of an old bottling factory. Its renovation was nearly complete. Gozo had just returned from a flying visit.

'How's it going, dear boy?' Eustace called from the office.

'The architect wants your final decision about the colour of the exterior paintwork,' Gozo said. 'Hallo Robert, how goes it?'

Amanda settled down behind the desk in the gallery and began the ticklish process of sticking a false nail on to the second finger on her right hand. She had broken the original that morning while dusting the pile of catalogues. Her secretarial skills were only average but she possessed the brand of modern looks that exactly fitted the Lombard image that Eustace, if not Bruno, sought to promote. She was tall with a short, sharp haircut and a very red mouth; though she was not particularly interested in art or artists, the job had seemed to promise more glamour than most. However, as it turned out there was less glamour and more solitary boredom than she had anticipated.

CHAPTER FOUR

Alice opened The Anchorage Gallery at nine thirty in the morning. Hester went with her. Paul had departed earlier carrying his folding easel, camp stool and sketch book.

The Anchorage was in the High Street, wedged between Wellands, the estate agents, and a greengrocer. Its shop window displayed a selection of watercolours, aquatints and turned wooden bowls.

'I'll have a word with Wellands at lunch time,' Alice said as she unlocked the street door. 'They could go up and give the Cider Press the once over while you're here.'

'If you've any doubts at all about selling, don't do so on my account,' Hester insisted. 'I'm in absolutely no hurry for the money.' The loan had been a private arrangement between herself and Alice. Robert knew about it, of course, for though they kept their financial affairs separate there was no particular secrecy on either side when it came to money.

'Well, I am, sweetie. And now's as good a time as later since with my usual immaculate timing I've managed to miss the property boom altogether.'

Hester browsed round the gallery, examining handmade pottery, carved wooden birds and tasteful ranks of local landscapes arranged on the hessian-covered walls.

'I must say I would love to have made a big splash with a truly upmarket outfit. Oh well. Dreams! Perhaps the shop is more my level after all,' Alice said, emptying a bag of small change into the till. 'Who knows? A classy gallery might have been more than I could have handled.' She shut the till with a clang. 'You'll notice I'm already indulging in comforting rationalisations.'

'I don't believe you couldn't have handled it. You just got the timing wrong. You have an infallible eye for quality.' Hester picked up a large hand-built pot. 'Look at this for instance.'

'I must admit I think that's gorgeous. She's made one or two huge one-off bowls with that glaze which I'd give my eyeteeth for.'

Hester returned the pot to its stand. 'You could still hold out until after the op of course.'

'No can do. As I said, I need the money.' As far as Alice was concerned the subject was closed. An early customer drifted in and Hester set off as arranged to re-acquaint herself with the town. At first she prowled aimlessly, sights and sounds peripheral to a dull sense of anxiety and a nagging conviction that she should be working. But at what? Beyond thought was the scolding clamour of gulls, the smell of paint, the metallic glitter of sun on water alternating with violet cloud shadow.

She almost fell over Paul deployed with his easel in a narrow street, a sunlit slice of river visible at its end. She stopped and watched. He worked with speed and accuracy.

'I don't do all my stuff in situ,' he explained without any hint of embarrassment. 'I've done this so many times before I could knock it off in my sleep. But being visible is good for business, especially when the grockles arrive. Accessible art, see.'

He squinted at her. His eyebrows were already bleaching out in the sun. Hester, aware that a mild attempt was being made to provoke her, merely smiled. She picked up one of the finished drawings. A view of the waterfront; the usual cottages, boats and river but from an unusual angle.

'I do loads of that one. It sells well. The hanging baskets aren't there at the moment but they will be. I have a very good visual memory,' he added matter-of-factly.

Hester put down the sketch and picked up another.

'So you trained?' she said coolly.

'I got a first at Brighton,' he said, without looking up from his work.

'Good heavens! What in?'

'Would you believe, macramé!' He roared with laughter, obviously delighted with his joke. 'No, sorry. It was painting. No shit.'

Hester perched herself on a low wall and leaned against some ancient railings.

'But have you never thought of using it? I mean really! You don't need a first to do this stuff.'

'What would you suggest? Teaching? Or should I have knocked on the door of the art establishment? Saving your presence, ma'am, hired myself to a Cork Street dealer. Sorry, no thanks.' He threw her another quick glance, his 4b pencil hardly ceasing to move on the surface of the paper. Hester came to the conclusion that he was older than she had first thought. Perhaps thirty. He seemed faintly disappointed at her lack of reaction to his jibes. She had heard similar salvos from Amy, usually directed at Robert rather than herself.

'You think I'm having a go?' he said. He had almost finished his sketch.

'Aren't you?' she remarked drily. 'And you're entitled to your point of view, naturally, if this is all you want. If you consider producing this stuff for the tourists is so much more virtuous.'

'Look at it this way,' he said, suddenly in earnest. 'This isn't great art but it's not rubbish. I give the grockles value for money. I mean I draw bloody well compared with some of the crap that's off-loaded on to the poor sods. So at least they'll have something decent to hang on the walls of the old homestead to remind them of their fortnight on the Costa Devonia. There's this too. I don't suffer from any high-minded angst. In the summer I wind-surf and swim when I'm not painting. I enjoy myself. As a way of life it's hard to beat.'

He grinned and Hester had no doubt about his success with the summer visitors. 'Grockles' as he called them.

'It gives me a buzz when the punters like my work to the point of shelling out hard cash for it,' he went on. 'Some of them come back several years running. There are actually houses in Walsall and Welwyn Garden City that have a Paul Finch in every room. They're collectors, just like Paul Getty. Not as glitzy, I admit.'

He stood up and began to pack away his sketching things.

Smug, she thought, and arrogant but with a persuasive line in patter.

Aloud she said, 'Well, let's hope you continue to keep alive the cause of art in deepest Devon.'

He sucked in his breath. 'Ouch! Below the belt!' But he was still grinning. 'Let's face it, it's just a case of finding your own level, wouldn't you say? I expect that if I could have painted like you I would have done what you did. I just wasn't up to it. Besides I'm too lazy.'

'I don't know that I believe that.'

'Well, time's money and all that. I'm off to the next. Do you want to keep me company or have you planned something more exciting?'

'I've decided to walk to the headland.'

'Ah, yes. The sea stacks. Great. I tried them but they didn't sell. Folks prefer something with more civilised connections. They weren't too keen on nature in the raw.'

'How odd.'

'Not really. Cottages and boats suggest people. More comforting and familiar, see?' He stopped. 'I shall mooch round here for a bit.

If you're going beyond the point, remember high tide's at three thirty.'

'I'll be back long before then.'

She left Paul squinting through a small rectangular view-finder while she continued up the High Street which led into what was known as The Strand. The end of The Strand was marked by a pair of former coastguard cottages, one of which still boasted a weather-beaten flagpole in its front garden. The road gave way almost immediately to a narrow stony beach littered with piles of lobster pots and a ragged line of fishing boats pulled up beyond the high tide mark. Pebbles and dry seaweed crackled underfoot and soon the great red cliff, its perilous brow topped by a fringe of trees and bushes, loomed overhead on one side, seeming to cast a well of darkness at its foot. On the other side the river met the sea, a glittering line beyond an expanse of sand.

There was no one about. Even in summer the place attracted few visitors, for the estuarine currents made bathing dangerous and the high tide covered the beach completely.

The brisk, cold breeze of the last two days was still blowing, driving the heaped white clouds like a flock of sheep across the sky. Shadows came and went, making dramatic changes of colour and tone.

It took longer to reach the furthest headland than she remembered from long-ago expeditions. The cliffs had the habit of throwing out further ramifications or drawing back into small hollowed bays without warning and these effectively blocked the view ahead. The beach had given way to a wide shelf of rock, pockmarked all over with pools, gleaming like pieces of blue mirror. Larger pools shimmered with azure and jade, then unexpectedly pink and straw yellow. And now, rearing up from the rock shelf, on the edge of the surf or still further out in deep water, were the rock stacks.

The impression was of gigantic piles of chipped and rusty plates, both precarious and sombre. On turning the corner she was immediately confronted by a hundred-foot arch of rock that on leaving the cliff hurled itself into space and descended on the seaward side in a series of sculptural ridges, knuckles of hard red rock layered between cushions of softer sandstone. Slashes of brilliant viridian marked the uneven course of streams down its side and sea birds dived through the arch like fishes swimming through blood-red coral. Beyond, the coast withdrew into the distance in a maze of spurs and stacks.

She approached the arch and pressed her hand against its surface.

It left a film of rosy dust on her palm. A school geography expedition. A magnifying glass revealing that yellow grains of sandstone were coated with something called haematite which turned them and the cliffs to rose, carmine, rust or blood red depending on the light.

Directly overhead the arch vaulted upwards in a dizzying parabola, a Gaudiesque succession of ledges and hollows. In the cliffs themselves these hollows became deeply scoured sockets excavated by the sea's ceaseless pounding.

Her head reeled, a sensation not at all like the claustrophobic weakness that had threatened her at the private view, more like an elemental panic in the presence of the potent forces of wind and water and the heave and thrust of mysterious underground collisions.

For much too long she had been shackled to the comprehensible spaces of studio, streets and cities, breathing in carbon monoxide and the sterile air of urban galleries. Energies like the ones that confronted her here challenged all her comfortable certainties, producing a profound astonishment. She had not always lacked contact with landscape, with trees and grass, air, water and rock. Had she not spent working holidays in Italy, France, Mexico? But always, she now realised, with eyes only for the selected image, for its potential for the abstract painter and the fascinating process of filleting the subject to make it palatable to an effete audience.

The events of the last year and a half had stripped her of the protective callous that had grown over her earlier sensitivity. The embryo soul that she had nurtured for a few months had bequeathed her, at least for the moment, its own unclouded vision and raw vulnerability.

Seeking support and comfort she spread her arms over the rock pillar and leaned her head on its crusty skin. If only she could stay in this place long enough, it might just have the power to replace permafrost with warmth and incoherence with meaning.

But it wasn't possible. In a few days she would return to Bristol, to Robert, to her studio where the dust was already settling on the cool, abstract canvases that had brought her money and kudos. Alice had told her that there were plenty of wide-open spaces here where she could feel free to howl if she felt like it but it was either too late or too soon; no tears came and no sound.

She sat on a rocky outcrop until the glittering fringe of the incoming tide reminded her that it was time to leave. It reminded her too that here she was an irrelevance. She should go back to where she came from. She realised that she was cold. Stiffly she got to her feet.

CHAPTER FIVE

Clifton was one of the areas of Bristol that the guide books liked to call 'historic', not only for Brunel's suspension bridge but for the terraces, crescents and squares of grand regency houses.

Salisbury Square was no exception. It was almost completely enclosed, with a large green area dominated by mature beeches in its centre. This was fenced and bore a notice which said 'Residents Only'. The terraces on every side were of classical proportions, the central house in each case being larger than its neighbours and dignified by a triangular pediment and a columned porch. Number twelve was one of these.

Amy ran up the steps, fitted her key in the lock and pushed open the massive front door. In the hall she dumped the kit bag she had been carrying on the floor and banged the door shut with her foot.

'Anyone home?' she yelled and her voice rang hollowly through the hall which was large and high ceilinged with a staircase of stripped and waxed wood rising gracefully from the tiled floor. The walls had been painted a dull red under a cornice of moulded plasterwork, their most conspicuous decoration being two large Turkestan rugs. A giant papyrus was brooded over by a nine-foot Buddha with a curled lip, said to have been part of a Javanese post carving. Its grey surface, split and cracking with age, held faint traces of paint. It could hardly be said to provide a welcoming ambience but since it was a familiar part of home Amy scarcely gave it a second glance.

In the kitchen she filled the kettle and switched it on before looking into the two studios that had been built on at the back of the house. The door of her mother's stood open and was unusually tidy, practically empty of all the normal artistic clutter. What canvases there were had been turned to face the wall. All the sketches, working drawings, colour experiments, photographs and objects of interest that usually adorned the walls had gone. Most of the gobs of paint that had once adhered to the floor had been scraped off, even the paint-stained coffee mugs were missing.

Amy frowned and moved on to her father's studio. There was no change here at least. He had an entirely different way of working, being almost obsessively neat and methodical; the only hint of disorder was the full ashtrays and the empty packets of Marlboros. Most of his recent canvases were now on show at Lombards but all his equipment and paints were arranged in the customary order on a long trestle table that extended the length of one side. Opposite the table under a glazed roof light was the area where he worked. At the far end was a double door to facilitate moving large finished paintings. Beside it a long slit of a window provided the only view of the walled garden that lay beyond. On the wall was pinned a collection of preparatory painted sketches. Robert himself was not present.

Amy surveyed the scene with mixed feelings. Part of her was touched by his meticulous preparations. He was hugely talented and she was proud of him, of both her parents. But another part of her was highly critical of Robert; irrationally she looked on his work, as an occupation for a man, as ridiculous. Other people's fathers were doctors, lawyers, shopkeepers or dustmen. A father who spent his time in his own private world messing about with paint seemed to her like an aberration. While she had been at school she could remember being slightly embarrassed by it. It hadn't mattered that his occupation had made him a comparatively rich man.

As there appeared to be no one home and it was not Phoebe's day to come and clean, she went back to the kitchen where the kettle had boiled. She made herself a cup of coffee and carried it through to the hall where she picked up her bag and made her way to her room on the second floor.

She stripped off the man's tweed jacket that she had found in a charity shop in Leeds, then her grey shorts and navy jersey; finally black leggings and a cotton bra and briefs joined the pile on the floor. She deserted her own shower room and chose instead the bathroom on the first floor which was altogether grander, all original mahogany, brass taps and polished pipework, or at least as polished as Phoebe's efforts could achieve. The monster bath took an age to fill so she sat naked on the edge and drank her coffee. Nude, she somewhat resembled a European version of Gaugin's Tahitian woman; small, well-covered bones and a smooth unblemished skin, in Amy the very palest olive.

She needed time to think and to amass verbal ammunition for the battle to come. She hated and detested discussing her affairs with her father because it always, absolutely always, turned into a row. He invariably pounced on the weakest aspects of her argument, however trivial, and blew them up out of all proportion. His attention to detail was part of his work, she realised that, but then it was part of Hester's too though not so obsessively. Why he could not grasp the validity of her central point and let the rest work itself out she could never understand. It had always been the same, ever since she was a tiny kid, and she was getting absolutely pissed off with it. She stepped into the water and began lazily to soap herself all over with Hester's Seaweed and Loofah Bodybar. Then she did something that she had tried very hard not to do, she began to think about Steve.

'I thought we agreed not to get heavy,' he'd said.

'I'm not getting heavy. I just think you could have told me you were going out with Kate.'

'You see! You *are* upset.'

'Only because you promised that we'd go to see Henry V together and you went with her.'

'Look, I've said I'm sorry.'

'So it was a one-off, was it?'

Silence,

'So it wasn't!'

'Look, Amy, if you must know I'm finding this thing we have is getting too difficult.'

'What d'you mean, difficult?'

'You're so intense.'

'Intense!'

'Stop repeating everything I say.'

The argument had rumbled on but the outcome was never in doubt. She had lost Steve to Kate. He found her, presumably, less 'intense', more restful; like an old sofa, she thought bitterly.

She got out of the bath and wrapped herself in a huge but ragged bath towel, the only one she could find. Later, wearing a long floral skirt and an outsize jersey, she ransacked the fridge and put together a meal of tinned tomatoes and a vegetarian pizza which she covered with a layer of French mustard and extra cheese. She added five pickled onions, all that were left in the jar. She laid a place at the kitchen table and was just sawing herself a chunk of bread when she heard the front door open and close. There were footsteps in the hall and Robert appeared in the doorway.

'Hi,' Amy said.

'Amy.' Robert betrayed no astonishment at her unexpected presence. With his usual economy of movement he put down the overnight bag he was carrying and went to make himself some coffee.

'How did the opening go?' Amy asked cutting chunks off her pizza and ferrying them to her mouth.

'Very well. Better than I thought given the present economic climate.'

'I shouldn't think that would effect your work much.' She said with her mouth full.

'I'm glad you are able to feel so sanguine on my behalf.'

Robert measured coffee into the filter. There was a pause.

Amy skewered a pickled onion with her fork.

'I take it there is an explanation for this unexpected visit,' he said at last.

'You bet,' Amy said with more assurance than she felt.

'Yes?'

'Uhu. I have an interview at the art college tomorrow morning.'

Robert poured boiling water on to the coffee. 'This is an obscure assignment with some relevance to Modern Arabic, I take it?'

'Of course not.'

Robert waited, looking at the top of his daughter's head as she bent over her plate. Since she had been at university she had cut her long chestnut mane into a pudding-basin bob. It reminded him of old photographs of the painter Carrington in the twenties. Her eyes were hooded like his own but hers had a perceptible oriental appearance.

She glanced at him quickly but continued to eat. 'I've left,' she said, then gabbled on rapidly. 'The course had been going really badly for weeks and in any case I've decided that it's just not the right thing for me. They thought it was pointless hacking on if I didn't intend to do the work because from now on it gets seriously tough. So there was only one thing to do.'

Robert leaned against the antique dresser, stirring his coffee with deliberation. 'I see.'

'I'm really sorry and all that,' Amy said. 'I mean, about all the expense and so on but I didn't think that in the circs you'd be too keen on chucking good money after . . .' She hesitated.

'Bad, you mean?'

'No. It's not like that. Nothing's wasted, is it?'

'I'm glad that you're able to be so philosophical about it.'

Amy groaned. 'I *knew* you'd give me a hard time,' she said.

'I would be less inclined to give you a hard time, as you put it, if you could have seen your way to letting me know your intentions earlier . . .'

'But . . .' Amy tried to interrupt but her father ploughed on inexorably.

' . . . as it's perfectly obvious, since you already have an interview elsewhere, that this has been planned for some time.'

Amy's face was aflame. 'It isn't like that!' she said, raising her voice. 'I didn't think that even you would want me to go on with a course I hated. Christ! Anyone would think that this was the first time in history anyone changed their minds about what they wanted in life!'

She got up, snatched up her plate and with a dramatic gesture, scraped the remains of her meal into the bin.

Robert appeared unmoved by these histrionics. 'Am I to understand that the interview at the art college has some bearing on your future plans?'

'I've applied for the Foundation course,' Amy said gruffly.

Robert took out his cigarettes, lit one and returned the packet to the breast pocket of his denim jacket. He let out a smokey breath. 'Ah,' he said.

'What's that supposed to mean?' Seizing the initiative she added, 'Hester doesn't like you smoking in the kitchen.'

'Let's get this straight, shall we,' he said, ignoring her efforts to side-track him. 'In spite of first class 'A' levels you opted against Fine Art and insisted, I repeat, insisted on reading Arabic. Let me remind you of your objections to my advice at the time. You said that a Fine Art degree would inevitably lead to slavish dependence on the male-dominated art market. And having to . . . what were your words exactly . . . ah, yes . . . kiss the arses of rich collectors. Would I be right in thinking that you have now waived these objections?' He saw her rejection, juvenile though it was, of his way of life as a rejection of himself and it had touched a raw spot in his psyche.

Deliberately shunning the dishwasher, Amy turned on the hot tap and sent scalding water gushing into the sink. She squeezed washing-up liquid into it and slammed her plate and coffee mug into the bubbles. Water slopped over her feet.

'Fuck it!' she yelped. 'I knew you wouldn't be able to resist chucking *that* in my face. I just knew!'

'I would actually rather like to know what has brought about this sudden change of heart since it seems that I shall be expected to finance it? I do hope you're not under the impression that Fine Art will be a soft option? And by the way, most fine art graduates would be overjoyed to be dependent on *any* kind of art market.'

Amy flushed. 'I don't *mind* hard work. I like hard work, as long as I'm sure that what I'm doing is the right thing. In my innocence I thought you'd be pleased I'd decided to do art after all.'

Robert said drily. 'You thought reading Arabic was the right thing not too long ago. In fact you waxed quite lyrical about it, I seem to remember.'

'So I was mistaken. People make mistakes. It's no big deal.'

'As you say, no big deal, indeed. What's the odds. Arabic, English, Classics, Art. Who cares!'

'I don't believe this! Look, if someone had told me that it was possible to be an artist without being dependent on the fashionable art market I would have made a different choice in the first place,' she said accusingly.

'What did you have in mind?'

'I believe an artist should and can work in the community, especially women artists.'

Robert smiled. 'You haven't been talking to Melanie Sofford, have you? Look, in fact I quite agree with you. I'm absolutely in favour of art serving the community. I just hope that by the time you're in a position to need its financial support you'll find the community will be duly grateful.'

'You're an arrogant male cynic of the worst kind!' Amy shouted, unable to restrain her anger. This was not how she'd hoped to conduct this discussion at all. For a start, she had not reckoned on Hester's absence. Her mother would have understood and could at least have been reasoned with in a civilised way. Why did she always have to lose her temper with Robert and why did he always remain cool and in control? Even if he meant to back her eventually he would make quite sure that she sweated blood first.

'Listen, Amy,' he said patiently. 'For a start I'm not being cynical, I'm being realistic and if that offends you, I'm sorry. But I've lived in this world somewhat longer than you and I know how it works. And I know the art world and how *that* works a bloody sight better than the fuzzy idealists you've obviously been talking to, well meaning though they may be.'

'So you'r not prepared to pay for the course? That's what it all boils down to, isn't it? I wish to God you were poor, even the stingiest local authority wouldn't make this much fuss over giving me a grant!'

Robert was taken aback. 'Now there, my girl, you're absolutely off track.'

'Oh yes?' she said on a high note. 'Well, that's me all over! Amy's boobed again. But don't think about it, it all stems from me being too *intense*, I expect. In any case, if you won't help me at least Hester will. *She* won't throw my mistakes in my face and will make *some* effort to understand. Where is she, by the way? I want to talk to her.'

'Hester is staying with Alice in Devon. And you are not to pester her with your demands . . .'

Amy's eyes widened. 'She's all right, isn't she? The miscarriage. Have there been complications?'

'No. She's taking a break, that's all.'

'Is that why she hasn't been painting?'

'Something like that.'

'I want to see her.'

Robert spoke with unexpected intensity. 'If you want to discuss your future you do so with me, do you understand?'

'Sod you, Robert! You can stuff your shitty advice *and* your money!'

'All right, since you obviously think you can get along without either we'll say no more, but when you decide to grow up and stop behaving like a spoilt brat perhaps you'll let me know. Meanwhile I suppose I'll have to get on to the university to hear their side of it.'

'Don't you dare,' she cried, 'I absolutely forbid it, I'm not a child and I'm going to that interview tomorrow!'

To hide her humiliating tears she stamped out of the kitchen and slammed the door behind her.

The telephone rang and Robert answered it. It was his mother.

'Oh, Robert. You're there.'

'Mother.'

'I rang before but you had that machine switched on.'

'Why didn't you leave a message on it . . . was there anything urgent?'

'Not urgent, dear, no. Except that Dad and I rather wondered how your private view went.'

'Yes, the private view. It went well, thank you,' he said, noncommittally. 'How are you?'

'Well, thank you. Quite well.'

'And Dad?'

'His cough hasn't been too good lately. The doctor is insisting that he give up smoking altogether.'

'Perhaps he should.'

'Just try telling him that, that's all,' she said, then added tentatively. 'You still smoke a bit, don't you dear? Perhaps you should both think about giving it up. After all one hears such horror stories.'

Robert remained silent. His mother, quite unmistakably anxious not to appear to be criticising him, added an enquiry about Hester and Amy.

'They are both well. Hester's away. Taking a few days' break.'

Mrs Gibb had been told nothing about the miscarriage. Robert rationed out information in strictly limited portions. Grateful as he was for his mother's early encouragement, he frequently wished there was a way of detaching himself from his parents and from his background in such a way as to cause no pain either to himself or to them.

'What about a holiday for you, dear? I'm sure you could do with one,' his mother continued. 'You should think of yourself sometimes. How are you managing while she's away?' Her tone of voice was such that Robert always half expected her to call Hester 'that woman'. She had never accepted Hester as an artist in her own right and was genuinely bewildered by his tolerance of not being looked after by his wife as she herself had once fussed over him, her gifted only child. Evidently, she saw no role for a woman other than as a helpmeet to her husband, in spite of the fact that for years prior to their retirement she had taken the lion's share of the responsibility for their newsagent's business. But she took sole charge of the cooking and housework too. There was part of Robert that yearned for Hester to take the same dual role but because it was quite illogical, besides being impossible, it was a feeling he firmly suppressed.

'I've been in London, Mother,' he said.

'And have your paintings sold well this time?' Robert had once told her sharply not to call them pictures.

'Yes, tolerably, I'm glad to say. There is, in fact, the possibility of a New York commission.'

'America! Robert, that's lovely! Why didn't you tell me before? Tell me about it. Will they pay well?'

Robert immediately regretted his momentary lapse into confidentiality. His mother had absolutely no understanding of his world (how could she?) and invariably embarrassed him by bringing things down to the most mundane level, as if he were selling a packet of fags over the counter.

'Money hasn't been discussed, at least not with me. I daresay Eustace is negotiating.'

'Eustace?'

'My agent, Mother.'

'Oh, yes. I remember.' She didn't understand what Eustace did apart from relieving her son of some of his hard-won income and it would never be possible to explain.

'Well, I hope he tells those Americans how good you are! I was watching a programme on the television the other day about an artist . . . what was his name now . . . Hodgson . . . something like that. From what I could see of it his paintings were just coloured daubs, all splodged on anyhow. I thought at the time how much better yours were, dear . . .' She stopped as if suddenly aware that she sounded garrulous and ignorant, then continued in her usual clipped voice, 'But then I know nothing about it, as you know.'

'Was there anything else, Mother?'

'How is Amy's course going?'

'I think reasonably well,' Robert lied.

'I expect she's quite grown up now. Her studies must keep her very busy.' Too busy to pay us a visit, naturally, he could almost hear her adding, though the little minx had always managed to find time for her maternal grandmother before that lady died. Presumably the attractions of Devon outweighed those of Swindon. She was actually saying, 'You'll give her my love when you see her, won't you. We'd love to see her sometime. We always love to see all of you. As a matter of fact, Robert, there was something I would like to discuss with you rather urgently. But not over the phone. Is there any chance you might pay us a visit.'

'I'm afraid not in the near future. Why don't you write?'

She sounded disappointed but not surprised. 'If you're sure you can't spare the time.'

'It's very difficult at the moment. This American business . . .'

'I quite understand, dear. Perhaps I'll write.'

'Yes, do that. Regards to Father.'

For a minute after he'd rung off and re-set the Answerphone, Robert stood with his hands in his pockets, staring at the floor. Then instinctively he reached for his cigarettes, lit one and remained deep in thought.

His immediate reaction to his mother was irritation, followed by guilt because he knew that lurking somewhere in his sub-conscious was a furious anger towards both his parents simply for being what they were. Their corner newsagency and tobacconist had never made them exactly prosperous but his mother, in particular, had diligently nurtured his early precocious talent. On his sixth birthday she had presented him with a beautiful box of Windsor and Newton's watercolours, artists' not students', because she had been careful to ask the man in the shop and he had told her they were the best, and nothing was too good for her son. When he had seen the gorgeous liquid colour flow from his brush on to the precious piece of Watman paper he knew that the only thing he would ever want to be was an artist. Not that he could have said at the time what an artist was, he'd never met one; though he knew that someone must have originally drawn Desperate Dan or Korky the Cat and the pictures that went with advertising slogans like 'Guiness is good for you.'

At school he had been a loner. If it could have been afforded he would have been sent to a private school. Short of this he somehow got the message from his mother that the children he had perforce to associate with were inferior. He was special. As a result he spent a great deal of time alone with his paintbox while his parents worked in the shop and his classmates played outside in the street.

At forty-four Robert was not unaware of the effect on his character of such single-minded devotion nor his mother's irritating deference towards him now; but he did not see what he could do about it either. That she lived in fear of saying the wrong thing or of appearing to like the tawdry and crass had ensured that their relationship was forever strained and that the small house in Maple Road had been scoured of all hint of character just in case it should appear to Robert that she was lacking in taste and sophistication.

He knew very well that she was bitterly disappointed at being denied a share in her son's success and that she resented the length of time he allowed to elapse between visits but he just could not tolerate either their dreadful little house or the look of reproach on his mother's face.

In the studio his anger subsided as he became immersed in work; he forgot about the problems of both his mother and daughter.

CHAPTER SIX

There was very little space to move in the room behind the shop; this was mostly because as well as accommodating stock, a place had been found for a work table and a printing press. Alice glanced at the clock. Five-fifteen. All she'd sold was a birthday card, (the birthday cards were a financial compromise), and a turned beechwood lightpull. Total, three pounds fifty. In a quarter of an hour she would call it a day. As she turned off the fan heater in order to save fifteen minutes of electricity, she heard the discreet clanger of the shop doorbell. Too much to hope that it would be a customer bent on making a wickedly extravagant impulse buy. Certainly too much to hope for in view of who it was.

Ezra Judd was more likely to want to sell *her* something.

'Alice, my old mate!' He greeted her like an old friend giving the fleeting impression that but for the counter and the bulky package he carried, he would have lunged forward and enveloped her in a bear hug. In fact she had met him only once before, perhaps twice; but gossip about him, probably exaggerated, abounded.

'Nice to see you again, Ezra. How did that exhibition go after all?'

His face creased in thought, at least what was visible of it behind a beard streaked with silver and something else that might have been paint.

'I forget which one that was,' he said. 'Must have been at the Bridge Art Centre, yes? A lot of water has flowed under it since then, alas.' He grinned. 'How's business or mustn't one ask?'

Alice shrugged. 'Bloody awful, if you must know.' She eyed the parcel he was carrying. She hoped he didn't have some idea of off-loading some of his least successful paintings on her or a clutch of pot-boilers knocked off in an afternoon.

'Are you exhibiting anywhere at the moment?' she asked.

'Not a one-man. Just the usual collection of bits and pieces. I'm not fashionable, you know. I sell only to the enlightened and there are precious few of them around. Though I did manage to shift a whopper at the West of England.'

'Good for you. What was it?'

'Two thousand.'

'I mean, what was it? Landscape? Portrait?'

'I get you. Tregardock Beach. Low Tide.'

'You're still living in Cornwall?'

'Yes, still in Rosepound, where I continue to live in a state of ambitious poverty, as they say.'

'I take it business isn't too good for you either?'

'I've come to the conclusion that skating on thin ice is an unavoidable activity for the creative artist so I don't complain. What really pisses me off is lack of time. If one is not a Raphael or one of those brilliant short-lived blighters one does need time; artists should be given a special dispensation in that department.' He gave a gusty sigh, dumped his parcel on the counter and with an exaggerated gesture passed a hand over his eyes. 'Christ, Alice, middle age! I can't stand it. Do you know how old I am?'

Alice laughed, not hazarding a guess. His creased and tanned features, his beard and his quantity of white hair suggested fifty-five at least, probably sixty, but he had the physique of a much younger man. At the time when she was going through a phase of being attracted to older men (usually married, it went without saying), she might have been susceptible.

'Tact is the better part of valour, eh? Well, I'm fifty. In fact today is my fucking birthday!'

'Many happy returns. I take it that you don't like being fifty?'

'A lot less than I liked being forty and even thirty I can tell you . . . What about a drink? Surely you can close up now. We can adjourn to the pub and drown our sorrows together.'

'Sorry,' Alice said, thinking of Hester. 'Not today. What's in this parcel?'

He gave a start. 'Gor blimey! I nearly forgot! I was going to offer you first refusal of these chef d'oeuvres.' He fumbled clumsily with the brown paper.

'Careful. You're tearing it,' Alice said, fearful that if their wrapping was demolished she would feel dutybound not to allow them to go back naked into the world. He produced a painting like a rabbit out of a hat.

'Stormy day. Bodmin moor.'

The painting was not much more than twelve inches by eight. Several assured sweeps of black and gunmetal grey, ochre and dirty white with glimmerings of hot blue underneath.

'What d'you think? Not bad, eh? I think I got down to the guts of it. D'you know Bodmin?'

'I've been there, yes.' At least it was recent work and hadn't been gathering dust in his studio for years. She touched it with a tentative finger. The paint was barely dry. He produced two more. A small Tregardock beach and the church at St Winnow.

'They're extremely good, Ezra,' Alice said.

'Don't sound so damned surprised! I am good.'

'I like your work, at least what I've seen of it; but you know I couldn't sell them here.' She glanced round the shop. 'As you see, it's mostly prints and watercolours.'

'But what about the new gallery? I was expecting to see it done up, glistening and open for business. And of course with the possibility of a nice little one-man in it for me.'

'Sorry, but it fell through. The money ran out, otherwise I should have been delighted to give your stuff a whirl.'

'Never mind. Story of my life. All the same, rotten luck. Couldn't you drum up enough backers? I would have chipped in but you know how it is. I can't even afford to get my motor though its bloody MOT.'

Alice picked up her coat and bag as the hands of the clock moved to five-thirty. 'It wasn't only the money.'

Ezra watched her thoughtfully. 'I get your drift. What a sod. So what will you do with the gallery? I heard through the grapevine that it was nearly finished.'

'Sell it, I expect.'

'My name is Might-Have-Been. Also called No-More, Too-Late, Farewell. There are few enough galleries that are prepared to handle my stuff these days. Mind you, if I'd been into hurling the old Dulux at six square yards of best cotton duck or casting the contents of my dustbin in plaster I might have been in with a chance. In my misguided youth I actually had a bash at that sort of thing. Bugger this for a game of soldiers, I thought, there's nothing in this caper for a dyed-in-the-wool painter. So I packed it in.'

'But things are getting better now, aren't they?'

'Not so's you'd notice. Too much sterling, dollars and yen tied up in the bloody stuff, you see.'

Alice opened the door. 'Ezra, I have to go. I have someone staying.'

'Aha! Do I smell an "affaire"? Of course you don't want to go drinking with an old reprobate like me when there's a grand passion on the go.'

They stood in the street as Alice locked the door.

'Nothing like that, I'm sorry to say. Have you heard of Hester Eliot? Well, naturally you have.'

'Hester Eliot! Now there's a name to conjure with. But of course. One of the great courtesans of the art establishment. Don't tell me you know Hester Eliot!'

'Before you say any more, she's a very old friend . . . and my guest.'

'I wasn't speaking of her sexual morals.'

'Nor, I hope, of her artistic ones.'

'Now come on, Alice. Loyalty can go too far.'

He tucked her arm against his yellow oilskins. 'Which way?'

Alice attempted to pull away. 'Thank you, but I don't need help. And it's this way.'

Ezra reclaimed her arm. 'I'm not offering help. I think that true believers should stick together. I need the reassurance if you don't.'

Alice gave in. They made their way up the High Street.

'Where have you left your car?'

'Up by the church.'

'It's all double yellow lines up there.'

'Oh, what the hell!' he said.

'I'm truly sorry I couldn't take your work but a high street shop is hardly the place for it.'

'I know, I know. All wrong as you say. I thought the gallery might be up and running. So, am I to meet the darling of Cork Street?' He chuckled, a deep rumbling that transferred itself through Alice's arm.

'Not if you're going to be rude to her. She'll think it's just sour grapes.'

'Is that what *you* think it is?'

'Look, I'm well aware of the dangers of fence sitting but I both appreciate your point of view and admire her accomplishments which don't include chucking Dulux at canvas, by the way; she's better than that, a lot better.'

The ghost of an idea entered Alice's mind which she might have labelled 'creative mischief' if she'd had to explain it.

'I can't come to the pub with you,' she said, 'but why don't you come back with me for a drink. Just as long as you understand that Hester is staying with me for a rest. She hasn't been too fit lately and I won't have her insulted by itinerant painters.'

Ezra turned an innocent beaming face in her direction.

'Credit me with a little tact, for Christ's sake!'

'A commodity you're not famous for, as I understand.'

'Do you think I would dare insult one of Britain's Greatest Living Painters?'

'Like a shot. But not in my house, eh?'

'A truce, Alice dearest.'

'I'm not your dearest either.'

'So, is your G.L.P. suffering from sickness of body or sickness of soul?'

'Shall we change the subject?'

They did.

Hester had returned from the red cliffs in a strange frame of mind, though it was a mood that extended beyond her mind, engaging tracts of personality that had lain untouched for so long that she'd ceased to be aware that they existed. The experience, out there by the red cliffs, had awoken far echoes of childhood, when she had first consciously discovered the emotion of wonder. The amber coins of lichens on granite, light through the petals of a field poppy, the rainbow encompassing a waterfall; all long since forgotten.

For an hour she had been sitting in The Riverside Tea Rooms, which was another example of a territory unvisited since childhood. It had been empty apart from a couple of elderly women in the far corner. Logs crackled in the grate of what must once have been the front parlour of a cottage. Old fashioned blue and white tureens had been placed in niches to provide atmosphere and some of Paul's watercolours hung on the walls, discreetly price tagged.

Hester's intention had been to meet Alice at the Anchorage and walk home with her but instead she sat over successive cups of tea, thinking; though thinking implied a logical, linear process rather than the confused brooding which was what was actually taking place. As far as she could see what it all boiled down to appeared to be a profound discontent. Discontent that had first manifested itself in her painting but now clearly permeated her whole life. She felt herself imprisoned. Matisse had warned artists that they should never become prisoners of their own success and had cited the example of the great Japanese artists who were said to change their names several times in the course of their lives to safeguard their own freedom. If she thought it would help she would do the same. She was unwilling to shatter her mood with conversation, even with Alice, so by the time she paid her bill she knew that the Anchorage would be closed. She made her way past shops also closing for the day.

There was a sense in which she felt as if a layer of her skin had been peeled away leaving her exposed and susceptible. Colours seemed brighter, sounds impinged more, the smell of the river, fish, tar and paint were more acute. The sensation was on the edge of pain and she felt very much in need of a shell. When she reached the house, opened the kitchen door and heard voices her heart sank.

Alice called her name and she went unwillingly into the parlour where she was introduced to a bearded man whose size made the small room seem overcrowded.

'Ezra was hoping to show some work at the Cider Press,' Alice explained.

'And discovered that it was not to be,' he said. 'Never mind.'

'What sort of thing do you do?' Hester enquired, making an effort.

'Ezra's a painter,' Alice said, putting a drink into Hester's hand. 'Sit down, Hester. You look a bit done in. How far did you go, for Christ's sake?'

'You know. Along the beach to the Arch,' Hester said vaguely. 'How was business?'

Alice pulled a face and bent to throw a log on the fire. Hester got the benefit of the full blast from Ezra's bright blue eyes. The artist as an old dog, she thought savagely, summing up a type she knew well.

'This arch,' he said. 'Would it be the Belstead Arch?'

Hester nodded.

'I've heard of it but I don't know the local landmarks too well, more into the Cornish scene myself. But landscape doesn't cut much ice with sophisticated London painters on the whole, does it? A bit *vieux chapeau*, eh?'

Alice said sternly. 'Hester isn't a London painter. She lives in Bristol.'

Unmoved, Hester watched the new log catch.

'And you live in Cornwall?' Glancing at him briefly.

'Little place called Rosepound just over the border.' Cradling his glass, he leaned back stretching his legs towards the fire. He looked very much at home.

'Now this I call a very civilised way to wind up an otherwise fruitless day,' he said. 'And I'd like a chance to repay your hospitality. In fact, why don't the two of you trot down to my part of the world while Hester's here? Rosepound is a pretty magical place, you know, having just about managed to escape the worst this God-awful century can hurl at it, thank heaven.'

'I'm afraid I'm not staying long,' Hester said quickly.

'Ah, do I hear the siren song of Cork Street,' he said. 'And doesn't it make me glad I'm tone deaf.'

'Galleries are not finding things quite so rosy as they did six months ago,' Hester said sharply. 'I'm bloody glad that Lombards keeps going, that's all.'

'Quite,' Ezra said. 'Otherwise where would one be.'

Hester glanced at Alice but Alice was sitting comfortably gazing at the fire with an expression on her face as smug as that of the bride in Brueghel's 'Wedding Banquet'. It had been her idea to ask the man in for drinks so why was she abdicating from her social responsibilities?

'I gather you're having difficulties finding exhibition space?' Hester said.

'There are exhibition spaces and exhibition spaces as I'm sure you know,' he said. 'Some I could mention just aren't worth the candle. You finish up having sold nothing and what's more some clumsy sod has put their foot through one of your best canvases or has lost the bloody thing altogether.'

'I think I can safely say that Lombards would not be guilty of that.'

'But on the other hand, I can't see them taking my stuff in the first place!' He roared with laughter. Alice topped up his drink. Why was she encouraging him dammit! Hester thought.

'Are those some of yours?' she indicated the untidy package beside Ezra's chair.

'Don't tell me you're prepared to endure that most ticklish of predicaments,' he said. 'Having to find something nice to say about another painter's work. No, I'll spare you that.'

'As you wish. Though I assure you I don't bother to say nice things about work if I don't mean them.'

'I'm sure you don't,' he said.

Abruptly coming to life, Alice reached across, extracted one of the paintings and held it up for Hester to see. Ezra grinned, shrugged, absolving himself from responsibility.

'Now Hester,' Alice said. 'What about this?'

The brushwork was agile, precise, the kind that Hester knew could be achieved only after years of experience. There were no short cuts to that level of skill. She was surprised at the evident sensitivity, the awareness of place which she would never have guessed at in the man himself. And yet . . . And yet, there was the impression that the painter had ceased to set himself new challenges and was working in a well-worn groove. All too familiar to her.

'Self-parody is a horrible temptation for an artist,' she said.

'I told you she wouldn't pull any punches,' Ezra confided to Alice.

'I was speaking generally,' Hester said. 'I'm sure you know what I mean.'

Ezra sipped his drink, watching her attentively.

'In fact I like this,' she continued. 'I like it very much. You obviously love the moor.'

'Aha. Is that what you see in it? Love?'

She nodded.

'The kind that doesn't tarnish,' he said. Then with a laugh. 'Other sorts all seem to give way to tedium sooner or later. But then I'm an inconstant bugger . . . You're serious about this business of self parody, aren't you?'

'I'm an expert on it, believe me.'

Ezra looked at her quizzically, apparently unsure how to take her meaning. He finished his drink.

'It seems to me that this warrants further investigation,' he said, heaving his large frame out of the armchair. 'What a pity we won't have time. Promise me you'll both visit me at Rosepound . . . perhaps in the summer? Now where did I leave my coat?'

Hester had been certain he was the kind to overstay his welcome but he thanked Alice pleasantly for the drink and was gone. She was about to grill Alice about her uncharacteristically reticent mood when Paul turned up burdened with his painting things, and the opportunity was lost.

The Old Cider Press could be reached either by the road that served the houses on the top of the hill or by taking the short cut up the lane that ran beside Alice's house. Hester chose the latter route which snaked up the hill, accommodating itself to the random distribution of dwellings and occasionally breaking into flights of steps where the way became steeper. Her first look at the Cider Press had been with Alice before the builders had moved in, when it had been one step away from dereliction. Today she came alone since Alice was busy in the shop and Paul had been up early to catch the light before the threatened rain arrived.

On each side doorways and open gates afforded glimpses of the bright cadmium yellow of daffodils or a cascade of purple aubretia beside washing lines hung with sheets and towels not destined to dry, for the weather was already closing in, bringing a soft drizzle. From doorways and windows came sporadic snatches of domestic conversation or the sound of radios. Strangers she met smiled and wished her 'good morning'. It was a different world. According to Alice the place was awash with feuds, passions and all manner of intrigues but to Hester it seemed warm and hospitable. A safe haven. A good place for reflecting and licking wounds. Robert would certainly have called it a funk hole. Boring and parochial.

The final flight of steps ended in a kissing gate which gave on to a wider lane, once surfaced after a fashion but now fissured and weed grown. The lane was wide enough for a vehicle though it ended abruptly a few yards beyond the Cider Press with a stone wall and a tangle of hawthorn and bramble, after which the ground fell away steeply. Directly opposite her was the wall of the Cider Press itself and next to it a rusting iron gate set in a high hedge. There were signs that the gate and the hedge had not long ago been wedged open and cut back to give access to builders' lorries and equipment but nature was already recolonising: cow parsley, alexanders, goose grass and the minute fists of emerging ferns pressing up greenly.

Inside the gate and alongside the building was a small overgrown paddock. A concrete mixer still stood with its feet in mud and grass but a path had been cleared round the footings of the walls and temporarily surfaced with hardcore. On the side furthest from the lane there were two doors, one at ground level and the other high up, reached by an exterior wooden staircase.

Hester selected the key that opened the lower door and went inside. The windows had been boarded up as a safety precaution but following Alice's instructions she found the main switch and surveyed her surroundings by the light of a string of naked bulbs that had been fixed up for the convenience of the builders. The architect's plans had been coming together nicely. Susan Orchard apparently had all the right ideas, leaving the original structure and materials intact wherever possible so that the place still had a look of age and retained its character. In fact the work was further ahead than she'd anticipated. She was standing in an anteroom or lobby, to one side were spaces she knew were intended for an office and cloakrooms and beyond, separated by a wall of planks deliberately left rough and uneven, was the area that had been destined to be the gallery itself. Here the slate floor had been relaid and the windows repaired and reglazed where necessary. The huge beams over her head were sound and would last as far into the future as they had in the past.

It was about forty feet long and twenty-five wide; it would have made an excellent gallery.

She went back outside and up the staircase, sound but still with its peeling dark brown paint. Opening the small door at the top she stepped inside. Here the windows had not been boarded up and in spite of the rain the place seemed flooded with light, most of it streaming in from a large arched window in the end wall; invisible from the ground outside because of the steep slope, it faced west, towards the estuary. Its arch and the high restored rafters lent the old apple store an ecclesiastical air of tranquillity; she could almost smell the ripening fruit along with the faint odour of wood preservative. She had already noticed that the roof had been repaired, together with the guttering and downpipes, and she now saw that the space between the rafters had been relined with planks. She was glad that so much old timber had been reused. The renovations had restored its character rather than destroyed it, thank God. The floor had not been attended to but the wide elm planks looked sound enough, the cracks between them could be dealt with by taking up and relaying. She walked across to the window which reached practically to floor level. Even in the rain the view was magnificent. Directly beneath her a wilderness of trees and shrubs, bedewed with moisture, gave way eventually to a tumble of gleaming roofs complete with sentinel gulls. Beyond them was the estuary and on the further side, Tidemouth. Through the drifting curtain of rain she could see as far as the frilled white crescent which betrayed the position of the sand bar at the mouth of the river. Cliffs were veiled in mist and headlands receded into a mysterious distance. It was very quiet, the fine rain made no sound, only the usual mewing of gulls reached this lofty eyrie. It had a distinct atmosphere; more than just tranquil. Expectant perhaps.

Conscientiously she turned out lights and locked doors but instead of turning back to the lane she explored the further side of the paddock where another, smaller gate, jammed fast with brambles, led to a path across the headland. She fought and kicked her way through, then followed the path until it petered out in a small wood and a tangle of undergrowth and stunted trees at the cliff's edge. A short distance farther on, a perilous place of steep turfy slopes and rocky outcrops marked the spot where the Belstead Arch was as yet still anchored to the land. Below, the high tide besieged the base of the arch and the stacks in a milky chaos of contrary surges. Nesting seabirds screamed their protest at her intrusion. Suddenly it was a place of legend, wild and Promethean, the turf untrodden by the human species, the air off the sea raw and unpolluted. She filled her lungs with it, discovering tears on her cheeks, or it might have been the rain, which was heavier now. It was a wild place but she felt at home here as if this was where her origins lay. Reluctantly she turned away and retraced her steps.

It could scarcely be said that she had a place of origin. Her Scottish grandparents, Elsbeth and Donald, had emigrated to Texas where they had run an unsuccessful sheep farm.

'The prairie was white with bones of sheep,' her grandmother was fond of saying, 'as far as the eye could see.'

'So then what did you do?' As a child Hester had known her prompt lines.

'We headed south for Mexico,' Elsbeth said dreamily. They had somewhat ineptly sold the farm to a rancher who one year later discovered oil on the property and made a fortune. In Mexico Donald had tried his hand at exporting shellac but under the brand new constitution foreigners became fearful of their position, believing the country to be under Bolshevik rule.

'The fighting as a whole had died down but there were still guerrillas and bandits about,' her grandmother had said. 'We were once on a train and came under attack from a gang of *cristeros*. We had to hold cushions to the windows to stop the bullets.'

'What good did you think cushions would do!' Hester's mother, having heard the story a thousand times before, dissolved into paroxysm of laughter, but to the child Hester it made perfect sense.

Plans were made to return to Britain but before they sailed from Veracruz, Donald, who was fifteen years older than his wife, died of yellow fever. Inez had always suspected that he had not been her real father though Elsbeth strongly denied this. Since both Inez and Hester had inherited a dominant gene bestowing black hair and pronounced aquiline features, there did seem ample grounds for suspicion, especially as both parents had the typically Scots mixture of reddish-brown hair and grey eyes.

Elsbeth's intention had been to return to Scotland but she never managed to get further than Southampton where she lived until her death. Inez on the other hand had spent her life wandering from place to place until she met and married Hester's father Rupert Eliot. Together they had started a small rural pottery which lasted four years, the same length of time as the marriage. Rupert emigrated to New Zealand and Inez took up her peripatetic existence again, this time with Hester in tow.

Hester became all too familiar with the overtures to a new move.

'What d'you say to living on a farm, Hester? You'll love it. All that fresh air and all those animals!' A housekeeping job for a battery chicken farmer in the back of beyond.

Or, 'It will be just what you like, lots of other kids to play with!'

A cold, damp commune in the Forest of Dean.

Lastly, 'A darling little flat in this absolutely enchanting village.' Two cramped rooms in a Devon village in exchange for running the antique shop underneath. Surprisingly Inez stuck this long enough for Hester to attend the local grammar school and even acquire some fairly creditable 'A' levels. The commune, or rather the ever-changing colony of arty characters, had ensured that she was accustomed early to nakedness, overt sex and holding her own against other people's half-tamed children; above all to having apparently limitless access to paints, drawing materials and at least semi-professional, though casual, tuition. Her relationship with her mother was close though her nurturing was haphazard, for she was expected to shift for herself at an early age, rather like a young animal. From her present perspective she regarded such an upbringing as nearly ideal for an artist. True, she had frequently felt insecure, afraid even, but Inez had an unshakeable, and infectious, conviction as to the benevolence of the world in general so it was impossible to remain fearful for long. Her mother could never be said to have been irresponsible, it was just that she bore responsibility lightly. All the same, from quite a young age Hester had seen it as her role to suggest strategies for their joint survival. Later, in their married life, Robert had come to depend on this useful aptitude.

The village of Sandford Bishop, if not the flat over the antique shop, had turned out to be Inez's most permanent home for she had remained there until the stroke put an end to her life. Her death had been as unconventional as her life. She'd had a part-time job at a garden centre where she had been found, quite dead, lying as if peacefully asleep in a display of primulas. Hester still found it almost impossible not to believe that sooner or later she would hear her mother's voice come over the telephone, breathless with some new venture.

'What d'you think! I'm working for the Cat's Protection League. Isn't it a hoot!' or, 'Guess what? I'm driving a taxi!' Both of which jobs she'd done at some stage, though the taxi driving hadn't lasted very long as Inez had a very poor sense of direction.

Hester attended the funeral in an unreal state of shock, noting only that it was unexpectedly well attended; Inez appeared to have a great many friends who all spoke affectionately of her. Robert had been in Tokyo and unable to accompany her. Besides he didn't like funerals and probably wouldn't have come anyway.

Hester heard from her father once a year at Christmas time.

Evidently, he no longer moved in artistic circles and was apparently unaware of his daughter's achievements. She felt a frustrated sense of loss over her father. Frustrated because she had never experienced how a father should be except in a second-hand capacity from the somewhat haphazard variety available at the commune. So neither she nor Robert really knew much about fathering since the directing force in his family too had been his mother.

Hester made her way back to the Cider Press. A figure in a greasy waxed jacket was standing in the rain gazing at it.

'Tis a praper shame to let 'n bide like this yer.'

Long ago conversations with the inhabitants of Sandford Bishop echoed in Hester's head.

'I'm sure it won't stay like this for long.'

All she could see under the hood of the jacket was an enormous purple nose down which the rain cascaded in a succession of large drops.

'I reckon 'twas all coz they did send a lil maid to see to 'n.'

'If you mean Miss Orchard, that's nonsense. She's a highly qualified architect.'

The hooded figure shook his head sadly and the hood slid off, revealing dark strands of hair pasted over a bald pate. Hester was already moving in the direction of the lane.

'Tidn't the same,' he called, 'They'm too flighty. What could 'er expect wi' a flighty lil maid seeing to 'n. I do reckin th' ol' roof do still leak like a colander. If Miss Ruddock had taken my advice 'er would've 'ad ol' man Buddle fix 'n up for 'n.'

It dawned on Hester that she was speaking to Reg Gammon, Alice's faithful admirer and donator of mackerel.

'I'll tell her what you said.' Hester went out of the gate.

'An' tell 'n to watch out fer thic ol' artist what was yammerin' 'is 'head off down th' Cutter las' night.'

So Ezra was still in Coombe Ferrers.

'Tis never right, 'oman alone like that,' was Reg's parting shot. She left him standing in the rain and went back down the hill.

CHAPTER SEVEN

'Have you any objection to a tape recorder?' she asked. Robert shook his head. He took out his cigarettes and offered one to Caroline.

'Not for me thanks, but you go ahead,' she said, answering a question he never asked.

Robert perched on a high stool beside the table on which his brushes and paints were arranged. He was thankful that Amy was not in the house. She had taken herself off early carrying a folder of work. Her interview was at eleven. He felt vaguely uneasy and restless. He put it down to the fact that Hester was away.

Caroline pretended to fuss with the tape recorder although it was already set up. This was the first time she had been alone with Robert but her cool exterior perfectly contained the turbulence inside. Level-headedness was one of her strengths, various degrees of dissimulation had landed her progressively more prestigious jobs. She had no doubt that being assistant editor of *Painting Now* would lead inevitably to being its editor or to being editor of something very like it. After all she had laboured long and inconvenient hours to get this far. She had attended private views and auctions, she had read omnivorously anything on art history she could lay her hands on, she had wangled introductions to and picked the brains of anyone she thought worth knowing in the art establishment and she had kept herself informed about the international art market. Even before she'd held any official status she had made sure that she had an invitation to important events in the art calendar. Her views had once been sought by a television reporter covering the Turner Prize when she had been a very minor cog indeed. This surprised no one who knew her. She radiated a mesmeric blend of confidence and polish. The fact that this overlaid a streetwise toughness had never been a disadvantage; in fact it frequently gave her the edge over rivals with twice her knowledge and understanding of art.

What she liked best was having the entry to the artists' private studios, being part of what she thought of as a specialised and enclosed world, the furnace that drove the engines of the art industry. It had happened that interviews with male artists had led to more intimate relationships but so far she could never have claimed that her emotions had been very much engaged. Robert Gibb was different. His very aloofness was a challenge, for it was notoriously difficult to get to interview him (she had been trying to set this up for months), but his elusiveness only added to his mystique. One or two of her colleagues who had been less successful in this direction claimed that Eustace Tench's reluctance to grant interviews with his client was because he knew how deadly boring Gibb could be, if only because of his refusal to be outrageous or to give anything away. Caroline didn't accept this. She hadn't met many boring artists. Opinionated, arrogant, reclusive or vulgar, yes. But totally unamusing? Very few. Certainly not Robert Gibb. Robert was the most exciting man she had ever met.

'I'm sorry Hester couldn't make it,' she lied. 'it would have been good . . . you know husband and wife, both painters . . . Hester did call me to explain. It's good of you to see me all the same.'

'Yes . . . well.' Robert tapped ash into an overflowing ash tray.

To put him at ease she began with innocuous questions about the current exhibition; flattering and knowledgeable. Naturally she had done her homework which this time had been far from a chore. Questions on the creative process he also handled easily but on the subject of his origins and his private life he immediately clammed up. Too soon. She wished she could have primed him with booze but this was difficult on his own territory. She continued with questions about his future plans.

Robert hadn't wanted this interview but Eustace had, unusually, pushed quite hard over it, although they had both visualised Hester being present. On a purely social level Hester handled these things so much better than he did; besides, photographers loved her. Eustace had waxed lyrical in support of a few moody, black and white photographs of them both in their respective studios, he would not be pleased that Hester had obdurately refused to take part. Robert himself was deeply angry with Hester. Angry first of all that she had chosen to distance herself from his recent success, angry over her moodiness during the opening at Lombards, angry that she was doing no work, angry that she had left him with Amy's problems to sort out and angry in the knowledge that Hester would undoubtedly back Amy up against him.

His thoughts were jolted back to the present. He had been asked a question.

'I'm sorry?'

'Successful painters are often bitchy towards each other. I was just asking if there was any rivalry between you and Hester?'

'No, never. Fortunately we have always been very supportive of each other. There has never been any question of rivalry.'

He wondered if this were true. Recent events were casting some doubt on the apparent reliability of the arrangement that existed between Hester and himself. If this were disturbed in any way he was not at all sure whether his past assumptions would remain intact.

'What about when you were at art school together? Was there rivalry then?'

'I wasn't aware of any. But our styles were very different.'

'Would you say that your styles are more alike now?'

Robert crushed out the stub of his cigarette thoughtfully. He was still perched on the high stool. With his head higher than Caroline's he felt more in control. She seemed untroubled by this arrangement, manifesting only professional composure and friendly interest.

'Not really. Though a degree of influence is possible.'

Caroline allowed the silence to lengthen as if she expected him to enlarge on this.

'Do you envisage any change of direction?'

'One is always changing direction but the deviations are often too subtle for the uninitiated to perceive.'

She laughed. He supposed she took it as a put-down, which perhaps it was. He smiled wrily, beginning for the first time to take notice of her. She was worth noticing; only his apprehension of the coming interview had stopped him doing so before. She sat easily on the only comfortable chair in the studio, her short skirt displaying good legs in sheer black tights. Her hair was of a Scandinavian blondeness cut to an inch all over; there was a fragile quality to the bone structure, like an ethereal boy. Something decisive passed between them.

'Your paintings are celebrated for their size and layers of thin glazes. Do they take a long time to do?'

His hand hovered over the pocket that contained his cigarettes. 'It's hard to say. I work on several at once. Let's say months rather than weeks.'

'And your sources?'

Robert looked at Caroline's legs thoughtfully.

'Do you understand this? Some things are buried in the unconscious and emerge years later when they could surface as an inspirational driving force or as a problem of logistics.'

Caroline asked him about his routine.

'I work long hours. I need very little sleep.'

'What about Hester? How does her routine fit in with yours?'

'Not at all.' Robert said crisply. 'Hester has no noticeable routine. She might spend ten hours at a stretch in the studio and then do no work for one or two days.

'Like now?'

When Robert didn't answer she followed up her question with another. 'You work in separate studios. Does this mean you don't see each other very often?'

'I suppose we see as much of each other as we would if we had conventional jobs.'

'Right.'

It dawned on Robert that her interest in him was more than professional. There had been small give-away movements; a re-adjusting of the position of her legs, a tongue just brushing her top lip, the faint clash of the bunch of silver bracelets on her insubstantial wrist, a lowering of her eyes to her notes after a gaze that held his a moment too long. He was intrigued, definitely. She reminded him of how much on occasion he missed teaching. He had always felt reassured by the overt admiration of a certain type of female student. The ones who regarded him as a kind of secular god, the ones untouched by student politics and strident feminism. He picked his women fastidiously. He was not promiscuous compared to other men of his acquaintance, there had never been an endless procession of mistresses nor any long-standing affair; he had always avoided emotional entanglement, in fact he never allowed a relationship to continue to the point of familiarity. He was proud of the fact that none of them had ever threatened his work or his marriage or the indispensability of Hester. He thought it possible that Hester had known about some of the women but being Hester had said nothing. She was a realist when it came to these things. Without realising it she represented his insurance policy against importunate females.

'Which artists have influenced you? Whom do you admire?' Caroline continued.

'I don't know about influence but I admire Rothko as I expect you already know, especially the earlier paintings. Then there's Clifford Still and Miro.'

'All moderns.'

'As you say, all moderns.'

'Why? I mean, what about earlier painters.'

'You mean Rembrandt, Velasquez et al?'

'Yes.'

'I admire them at one remove. I can't relate to them except in an historical context.'

'Some people would say that was heretical.'

'I'm aware of that. But then very few people think for themselves. They revere what they have been taught to revere. Those men were human. We approach their work blinkered by history, tradition and preconceptions of every kind. It gets in the way of pure seeing.'

'Aren't there preconceptions about modern art too?'

'Of course. Mostly negative.'

'Why is that, d'you think?'

'Historically the man in the street had nothing to do with the production and consumption of art, he had no access to it, except perhaps in churches, therefore he had no opinion about it. The difference now is that his opinions are solicited on every issue, he thinks therefore that his views on art are as legitimate as those of the professional who has made it a lifetime's study . . .'

He was beginning at last to feel at ease and expounded his ideas at some length.

This is good, Caroline thought. Just the kind of stuff that would go down well with the readers of *Painting Now*. There would be a satisfying clutch of follow-up letters praising or castigating Robert's elitist position. Now that she had him talking he needed very little further encouragement. She watched him hungrily, trusting to the tape recorder to listen to Robert the professional while she concentrated on Robert the man. She was intrigued by all that he refrained from saying about himself but by this time she knew there would be other more private occasions to find out what made Robert Gibb tick.

'Thank you. That was absolutely marvellous.' She pressed the stop button. 'You're a terribly good subject. Some people clam up or start spouting the most awful pretentious rubbish.'

He smiled an acknowledgement and lit another cigarette. As an afterthought he offered the packet.

'I think I will, thank you.' Normally she never smoked and drank very little, disliking the way alcohol clouded her perceptions. This was different, there was a moment of mutual relaxation of tension, as if they had just made love, which justified breaking her rule.

'Are you staying in Bristol this evening?' he said. 'I thought we might go out for a meal.'

She hesitated. She would like to have been sure that he was alone. On the phone, Hester had apologised for missing the interview and had given as her excuse for doing so, her pressing need for a break, which was intriguing in itself because Hester was known to be both reliable and professional. But none of her leading questions produced any further explanation. Anyway, she was more than glad to have Robert to herself. There was no sound beyond the door and the other studio appeared to be closed and unoccupied. Robert seemed to sense her reason for not answering immediately.

'Hester won't be back for a few days,' he said quietly.

Caroline stood up and stowed the tape recorder away inside her capacious bag.

'I'd love to. Thank you. Shall we go in my car?' She already knew that he disliked driving, besides she preferred to have control over her own transport.

'I'll look forward to it,' he said but his voice gave absolutely nothing away.

CHAPTER EIGHT

Hester completed the unfamiliar domestic tasks of vacuuming the shop carpet and dusting the turned bowls and hand-made pottery. Alice had gone to Exeter for a check-up at the hospital and as Paul had art materials to buy it was arranged that he should take her. Alice was finding it increasingly painful to drive. Hester put herself in charge of the shop.

'See she does something nice as well, Paul. Has her hair done or buys some scent.'

Alice's condition worried her; she had even offered tactfully to pay for private treatment but had been briskly turned down. *No,* Alice would *not* either pay for private treatment herself nor allow anyone else to do so on her behalf.

On an impulse Hester looked up the number of the potter whose work Alice so much admired. She got through to the potter herself and ordered one of the bowls she remembered Alice saying she'd give her eyeteeth for; well, eyeteeth would not be necessary, she would have it as a post-operative present. Besides her birthday was coming up later in the summer.

After that she kept her restlessness at bay with various odd jobs. She had never been much good at leisure, for leisure and work amounted to the same thing as far as she was concerned. She wondered how Alice coped with boredom, but then Alice's life had changed radically; now it was not only entirely different from her own but entirely different from how it had once been for Alice. Arthritis had created an uncharacteristically philosophical Alice, or so it seemed on the surface. The turbulent days when her friend had careered from one passionate and usually ill-fated love affair to the next seemed to be over. As ever she sailed majestically through life, but the trail of emotional wreckage behind her was missing. By comparison Hester's own love life had been serene to the point of dullness. There was never time or passion left over for affairs; her emotional energy was expended on her work, on Amy and on Robert. Besides after she had married Robert, she had made a conscious decision not to mess up her life sleeping around; she had already, she realised in retrospect, done rather too much of that as a student. Affairs that had been every bit as tumultuous as Alice's.

This current lack of work had cut her adrift from familiar landmarks. Would she now become just the helpmeet to a fashionable and busy artist? Something inside her recoiled at the very thought. She was not unaware of the fact that she already provided Robert with essential moral and emotional support but could not conceive of that being a full-time occupation. She knew all about his women, of course. His child women. He conducted his affairs with extreme secrecy, she had the impression that he would have been thrown into a state of panic if she mentioned them. Yet he must know that she knew. She could only believe that he had deliberately expunged the knowledge from his conscious mind because his need for a woman who was both unthreatening and who approved of him unconditionally was too pressing. His mother had always adored him absolutely and Hester had long since schooled herself to modify her own criticisms to protect his vulnerable ego, hoping that time would make him stronger. This had never happened; instead he sought additional reassurance from other women. As he could no longer persuade himself that Hester accepted his every word and action without question, it was easier for him to look elsewhere for unconditional worship.

The Hester Eliot – Robert Gibb duo was practically an institution in spite of the fact that his affairs were fairly common knowledge, for no one took them seriously. Few people she knew would have been able to imagine Robert without Hester. She wondered if they would be able to visualise Hester without Robert.

The shop bell rang for only the second time that morning. Ezra was evidently hoping to surprise her by his reappearance.

'Surely you know about the grapevine in places like this,' she said. 'I knew ours was in good working order when I heard you were still here last night.'

'Ah, yes. Well, I had expected to be back in the old berth by now if it wasn't for my tedious old jalopy.'

'What's the matter with it?'

'Flat battery,' he continued blithely. 'The place up the road have put it on charge overnight. Damn thing's always letting me down. I think it's going senile. Where's Alice?'

'I've taken over for the day. She can hardly keep me in idleness. Did you want to see her?'

'Not for anything in particular. Christ! I never thought I'd see

Hester Eliot behind a counter. Do you think I should make a sketch for posterity?'

'It's no joke. You may see stranger things yet.'

'Don't tell me! Something's afoot. Want to bend Uncle Ezra's ear with it? I can be both sympathetic and discreet when I choose, believe it or not. Would I be right in thinking that you and Cork Street have fallen out?'

She hid her astonishment at his near guess by picking up a wooden bowl and a duster. 'It has nothing whatever to do with Cork Street,' she said busily dusting, 'I am allowed time off occasionally you know.'

'Look, it's nearly one. What about a pint and a pasty at The Cutter? We can discuss our respective woes.'

Hester hesitated. Normally she would have turned down an offer from the likes of Ezra Judd and she didn't have to look far for the reason: he was not in her class as an artist. In other words he was unsuccessful in the artistic circles in which she moved. She practically blushed at the thought. How could she have become such an arrogant and snobbish cow without noticing? Ezra's work, what she had seen of it, was good. With the kind of promotion she'd had herself he could have gone far. But a man like Ezra would never compromise or modify his style to suit the market. He was far too stubborn. In any case it was too late now, he had on his own admission turned fifty. Galleries were looking for new bloodstock, not old warhorses.

She found herself agreeing to his suggestion and closed the shop for the lunch hour.

They chose a table in the saloon bar next to a window that overlooked the river. The public bar was already noisy and crowded and Hester guessed that left to himself Ezra would gladly have thrown himself into the scrum. Reg Gammon and a few of his cronies were already signalling to Ezra as if they were old drinking pals but clearly he expected her to talk, to unburden herself in peace. She was damned if she would.

On his insistence she agreed to try the local beer and he went off to track it down. The Cutter was one of the oldest buildings in Coombe Ferrers and had been a pub for its entire life. Its foundations were of stone, for on one side they were under water at high tide; its upper stories were timber and cob. Inside, the timbers were dark with centuries of smoke and polished by generations of hands, feet, elbows and bottoms.

Ezra returned and dumped down a pint for himself, a half for

Hester, some crisps and a couple of pasties.

'I thought the pasties looked quite decent,' he said, 'For Devonshire ones, that is.'

'Good. I'm hungry.'

He watched her, amused, while she bit into the honey-coloured pastry.

'I rejoice to think that there is still something I can offer such an esteemed painter, even if it is only a humble comestible.'

'You can stuff your sarcasm.'

'There was me thinking I was just being honest.'

She raised her eyebrows to signal her disbelief and took another bite. 'When will your car be ready?'

'They put the battery, such as it was, back in this morning, then they found something wrong with the distributor. Don't know anything about the bloody things myself so I have to trust the blighters. I wanted to get away by this afternoon but, what the hell! It's given us a chance to have another yap.' He obviously assumed that she was as delighted with the opportunity as he was himself.

'This is jolly,' he said indicating the view through the window. The rain was clearing away from the west and a watery sun silhouetted the moored craft on a background of quicksilver.

'The other night,' he said. 'You raised some pithy questions. Made me get down to some serious thinking. And it occurred to me that you may have struck a bit of heavy weather. Right?'

He bit into his pasty, holding it with both hands, which she noticed were unexpectedly attractive; square and capable looking with well-shaped fingers, though the cuffs of his seaman's sweater were ragged and ostentatiously paint stained.

'Don't most painters experience times when they have to re-think? Surely you do? Or perhaps you don't.'

'Are we speaking emotionally, personally or professionally here?'

'Professionally, of course. Though I'm not sure they can be compartmentalised like that.'

He grinned. 'Quite right. A dicey love affair plays havoc with one's work, don't you find?'

'I wouldn't know.'

'Aha! Don't tell me that all the hype about Mr and Mrs Robert Gibb is true?'

Hester was getting fed up with his unrelenting facetiousness.

She looked at her watch, a man's Tag Heuer. It was still only one-twenty. The gesture was not lost on him.

'Sorry,' he said. 'Point taken. All right, let's be serious. You said something about self-parody and I'm quite prepared to accept the criticism.' He thumped his chest. 'Mea culpa and all that. I've been ploughing the same ruddy furrow for years because, to be honest, I don't know how to change and I can't actually say that it's occurred to me to do so. So what you're saying is that you're in a rut and feeling it?'

'It's not quite like that. I've been happily exploring the same furrow, as you put it, for some time but a few months ago I discovered that it was actually a futile activity and a complete dead end. Since I realised that, naturally it was pretty pointless to go on. To change for change's sake is likewise pointless. Just swopping one rut for another, leading nowhere. I've decided to quit.'

For once Ezra was speechless. Then in a shocked voice, 'You mean for good?'

She nodded. She must be mad confiding all this to a very possibly indiscreet stranger. The last thing she wanted was for it to get back to Eustace before she was ready to tell him herself.

'Give it all up!' he said. 'I don't believe it. Once a painter always a . . .'

'Not so.'

'Listen, you say that now, but I'd give you a month at most. A month of enforced idleness and you'll be reaching for the old number twelve best hog, pining for the smell of the oil paint and the roar of the critics.'

'It's already been two months.'

'Then you need a kick start, my old mate. A great new revelation, a stop-me-dead-in-my-tracks-and-call-me-Rembrandt jolt. A Whatsitsname . . . an epiphany.'

'My epiphany came when I saw my work for the trash it is . . . and not only my own work either, as a matter of fact.'

'If you can see that, and I think you're being a bit rough on yourself, then you have some hope of recognising the genuine article when you clap eyes on it. You should at least give yourself a chance. Me, I daresay I shall slog away at the old pot boilers until I drop. You're obviously intended for higher things.'

He tossed off the remainder of his pint. 'Drink up. I'll replenish these. When I come back I'll tell you what you have to do. After that I think we should get ever so slightly pissed.'

'No,' she said getting up. '*I'll* replenish then, then you can tell me what to do if you must. Same again? This local brew's not bad.'

He nodded, grinning. 'Told you so.'

'And another pasty?'

'Why not.'

She returned with the drinks and a fresh supply of pasties. He tasted his new pint and then laid the glass on the table thoughtfully.

'Solution to problem,' he said. 'Item one. A cracking new love affair.'

'Why didn't I guess you'd say that! Sex as the panacea for all ills. If I may say so, the typical male solution.'

'No? It's worth considering all the same. All right then. Item two. A change of scene.'

'I'm having it.'

'Not temporarily. A total change of scene. A Van Gogh-Provence-Gaugin-Tahiti-type change. Shift your studio. Yours is in Bristol? Right, then move to Cornwall. It's worked for other folks. Though you needn't take me as a shining example, of course.'

'Come on now! That's thirties stuff.'

'Somewhere else then. Abroad for instance, or here? What's wrong with here? Coombe Ferrers is a nice spot. Not too far away from the Metropolis. Find yourself a cosy studio somewhere?'

'What would be the point if I can't paint and don't intend to?'

'Now then! Give yourself the benefit of the doubt at least.'

'In any case I'm used to working on a large scale. A cosy little studio would hardly be the answer.'

Ezra started on his second pasty. She followed suit and they ate in silence for a few minutes. He dusted crumbs of pastry from his beard.

'You could always take over Alice's old Cider Press,' he said. She was staring out of the window considering the dark shape of a cormorant perched on a post with wings outspread. The salty smell of seaweed drifted in.

'Did you hear what I said? What about Alice's old Cider Press? Now that's a brilliant wheeze. Do you both a favour. And you can't say that it's not big enough.'

'Out of the question.'

'Why? Come on, tell me why?'

'Expense, for a start. I can't afford to run two studios.'

'Let the Bristol one.'

'Robert wouldn't wear that! A strange painter right next door!'

'Then rent the Cider Press for a trial run. Say six months.'

'Where do you suggest I live?'

'Ah now. That gets us into tricky personal stuff. I leave that to you.'

'Thank you!' She was shaking her head. 'It's out of the question, anyway.' she repeated.

He heaved his shoulders in a massive shrug.

'Have it your own way. But, look here, Alice is serious about selling. If you don't make up your mind soon it will be too late. Some joker will have snapped it up and turned it into flats before you can say fitted kitchen.'

'My mind is made up.'

'Then we're left with solution number one. And before you make up your mind about that too I'd like to put myself forward as a likely candidate.'

Hester gave a short explosive laugh. 'I'll say this for you, you have the most astounding nerve!'

'I'm noted for it. So that's out of the question too?'

Out of the question! There he sat, bumptious and self-assured, with his shock of unruly white hair, his greyish beard with its sprinkling of pasty crumbs in spite of his efforts, his awful old jersey and his paint-stained jeans. A likely candidate indeed!

'Why not?' he asked as if in reply to her thoughts. 'Have you strong views about marital vows?'

'Not particularly. But hasn't it crossed your mind that I might just care to exercise some discrimination in the matter.' She looked at him again. On the other hand, it was a long time since she had met anyone so unaffectedly warm-hearted and sympathetic, and it was quite apparent that in spite of the painterly scruffiness he had not allowed himself to go to pot physically. And he had beautiful, sexy hands . . .

'Ah,' he said. 'I'm with you! Yes, I'm an unprepossessing bugger I admit, but I do have a few good points if you can get over the initial snags.'

His eyes were as blue as lapis, urging her to laugh at his expense but she looked away unsmiling.

'Where are you staying?' she asked.

'Changing the subject, are we? Very wise. I'm afraid I crash landed on an old chum who teaches at the art college. Luckily he doesn't mind. Divorced. Lives in an old barn just off the Exeter road. Place is a bit of a tip so I fit in perfectly. He hardly notices I'm there.' He subjected her to a steady scrutiny. 'Of course I might stay on if I thought there was any chance of us having a whirl round together.'

An involuntary gasp of laughter escaped her. She got up from her chair. 'I don't go in much for "whirl rounds" as you put it. As to you staying on, you must please yourself. Don't linger on my account.'

Suddenly he leaned over the table and put a restraining hand on her arm.

'Listen, Hester,' he said earnestly. 'Don't go jacking the whole thing in. What's wrong with your work is no more and no less than what's wrong with pretty well every painter's of this God-forsaken generation. What you need, what we all need, is a bloody great shot of humility and a bloody sight less arrogance.'

'How do you suggest we go about getting those?'

'Well, I'll tell you one thing for nothing. You won't find what you're looking for in West One. The gurus of Cork Street can't help you now.'

'I already know that. Why do you think I came down here.'

'So you *are* still looking? That's a good sign, anyway.'

'I never said that!' she replied with finality. 'Look Ezra, I have to go.'

'Me too. I have to see how much of a hole the ruddy Deux Chevaux will make in my bank account.'

'Can't your art school friend get you some teaching at the college if you're so hard up?'

'My dear old mate! Don't think I haven't taught in my time! Unfortunately art schools and I had a great falling out many moons ago. A case of the men in the grey suits versus the last of the Mohicans!'

She grinned and felt more cheerful as he walked back with her to the Anchorage.

'Think about what I've said, old mate,' he said as he left her. 'I shall be asking questions later!'

She locked up the shop at five-thirty. Paul and Alice were not yet back, but a visitor was sitting on the garden seat under the verandah, reading.

'Amy!'

'Hi, Mum. You took your time.'

'I've been at The Anchorage. For goodness sake! Why aren't you in Leeds?'

'Yes, sorry, I suppose I should have phoned but it was a spur of the moment thing. I thought Dad might have got on to you.'

'I think he's in London, on the way to New York.'

'Yeah. He left after the interview with that weird woman.'

'Weird woman?'

'From some magazine or other. He said you were supposed to be there.'

'Oh, yes. *Painting Now.*

'Had you forgotten?'

'No. Don't let's stand around out here. You'd better come inside and tell me why you've come.'

Hester unlocked the back door. They made tea and stood in the kitchen drinking it out of mugs, a habit Hester fell into as if they were in the kitchen at home.

She scrutinised her daughter closely.

'Now,' she said. 'What's wrong?'

'I've chucked the course.'

'I see,' Hester said more calmly than she felt. 'Why? I thought you were liking it?'

'I liked Egypt. But after I came back I began to think about things. I met an art student in Cairo and we talked about her course and she told me her ideas about art and so on . . .'

Hester waited.

'So when I came back I applied for the foundation art course in Bristol.'

'Amy! For God's sake, why didn't you tell us?'

'If you must know it was because I knew Robert would throw a wobbly. I was afraid that he might even fix it for me so that they cancelled the interview.'

'Why on earth should you think he'd do that?'

'You know Dad! I knew he'd be obstructive just to ram it home that I should have chosen art in the first place.'

'You did put forward some fairly acrimonious views about the art establishment.'

'I know I did. I still have them as a matter of fact. But I see now that there's a strong scene in alternative art if you know where to look for it.'

'When is your interview at the college?'

'It was today. I'll hear in a few days but I *think* I got in.'

Hester saw her daughter battling to suppress a cocky Cheshire cat grin.

'What had you intended to do about Leeds?'

'I talked it over with them. I told them I'd made up my mind. It's more or less a *fait accompli.*'

Hester emptied the dregs of her tea into the sink with an exasperated gesture.

'What's wrong?' Amy had been so sure that her mother would be on her side.

'You may well ask what's wrong! You must have decided months ago that you wanted to change. In fact you must have been taking active steps to bring it about before Christmas and yet you said absolutely nothing about it to us then. You talked it over with some bloody art student in Cairo and probably with Steve and all your friends at Leeds, yet you never so much as breathed a word of it to either Robert or me. What's wrong is that I'm very disappointed. I thought we were on better terms than that, yet you've treated us as if we were . . . as if we were Granny Gibb and not to be trusted with the truth. I find it insulting and hurtful.'

Amy's face was aflame. She sat down suddenly at the table. 'Oh God!' She sank her head between her hands and clutched at her hair. She was wearing knitted mittens.

'Sorry, sorry, sorry. I got it wrong, didn't I?'

'I should damn well think you did!'

'Only you and Dad were fully occupied with other things. Dad with the preparations for his exhibish and you preggers and in a funny mood. There just didn't seem to be a right moment.'

Hester calmed down, remembering how it had been. Remembering how preoccupied she must have seemed.

She nodded. 'Yes, well I suppose it was all rather fraught.' She stroked Amy's coppery hair.

Amy raised her head. 'How are you anyway? Are you better now?'

Hester smiled at the childish phrase. Her daughter was still a disconcerting mix of would-be adult sophistication and childish candour.

'Yes, darling. I feel a lot better.'

'How long will you be staying with Alice?'

'As long as she'll have me. I might even put up somewhere locally if I decide to make a protracted visit. But let's get back to the matter in hand; if you intend to start the foundation course next September we shall have to talk money, shan't we?'

'I won't be eligible for a grant. Robert doesn't want to pay so I'm getting a job until the course starts.'

'That won't do much more than pay for your keep.'

'I know, but I will *try* to save. Do you mind awfully forking out for it? Dad wants me to grovel, I know he does!'

'Don't be melodramatic. I'm sure he doesn't.'

Amy sighed. 'You're so loyal. You don't have to present a united front for my sake you know. I'm not a child!'

'I don't know what you mean by that. In any case it has nothing to do with it. I'm trying to be realistic. Yes, I will pay for your new course. Naturally I will if it's what you really want to do.'

'It really is.'

'You're absolutely sure this time?'

'Absolutely'.

I will pay for your new course. And how, Hester thought, do I intend to do that? A cold feeling of panic closed on her. She had money saved, for she had never assumed that success would follow success indefinitely. The art-buying public had supported her handsomely, at least her own loyal following had, but if she never worked again, what then? She couldn't expect or allow Robert to keep her. She was sure that once Robert had made his point he would certainly relent where Amy was concerned but for herself there was little hope of her money lasting for more than eighteen months or so. She would have to get a job, something ordinary, certainly not teaching. The future was a complete blank; except for one thing. It was dawning on her with ever-growing clarity that she was persistently visualising a future without Robert.

Scarcely had the thought floated into her mind than the kitchen door opened, banishing it. Alice and Paul had arrived home.

CHAPTER NINE

The flat was almost completely monochrome. The walls had been faked to look like white marble, the curtains were drifts of white muslin, the armchairs and sofa were covered in sharply tailored ivory linen. At one time there had also been a white fitted carpet but since she had worked for *Painting Now* Caroline's taste had undergone some modification. The carpet had been slung out and the floorboards painted white instead. A few black metal chairs made, in the words of the magazine that had inspired the idea, 'a calligraphic statement' against the pristine background. This turned out to be their only function as they were too uncomfortable to sit on. The metal table was fractionally more practical. On its marble top Caroline laid a circle of ticking with a pale grey stripe; on top of this went a slightly smaller damask cloth and a branched candle-holder; (another calligraphic statement), supporting three reed-like candles.

The room possessed a minimum of decorative clutter; there was an ivy with dark green leaves cascading out of a black painted bird cage, an alabaster bowl filled with pastel coloured pot-pourri and a few meticulously positioned photographs in silver frames. On the floor was a much-prized grey and white rug, the work of a degree student at the Royal College of Art. Otherwise the only colour, and that restrained, was in the paintings on the walls. These had been purchased at very low cost or were outright gifts, mostly from painters who at the time had not yet 'arrived' but whose work had subsequently been featured in the pages of *Painting Now.* The most nearly representational was a small portrait of Caroline herself done by an up and coming painter who not so long ago had been her lover. It was satisfyingly dark and scumbled, ascribing to the sitter less prettiness and more character than the painter actually believed that she possessed. Caroline was very proud of it.

She had cleaned the flat and put the food to keep hot. It had been cooked and delivered by a very efficient young woman whose services Caroline had used before; spinach soup, sole meunière with celeriac potatoes and mange tout followed by chocolate mousse.

Then she had spent a luxurious hour in the bathroom and dressed with extra care. Her minimal black dress had been very expensive, its cost in inverse ratio to the amount of clinging jersey that had gone into its creation. It was long sleeved and skimmed her shoulders at one end and her mid-thigh at the other like a bandage. There were good pieces of gold in her ears and on her right arm one huge barbaric bracelet. Her neck was bare and with her cropped hair, long childish legs and flat chest the effect was unmistakeably androgynous. She looked in the full-length mirror, satisfied with what she saw. When Robert arrived it was evident that he was also.

He brought wine, pale and expensive as if he had an explicit understanding of the meal, the flat and the woman. Despite momentous events in New York he realised that he had been looking forward to seeing Caroline again for the entire week since the interview in his studio.

'Hm, lovely,' she said, kissing the air by his cheek.

'It should still be quite cold.'

'I'll put it in the fridge anyway. It will go beautifully with the meal. Sit down. The drinks are on the side. Help yourself.'

They sat on the white linen sofa. He said he admired the flat.

'How was New York?' she asked.

He turned the glass in his hands, sipped and allowed seconds to pass as if waiting for the familiar warmth to circulate.

'Energising,' he said at last. 'Chaotic and invigorating. I think I need quite large doses of New York at regular intervals.'

'And the contract? Did Hirsch come through?'

He drank and nodded. 'It's all fixed,' he said without elaboration.

'Robert! That's wonderful! I do congratulate you. You deserved something like this, I've thought so for a long time.'

Robert looked at her speculatively. 'Have you?'

'But of course! This will bring your name before a much larger international public.'

They spoke of art in general, of recent shows, and professional gossip, with Caroline doing most of the talking. She was becoming familiar with his austere silences, yet was made both uneasy and excited by them. She was aware of his eyes covertly assessing her legs, her small breasts, her expressive hands, her stem-like neck.

Robert hardly listened to what Caroline was saying although he gave the impression of attention. The fact that he found her opinions facile and superficial in no way detracted from his feeling of wellbeing. It was an odd sensation, a mix of fatigue, very slight intoxication and of knowing for sure that he was unconditionally appreciated. He relaxed. The white flat, the black-clad girl gave him the faintly unreal impression that he was taking part in an old black-and-white movie. It was not unpleasant. He felt that as a result anything could happen without any initiative on his part, as if he were merely a spectator.

The meal turned out to be delicious. It didn't bother him in the least when she admitted to not doing the cooking; since his affairs were strictly short term, such things were unimportant, he was not looking for 'wifely' qualities. She was meticulous not only about the appearance of the flat but about the presentation of her own person. He liked that; and he liked the way she used her delicate child-like hands for emphasis. She looked young, clean and wholesome.

Caroline set a tray with a glass cafetiere and two white bone china cups and placed it on the small table beside the sofa. She put on a Nigel Kennedy tape and hoped that the intimate atmosphere and the wine would assist her in probing the enigmatic facade of Robert Gibb. After half an hour she seemed to be getting nowhere, yet she was convinced by the way he appraised her from beneath drooped lids that he fancied her like mad. Yet he made no move towards her. In Bristol there had been neither the time nor the opportunity for anything more intimate than dining together.

'So now that the First New World has given you the commission, would you say that you have everything you want, Robert?' she said. 'There's nothing missing from your life?'

He regarded her thoughtfully. 'Do you mind if I smoke?'

She shook her head and laughed softly. 'Was that all that was missing?' she teased.

He lit the cigarette, letting out a satisfied, smokey breath.

'How old are you, Caroline?'

She didn't know if she wanted to admit to twenty-six. She had heard through the grapevine what sort of girls he liked, and twenty-six was hardly pubescent.

'How old do you think I am?' she countered.

'You must be in your mid twenties but just at this moment you look about seventeen.'

'Do you like that?'

'Yes,' he said. Very gently he stroked the skin of her shoulder with two fingers. 'Your skin has that unused look.'

She looked at the place he had stroked as if she expected to see a fiery brand printed on her skin.

'There's more,' she said quietly.

He looked at her quizzically.

'More?'

She got up from the sofa, forcing herself to move slowly and fluidly and, standing on the grey-and-white rug she kicked off her shoes and then began to peel the black dress from her shoulders, then from her minimal breasts and over her hips. Finally she stepped out of it, leaving it on the rug. She was completely naked. Her skin gleamed like a candle. Her nipples were faintly pink and her pubic hair was blonde and silky like that of a very young girl.

Robert pressed out his cigarette in an ashtray made of a solid chunk of glass. He didn't take his eyes off her. The sensation of unreality had increased but so had the feeling that he was not responsible for what was happening. Then he knelt forward on the rug and leaned his head against the cool flesh of her flat, nearly concave stomach. His hands cupped her boyish buttocks. She let out a small sigh and leaned over him.

Her response to him was powerful and gratifying for although she took the initiative at every stage she did so subtly, like a provoking child, alternately urging and teasing, making it seem that she was powerless in the face of his overwhelming masculinity. For the first time for many months Robert's desire was fully awakened. He needed a very particular set of circumstances in order to be aroused at all and for this reason Hester and he made love less and less frequently these days and for this reason too he found himself feeling ridiculously grateful to Caroline. Of all the child women he had slept with, she came closest to his ideal. Her body was perfect and she was as pliable and unquestioning as if this was a new experience for her and he was in control, yet paradoxically there was an undeniable knowingness about everything she did that was as old as time. After he had entered her he even had to allow a moment of luxurious stillness before he finally reached his climax. Afterwards he couldn't remember if she had reached hers at the same time; he believed that she had.

Caroline rolled on to her stomach and reached for Robert's cigarettes. His habit seemed to be catching. She lay back on the rug, letting a dribble of smoke out of her mouth. She looked at Robert. He was still asleep. She smiled and closed her eyes momentarily; she felt triumphant. She'd had Robert Gibb. Correction; she had Robert Gibb. It had been a less than sexually satisfying encounter as far as she was concerned but that was not the point. She already knew where and how she could get sexual gratification when she wanted it, for after many bitter experiences she had long since come to the conclusion that she herself was the only person in the world capable of bringing her to orgasm. The point was that she knew Robert's secret. His problems with women he masked with a show of coolness and aloof indifference. If her narrow body had the power to turn him on by virtue of a quality of unthreatening femaleness then she would make sure that it continued to do so. In view of this she brushed her sexual disappointment aside for she had achieved more than she could have reasonably expected. At first she had wanted him for what he represented, a feather in her cap, a head worth hunting; then she had desired him as a man almost to the point of obsession. Now his inadequacies and idiosyncrasies were apparent she saw that the tables were turned. Now Robert Gibb had good reason to defer to her.

CHAPTER TEN

Alice's house suddenly seemed overcrowded though Amy airily assured everyone that she was staying only one night.

'If you don't mind putting me up, I don't mind sleeping on the floor,' she told Alice. 'I have my sleeping bag.'

'Sweetie, stay as long as you like,' Alice said. 'I don't seem to have seen you for ages.'

'I've applied for a job in market research for the summer. I have to get back to see if they're going to offer it to me.'

They sat alone by the fire. Hester was in the hall speaking to Robert on the telephone. Paul had gone to fetch milk from the late-night store.

'So you might get the op this summer?' Amy said.

'I'm not counting on it. It rather depends on the results of this latest crop of X-rays.'

'Poor you. What a sod.' Amy, who was sitting on the floor, toyed with a piece of bark she'd found on the hearth, lighting the end of it and watching the dry moss catch. 'I love open fires, people don't have them much these days, do they? I'm sorry about your hip. It must be foul not to be able to do the things you used to.'

'One manages.' Alice said succinctly. 'I try to ignore the bloody thing. I'm not the martyr type.'

'If you did have the op this summer, what about me coming to look after the shop?'

'That's quite an idea. We must think about it. Would you like to?'

'I'd adore to. Besides it would get me out of Robert's hair.'

They both laughed. A spurt of flame from the fragment of bark seared Amy's hand briefly and she dropped it into the fire.

'Bugger!'

She turned to Alice. 'How do you think Hester looks?'

'A damned sight more relaxed than when she first came.'

'She hasn't been doing any work, you know. Her studio has been completely cleared.' Two creases furrowed Amy's brow.

'I think she's needed a respite and a re-think,' Alice said. 'She's kept up the pace now for twenty years, don't forget. Don't ask me how! But even Hester must run out of steam eventually.'

'Mm. Granny Eliot snuffing it like that upset her a lot . . . not to mention the miscarriage, though I don't think they wanted another kid.'

'I thought you were quite fond of Inez yourself.'

'I was. I adored her actually, even though she was slightly out of her tree.'

'Just mildly eccentric, surely?'

'That's what I said.' She gestured towards the door that led into the hall. 'That's Robert on the phone. I expect they're talking about me and my future. Christ! It makes me feel like a frigging kid! I wouldn't put it past Robert to have rung the university.'

Hester already knew about Robert's success in New York; he had telephoned her from there as soon as the deal was complete, but playing his cards close to his chest as usual he offered no details. Now he wanted to talk about Amy.

'You know she's here, I suppose,' Hester said.

'In Devon, you mean? With you?'

'She turned up an hour or two ago.'

There was an ominous silence. Then in the clipped tones he used when he was very annoyed indeed he said, 'I thought she'd gone to see her friend Gina. I told her not to concern you with this just at the moment.'

'I'd have to know about it sooner or later since she seems so set on the idea. I think we should bow to the inevitable.'

'I rang Leeds but they as good as told me that it was Amy's decision and better to cut her losses now than later. *Her* losses! I must say I find her rationale for the switch unrealistic in the extreme.'

Hester felt a stab of irritation. Like a stranger she was all at once made aware of his habit of distancing himself by his tone of voice and a formal turn of phrase.

'I'm sure she'll get into the art college,' Hester said. 'Her 'A' level work was good.'

'Well, of course she will,' Robert said. 'There is no doubt in my mind about that. What is cause for concern is the possibility that she will approach the new course in her usual uncompliant frame of mind and with a whole raft of half-baked ideas. She has become so touchy and rebellious that I must say I hardly recognize her these days. And trouble with the polytechnic I can do without.'

'Touchy and rebellious!' Hester hissed into the receiver, not putting as much feeling as she might into the words for fear of being overheard by Amy. Amy would have very strong feelings about being discussed. 'Robert, you can't be serious! Amy is an absolutely normal, intelligent young woman. She wants to change her course, yes. But she's not, as far as I know, pregnant, she's not on drugs, she hasn't got AIDs and she's not in trouble with the police. What more do you want these days, for God's sake!'

Robert drew in his breath. 'I see she's done a pretty exhaustive PR job already.'

Hester kept her temper with difficulty. 'Look, she said. 'I think we better discuss this again when I get back and when Amy is present.'

'As you like.' There was a silence.

'Anyway I'm glad about the commission.' Hester said. 'Are you pleased?'

'Well, naturally. All the same you know how I feel about commissions.'

She did know. Commissions for a specific site for a specific client could go wrong. Both she and Robert preferred a collector or, better still, a museum to be waiting at the studio door to snap up the latest painting hot from the easel.

'It might lead to your work being bought by M.O.M.A.' To see his work in the Museum of Modern Art was Robert's, not to say Eustace's, next goal. It had once been hers.

'What will the new thing consist of?'

'Six large paintings.'

'What is the site like?'

'Huge. There are a few potential snags but they say they'll cooperate.'

She knew very well that he was tremendously pleased at being offered the commission but being Robert would consider it too unsophisticated to express it. Besides he had a superstitious fear of tempting Providence. He had never been confident as to how long he would continue in favour, he had nightmares about being superseded, becoming a back number, unappreciated by a new generation of collectors. After all, it could and did happen. It was not the loss of income that worried him so much as a loss of reputation; the keen pleasure he derived from seeing his work change hands for a large sum of money was simply because this was the barometer of success. He rarely discussed money as obsessively as most artists of her acquaintance; in Hester's experience lively conversations about art and aesthetics were invariably conducted by bankers and accountants, but where two or more artists were gathered together one could absolutely count on the likelihood of the talk coming round sooner or later to cash.

'There's something else,' Robert said. 'I think there's a possibility that I might have to find a studio in New York.'

'Good God, why? It would cost the earth!'

'Not necessarily. Hirsch knows someone who might rent me the space for a nominal amount. He owns property in SoHo. I had my doubts all along about the adequacy of the Bristol studio. Now I'm sure. I don't think it will be large enough. How would you feel about living in New York for eighteen months or so?'

'This is your commission, Robert. What would I do in New York!'

'It would be an absolutely unprecedented opportunity for you to become better known on the other side of the Atlantic. Surely I don't have to spell it out for you. As a matter of fact Hirsch himself is quite keen on the idea.'

'So you've mentioned it to him.'

'*He* mentioned it to *me* when we were discussing the advantages of my working on the spot.'

'I see.'

Hester took a deep breath and sat down on the little petit-point covered spoon-back chair beside the telephone.

'Listen, Robert,' she said at last, 'You'll have to ditch that idea absolutely and completely. New York has no appeal at all for me at the moment. You must do what you like, of course.'

'I didn't mean immediately. You probably don't want to make a decision right away but when you're really fit and back in Bristol you'll feel differently. Eustace thinks it's the opening we both needed.' He stopped speaking and there was murmuring in the background, then Robert's voice came again. 'Actually I'm phoning from Lombards and Eustace has just walked through the door. I'll put him on.'

'No!' she cried. But it was too late.

'My darling girl!' Eustace's voice boomed in her ear. 'How goes it in the great outdoors. Firing on all cylinders now? What d'you think of the news?'

'Hello, Eustace. Thank you, I'm much better and I'm very pleased Robert made a hit with the First New World and Union Bank. Congratulations! I know you worked your socks off for this.'

'Can't say I didn't, can't say I didn't. Well, there you are, it's all fixed. The boy told you about the brilliant notion of the two of you working over there for a spell. What about it, eh! Making it in the Big Apple? The timing's perfect, couldn't be better career-wise. For both of you.'

'The thing is, Eustace,' Hester said carefully. 'I don't want to go to New York.'

'Well perhaps not right away. I daresay you'll need a bit more time. But Hester . . . ?'

'Yes?'

'Not too long. Strike while the iron's hot and all that.'

'Listen, Eustace. I think we have to talk.'

'Of course, dear girl. Funny you should say that. I was thinking of coming down there to see you.'

'Down here! To Devon!' Hester gazed panic-stricken at the hall window with its delicate insets of red and blue glass as if she expected to see Eustace come crashing through it.

'But Eustace, you hate the country! You don't even know where Devon is!' she cried weakly.

'I daresay I'll find it somehow. They have hotels down there, don't they?'

'Well, yes.'

'Then I shall be there tomorrow and we can have a nice chat. Don't worry, I'll get the phone number from Robert. Do you want to have another word with him?'

'No,' she said. 'No, not now.'

'Then I'll be in touch. Au revoir, dear girl.'

Hester put the receiver down and stood looking helplessly at it. The shock of the New York suggestion and the news of Eustace's impending visit fused all her instincts into one overpowering urge for self-preservation: personal, emotional and spiritual. The mishmash of anxieties, sensations and half-formed thoughts erupted without warning from the dark room somewhere in her mind in which they had been confined. The moment was now and she felt wholly unprepared for it. She would have to have her answers and explanations ready for Eustace, and for Robert too, if he persisted in the New York idea.

The back door slammed. Paul was back. Amy sauntered into the kitchen and from the parlour Hester and Alice heard the rise and fall of their voices punctuated by laughter.

Paul put three cartons of milk in the fridge and dumped a couple of rosy-shelled crabs on to the draining board.

'Present to Alice from an admirer,' he said. 'Reg Gammon,

poacher and piss artist of this parish.' He laughed. 'Alice will go mad.'

Amy studied the creatures, poking them with an inquisitive finger. 'Why?'

'He dotes on her and keeps giving her stuff; and she's too softhearted to tell him where he can stick it.'

'What will she do with them?'

'She'll put them on the floor and use them as door stops . . . what d'you think she'll do with them! We'll eat them, won't we.'

'Yuk. You can if you like. Do you know how they're killed?'

'Are you a veggie?'

'I don't believe in eating my fellow creatures if that's what you mean, especially ones that have been boiled alive.' She picked up one of the crabs and explored its smooth shell.

'Well, it looks as if these fellow creatures are going to be on the menu tonight.'

'They won't, you know. Hester's taking us all out to eat. You too.'

'That's praper 'andsome of her. We'm zelebrating then?'

'Celebrating?' Amy turned the crab over and examined its underside. 'This crab has tar in its joints.'

'They sometimes do. Alice chucked out the last lot. Yes, celebrating. Hasn't your Dad just made a killing with the Yanks? And aren't you all set to jump aboard the gravy train?'

'What gravy train?'

'Like father, like daughter . . .' Paul pulled out a chair from the kitchen table and sat astride it.

'You must be off your chump! You're not suggesting that art students see their futures in terms of gravy trains, for Christ's sake!'

'All the same, I can't see the daughter of Robert Gibb and Hester Eliot *not* making the big time.'

'I see. Serious sour grapes. Anyway, since you appear to have my interests so much at heart I have to disappoint you, I'm afraid. I have absolutely no intention of messing with the male-dominated art establishment.'

'That's telling it like it is, sister! What had you in mind?'

'The alternative scene. Art that has some reference to ordinary people, particularly women.'

'Like mine, you mean?'

'I don't call ripping off the grockles art for ordinary people.'

'Get this, chum. My stuff is okay so don't knock it. The trouble with you is that you're a hopeless bloody dreamer, d'you know that!'

He laughed good-naturedly and stretched his long legs across the floor. The thigh sections of his jeans were covered in multi-coloured flecks of paint where he had wiped his brushes. His arrogant posture, his white teeth and his golden hair acted as kindling on Amy's smouldering feminist principles. She tossed the crab back on to the draining board.

'You've got a frigging cheek! You haven't a clue what I've been talking about.'

'And you haven't a clue what I do. You haven't even seen my stuff.'

'Your name's Paul Finch, isn't it?'

'Uhu.'

'Then those are your watercolours in the hall?'

'That's very observant of you. So you, with your vast experience, think they're crap?'

Amy shrugged. 'No. As a matter of fact I think they're quite good.'

'Oh, wow! Thanks a bunch.'

'I only said "quite".'

Clad only in tee shirt and knickers Amy unrolled her sleeping bag and laid it out on the floor of Hester's small attic room.

'I'm sorry for muscling in like this. I didn't want to give you any grief but I promise I'll go back tomorrow.'

Hester squeezed an inch of hand cream on to her palm and smoothed it into her skin, a nightly ritual against the ruinous effect of paint, turpentine and all the other tools of her trade.

'I'm glad you came down, darling. Don't worry about the fees, I'm sure we can sort something out. When would this job you applied for start? What did you say it was?'

'Something to do with market research. They said it would start more or less straight away. Suits me.'

'You mean stopping people in the street?'

'No, you go to people's homes and ask them a whole pack of questions. The pay's not much but I shall still have time to get on with the projects I'm supposed to submit to the college at the beginning of the foundation course. If they take me, that is.'

She paused and looked at Hester before thrusting her bare legs into the sleeping bag.

'By the way,' she said. 'Thanks for the meal tonight. Their vegetarian menu was pretty decent.

'It wasn't bad, was it.'

Amy glanced at her mother. 'It is all right about the new course, isn't it? I mean, you're not terribly disappointed about the Arabic?'

'To tell the truth I was never one hundred per cent convinced that it was right for you but since you seemed to be enjoying it, at least at first, I came to the conclusion that it must be leading somewhere. You always showed so much aptitude for art that naturally I was disappointed when you didn't go for it in the first place.

Amy sighed. 'Ah me! The down side of being multi-talented!'

Hester glanced at her daughter severely. Amy's ability to bounce back was only matched by her emotional extremes.

'So you're really very set on the idea of a degree in Fine Art?' she said.

'I've never been surer.'

'What does Steven think about it? It's going to mean a parting of the ways, isn't it?' She thought she might as well mention his name since Amy, very conspicuously, had not done so. Steven was reading English at Leeds and he and Amy had had a steady relationship for two years.

'Steven and I split last month,' Amy spoke with an air of nonchalance while she busied herself taking off her watch and laying it beside her on the floor.

'Finally?' Hester asked.

'Yup. He started going out with a first-year student.'

'Did you mind?'

'Well, yes. Actually I did.' Amy's voice was crisp with the effort to seem normal.

Hester had been putting the lid back on the tube of hand cream; she paused and glanced at Amy. 'Darling, I'm so sorry. Do you want to talk about it?'

'I might some time but not now. I just want to sleep.'

'Of course. Sleep well, darling.'

Hester turned out the light. There was a period of quiet snuffling while Amy in her makeshift nest, fought to keep her tears inaudible, but this turned at last into soft regular breathing. Hester lay awake. Poor Amy, her first big emotional disappointment. Hester hoped very much that it had not been an important factor in Amy's final decision to leave the course. It seemed that at the moment Robert was the only member of the family whose immediate future was fixed.

She reached for her glass of water, drank some and tried to sleep. Her ability to drop off instantaneously after long stints of work, to sleep soundly and wake refreshed after only a few hours, had been entirely disrupted since the miscarriage. Lately she had remained awake far into the night, her mind in turmoil and her eventual sleep disturbed by cryptic dreams. After the first night in Coombe Ferrers they had played themselves out in vivid colour. She found this strange and disturbing, it reminded her of the uninhibited way she had used colour in her early career; now the hallmark of her work was restraint. Polite, monochromatic, tasteful.

She fell asleep at last and found herself being whirled into a towering peach-coloured cloud whose deeper reaches glowed with ruby and carmine. Finally the colour solidified and became the familiar red cliffs. She was embedded in their interior, curled like a fossil or some antediluvian creature. It was both terrifying and rapturous and it woke her up. She was bathed in sweat and her throat was on fire with thirst.

The glass by her bed was long since empty and quietly, so as not to wake Amy, she thrust her arms into the sleeves of her dressing gown and tugged it round her. Her feet bare, she started down the stairs to the bathroom which was on the floor below. She paused when she heard a door open and glanced through the banisters. In the dim light that filtered through the landing window she saw Paul emerge from Alice's room. The short towelling robe he was wearing hung carelessly open. Under it he was naked. He disappeared into his own room and closed the door, after which there was silence.

Why Hester was surprised she didn't know. Alice was hardly noted for her celibacy and Hester couldn't imagine why she had looked no further than the landlady-lodger relationship. Had she allowed Alice's disability and Paul's youth to get in the way of her usually sharp perceptions? Obviously she had, and ought to have known better. Now certain atmospheres and undercurrents were explained. It wasn't that Alice used affectionate language when she talked to him; she did that with everybody. It was something else which of course she should have noticed earlier. Why had Alice not mentioned it? She had never been reticent in the past about her affairs. Could she be embarrassed by Paul's youth, his brashness or because she sensed that Hester didn't like him? It was much more likely, Hester thought with a twinge of conscience, that she thought Hester had been too self-absorbed to care. All the same she couldn't help feeling the slightest bit hurt that Alice had not thought fit to confide in her; after all they had been friends for a long time.

But there it was. Alice and Paul. Was it to be another of Alice's ill-fated love affairs? Sitting on the stairs in the dark, Hester frowned. She very much hoped not.

CHAPTER ELEVEN

Once he was comfortably dug in at the very superior Greyve Manor hotel, all the vague misgivings that Eustace had experienced as soon as the Intercity 125 passed Reading abated to an acceptable level. Although the great outdoors was very much in evidence, sloping lawns, majestic chestnuts and cedars, and beyond them glimpses of an amethyst-coloured moor, they were all at several removes. To his surprise a few people were actually outside taking their coffee on the terrace. He himself sank down into an easy chair in front of the cosy log fire, safe in the warmth and civilised elegance of his surroundings. He had the deepest suspicion of the countryside; fortunately he had no idea that the shadowy hills he saw in the distance were part of a wilderness that would have shocked him to the core had he experienced it at first hand.

He lit a cigar and put his feet upon a handy footstool. His coffee and brandy were by his side. Next to the splendid Adam fireplace a table lamp cast an apricot glow, even though outside a tentative sun had at last broken through. If he had to be so far from his habitual stamping ground this at least partly made up for the disruption. He let out a long, steady lungful of smoke and air.

In spite of, or perhaps because of, Robert's reassurances over Hester's mysterious defection, he was deeply worried. Naturally she had taken breaks before, had buzzed off to some pretty remote places but never in so *furtive* a way; and he didn't believe Robert's story that she was preparing new work. In the past she had always let him know when something was in the offing; no details, just a general sense of excitement that followed fresh ideas. She rarely showed her hand in the preparatory stages and that was as it should be. But this elusiveness was disturbing and what was more, deliberate. His task today was to impress upon her that now was just about the worst time she could have chosen to take an extended break, unless it was to undertake the necessary rehearsals for a great new burst of activity. However, he very much feared that this was not the case. As far as his two protégés were concerned the market was comparatively buoyant but if the supply failed to keep up with demand then collectors and galleries got bored, drifted away, found other outlets for their money. This hiatus just would not *do*. Hester had to be made to see that.

There was a stirring of interest amongst the scattered guests when Hester walked in. In an English setting there was something so striking and unusual about her appearance that more or less guaranteed attention. She had on blackish-purple trousers with a jacket of the same colour which he approved of, especially with the high-necked jersey that was the same colour as her amber earrings. He hoped that those slightly challenging objects weren't a sign that she was here to do battle.

But there was no sign of defiance in her demeanour as she approached. He struggled to his feet to greet her. She deposited a kiss on his cheek and sank into the chair next to his.

'Ah, darling girl. You look so much fitter! Don't tell me that this Devon air suits you?' An exaggerated shiver caused a small seismic disturbance to run through his ample frame.

'Perhaps it does,' she said noncommittally. He thought she seemed unusually distant.

'Nice fire,' she said nodding towards the welcoming blaze.

'Never mind the fire. What are you going to drink? I've reserved a table for one o'clock, that suit you?'

'Yes, fine. I won't have anything to drink.'

'Of course you will. Just an aperitif, there's half an hour yet.'

'All right then. I'll have a tonic.'

Eustace pulled a face but summoned a hovering waiter.

'Ice and lemon?'

'Yes. Thank you.'

Eustace kept the conversation on a safely innocuous level. They talked about Robert's exhibition, the New York commission and how the new Lombards gallery was coming along.

'I'm hoping that we shall be able to announce the date for our grand opening quite soon,' Eustace declared expansively. 'Sometime in August all being well, starting with a showcase exhibition of all our best talent.'

'I do hope it will turn out to be a good move,' Hester said.

'I'm sure of it. One has to do something in these precarious days.'

He mentioned a neighbouring gallery that had just closed its doors for good, just to demonstrate to Hester that not everything in the garden was as rosy as it had once been.

'Is Bruno pleased about the move?'

'You know Bruno. Cautious old bugger.'

'Perhaps he's too softhearted for today's tough dealing.'

'Knows his stuff though.'

'Possibly more than anyone I know.'

'Sixth sense. You know he came out of Germany on one of the last trainloads of Jewish kids? Brought up by foster parents.'

'Yes. He told me.'

'Right. Well, let's go and eat. I think our table's ready.'

For lunch they ate fish pâté, duck with small carrots and mushrooms and a dessert with chestnuts and cream. Eustace chose an expensive wine and spent the meal urging her to 'drink up'; but he noticed that she did so sparingly, almost cautiously. A bad sign. Why did she think it so important that she kept a clear head?

Afterwards, back in the spacious drawing room, separated from the scattering of other guests by acres of carpet and groups of comfortable chairs, they sat with cups of black coffee and a bowl of petit fours by their sides. In spite of the fact that Hester remained alert for the leading question or seemingly casual enquiry Eustace managed all the same to catch her off guard with an apparently innocent remark.

'You know, Kandinsky said that the artist is not a Sunday's child for whom everything immediately succeeds. The task assigned to him, or shall we say her, is painful.' Eustace looked at her searchingly.

Hester put down her cup.

'What does that make me? A Sunday's child surely. I've been lucky, haven't I?'

'Not you! More like Saturday's since you work hard for a living. And our Wassili also said something else. He said the abstract artist must be a true poet.' Eustace was sitting with his legs in their crumpled snuff-coloured corduroy stretched comfortably out before him, his chubby fingers laced across his snuff-coloured waistcoat. Several of his chins were buried in an electric blue shirt above a rust bow tie. He was staring thoughtfully into the fire.

Hester waited.

'Dear girl,' he said at last. 'Do you trust me?'

The question surprised her.

'That depends,' she said with a ghost of a smile. 'All right then, yes.'

'Then why are you holding out on me? Don't you think I don't know about pain, doubt, grief?'

Hester nodded. Eustace had watched his mother, to whom he

was devoted, die after three years in a long and painful struggle with cancer. It had not left him unscathed.

Abruptly he reached over and covered her hand with his, shaking it gently.

'Tell me, aren't you well? Is there something I don't know?'

'There is nothing wrong with me physically. Not now. I'm perfectly well again.'

'That only leaves the soul. Tell me, Hester. How is your soul?'

She glanced at him as if to assess his preparedness.

'My soul as you call it is sick to death.'

'Ah, now we have it,' Eustace said. 'And could you say what it is sick to death of. Is it art, life, the human race . . . what?'

'You could say all,' Hester said warily. 'But principally art.'

'Art!' Eustace sat up in his chair. Of all the replies he had half-anticipated this was bottom of the list. In fact he had a fixed notion in his head that she was going to complain about Robert's infidelities and he had been ready with the usual bromides to the effect that these affairs were of no significance, that the one woman in the world who was essential to Robert as a man and as an artist was Hester. In fact, he believed this to be true. He feared that Robert might not be able to function as a painter without Hester. The man's emotional dependence sometimes worried him. Thank Christ at least that the marriage didn't appear to be the area of difficulty.

'Art,' Eustace repeated. 'Surely you're not having problems with the work? You've never had problems with *that*.'

'Well, I am now. To be absolutely honest with you, Eustace, since you asked if I trusted you, I have to tell you that I have completely lost any desire to paint . . . and especially to paint the sort of meaningless crap I've been doing lately . . .'

She hadn't meant to be so blunt for by implication she was, after all, casting doubt on Eustace's own judgement. But there it was, she'd said it.

Eustace didn't react. He merely nodded sagely as he smoothed down a couple of hairs that had gone astray.

'I wondered myself,' he said eventually, 'if you might not be ready for a change of direction. Not that your stuff isn't a huge success . . . but I quite see that you, as an artist, can't stand still.'

'You don't understand,' she said, speaking with quiet intensity. 'I loathe the work I've been doing. It's effete and insincere. In fact I think it stinks. Mind you, I don't actually think it's any worse than most of the stuff you see around but I don't want any part of it anymore,' she paused for breath. 'I'm going to chuck it in!'

She had wanted to stay cool and rational, arguing her position with unassailable logic. So much for that!

Eustace had gone dark red but he stayed outwardly calm. One glance at her face was enough to read there a mixture of defiance and despair. He wondered briefly if here was a case for his psychotherapist friend in Bayswater. He doubted it. There remained other ways of dealing with 'painter's block'.

He reached for a cigar, making something of a production of lighting it in order to give himself time to think.

'I hear what you say,' he said when his cigar glowed to his satisfaction. 'So let's look to the future. Incidentally I think you're very wise to have recognised when a complete change of direction is indicated . . .' He held up his cigar to prevent her interrupting. 'Now I was just thinking about that Mexican jaunt you did, remember? And the trip to Rossillon? You need to find your Arles, dear girl. To be ravished like himself, by what you see . . .' He glanced at her. She had on her stubborn look. 'Or perhaps just the stimulus one gets from mixing with the greats. In fact, I think that's the answer. Yes, I'm convinced of it.'

'What do you mean?'

'Why, I mean New York, the Big Apple, of course! London has its advantages but you need the sort of kick-start that only New York can give you, dear girl. Listen, now that I come to think of it, it's got to be the answer, both for Robert and for you. In fact, it's perfect.'

'I already told Robert, no.'

'But did he tell you there might be another studio for you?'

'No, but I wouldn't be interested anyway.'

'Not interested in a studio in TriBeCa! Look, you think about it very seriously. Hirsch isn't a man whose offer one turns down. It tends not to get repeated.'

'Just at the moment, Eustace, I can't think of anything I should hate more.'

'It's my considered opinion, Hester,' Eustace said with an effort to control his intense irritation. 'That you need the stimulation only New York can give you.'

'I don't need stimulation,' she snapped. 'I need peace. Time to think. For years I've been stimulated, over stimulated; but it's all been superficial, like constantly stirring the surface of a pool without ever penetrating the depths. If there are any depths to penetrate, that is. What I should like is a chance to find out.'

Eustace nodded slowly. 'You're serious about this?'

'Of course I'm serious, damn it! But listen, Eustace, even if I had the time I couldn't promise anything at the end of it, that would defeat the object. There may not actually be anything at the end of it.'

Eustace's mind was busy. 'How much time are we talking of here?'

'I can't tell you that.'

He leaned back and drew on his cigar. 'All right then . . .'

Hester waited.

'What d'you say to this.' Eustace went on. 'Say you took six months. No pressure. Call it a holiday. You could go to New York with Robert, do some looking at galleries, do some shopping, meet some folks, what you like. Be there for Robert, he's going to need you. This commission is the best thing that's happened to him but it ain't going to be no walkover!'

'I can't do that, Eustace,' Hester said evenly. 'As I said, and I do hope you'll take it in this time, I need peace.'

Eustace took the cigar out of his mouth and studied the glowing tip. 'Don't you think that's being just the tiniest bit selfish, Hester, darling girl? As I said this is the biggest thing that's happened to Robert and if you honestly believe that you might not be actively creative in the foreseeable future then I think that you should at least be looking at the . . . let's say the *fiscal* angle. The old bread and butter side of things. Robert's going to need you. I didn't say this before but I think that I should stress that in the event of Robert taking that studio, which I'm sure he will, it's going to be essential that you accompany him to America.' Eustace was very fond of Hester, their relationship had always been warm but if she was serious about opting out as an artist even for six months he might have to reconsider his position. He was only too aware of the 'hungry generations' of young artists waiting in the wings. If Hester couldn't deliver then she must be made to see that her place was beside Robert.

Hester had seen that expression on her mentor's face before; specifically when dealing with creditors who wouldn't or couldn't pay or a client who reneged on a deal. It demonstrated a side of him that she was glad never to have come up against herself. The iron man behind the clown's outfit. She felt a slow and inexorable anger building in her.

'The hell I will! All I can say to that is that it's too fucking late. I've already made other arrangements.'

'Other arrangements! Now listen . . .'

'No, you listen! I've just put six months' rent down on a studio in Coombe Ferrers.' The words sprang out of her mouth from nowhere, without apparent volition on her part.

'Coombe Ferrers?' Eustace had taken his cigar out of his mouth again, an expression of bewilderment on his face.

'Coombe Ferrers, Eustace! Where I'm staying. There's a newly renovated studio overlooking the estuary. I've rented it.'

'I thought you said . . .'

'I know what I said,' Hester snapped. 'I just didn't want it to get around.'

'That's what you call trusting me, is it?' Eustace's features were dark with rage.

'I didn't want you to go reading too much into it, that's all. It might be a total failure . . .' She stopped speaking abruptly before she embroidered the outrageous lie any further; but to keep Eustace off her back it might be necessary to perpetuate it for some weeks or months. Ezra's suggestion had come in useful after all.

Eustace protested and blustered but agreed on some kind of uneasy truce. He said he would give up the idea that she should go to New York but only providing Robert was agreeable.

She drove away from Greyve Manor knowing that she had bought some time, but nothing more.

CHAPTER TWELVE

'You must think I've taken leave of my senses,' Hester said. 'He's not going to believe it for long and then he's going to try to insist I go with Robert.'

Alice was shaking with laughter, her round face pink under her diffuse halo of hair. 'I think it was inspired,' she said when she could speak.

'Inspired by Ezra when he was in his cups, that's the truth of it! Alice, for God's sake tell me what I'm to do.'

Alice turned back to the display shelves of the Anchorage, flicking them industriously with a feather duster. Hester sat astride the only chair, her arms across the back.

'Well, there's only one thing you can do, my duck,' Alice said.

Hester's head came up.

'You'll just have to move into the Cider Press, won't you. Pity I told Wellands to measure up today. I'll have to go next door and cancel it.'

'Be serious, Alice, please.'

'I am,' Alice said, ceasing her activities and fixing Hester with a round-eyed stare. 'I don't believe all that crap about you not being able to paint and I don't think you do, at least not any longer. What I think we ought to do is to temporarily fix up the Cider Press and that you should move in, say for six months as you suggested.'

'I didn't suggest it! Eustace drove me to it. The whole idea's preposterous. Besides I thought you desperately needed to sell it.'

'You forget that things aren't as straightforward as all that. Even if I let Wellands go ahead and put it on their books today, it will be at least six months before it sells. Probably a damn sight longer. In fact I wouldn't be surprised at two years.'

'Two years!'

'That's how things are these days, especially as its only possible uses would be a gallery, a studio or conversion into flats. When it does eventually go, naturally I'll pay you back for the money you sunk into the renovations but in the meantime the least I can do is to let you have the place rent free. It will be doing me a favour, stop it deteriorating.'

'I would never dream of taking it on those terms . . . What am I talking about? I don't need another studio!'

Alice shrugged and turned back to her dusting. 'Have it your own way but have you thought what you're going to tell Eustace? And about what you're going to do from now on. Go to New York? Mope about in the Bristol studio? You tell me!'

Hester rose from her chair abruptly.

'Look, I'm going for a walk,' she said. 'When I come back I'll tell you what I'm going to do.

In the High Street Hester made her way past the shops, the Riverside Tea Rooms, the Cutter and the coastguard cottages. Paul was not in evidence today, he'd left early with a stack of work to do the rounds of potential outlets in the more popular resorts. Hester had taken Amy to Exeter St David the day before on her way to lunch with Eustace, Amy was hoping for a letter or a telephone call from the art college.

Hester stepped on to the beach which was strewn with the usual detritus; dry black seaweed, crab shells and pieces of teased-out nylon rope, orange and blue. The smells were the usual ones, fish, fresh paint, salt breeze, a whiff of diesel. The tide was further in than it had been last time. Going out or in? She would have to remember. The air was warmer, scents blew down from the looming cliff redolent of cut grass and new growth. New growth. The seed of the idea that Ezra had planted in her mind had germinated, taken root and was now growing vigorously out of control. Of course it was all wildly impractical, apart from the fact that Alice could do with the rent. She was still slightly shocked from the interview with Eustace; she knew with perfect certainty that their relationship had changed and become almost confrontational. Desperately she longed for the familiar and reassuring agitation that heralded a need to work. To get her hands on a pencil, a paintbrush, a piece of charcoal. For the sensation of gooseflesh and the state of mind alternately restless and exhilarated. It could be that the only way to summon it up again was to provide the right conditions, peace, solitude and a place to be. A place without associations. A blank canvas. Perhaps when she had held forth to Eustace about the Cider Press she had spoken more wisely than she knew. She needed to think, and fast, or events would overtake her.

She arrived at the place where the stacks stood silently apart, their roots either drowned by the green water or desiccating in the warm sun. The breeze was off the land so the sea was almost motionless here, reflections rock steady. The Gaudiesque cliffs with their hollows, convexities, crags and clefts were madder red in the sun, a painted desert which was what this sandstone had once been, but was now solidified and rough-hewn by a new sea.

In her curious dream she had been embedded in a cliff like a shell or the fossilised remains of some long-dead creature or a creature yet to be born, by the abrading action of the elements.

Attachments were being severed. First her mother, then the unborn child, soon Amy would conduct a completely separate life. And Robert?

She leaned against a part of the cliff that rose above her like a sculptured wave, partly enclosing her in its arrested fall.

She was a creature in between, half way through life, with substance and experience gained but with the possibility that she had amassed no wisdom apart from the day-to-day prosaic variety. One more cutting adrift was inevitable, one more disconnection had to be made. Robert would be in New York, and perhaps that would make it easier for him. She sincerely hoped that Eustace had exaggerated when he'd said Robert needed her there, Eustace in any case had ulterior motives for wanting her in the forefront of what he saw as the artistic scene. All the same she was profoundly doubtful of Robert's ability to manage without her unless, that is, he found other willing shoulders on which to lean. Stella Bowen had written that female devotion was a drug on the market. It was still more or less true in spite of the Melanie Soffords of this world. Hester had inherited the burden from Robert's mother (though of course she hadn't regarded it as a burden at the time). Now Kathleen Gibb had been left far behind, her son had become a bright, visiting comet, not a dutifully orbiting satellite. Could Robert find other supports, more suited to his needs? Perhaps it was not too much to hope that one of his string of child-women might actually have some substance to her and undertake the role.

For she, Hester, could no longer fulfil it. If she was to survive, she would have to leave Robert. Leave Robert and disconnect herself from Eustace, Lombards and the whole of that world, for their preoccupations were no longer hers. There had been something vital missing from her life and her marriage for a long time but she had been too busy to notice. While she was painting it hadn't seemed to matter, at least it wasn't a priority, but now that she had been forced to stand back the hollow centre of her life gaped like an abyss. If she had studied her own painting sooner and more closely she would have seen the precarious thinness of her emotional resources. It had to change. She had to save herself from the abyss.

The edge of the quiet water was creeping closer, she would have to return, though her impulse was to stay. At her feet were shells, on the rocks and in the pools. Tangerine coloured, primrose yellow, chocolate striped, metallic grey, fondant pink. The sort of shells she had so obsessively collected on rare visits to the seaside with her mother. She had delved into pools, stirred the fronds of anemones, fed the crabs with scraps of bacon left over from the guest house breakfast, seen her brown, childish fingers pale and magnified under water.

She put a small collection of the shells in her pocket, aware of a heightening of her perceptions. Rocks the colour of rubies, the multi-hued shells, the sea stretching away from her feet to the horizon in bands of jade, peacock and amethyst. Gulls soaring paper-white against the cliffs. All precious, fragile, transitory.

There was a sense of urgency about her return, a need to precipitate action, a feeling that too much time had already been wasted. Now she knew what she had to do.

At the top of the steps that led from the beach to the Strand she collided with Ezra. He was carrying a large plank.

'What d'you think of this for jetsam, then?' he said. 'Solid two inch beech. Came in on the tide.'

'What will you use it for?'

'I'll think of something. Can't let it go to waste.' Balancing it on one shoulder as if it were a small piece of plywood, with his other hand he possessed himself of her arm. 'Now, what's the rush? I thought your hustling days were over.'

'And I thought you would have been back in Cornwall by now.'

'Now there's a greeting! Makes a chap feel wanted.'

They began to walk slowly along the road, being given a wide berth by other pedestrians due to Ezra's ungainly burden.

He said. 'I was watching you dashing along the beach in a purposeful manner so I waited to see if there was a chance you could make it for a meal tonight? If you're not too busy to spare a chap an hour or two, that is.'

Hester looked at him obliquely. 'Humility doesn't suit you, Ezra. Even less when I tell you that I'm about to put one of your suggestions into practice.'

'I didn't think you'd be able to hold out against my charisma for long.'

'You'll be amazed to hear that in fact it wasn't that suggestion I had in mind. All the same I'd like to come out to dinner tonight.'

'Well now, that's encouraging anyway. You must tell me about all the new developments. What time shall I call for you?'

'The car's all right now, is it?'

'As it'll ever be.'

'Then what about eight o'clock?'

'Do you mind making it seven? To tell the truth I get a bit peckish by then.'

She looked amused. 'All right. Seven then.'

Reaching the Anchorage door she paused before going in. 'I hope you find a use for your plank.'

'Sure to. I'll see you later and take what that sweet hour yields,' he said as he went.

Inside the shop, four customers at once practically constituted a riot. While Alice dealt with the other three, Hester managed to sell the fourth a watercolour. Eighty-five pounds. She took it as a good omen. When they had gone she told Alice that she had come to a decision.

'I'd like to rent the Cider Press for as long as it takes to sell it,' she said.

'You realise it will have to have a bit more done to it to make it usable,' Alice said composedly.

'Whatever it takes. I don't want anything elaborate.'

Alice's face broke into beaming smiles. 'Sweetie, I'm absolutely delighted. I'm sure it's the right thing. Convinced, in fact.'

'I hope you're right.' Hester found herself smiling too, foolishly and with a childish sense of excitement.

'I'll get on to Susan Orchard right away,' Alice said, bustling about out of sheer pleasure.

'Susan Orchard?'

'The architect. You remember,' Alice said. 'She'll be able to tell us what's the least we can get away with to make the place habitable.'

She telephoned and made an arrangement to meet Susan Orchard outside the Cider Press the following morning at nine-thirty.

'You seem to be taking it very much in your stride,' Hester said. 'About me taking on the Cider Press.'

Alice looked at her consideringly. 'I thought you might. Once you'd had a chance to think it over.'

'It seems everybody knows my mind better than I do myself,' Hester said mildly. 'But I suppose you know it won't be approved of, this decision?'

'I'm quite sure it won't,' Alice said. 'Are you ready to face the flak?'

'I'm quite sure I'm not but tomorrow, after we've seen your architect friend, I shall go back to Bristol. I shall have to tell Robert. There will be all kinds of things to sort out.'

And that, she thought with a flicker of apprehension, was to put it mildly.

CHAPTER THIRTEEN

Caroline swung her legs to the floor and sat on the side of the bed. She grabbed the satin robe that lay discarded from the night before and pulled it round her naked body. She thrust fingers skinny as claws through her pale crop and was then one hundred percent awake. Adrenalin, to which she was addicted, began its daily coursing through her bloodstream. She leaned over Robert, reaching for his cigarettes. She lit one, watching him. Asleep, the habitual tautness of his facial muscles relaxed. He looked boyish in spite of the streaks of silver grey above his ears. Their lovemaking had failed to satisfy her once again but that was nothing unusual, she hardly expected it to. It was not that he was a rotten lover, once he was aroused, certainly no worse than many she'd had, but like them he was able to excite and tantalize without being able to satisfy her. She realised that the fault was hers but this knowledge did nothing to diminish her anger. Her ways of satisfying the desire that men aroused in her but never assuaged were solitary. Before she had learned to fake orgasms she had suffered at the hands of lovers. There had been well-intentioned but exhausting marathons that had left her sore and angry and violent near-rapes that had resulted in bitter recriminations and the end of relationships. She had once been hooked on a quest for the possibility that a man existed who would be able to bring her to fulfilment but since this appeared to be increasingly unlikely, an illusion in fact, her second priority had recently been much more on her mind. The image of herself as consort to a powerful man.

Of course this did not mean powerful in crude financial terms, but powerful through the mystique bestowed on him by his position in the exclusive hierarchy of the art world. Since she had first set eyes on Robert Gibb this second option had emerged as paramount. It was now ten days since she'd interviewed him in his studio.

She left him sleeping and went to have a shower. She returned rubbing her short hair in a thick, white towel. Robert was still asleep. She drew the sheet down from his relaxed body and looked at him attentively. His skin was almost as pale as her own but with a sprinkling of freckles over his shoulders. His arms were surprisingly muscular for such a slender man, she supposed as a result of the physical nature of his occupation. His hands were elegantly shaped but stained and scarified. There was a black bruise under one of his nails, a fine sprinkling of white paint on the almost hairless back of the hand that lay along the pillow. So this was Robert Gibb. The images that found their eventual home on the walls of prestigious galleries and international collections began here in this narrow skull, by way of these hands which now lay motionless in her bed. In her power. She had no doubt that Robert could be manipulated. For all his intellect and sophistication she had glimpsed the frightened little boy. An insight she had first thought too much of a cliché to be true. But she recognised it as a fact and it gave her the greatest satisfaction.

She knew about fear. It was something she had always understood, even from the playground of her Cheltenham primary school. How it felt; how to induce it in others. Later, as a result of stringent economies on the part of her parents she was sent to a private school with a reputation as a crammer where she learned further refinements in the art of manipulation. When she was fourteen her parents separated, after which she was twice hospitalised as a result of illnesses induced by anorexia. At the time her periods disappeared and had never since been reliably regular. Sometimes she went without one for six months at a time.

She had emerged from anorexia and illness eventually, understanding much more about herself, her mother and her now absent father. She discovered that a price could be exacted from parents who let a child down. She had exacted it: from her mother in particular who was afraid of her; from her father on a less regular basis in terms of cash. Although anorexia still lurked in the background of her consciousness, a new-found power relegated it to a memory. A well-learned lesson.

As if alerted by her prolonged scrutiny, Robert woke up. The muscles of his face responded almost at once to consciousness, hastening to preserve his public mask. His eyes were immediately wary, his mouth controlled. Automatically he reached for his cigarettes. Turning away as he lit one he said, 'I'm not crazy about being looked at when I'm asleep.'

'Why not? You looked gorgeous.'

'For God's sake, Caroline,' he said testily.

It was early in their relationship. She had to be careful. Reaching out she placed a caressing hand on his chest. It was smooth, almost hairless. She allowed her robe to fall open invitingly but he turned away as if there was suddenly something repugnant about her nakedness. He picked up his watch and, glancing at the time, put it on.

'I have to go,' he said abruptly. 'Now that New York's been decided upon.'

'Stay,' she said. 'It's Sunday.'

'I'm not a wretched five-day-week clerk,' he said. 'I have to catch the eleven-thirty train.'

'What's the hurry. I'll drive you down later if you must go today.'

'I don't like cars. You know that.'

Abruptly she rose from the bed, tugging her robe tightly round her waist, tying the sash.

'I thought you liked last night,' she said crisply. 'You said it was good.'

He responded angrily. 'Don't tell me what I said!' Then he relented, holding out a hand. 'Caroline, come here.'

She went. He balanced his cigarette on the glass ashtray and pulled her gently to him.

'Sorry, darling. I'm a shit. Of course it was good.' He kissed her forehead chastely. 'Of course it was.'

'But you're not going to stay all the same?'

'No,' he said, closing the matter. 'I have work to do.' He let her go and crushed out his half-smoked cigarette. 'I'd like a shower.'

'Help yourself. The water's hot.'

He shut himself in the bathroom, excluding her. She went into the kitchen which was minimal in size and sparsely furnished like the rest of the flat, though it was well supplied with time-saving gadgets. She measured out coffee, filled the kettle with water and turned it on. She cut a grapefruit in half and sliced bread for toast.

Robert came into the kitchen, his hair still faintly damp. He was dressed in the usual cashmere sweater, pearl grey under a peat-coloured Armani suit, casual chic. He sat down and she put a cafetiere of coffee in front of him and sat opposite. He poured, tasted and grimaced.

'Has this got fig in it?'

'Half a teaspoon, yes.'

'Sorry, but I hate fig.'

'I didn't know. I'll make some more.' She emptied the cafetiere down the sink and refilled it, this time without the fig. He helped himself to a slice of toast and a cigarette. She had half a grapefruit.

'You do understand why I have to go back, don't you?' he said.

'It's essential for my work that I avoid distractions or commitments.'

'Of course I do. I *know* about artists, for Christ's sake!'

'It means that I never know when I'm going to work through the night, for instance, or when I'm going to be able to see you. It isn't something that can be prearranged, especially now.'

'You don't have to tell me, I understand.'

'I knew you would. You're an unusual woman. I don't see you ever acquiescing to orthodoxy. You have your own life, your own career. You obviously can't afford entanglements any more than I can.'

'Come on, Robert,' she laughed briefly. 'You're married, for God's sake!'

'Quite. But that's different. Hester and I have an understanding,' he said curtly. 'But we must do this as often as we can, don't you think? You do believe we have something to offer each other?'

She nodded. 'Yes, I really believe we have.' She would like to have probed him on the exact relationship between himself and Hester. She had tried last time they'd met and nearly had her head bitten off. Hester was for the moment a taboo subject apparently. Like a holy, bloody cow, she thought savagely. And how had it come about that she, Caroline, the independent woman, was not only listening to what from anyone else she would have condemned as chauvinistic crap, but willingly condoning it? She must have flipped. Either that or she was engaging in more subtlety than she'd previously thought herself capable of; if it was what Robert wanted to hear, then that is what she would provide. In any case, he was not some deadbeat painter, she'd known plenty of those. He was Robert Gibb. Successful, rich and glamorous. He'd earned his right to dictate his own terms. Hers would come later.

She smiled at him, her urchin features softened unexpectedly almost to sweetness. She put a narrow hand over his. 'Darling Robert,' she said. 'I am so glad about the new commission. If there's anything I can do you'll let me know, won't you? I think you should accept this offer of a studio in New York. It could lead to other things. I only wish I could be there myself.'

'So do I, Caroline,' he said and was surprised to find that he meant it.

'I shall have to see what I can do,' she said jokingly.

CHAPTER FOURTEEN

Ezra let out an agonised yell.

'Christ Almighty! What's happening!'

'I'm not sure but I think the engine's on fire,' Hester said.

Ezra pulled into a gateway at the side of the lane, their view through the windscreen now totally obscured by rising clouds of smoke and steam. Both doors opened simultaneously and they struggled out, hampered by an ooze of squashy brown mud underfoot. Ezra bent to release the bonnet catch.

'I don't think you should do that,' Hester said. Ezra being engulfed by a sheet of flame seemed a distinct possibility. 'Unless you happen to have a fire extinguisher handy.'

'Extinguisher! You're joking. How are we going to put the damn thing out? Perhaps we could scoop up water from the puddles?'

'I think we should wait. The smoke seems to be less.'

Ezra kicked the wounded vehicle viciously.

'Bugger it! What d'you think can be wrong with it *now*?'

'It could be the thermostat.' She wondered how she had been so misguided as not to insist on taking her Peugeot. Pandering to Ezra's *amour propre* had been a mistake.

The smoke did in fact appear to be lessening. Only a few wisps were now emerging but the smell was evil. Ezra sat himself on the granite stile that was set in the hedge next to the gateway.

'That's it, I suppose,' he said bitterly. 'This isn't at all as I planned it. Dinner, then back to my place for a spot of seduction was what I actually had in mind.'

'I see. Your place?'

'Well, Richard's place.'

'Isn't Richard in residence?'

'No, he's abandoned the barn to me and is currently shacked up with his rich girlfriend in Totnes. We would have had the barn to ourselves.'

'Oh, well. I'm glad you put me in the picture.'

'Don't mention it. It was to have been an optional extra you understand, which I hoped you'd fall in with, naturally. Ah, the best laid plans! Come and sit here while we think what to do.' He moved along the flat piece of stone and reached down to hoist her up.

The lane was unfrequented; one of those bordering Dartmoor, narrow and flanked by the typical turf-covered stone walls inextricably bound by the roots of trees that balanced, apparently precariously, on top.

Ezra glared at their failed mode of transport.

'This,' he said, 'is typical of my life. Sums it up in a nutshell.'

'Trouble with cars?'

'Trouble with cars, trouble with the establishment, trouble with money, trouble with women; but mostly trouble with money and women. Now that's a bummer.'

'I wouldn't know,' Hester said drily.

'All my own bloody fault,' he went on gloomily. 'Only an idiot would end up with one duff car, two ex wives and two sets of alimony.'

'Two!'

'Two.'

'That's what I call mismanagement.'

'That's what I call being up shit creek. You see, the trouble is that the first one left me, went off with an estate agent of all bloody things and I, in an incomprehensible fit of gallantry, agreed to be the guilty party. It was like that in those days. Mind you, she did claim that I was just the tiniest bit guilty anyway but it didn't penetrate my thick skull that I'd be forking out for the rest of my natural.'

'Were there children?'

'Not from that marriage. Two from the next though. Grown up now and in sensible professions like design technology.'

'What about now. Are you living with someone now?'

His substantial frame shook with ironic laughter. 'What d'you think. No chance of anything permanent with this millstone round my neck.'

'Do you want something permanent?'

He grasped one of her hands and enclosed it in his.

'Alas, the old buffalo's rumbustious days are over. He's drawing in his horns and would be happy to settle for quiet browsing in the backwaters.'

'Why do I get the impression that that's a load of balls?'

He laughed again. 'You're a cynical woman.' He waved an arm about to indicate the scenery. 'Now tell me, as an urban artist how d'you rate the view? Would you be cynical about that too?'

Before them a ploughed field tilted down towards a wooded valley. The level rays of a sinking sun picked it out in strips of purple and cinnabar against the shadowed inkiness of the as yet leafless birch. Beyond, a field of new corn flashed yellow green before the ground soared away to form a background of tan, violet and peat brown with the occasional golden banner of gorse. Hovering above the secret valleys and sweeping uplands could be seen the rocky outcrops of the Tors, mysterious and remote against an amber sky. Cloud shadows passed, turning the moor from a landscape of colour and delight to a threatening wilderness and back in a matter of minutes. The only sound was of a lark singing overhead and the wind in the trees.

The atmosphere of the place acted like yeast on a part of her that had been too long inert.

She grinned. 'It's been done,' she said.

'I thought you'd like it. Listen! D'you hear that?'

He jumped down from the stile.

'What?'

'I think I hear the sound of possible rescue.'

He plunged into the road in the path of the oncoming tractor, waving his arms like a lunatic. The tractor ground to a halt and after a short discussion with its grinning driver, Ezra managed to negotiate a lift to the next village. He fished out his well-worn oilskin from the Citroen and laid it on the bare boards of the trailer. The young tractor driver and his untrustworthy-looking black mongrel looked on with undisguised amusement while Ezra helped Hester aboard.

'Don't stray off the oilskin,' Ezra said. 'The last occupants could well have been pigs.'

No conversation was possible over the racket of their progress but the driver looked frequently and mirthfully over his shoulder. The dog had turned round to face them. By the time they reached the village it was too late to ring the garage at Coombe Ferrers, in fact it had been too late for some time.

'What the hell!' Ezra said. 'Let's leave it where it is for the night. All I want is a decent pint.' He turned to the young man who had thoughtfully drawn up outside the pub.

'Fancy a pint yourself . . . what's your name, by the way?'

'Terry.'

'Right, Terry. Have a pint on us.'

The Queen's Head was not much bigger than the cottages that

flanked it on either side, Ezra at least had to stoop on entering. It had been built before there had been machines to coerce its timbers into straight lines and they had since settled down to a comfortable old age, dark and beery.

The appearance of strangers caused a slight stir especially after Terry, high on the prospect of a free pint, had regaled the clientele with the story of his gallant rescue.

'The discomforture of "grockles" seems to be a popular topic,' Hester said when they were able to retreat to a quiet corner by the window. 'I can't say I blame them.'

'You're never going to forgive me for this, are you? Especially when you get home and discover that those beautiful trousers smell of pig.'

'Don't worry. I'll send you the dry cleaning bill,' she said straightfaced.

'Let's have another. Drown our sorrows.' Ezra returned with their drinks, the promise of sandwiches rustled up by the landlord's wife and the possibility of a lift back to Coombe Ferrers in Terry's Ford Escort; the latter depending on Terry's level of sobriety when the time came.

Ezra wedged himself back into the panelled alcove. The window embrasure itself was scarcely three feet square and framed a view of a few lop-sided apple trees and a tangle of overgrown grass and nettles.

'What will you do about the car?' Hester asked.

'I'm hoping that if I leave it there overnight someone will nick the bloody thing. At least then I can claim the insurance.'

There was an interruption while the sandwiches arrived.

'These will stave off the worst pangs,' Ezra said. 'Until we can reach civilisation and some decent grub.'

'This suits me,' Hester said, biting into the sandwich, which was at least fresh with generous amounts of cheese and pickle. 'I can and do exist on this sort of stuff.'

'No wonder you're as skinny as a bloody Giacometti. They're not bad though, are they?' He polished off half a round before he spoke again.

'So it's all go, is it? You're really starting work again?'

'I didn't say that. But I've arranged to rent the Cider Press from Alice until she sells it.'

'This is very sudden, isn't it? I seem to remember you swearing to God you were all washed up. You surprise me!'

'Maybe I'm not sufficiently in touch with my own motives . . .

though I think that's changing. The Cider Press will just be a place to be while I think what to do.'

He regarded her thoughtfully.

'This stopping to reflect on one's motives is a bloody good idea. I wish to God I could afford to do it. I have this bee in my bonnet . . .' He stopped to attend to his glass, dabbing the moisture from his beard with the back of his hand. 'As I was saying,' he continued. 'I have this bee in my bonnet. The inescapable fact is that there's too much art about. At least too much that purports to be art. All painters should be paid to stop painting every once in a while and be forced to consider what they're up to. In fact there are some painters I could mention who should be paid to stop painting altogether.'

'Like myself, perhaps?' Hester said, amused.

'Ah, now. I might have said so a few weeks ago,' he said. 'Now I don't think so.'

'As I'm doing precisely what you recommend . . . except that no one's paying me, unfortunately.'

He grinned at her. 'I reckon you'll surprise not only yourself but a few others into the bargain,' he said.

'You think so?' she said with only a touch of irony.

'Oh, yes. I do indeed.'

'And what about you? Do you think you should be paid to stop painting?'

'Oh, definitely. Build up a nice head of steam.'

'You'd cheat.'

'Of course I would,' he said cheerfully. 'And what about our "eminence grise", the sainted Robert? Still haemorrhaging banalities?'

'He's been offered a nice little earner from the First New World and Union Bank. New York.'

'A bank, you say?'

'Yes.' Hester polished off the last sandwich. Her appetite had come back with a vengeance.

'That figures. So the boy's hit the jackpot.'

'You don't like his stuff. Tell me why. I'm interested.'

'Don't you see it for yourself? No, perhaps you don't.'

'I want you to tell me.'

He lifted his glass and drank, then set it carefully on the seamed dark surface of the table.

'How can I best put it? Imagine this enormous table full of the most marvellous goodies. Great loaves of crusty bread, bowls of translucent grapes, huge baskets of apples, sides of beef, mounds of plums, strawberries, cherries and goosegogs. Heaps of gleaming fish . . .'

'I hope this is leading somewhere.'

' . . . mountain slopes of Devonshire cream. Now what do you choose to eat? Muesli.'

'I like muesli.'

'But I ask you, muesli for breakfast, lunch and dinner, morning, noon and night. That's Robert's painting. No food for the soul. What he needs to do is to muck in, get down to the nitty-gritty, do a bit of life drawing, for instance, and find out how bloody hard it is to be a real painter. But then I'll bet a penny for a pound that he came from the generation who never did any life drawing when they were at college.'

'My generation, you mean! As a matter of fact I did life drawing even though it wasn't actually on the curriculum.'

Robert had done very little. An academic anachronism, he'd called it. It was the fashionable view at the time.

'Perhaps you've always been a rebel at heart.'

'If you want to know the symbolism of Robert's work you should read Kurt Sagar on the subject.' Hester said with a grin.

'That time-serving git! What can Robert's paintings possibly be symbolic of? About the significance of squares à propos the ills of mankind, no doubt! I say balls. What the fuck do either of them know about anything!'

'You can't say that. You don't know Robert.'

'Stop playing devil's advocate! You know you agree with me otherwise you wouldn't have stopped producing the stuff yourself. No wonder he needed old Sagar to write twenty pages of explanation in the bloody catalogue. Just show folks that and forget the paintings, I say. Or put them in a bank, which is what he seems to be going to do.'

'This wouldn't be sour grapes, would it?'

'What a marvellously loyal woman you are! I wouldn't mind you on my side.'

'Are there sides?' she said. 'Look, if I had something to say about Robert's work, I'd say it to his face.'

'Then you're a heroine too. But I'm sure you'll say he's man enough to take it.' His eyes twinkled at her in the fading daylight and the glow from the few dim bulbs.

'That's his problem, don't you think?' she said sweetly. 'And mine.'

'Right. His problem, as you say. Don't think it's yours. You have your own, Hester my old sweetheart.'

'Don't call me that!' she said sharply. 'Anyway, that reminds me. I have to go back to Bristol the day after tomorrow.

'Oh, my God no! You can't do that!'

'Actually I can. And will.' Though she spoke of her intentions with firmness and equanimity the thought of return filled her with dismay. Even with the unforeseen mishaps she had felt perfectly at ease all the evening; she had also been stimulated, amused and, yes, happy and she couldn't remember feeling all those together for a very long time.

'What shall I do! We haven't even started to discover each other's possibilities yet. You simply can't go.' His voice dropped, becoming urgent. 'Please, Hester. Don't.'

'Obviously I shall come back.'

'But when? Tell me?'

'I don't know. Soon. I shall have to be here when work on the Cider Press starts.'

Ezra put his head in his hands, clutching his beard like a figure from Michelangelo's Last Judgement.

'This is a disaster,' he said.

'You're crazy! We've only just met.'

'What bloody difference does that make!' He dropped his hands, enclosing hers. They were warm and oddly comforting.

Hester shook her head. 'Ezra, you're insane.'

'You're a heartless woman.'

'As well as cynical and loyal! Look, don't you think we should do something about getting back?'

'And so sodding practical. Right. I'll summon our rude mechanical.' Reluctantly he lifted his hands from hers and signalled to Terry who came over, his grin still in place.

'You ready to go on now, mate?' Terry said jauntily.

'How the regional accents have been hybridised. It's a tragedy,' Ezra said but Terry simply looked blank.

'You want a lift or no?' he said.

'How many pints have you had?'

'Just the one you bought me. I'm skint, see. Only, if you're still keen I'll nip up the road and get the motor.'

Terry's red Escort pulled up beside the tractor five minutes later and in spite of its slightly ostentatious customising Ezra and Hester came to the conclusion that it was probably roadworthy, while Terry apparently came to the conclusion that they were probably worth a tenner and very likely more.

They sat in the back, Terry drove and his black mongrel faced then from the front passenger seat, dribbling on Ezra's shoes and watching them with an unreliable eye. When Ezra put a steadying arm round Hester it showed its teeth and growled a warning.

'Does your tyke belong to the Purity League by any chance?' Ezra grumbled.

Terry snorted with laughter, 'He always does that.'

'Can't do much for your love life'.

Terry gave another hoot of laughter. 'Fat chance of that where I live,' he said philosophically.

He dropped them on the quay at the end of the Strand and Ezra pressed some notes into his hand.

'Ta very much,' Terry said, leaning out of the driver's window. He put the car in gear. 'Cheers. See yer.' He let in the clutch and roared off up the road.

'How much did you give him?' Hester demanded.

'Twenty.'

'You idiot, Ezra! No wonder he shot off at such a speed. He probably thought you were going to change your mind. You better let me give you half.'

'Not likely! Anyway, what the hell,' he said. 'No good having a bank manager and doing the worrying yourself.'

It was late. Only the Cutter was open for food but neither of them felt in the mood for any more pub fare. Ezra had another pint, Hester had a tomato juice and an hour later stopped her Peugeot outside Richard's ramshackle barn five miles from Coombe Ferrers.

'After such a disastrous evening I don't suppose I can persuade you to come in?' Ezra said gloomily.

'Some other time perhaps.'

'So you can't tell me when you're coming back?'

'You'll be in Cornwall, won't you?'

'I may stay on for a while. Richard's not coming back for a week or two. In any case he won't mind. I'll ring Alice every day just to check.'

'I hope you won't!'

'I'll ring you in Bristol then.'

'I hope you won't do that either.'

Ezra put his hand on the door handle. He sighed gustily.

'Look, I'm bloody sorry about this evening. In spite of what I said I don't usually make such a fuck-up of my arrangements, particularly when it's with someone special.'

He placed a gentle kiss on her cheek and then pulled her into his arms and did the job more thoroughly. An unfamiliar sensation, whiskers. Hester thought she could easily get to like it. She didn't delude herself that Ezra was either safe or reliable but at the moment his substantial body felt like a haven. A haven at least compared to the storms she had already faced and would face again as soon as she returned home. He was blessedly uncomplicated, as far as painters ever were uncomplicated. She put her arms round his neck and kissed him back.

'Much more of this,' he said into her ear, 'and you'll have to come in.'

She pulled away.

'Loyalty to Robert?' he said.

'It's not that. But there are things I have to sort out. I just don't need any more complications than there are already.'

'I see,' he said, not seeing. Briefly he laid the back of his hand against her cheek. It was like a promise and a reassurance. In a mood of utmost pessimism he got out of the car and watched while she turned it round.

'Say we'll meet again,' he called out as she drove away. But her answer was lost in the noise of the engine.

She arrived back to the news that Amy had telephoned. The art college had offered her a place. There had also been a call from Paul to say that he was staying overnight in Plymouth.

CHAPTER FIFTEEN

Directly below them a sandboat made its way downstream on a full tide, shouldering the sluggish green water into reluctant ripples that sucked at the mud on either side. From two hundred and fifty feet above, the boat could have been a working model and the traffic on the Portway alongside the river a string of mechanical toys. Paul, whose first visit to Bristol this was, craned to look over the parapet.

'I'm impressed,' he said. 'Isambard could certainly hack it.'

'I thought you would be,' Amy said. 'Men are always more impressed by the suspension bridge than they are by the gorge itself.'

'Come on, woman, this is supposed to be the jewel in Isambard Kingdom's crown.'

'Except that he never lived to see it built.' Amy turned her back on the view and gazed up into the massive girders. 'Anyway, you haven't told me yet what you're doing in Bristol. I thought you were nose to the grindstone in Devon.'

'I've brought some work up. Thought I might do the rounds with it here.'

'With views of Devon? You'll be lucky.'

'And I thought we might meet for a drink.'

'Long way to come for a drink.'

'The really good thing about being self-employed is that you can take a break when you feel like it. I felt like it. Spur of the moment decision.'

'I was in the sodding bath when you rang. I'd forgotten to put the Answerphone on again after I'd rung Gina.'

'Gina?'

'Friend. Lives in Bedminster.' She turned round and pointed. 'If you make an effort you can just see Bedminster from here.'

'Oh, I get you. Part of the city.' He turned to look at her. Strands of curling blond hair blew across his face in the updraught from the river; it amused her to think that some people paid good money to get that sunstreaked effect; and she noticed that his eyes were brown, not grey as she'd supposed.

'Is your pop at home?'

'Yes. He's working.'

'And when does Hester come back?'

'I'm not sure. Tomorrow, I think. Why? You wouldn't be soliciting to stay the night, would you?'

'I'm not sold on your choice of words.'

'So you *were*.'

'No. On second thoughts I don't think it would be such a great idea after all. Hester wouldn't go much on it if she found out. She doesn't like me. Probably thinks I'm a bad influence.'

'She hasn't said anything to me. Besides, you might give me credit for some independence of mind, for God's sake.'

'In that case, maybe we could go somewhere tonight?'

'We could go out to a meal.'

'Suits me. What sort of place d'you fancy. Classy or basic? What d'you like to eat? Spaghetti and gnocchi, sea food, sweet and sour, nouvelle cuisine, tacos, frogs in garlic, moussaka, sushi . . .'

'For God's sake!'

'Fish and chips, borsch and blinis . . .'

'I like pasta and I'm a vegetarian in case you forgot. I'll take you to a rather decent Italian place I know.'

He rested his hands on her hips. 'Good. What shall we do till then?'

'I have to start preparing a project for the new term.'

'Have you heard from the college?'

'This morning. I'm in.'

He grasped her round the waist and swung her off her feet, nearly knocking over a hurrying pedestrian.

'Watch it!' The man grumbled at them. 'You mind what you're doing on the bridge. It isn't safe to fool around.'

'Stupid old git,' Paul said, not waiting until the man was out of earshot. 'Anyway, bully for you. Tonight we'll celebrate.'

'Tomorrow I'm starting this job.'

'Doing what?'

Amy giggled. 'I'm taking part in a survey of people's tea-drinking habits amongst other things.'

'Sounds terminally boring.'

'Don't knock it. At least it's money. Not much, but something.'

They rested their arms on the parapet and watched the progress of climbers on the side of the gorge, tiny brightly coloured manikins strung together by a thread.

'What d'you do in the winter, when you're not in Coombe Ferrers?' Amy asked him.

'This and that. Bar work, mostly. West End wine bars, you know.'

'With a wee wifey stashed away somewhere, I've no doubt.'

'Naturally. Not to speak of the four kids and a whippet called Fido.'

'So you're not married?'

'What d'you think! Of course I'm not married, you dickhead.'

'And no girlfriend?'

'What's all this third degree stuff. And what's it to you anyway?'

Amy pursed up her lips in an expression of nonchalance.

'Nothing, believe me. Just making conversation.'

'And what about you. No nice middle class intellectual boyfriend then?'

'There was. It's over.'

'So we're both between relationships, as they say.'

'Don't use that word. I hate it!'

'What word?' Paul raised his pale eyebrows inquiringly.

'Relationships,' Amy said derisively, 'Yuk.'

'Okay. Please yourself. I'm sure you're not the type to rush into marriage since you have such a brilliant career already mapped out for you by adoring parents.'

Amy flushed. 'How can you say that when I've just had this big fight with Robert over changing my sodding course!'

'That's no big deal. Now if you'd suddenly opted for a life stacking shelves at Tesco's that would certainly be a mega insurrection.'

'Don't be ridiculous.'

Paul put an arm round her underneath her baggy jersey. 'I'm not knocking it, kiddo. Look what a sheltered life has done for you. All that education, good food, fresh air and general nurturing has all lead to an unmistakeable end product. No. I wouldn't knock it for the world.'

'Listen, I'm willing to bet that I've seen more real hardship and misery than you have, and not on the box either. When I was in Cairo I spent some time with the fellaheen out of choice.'

'More of your Dad's influential connections?'

'You're an ignorant shit, aren't you? The fellaheen are the poorest of the poor.' She shook off his arm. The last of the climbers had reached the top and were moving around collecting their gear, their distant shouts just audible.

'You forget I haven't had your advantages,' Paul said imperturbably. 'I think it's highly likely that you wouldn't have heard of the fellaheen if you hadn't happened to have read Modern Arabic.'

'As a matter of fact, I had . . . What's the matter? Why are you laughing?'

'You're so prickly,' he said, still laughing. 'And you take everything so bloody seriously.'

'Sod you, Paul Finch!' she said through clenched teeth.

'We get on a treat, don't we.' He pulled her against his Aran wool sweater and kissed her on the forehead. He smelled healthy and out-of-doorish and was already faintly tanned.

She disapproved of him but knew that she was already intrigued to say the least. He was far more attractive physically than Steve, though Steve would of course score higher when it came to integrity and intelligence she had no doubt; but Paul was older, he was financially independent and he was interestingly rugged from swimming and windsurfing. While she and Steve had still been at school Paul was already coming to grips with the problems of survival and had emerged from it with his insolent grin undimmed. That he was also just the kind of man to set her feminist teeth on edge was unfortunate; the trouble with feminist principles was that they tended to limit one's scope and while she was in no way promiscuous, in fact she was soberly conscious of all the current dangers of careless sex, she had all the same a normal share of sexual curiosity. Besides, the prospect of five months not only without Steve but without the friends she'd made at university filled her with panic.

She thought it appropriate that the first object she saw on waking was Bast, the cat-headed goddess of pleasure. Next to her on the bookcase was Isis, the Eternal Mother, then Hathor of the horned headdress and Selket with her scorpion, protector of the dead; even Sekmet was there, the terrible goddess of war. Amy thought they had been carved out of soapstone, all had come back with her from Egypt. Her eyes moved lazily to the mirror hung round with her collection of exotic beads, displayed but never worn. On the wall was a blowup of one of her own photographs, a pair of colossal feet laying in the sand at Luxor. Beyond that the window framed the branches of the beech trees in the square, misted with new growth. A sussurration of wings. Pigeons.

Amy stretched her arms deliciously above her head and pressed her feet down between the sheet and the duvet. She turned to look at Paul. He was already awake.

'Hello, ratbag,' he said, pulling her towards him and leaning over her.

'Hello, shit-head.'

He pressed his mouth on hers and then on her eyes, caressing her closed lids with his tongue. She felt him hard against her again. His hands stroked her breasts, gently, coaxingly.

'More,' he said.

Paul's lovemaking was so unlike anything she had shared with Steve as to make last night a new experience. Steve was enthusiastic but impatient, always pressing on to orgasm as if it were a train he had to catch. Sometimes he took her with him but more often he left her behind, cross and unsatisfied. Her complaints made no difference, he said he was unable to pace himself. His idea of foreplay was to search his pockets for a Durex. He was a good friend but a lousy lover. All the same, she missed him desperately.

Paul understood without asking. He read the responses of her body. He increased or decreased the pressure, he changed their positions, he caressed her with fingers, lips and tongue. He caressed her with the movement of his whole body, with the tip of his penis; without rush, as if they had all the time in the world. He waited and waited again until he was absolutely sure she was ready for him. When the mutual orgasm came it shook her with its ferocity and duration. It had never happened that way with Steve. She'd had no idea that orgasm could be different in scale. That it could be a ripple or a tidal wave.

Half an hour later she looked at her watch.

'Oh, Christ!' she sat up abruptly. 'It's twenty to nine.'

'So what?'

'I'm supposed to be at this place by nine.'

Paul leapt out of bed, naked and energetic.

'Come on then!' he said when she didn't move. 'Shift your arse. I'll drive you.'

Amy fell out of bed. 'I can't. It's too late already.'

'No, it isn't. Go and have a shower. I'll tidy this up.' In a daze, Amy staggered next door to the bathroom and turned on the shower. Paul joined her and a minute later they were dressed with their hair and other bits of them still wet. Amy flew downstairs and came back with mugs of coffee which they drank standing up. Then they went downstairs, circumspectly, their feet silent on the wooden stairs.

'Robert's in the studio. I heard him moving about when I made the coffee,' Amy whispered and then giggled.

'What the hell's that?' Paul indicated the nine-foot carving, its wood cracked with age.

'It's a post carving. Javanese.'

'It doesn't look too matey.'

'Look, come on. Never mind that now.'

Five minutes later they were in Paul's car hurtling through the streets of Clifton. Amy wondered how she could feel both enervated and invigorated at the same time, and how in hell she was going to be able to concentrate on tea for the next eight hours.

CHAPTER SIXTEEN

To save Alice the long pull up the hill the following morning Hester took her Peugeot and they approached the Cider Press by way of the road that looped round the back of the town. At its highest point they branched off into the rough lane that finished abruptly outside their destination. Susan Orchard's Land Rover was already there, parked close to the hedge.

Susan was a rosy-faced young woman with straight fair hair cut short at her ears; she wore a Barbour and carried a clipboard and a folder containing the original plans. She jumped out of the driving seat and came over, holding out a hand. Alice made the introductions.

'I'm tremendously glad you're having second thoughts,' Susan said. Her manner was brisk and cheerful.

'It rather depends on the estimate.' Alice was cautious. 'Though we're not thinking of going ahead with it as a gallery now.' She explained that they had been thinking of a studio.

'Sounds great,' Susan enthused. 'And it shouldn't be too difficult. Shall we go inside and you can tell me what you are hoping to do.'

The good weather was holding out. There was cloud and intermittent sun and a noticeable smell of spring in the air. The grass and weeds were already higher, wild arum and a scattering of primroses had made an appearance. There was a difference in the interior of the Cider Press too, even the ground floor area was lighter than Hester remembered for splinters of sunshine pierced the chinks in the boarded-up windows.

After a brief look round downstairs it was agreed it would be more sensible to start on the first floor. Alice sat herself on the bottom step of the outside staircase.

'You two go ahead,' she said. I'll wait for you here.'

Hester could easily have helped Alice to the top but knew her too well to offer. She and Susan went on alone.

The top floor was transformed. Hester had last seen it on a dull and sodden day and even then had been struck by its possibilities, its expectant atmosphere; but today the sun was flooding in through the window at the far end, bouncing light from the floor into the rafters overhead. Instead of the veils of mist and rain which were all that had been visible last time, there was a wide and sweeping panorama, the mouth of the estuary, a curving perspective of distant coastline containing a bowl of blue-green sea and on the far side of the river, a tumble of houses, their windows shooting bright, trembling reflections on to the far wall of the room. One way and another the whole place was filled with light.

In her mind's eye Hester already saw a studio. White walls supporting canvases, blank but awaiting the first decisive brush strokes or already shimmering with live colour. Not greys or monochromes, colour. She saw a long trestle with all the familiar tools of her trade arranged on it: brushes, palette knives, cans of oil and turpentine, boxes of charcoal and graphite, bags of pure pigment in powder form as colourful as an Indian spice market. Colour was the unexplored, the neglected, feared even; forbidden fruit because of its appeal to the spirit and to the emotions. She had only herself to blame for the state in which she found herself, for her neglect of her painterly roots, and the humiliation was almost too painful to bear. Insidiously she had absorbed an effete intellectualism, an attachment to the conceptual and a snobbish disdain of image without its accompanying dialectic. A dead hand had been laid on her imagination and her creativity and she had been too myopic and steeped in it herself to understand what was going on. Surely, if she detached herself completely from its chilling influence, she and her creativity might still stand a chance. If, in her fragile and muddled state she could yet find the courage . . .

'Are you all right?' Susan had been by the window admiring its outlook, waiting for instructions. She had turned to see Hester with closed eyes.

'I'm sorry? Yes, of course I am,' Hester snapped, taking out the pain of her thoughts on the well-meaning young woman.

Susan apparently put it down to the unpredictability of artists.

'You don't think it would work as a studio then?'

'Work?' Hester said. 'Oh, yes, it will work brilliantly. It just lacks the painter to go in it.'

'Really?' Susan was still faintly puzzled. 'What about the ground floor?'

'Storage, I should think, with the work space up here. Though one would need some kind of access for large paintings.' She crossed the floor and examined what appeared to be a large double door in the wall.

'We were going to fill that in with matching stonework,' Susan said. 'It must have been used for delivering the apples. The carts drew up underneath. There used to be an old chute in the floor here where they would shovel them into the hopper downstairs.'

'Leave the doors as they are for the time being, would you.'

Susan scribbled in her pad. 'Anything else.'

'It seems ridiculous to mention it on a day like this but there ought to be more windows.

'We could put in roof lights,' Susan suggested.

'Sounds a bit expensive. Estimate for them anyway, we shall have to see.'

'Heating?' Susan inquired.

'I hadn't thought. To tell you the truth I hadn't visualised being here in the depths of winter. I thought six months at the outside.'

'It would be freezing I should imagine,' Susan said with a grin.

'What do you suggest?'

'What about a stove. You can run radiators off some of them. They're quite attractive too.'

'Perhaps you can let us have some prices. Brochures and so on.' Hester spoke with a sinking heart. It was becoming more complicated than she had anticipated.

Susan wrote, looking thoughtful. Then she said. 'Miss Eliot, you've mentioned the expense and I think I agree that it does seem to be mounting up just for a six months' let. You might never get your money back; especially if it's sold for development as flats. They would obviously have a completely different set of requirements.'

'What d'you suggest?' Hester stood with her hands in the pockets of her trousers, frowning.

'Of course it's not for me to say but I was wondering if there was a possibility that you might require the Cider Press for longer?'

'There might be, yes.' Hester continued to stand, deep in thought. If there was a die to be cast, this was the moment. After today there could be no more shuffling of options in her head. Her only hope was to act as if she would paint again once she had broken free. To act at least, as if she had the courage . . .

She looked at Susan. 'Would it be possible to include living accommodation in the plan?' she asked after a long pause.

'Possible, yes.'

'But . . . ?'

Susan explained about planning permission. 'It would take twelve weeks altogether to receive planning permission,' she said.

'You're not still thinking of renting then?'

'No. I'm thinking along the lines of buying it myself.' Hester said quietly.

If Susan was surprised she didn't show it. 'You'd like me to apply for planning permission then?'

'Yes. Please. Then the work could start?'

'Certainly, if your builder was free.'

'What about the one who began the work? They obviously understand old buildings.'

'I could ask them.'

Hester began to walk restlessly up and down. 'Try to persuade them,' she said earnestly. 'Because you see, if Alice agrees to sell to me I would want to move in as soon as possible.'

Susan was intrigued by her client's change of mood. She scribbled a cryptic note in the margin of her pad.

'I think we'd better go downstairs and speak to Alice,' Hester said.

Alice was still sitting on the bottom stair.

'Is there a problem?' she asked. They had been rather longer than she'd expected.

'No, but we've had an idea,' Hester said unemphatically.

Alice glanced at her. Could this be the old Hester she knew so well? Intense, energetic.

'Oh, boy! What's up now?' she said, getting to her feet.

'I want to fix up living accommodation.'

'You want to *live* here?'

'Alice, we have to talk.'

'I'll wait in the Land Rover,' Susan said diplomatically, 'while you have a chat about it.'

Hester gave her a quick smile. When she had gone Alice said, 'What's all this about?'

'Alice, I want to buy the Cider Press.'

'Shit! Hester. How on earth d'you think you're going to afford it? Unless Robert agrees to sell your Bristol house . . . and I can't see him doing that.'

'No he wouldn't. Not to begin with that is. And in any case now that Amy's got into the art college she would need somewhere to live. Of course she could come here in the holidays, if she wanted to . . .'

'Aren't you forgetting something?'

'I know. Robert.' Hester suddenly looked downcast, checked in her headlong rush towards freedom. She prodded at a tussock of grass with the toe of her boot.

'Then you *are* thinking of leaving him?'

Abruptly Hester stopped prodding. 'Yes. I really think I am.' Converting the abstract thought into words suddenly made the next step of converting words into actions that much more inevitable.

Alice put her arm round her. 'Look, sweetie, don't you think you should get that sorted out first? I mean before you start talking about buying the Cider Press? It does all seem to be happening a bit quickly. Of course I'd adore to sell you the Cider Press. I can't think of anything I'd like better, but it does seem just the tiniest bit impulsive. I would hate you to regret it.'

Hester had a stubborn look on her face. 'Don't you see, I have to. I can't think why I haven't thought of it before.'

'Because, my love, you obviously haven't thought of leaving Robert before.' Alice made a move towards the gate. 'Look, I think this warrants a lot more discussion.'

Alice was right, of course, but now that her mind was made up Hester had no desire to discuss it further unless it was to agree a price. The decision, taken at reckless speed, would affect everything that happened from now on. Her marriage, her work, Amy, everything. The purchase of the Cider Press would take all her saved capital, she would have to borrow for the conversion if and until she worked again. Even now though, it was not too late, it could all be turned round if that was what she wanted. She could go back to Bristol, accompany Robert to New York, tread the sensible path. There would, however, be one difference: she would never be able to paint again. Not there with Robert, not in her old studio. If she went back now something would die. A third death for which she would feel responsible, or at least some measure of guilt.

'All right,' she said at last. 'We'll talk about it some more, but I warn you, my mind's made up. I suggest we let Susan go ahead with applying for planning permission all the same. After all,' she gave a small ironic smile, 'with planning permission I daresay you'd get a lot more for it if you decided to sell it to some rotten developer!'

'Don't tempt me!' Alice replied.

CHAPTER SEVENTEEN

Caroline slid the thick brown envelope across the table to Eustace. Then she helped herself to one of Armardi's anorexic bread sticks, snapping it in half with her equally fragile-looking fingers.

'There you are. See what you think,' she said.

'Let's order first, shall we,' Eustace said. 'That's if they actually serve real food here.'

The restaurant was Caroline's choice. All black and white marble, chrome and mirror glass. A young waiter approached dressed in a zebra-striped shirt and red braces. They ordered, Eustace without enthusiasm as he had abandoned the prospect of being served anything nourishing between these walls. Perhaps it was just as well; his doctor-inflicted diet was a constant thorn in the flesh. In any case he didn't see why Caroline had insisted on this meeting, she could more easily have sent the photographs by post.

'You must be very pleased with the New York deal,' she said.

'New York deal?'

She tapped the envelope with a filbert-shaped nail. 'Robert Gibb.'

'Ah, yes. I'm with you. It's more than time he had something big. He's exhibited everywhere: Cologne, Tokyo, Amsterdam, Milan and, of course, New York; but I always thought he could go even further.'

The waiter slid to a stop beside them with something called a Libraspritzer for Caroline and wine for Eustace. Caroline drank, lifting the bubbles from her lip with a small pointed tongue. Eustace tasted his wine, grimaced, shrugged and nodded, vowing to make it all up to himself this evening at dinner.

Caroline leaned over the table. 'But what about Hester? How much further were you hoping she'd go? The word is,' she said with elaborate casualness, 'that Hester Eliot is finished.'

'Hester, finished!' Eustace's astonished laugh rang out, attracting attention. He was not typical of this establishment's clientele who were mostly young, bright and ambitious; a Filofax on every table. 'Finished! That, if I may say so, my dear young lady, is the most extraordinary load of balls I ever heard in my life.' He leaned across the table and wagged a sausage-like finger at her. 'You know what? Hester hasn't even *begun* yet, and you can quote me. Do you know what Degas said?'

Caroline concealed her irritation. She detested being called 'my dear young lady', having Eustace's stubby fingers wagged in her face and being quoted at.

'I've no idea,' she said.

'He said that talent at forty was a damned sight more interesting than talent at twenty.' Eustace leaned back, precarious on his chrome chair, as if he had proved a point. Caroline was unmoved.

'You forget I went to Bristol, Eustace. I was in Robert's studio.'

'Robert is a very private person. You were particularly privileged. There aren't many people who can say they've seen the inside of Robert's studio.'

'Or for that matter,' Caroline said, 'can say they've seen the inside of Hester's.'

Eustace looked wary. 'I thought you said that Hester couldn't make the interview. In fact I know she didn't.'

Caroline sipped her Libraspritzer.

'Quite. All the same I happen to know that, judging by the state of her studio, she is doing absolutely no work at all at the moment. I must say I was rather intrigued.'

They were served with mushroom pâté and seafood mousse. Caroline ate tiny portions at a time. Eustace, mindful of his diet, resisted the temptation to polish off his mousse in one mouthful. In any case it behoved him to pay attention to Caroline Childs. Part of her power, and on occasion her usefulness, lay in her unerring nose for scandal and gossip.

He was not taken in by the fact that at first glance she looked about seventeen. He had known her for three years, since when he had found himself impressed by her encyclopaedic knowledge of what was happening in the art market besides all the latest gossip. It wouldn't be wise to underestimate her for he had absolutely no doubt that she would be quite capable of the deft stab in the back.

'You're on the wrong tack there,' he said. 'But then I wouldn't expect you to know about her other studio.' He leaned back in his chromium chair. 'It's not general knowledge.'

'Her *other* studio? Tell me . . . ?'

Eustace laid his finger alongside his nose with an absurdly conspiratorial gesture.

'In the West Country,' he said with an arch look. 'Watch this space.'

Caroline's sparse flaxen eyebrows drew together momentarily. If there really was a studio in the West Country, why hadn't Robert seen fit to tell her? When it came to anything to do with Hester he was quite infuriatingly secretive.

'Just Hester? Not Robert?'

'Not Robert.' He smiled complacently.

'Where in the West Country exactly?'

'Patience, my dear. All will be revealed but this is not the moment . . . "There must be a certain aura of mystery about an artist's work." Degas again.'

Fuck Degas, Caroline thought. Aloud she said, 'You wouldn't be trying to put one past me, would you?'

Eustace stretched out his hands in an expansive gesture.

'I do assure you I'm not. Why should I.'

'Have you seen it? The studio?'

'Indeed I have. Of course I have.'

Caroline finished the last piece of mushroom pâté. She leaned across the table.

'They're separating, aren't they?' she said silkily. 'Your two shooting stars.'

Eustace's hearty laughter echoed briefly through the black and white cathedral of current taste.

'Hell's teeth! What gave you that idea?'

'He in Bristol or possibly New York,' she said softly. 'And she in the west of England.'

Eustace pushed his empty plate to one side.

'Dessert?' he said. She shook her head and he signalled for coffee.

'Listen,' he said. 'What makes their marriage as solid as the Rock of Gibraltar is that it has all the right ingredients. They both understand about long hours in the studio and work taking precedence. Who else would put up with it?'

Caroline adjusted an armful of silver bracelets.

'Any number of people,' she said. 'You'd be surprised.'

Eustace speculated on the possibility of Caroline having heard about Robert's little affairs.

'Don't be misled by gossip,' he warned. 'In the twenty years I've known them nothing has come near breaking up that particular alliance.'

'No? Ah well. Now this studio in the West Country. Where did you say it was?'

'I didn't, my dear. Try again!' He grinned and pressed himself back in his chair while their coffee cups were filled.

'And she's working down there at the moment?'

Eustace's playful grin concealed a trace of anxiety. He fully intended to take a look at this so-called studio at the first opportunity. If it meant that Robert was busy in New York and Hester in Devon, so be it. Just so long as they were both working.

'All I can say is this,' he said, reaching into his pocket for a tube of sugar substitute and tipping four into his coffee. 'Prepare yourself to be astonished.'

'And Robert?' Caroline's eyes were wide and innocent. 'Do you think this commission will mean that he has to work in New York?'

Eustace reached for the brown envelope. 'It's a possibility.' He began to sift through the contents of the envelope, his thick fingers surprisingly deft. The photographs were black and white. Robert in his studio, face half hidden in cigarette smoke; or taken *contra jour* in his habitual pose, chin in hand. Sitting on a high stool contemplating a huge empty canvas. 'Who was your photographer? Fraser?'

'Of course.'

'They're all good. Not too keen on the one with the blank canvas though. It looks unproductive.'

'But moody. Mysterious. Like you said earlier.'

'Aha.' He stabbed a couple of them with his finger. 'Use that one, and this. Excellent.'

He let out a gusty breath. It was a pity about Hester. There would have been a lot more mileage to be got out of the original idea of Hester and Robert *à deux*. He would have to think of another angle for Hester. He thought he had successfully whetted Caroline's appetite with the Devon studio idea. At least it was something new. He must remember to make a date for another visit to Devon himself; stay at the Greyve Manor Hotel, take Gozo perhaps, if he could be spared. He passed the photographs back to Caroline and she shuffled them back into the envelope.

'You will let me know about the new studio, won't you?' she said. 'I might even get down there myself. Make a nice break.'

'You'll be the first to know, my dear young lady,' Eustace said, wondering how long he could keep her at bay.

CHAPTER EIGHTEEN

Later that morning, after they had returned from the Cider Press and done the shopping in the High Street, Hester and Alice climbed back up the hill to Alice's house.

Hester put cushions on the iron seat under the verandah and Alice, as always insistent on the small details of life, laid the circular table for lunch with a blue-check cloth, well-polished glasses and a basket of bread rolls. Hester thought of her own snatched meals taken as she worked, a piece of bought pizza and a mug of coffee half submerged in the clutter of paints and brushes; or, in contrast, meals taken at some expensive and fashionable restaurant alone with Robert or with Eustace and some rich potential buyer. Hardly ever at home or with Alice's sense of occasion.

They ate salad and several different kinds of cheese; Alice put a bottle of wine on the table.

'In case,' she said, putting the day's post on the bench beside her, 'we have something to celebrate. I haven't had a chance to open these yet.'

'Were you expecting something from the hospital?'

'If I'm not mistaken,' Alice attacked a small brown envelope with her knife. 'This is it.' She read the contents swiftly. 'The end of May, God help us!'

'Oh, Alice! At last. I'm so glad.' Hester put her arms round Alice and hugged her. 'What a relief!'

'It's one of those things that one waits so long for,' Alice said, touching her hair and re-arranging her strings of beads, 'That it's difficult to believe when it actually happens. In fact I *shan't* believe it until I'm coming round from the bloody anaesthetic.'

She turned to Hester as if only now could she acknowledge that there was a problem. 'When the pain is really bad, I would give everything I own just for half an hour without it. There's something so . . . so wretchedly alienating about pain. Like having an irritating companion who not only disgusts you but everyone else as well and who won't leave you alone even in bed.' She glanced at Hester. 'Even when you're in bed with someone else.'

'Someone like Paul, for instance.'

Alice sighed. 'I don't know why I thought you wouldn't guess.'

'Why the secrecy? You were never exactly reticent about these things before.'

'Okay. To tell you the truth, I was madly embarrassed. I thought you'd disapprove.'

'But I've always disapproved of your men. What's new?'

'His age of course, you fool. I thought you'd call him my toy boy. Well, he is, I suppose. But I do rather adore him.'

'I can see that, though at first I thought he was just an over-familiar lodger.'

Alice chuckled. 'Which he is, of course.' She began to pour the wine. 'Help yourself to bread rolls and cheese. We needn't starve just because life is beginning to get interesting!'

Hester took a roll and cut herself some Brie. She raised the glass that Alice had passed her. 'Here's to toy boys and hip replacements,' she said smiling.

'And to all women artists who want to be their own people,' Alice said. 'Whether they buy my Cider Press or not!'

It felt like a decisive moment to Hester and perhaps, she thought, to Alice. A turning point. She drank, knowing that something significant had taken place.

The garden steamed in the unexpected warmth. The houses and trees on the opposite bank of the river and the cliffs beyond were revealed with a newly washed clarity.

Alice turned her glass between knobbly fingers. 'So you're not shocked about Paul.'

'For goodness' sake, Alice! Just as long as you don't get hurt.'

'There are worse things than getting wounded in love. My whole life is a testament to it. As you know, in my own modest way I've always been a risk taker in that department.'

'And that's because you never managed to fall for anyone the least bit suitable, let alone available.'

'I wish I had. I wish to God I *could*. I'm quite aware of the fact that this thing with Paul can't last, in spite of the fact that he swears eternal love.'

'Does he indeed! Is he back, by the way?'

'He must have come back while we were out. His things are still in the hall.' Alice said. 'More cheese? This one with walnuts in it is rather good.' She poured more wine into both glasses. 'Now it's your turn.'

'My turn for what?'

'Confession. Good for the soul.'

'About what?'

'Come on, Hester! About you and Robert. I mean, what triggered this sudden decision? Was it Ezra?'

Hester gave a smothered squawk and covered her mouth with her hand. She went red in the face, coughed and took a drink of wine.

'Ezra!' she said when she could speak. 'For God's sake!'

'I didn't think he was that bad. Are you using him or is he using you?'

'Neither. Both. There's nothing between us. Nothing.'

'Will you sleep with him?' Alice asked blandly. 'Or perhaps you already have?'

'Alice!'

'Sorry. Not my business. Poor Ezra!'

'Why poor Ezra?'

'He's nuts about you. I meant to tell you that he rang this morning just after you'd gone to get the car.'

'He's just randy. He expects women to keel over like ninepins at his approach. Perhaps they did twenty years ago.'

Alice giggled. 'You're a hard woman, Hester.'

'It doesn't pay to be anything else with the likes of Ezra Judd, or most men for that matter.'

'As far as Ezra's concerned, I think you may be mistaken. Appearances can be deceptive.'

'What did he want?'

'Nothing in particular. Just to hear your dulcet tones, I think.'

'Was he back in Cornwall?'

'Just leaving, I gather.' Alice cut a bread roll in half and spread it with her own low-fat margarine. 'So if it wasn't Ezra, what was it that made you so sure you wanted to leave Robert?'

'As a matter of fact, it was the Cider Press.'

'The Cider Press!' Alice stopped spreading. 'Well, that's original anyway.'

'It's what it represents. To give myself a chance at last of doing work that is completely my own in a studio that is completely my own with none of the associations of the Bristol one.'

'Yes, I understand all that. And Robert?'

'I don't know if I can explain, but what has been wrong with my work was symptomatic of what was wrong with my marriage. Look, in the last few days I've been thinking about Robert a lot. And life. And what the hell I'm doing or supposed to be doing. If I stay with

Robert there is only one possible role for me and that's as a sort of behind-the-scenes helpmeet. You know, like Stella Bowen and Ford Madox Ford. Or Ida Nettleship and Augustus John. Or Gwen Salmond and Matthew Smith. Need I go on?'

'So there's no chance of staying with Robert and going on with your work?'

'Absolutely none as I see it.'

'You don't love him?'

Hester had been toying with a bread roll. Abruptly she left it on her plate and clasped her hands together on her lap.

'Yes, in a way I still do. But not in the way a woman should love a man, on equal terms. It would be so much easier if I could truthfully say I hated his guts. All the same, Alice, the marriage is dead. All the things that used to make it work seem to have disappeared. There's nothing left.'

The things that used to make it work and that had disappeared were the closeness of shared achievement as well as shared hardship and disappointment. The achievements they now took for granted and there were few disappointments and little hardship. There had once been shared ideas and shared moments of sheer idyllic happiness on the brief shoestring holidays in Dorset when they had watched the surf thunder over the rocks at Tilly Whim. And then there were the shared jokes. But there were no jokes now. Robert had become more serious, more morose even, the more successful he became.

Alice said. 'Not even sex?'

Hester laughed shortly. 'Certainly not sex.'

'But I think he depends on you for a lot of other things. How will he take this when you tell him? Presumably you're going to?'

'Of course. As soon as I get back. He'll make a fuss. It won't be easy. But I hope he'll get used to it. Perhaps New York will distract him. And he has his women to comfort him.'

Alice looked up. 'His women? Oh, I see. I didn't know.'

'He has a yen for very young, androgynous-looking females,' Hester snipped off the words matter of factly.

'My, God! Not under age, I hope!'

'Not as far as I know. Don't even think it! No, I'm sure not.'

'How long has that been going on?'

'Ages. Years.'

'Oh, Hester. I am sorry. I didn't know.'

'Yes, I suppose it must seem awful.' Hester fingered the stem of her glass. 'I'm so used to it that I hardly think about it any more.

One more fact about my marriage that I wouldn't face up to; until now, that is. When I was confronted by inescapable facts like Inez's sudden death and then the miscarriage, I started to think about my life in general and it seemed to me that it was . . . well . . . unsatisfactory. D'you see what I mean?'

'All too well, sweetie.' Alice said drily.

Hester glanced at her friend. 'Sorry, of course you do,' she said. A few white sails appeared between the roofs and chimneys below them. Alice nodded in their direction. 'The good weather has brought out the yachtsmen,' she said. 'It looks so tranquil and effortless from up here where you can't hear the swearing or smell the sweat. Personally I prefer to view it from afar. I get sick as a dog on boats. Come on, dig in. You're not eating.'

Hester went back to crumbling pieces of roll in her fingers. 'I want to talk about the Cider Press,' she said. 'Naturally, I'll have to take some advice about the finances and you must hit on a price. I don't see why estate agents have to be involved, you can save yourself their fees at least. But I tell you, Alice. I mean to buy it from you!'

CHAPTER NINETEEN

After just a fortnight away, her studio already had a faint air of dereliction. The great bundles of brushes of all sizes from six-inch house painting to Siberian sable, the tubes and cans of paint, bags of pigment and rolls of canvas could as easily be the memorabilia of another age as the paraphernalia of last week. Soon it would all have to be packed up and transported to the new studio. The thought gave her a frisson of fear, anticipation and also of impatience for it to happen.

She moved several of the canvases that were turned to face the wall. They were the ones that hadn't worked, those she had been unwilling to let go because they might have damaged her reputation, or they had been experiments made in the last disaffected phase when she had been struggling to find her way out of the stalemate. They were the runts of the litter but they still bore a strong family resemblance to her other, more successful paintings, those she had sent out into the world. To her fastidious eye there was no appreciable difference between the two, runts or prodigies. Now even the prodigies offended her; sophisticated, glossy little upstarts with no hearts. Eighties children. If she could she would have called them back from the four corners of the globe and done away with them.

She sat on the edge of a wooden platform that served as a model's throne (for unlike Robert she had never relinquished regular sessions of life drawing), and scowled at the unsuccessful canvases. These later ones in the usual subtle tones of grey were darker, altogether blacker than usual, but they retained the absolute control of form and proportion that was customary in her work. The shapes looked to her critical eye as if they could have been computer generated with no intervention of human emotion or human hand. If that satisfied current taste, she thought sourly, so much the worse for it. It sure as hell didn't satisfy her. Monochrome geometrics, with here and there a purposeful blurring or smudging exactly paralleled Robert's torn rectangles, a similarity which unbelievably she had never before detected. Now it stood out, as humiliating as discovering one had a hideous and previously unnoticed disfigurement. She put her head into her arms and, crouching on the edge of the dais, wept.

She heard Robert come back. The house had been silent. Amy was at work, doing her market research, and it was not Phoebe's day to tidy and clean. Robert must have seen evidence of her return but he went straight to his studio, assuming rightly that she was in hers. She was glad; she needed time, for she had no intention of confronting him in an emotional state. She would take a shower, change her clothes and compose herself.

'Hester. I saw you were back.'

She started. She hadn't seen him standing at the door and wondered how long he'd been there.

'Hello, Robert.' With the pretence of straightening her hair she dabbed at her wet cheeks. He came across and kissed her.

'You look better. More colour. How was Devon?'

'I'm fine. Devon was superb. I want to talk to you about Devon. Were you going to make some tea?'

'I put the kettle on, yes.' He put an arm round her shoulders. 'Darling, it's lovely to have you back.'

They left the studio. In the kitchen Robert rinsed two used mugs under the tap and reached for the tea bags while Hester began restlessly to pack the piles of dirty dishes into the dishwasher.

'Leave those,' Robert said. He handed her a mug.

'Yes, why not,' she said brightly, 'Everyone else does. How's the new work going?'

He looked at her, swiftly sensing something different.

'I think I've made a start,' he said cautiously. 'But I have finally decided to take the studio in TriBeCa. This one will be quite inadequate for the dimensions I shall be working to, and the new one is huge. In one of the cast-iron buildings . . .' He put his mug of tea on the dresser and fumbled in the back pocket of his paint-speckled jeans for the cigarettes he'd been out to buy. Lighting one, he gasped in the smoke. It struck her for the first time that she disliked the smell of tobacco smoke intensely, especially when it hung stalely in the air and on her clothes.

'The thing is, Hester, we have to make a decision about the other vacant studio. Hirsch is very keen for you to take it. I have an idea that he has plans for you too which I think would be a considerable mistake for you to turn down . . .'

Hester opened her mouth to speak but he forestalled her.

'All right. I know you're not particularly stuck on Hirsch but we wouldn't get far if we sold only to buyers we personally liked or approved of. This opportunity would consolidate your standing in the States as I'm sure you're aware.' Hester pulled up a chair and sat at the table. Abruptly she cut into Robert's patient, reasoned argument.

'Why won't either you or Eustace leave it alone,' she said, quietly patient. 'I am not coming with you to New York.'

Robert narrowed his eyes against a curl of smoke. He looked wary.

'I thought that when you'd had time to give the matter some consideration you'd see the sense of it.'

'There *is* no sense in it. Besides . . .' She paused and drank some of her tea. 'Besides, I'm buying a studio in Coombe Ferrers.'

'You're not serious?'

'Perfectly. That's what I wanted to tell you. I intend to work there.'

'I can't believe this! What sort of stimulus do you expect to find down there?' He laughed but there was no amusement in the sound.

'I've already found it.'

'Hester! For Christ's sake, *think* about it! Think what you're doing. This is not the moment to piss around with frivolous schemes . . .' He dragged smoke into his lungs.

'Look,' he went on reasonably. 'I believe this Coombe Ferrers business is just an expression of your need to get into something larger, more fundamental, more global if you like. I think we're both feeling the limitations of this place. In other words, we're ready to move on . . .'

'I agree with you. We *are* ready to move on, though I'm not sure yet if I shall be able to paint. I hope the new studio will help.'

'Hester, there's no need to dramatise what we both know is a perfectly normal period of regeneration. They're part of a painter's life, we've always been aware of that. I don't know about you but it's perfectly obvious to me that we've been too *English*, too parochial. You need to expand, take your work further, express something more universal, more cosmic if you like . . .'

'Bollocks! All I can express is something that comes from inside myself and if you were honest you'd say the same. If that's too personal, not cosmic enough for you or for Eustace, I'm sorry. The point I'm really trying to make is that I'm not even sure that there is anything left inside and I sure as hell can't speak for the bloody cosmos . . .'

'You are deliberately misunderstanding. Why?' His tone changed and he dropped his voice persuasively. 'Okay, look. All I'm asking is that you give New York a try, darling. If you won't come for your sake, if indeed you feel that this period of stagnation is likely to continue, then come for my sake. As you know this is an extremely significant break for me, for us, and to tell the truth I need you there.'

'Need me?'

'Of course I need you. You know I do.' He was impatient with her for doubting it.

Hester stood up and poured the dregs of her tea into the sink. Turning round she said, 'Robert, I don't like this beating about the bush. I might as well tell you now that I'm leaving you.'

The cigarette hovered in midair, half way to Robert's mouth.

'What did you say?'

'I said I'm leaving you. I'm leaving Bristol and I'm going to live in Coombe Ferrers.' She gripped the empty mug with both hands. It had the symbol of Aries the Ram painted on it, black on white. Aries was her sign. Amy's Capricorn mug was hanging on the dresser, Robert's Virgo mug had been broken.

'You mean leaving for good?' Total disbelief.

'Yes, leaving for good. You have to agree that things haven't been right between us for a long time. I think the moment has come to admit it and make a new start. Both of us.'

Robert crushed his cigarette into a saucer. Only the trembling of his hands betrayed emotion. 'Look, Hester. There is absolutely no reason to overreact to temporary stress or to confuse your current problems with your work, with the state of our marriage.'

'I do see the two as connected, as a matter of fact.'

'Come on now!' he said roughly.

'It's how I see it.'

'If you'd just give New York a chance it would at least give you some sense of proportion . . .'

'Shut up about New York!' she said loudly. 'And listen to what I'm saying. I'm leaving you, can't you understand that!'

The colour had come to Robert's face. 'Divorce. You mean divorce?'

'Yes, I mean divorce, damn it. Or a separation, I don't care.'

Robert reached again for his cigarettes, then changed his mind. He sat down at the table opposite her.

'No!' he said. 'No!' His breath was beginning to come in ragged gasps, he was sweating. 'No!' He continued to repeat the word while he clawed at his shirt as if it were obstructing the flow of air to his lungs.

For the next five minutes the sound of his panic filled the kitchen. It was a reaction with which Hester was already familiar, although it had not happened for several years now. The first time it had frightened her, she hadn't known what to do.

She dumped the mug and grabbed his hands. 'Look at me, Robert!' she ordered. She exaggerated her own breathing, making it slow. 'Breathe with me!' He was still fighting but she bullied him until his breathing matched her own, slowly returning to normal. He closed his eyes. The sweat was pouring down his face.

The first of his panic attacks had been at college when his assessment marks had once dropped below straight A. The second time was when she was in labour with Amy, the last she remembered was when one of his paintings had been damaged en route to a gallery in Cologne.

'You can't mean it,' he said thickly, when he could speak.

She held herself away from him now, for the first time since they had been together seeing him at one remove, detached.

'These things happen. You know they do.'

'Christ, Hester, of course I know. But not to us. For God's sake, we're different. We need each other. Our's isn't any old marriage . . .' There was a pause while he took several steadying breaths. 'Don't you see that the springs of our invention lie in our relatedness . . . our interdependence . . . they always have . . . you can't just cut through that and say it's finished!'

'We have to, Robert. What you say might have been true once, but not any longer for me, probably not for you either. We're both stagnating in every sense of the word. Our marriage is a burden and an obstacle.'

'A burden,' he said hoarsely. 'What the hell are you saying?'

Hester was silent. When he spoke again it was with heavy cynicism.

'I suppose the archetypal question on these occasions is why? Why now? Can you tell me that?'

'Because I feel smothered. Smothered and obstructed. Because we're different, our relationship has changed, it changed a long time ago and for the worse. There's nothing left, Robert. There is simply no reason for us to be together any longer . . .'

'No reason!' he cut in. 'There's every reason! You must know how much we need each other. We give each other the peace and security we both need in order to work. It's not a matter of choice, it's absolutely imperative . . .' He stared at her compellingly, holding eye contact. His breathing was still noisy. 'I assumed you knew that without it there is no possibility that I shall ever be able to paint again.'

'Now who's dramatising?' she said. She picked up the discarded mug and tapped it impatiently on the table.

'What you're telling me then,' he said, a dangerous edge to his voice, 'is that you're quite prepared to endanger my career, our two careers, for a self-indulgent whim?'

'I don't think there's any point in continuing this discussion if you refuse to take what I'm saying seriously, if you're going to insist on rubbishing my point of view . . .'

'But it comes to the same thing whichever way you look at it,' he said. 'Fact. You are planning to sacrifice my life as a painter to yours, which God knows is at present amorphous in the extreme. And,' he added grimly, '*don't* you choose your moments! I might just as well ring Eustace right away and tell him that the First New World and Union Bank deal is off.'

Hester put down the mug abruptly and paced about the kitchen. 'You bastard!' she said on a sharp indrawn breath. 'You blackmailing bastard!'

Robert got up from his chair with such violence that it crashed over backwards. He was unsteady and grasped the dresser as if for support. 'And you're a selfish, calculating bitch. You weren't like this before so I guess someone's put you up to it. Don't tell me! That embittered old cow, Alice? Or have you acquired some bucolic lover?'

For the first time the idea that Hester might have found someone else took hold of his imagination. 'So that's it!'

'No, it bloody well isn't,' she shouted in exasperation.

'Because if that's all it is there's no need to rock the boat because of it. Have your lover. Fuck around all you like but don't fuck around with our marriage!'

Hester strode across the room, grasped the discarded mug and banged it on the table.

'How dare you say that!'

The action seemed to trigger a violent response from Robert. He grabbed her arms and forced her against the dresser, the edge of which slammed into her back making her cry out in pain. He thrust an unrecognisable face into hers, his normally tidy hair disarranged so that it fell over his face.

'What's the matter with you?' It was like a child's thwarted howl. He began to shake her, all the more shocking because he had never before used violence towards her. His strength belied his appearance and it was minutes before she could break away, her head reeling and her arms bruised. She was very much afraid, for she had never seen his iron self-control slip so disastrously.

She put the distance of the room between them, nursing her bruises but holding a chair in front of her as a shield. Robert propped himself on the table, his arms rigid and his head hanging; his breathing was loud and tears washed down his face and splashed on to the table.

'You can't do this,' he moaned between terrible gasping sobs.

She said nothing, wondering if she could get to the door without precipitating another attack. She moved towards it but he forestalled her, by pushing roughly past and flinging himself out of the kitchen. He stumbled off in the direction of his studio and there came the sound of the door crashing shut after him. Shaken, she collapsed on to the chair she had been grasping and rested her head and arms on the table. Her teeth chattered with sudden cold while her brain stubbornly refused to believe what had happened.

Amy came into the kitchen with the post, which she dumped on to the table.

'All for you,' she said.

Hester let it lie, and drank her coffee. Amy finished her coffee without sitting down. She was dressed for work in a grey jacket and short skirt she had bought for four pounds at a charity shop, a compromise between her usual leggings, oversized jerseys and shorts and what the firm demanded. Hester and Robert gave her an adequate allowance but she refused to buy new clothes. She said it used up the earth's precious resources, but Hester guessed that it was also something to do with keeping herself in line with her impoverished friends at university. Her chestnut hair, cut like an inverted bowl, shone fresh from the shower.

'What will you do about Robert?' Amy said. She nodded in the direction of Robert's studio. 'He's been in there for two days.' It was near to being an accusation.

'He must have come out sometime. There's food missing and I heard him come up to the bathroom in the night.'

'He's not working, you know. I always know when he's working.'

'I'm quite aware of that. You don't have to tell me.'

'What are you going to do then?' Amy persisted, her mouth set in a stubborn line.

'Nothing. He needs time to think.'

'Eustace will throw a wobbly if he finds out he's not working.'

'Look, Amy, leave it to me. I'll explain to Eustace if necessary. Go to work and don't worry.'

'In other words, mind my own frigging business.'

'No, not mind your own frigging business,' Hester repeated with an attempt at humour, though she had never felt less amused. 'Darling, I know this has been a shock for you. I've tried to explain my reasons for needing a separation from your father. Believe me I wouldn't, couldn't, do it unless I felt that I just couldn't go on as we were . . .'

'I don't see why not. What's changed?'

'It hasn't changed suddenly. It's been a long process of estrangement.'

Amy frowned and said nothing. It was difficult to refute the evidence of her own eyes but that didn't stop her feeling deeply aggrieved.

'Amy,' Hester said gently. 'Naturally you're upset. I realise that . . .'

'Too right,' Amy said drily. She looked at her watch. 'Look, I'm late already. See you later.'

She left the kitchen but a moment later put her head round the door.

'I shall be late so don't worry about food.'

Food. Hester hadn't even begun to think about food, never having felt less like eating.

'Paul and I are eating out.'

'Paul?'

'Yes. Paul.'

'Which Paul is that?'

Amy's head disappeared. Her disembodied voice floated in from the hall.

'You know, MCP Paul, Paul from darkest Devon. Paul Finch.'

Hester left the table and caught Amy as she was opening the front door.

'Paul *Finch*?'

'Right. Okay, don't tell me. You don't like him, but then it's not you he's asking out.'

'Amy, darling. You mustn't!' Paul who lied, Paul who cheated, Paul who was supposed to be elsewhere, certainly not in Bristol.

Amy hesitated at the door.

'*Mustn't*! Look, I'm late . . .'

Hester pulled Amy in and shut the door, leaning her back against it.

'What . . . ?' Amy began.

'Amy, how could you! What about Alice?'

'I don't get it. What about Alice? What's she got to do with it?'

'Hasn't he told you, then? Hasn't he told you how things are between them?'

'I still don't know what you mean.'

'Oh, my God! He hasn't! He and Alice are lovers, Amy.'

'You're joking.'

'Why should I be joking? D'you think she's too old? Or too ugly? Or too incapacitated?' Hester felt a twinge of conscience. After all, it had come as a surprise to her too.

'I don't believe you.'

'Well, it's true. So do.'

Amy stood still, frowning at the floor. 'Okay, he should have told me but I don't see what difference it makes.'

'You don't see . . .' Hester stared at her daughter. 'Do you intend to go on seeing him?'

'Sure. It's quite all right, you know,' Amy assured her. 'We're not in love or anything. And personally I don't think you're in any position to talk about principles. Alice doesn't need to know, unless you tell her, that is. Besides, she can't expect to hang on to him indefinitely, can she?'

Hester never intended what happened next. She had never laid a finger on her daughter, not even when she was an exasperating four-year-old or a recalcitrant fourteen. The sound of the slap echoed round the hall. Amy's face jerked away, her eyes watering, the glowing trace of Hester's hand already visible.

She shoved Hester aside and tore at the front door, slamming it with a resounding crash. Silence closed in. Hester was left standing beside the giant papyrus and the Buddha with the curled lip, cursing herself for her stupidity. Tears came again but this time never fell but remained burning in her eyes. What was happening to them all? How could Amy not be concerned at what she was doing? How could she herself have struck her daughter under any provocation? This was becoming a house of closed doors, non-communication and sudden uncontrolled eruptions of violence. Were they all losing their minds?

Ever since she had told Amy about the separation, ever since Robert had locked himself away in his studio, Hester had been aware of Amy's scarcely disguised hostility. In the past all Amy's battles, all her antagonism had been with or directed towards her father. She and Hester had always been particularly close. Other people had remarked on it and called her fortunate. Now, in Amy's eyes, Robert was the injured party, Hester was guilty and the cause of all the disruption. The manner in which Robert had remained stubbornly incommunicado had affected Amy badly. Even though in the past her erratic contact with her father had been punctuated by explosive rows or nagging hostility, she now behaved as if she and Robert had been the closest of allies. Hester had no doubt that the rows, challenges and the criticism had all been a complicated expression of love; love offered, love withheld, love that strove to dominate, love that on Robert's part might not be love at all. She wasn't sure if Robert was capable of love, it now seemed more like self-interest or a need to control and compel. She wasn't sure if Amy knew or suspected this to be the case. The constant challenging of her father could have been her way of trying to find out.

Of Hester's love she appeared to have no doubt, never having seriously questioned it or put it to the test, except perhaps once or twice during her adolescence. It could be that it offered such security that the blame for all their present afflictions could safely be laid on Hester's broad shoulders.

Yet she remembered something that Amy had said not so long ago.

'You're so loyal. You don't have to present a united front for my sake, you know. I'm not a child.'

She must have guessed then that things were not as they should be. She was a bright, perceptive girl. She probably knew about Robert's 'girls' too, although strangely they seemed to have only a marginal bearing on their present predicament. Hester stood for minutes with her hands over her face. Then abruptly she made a lunge for the downstairs cloakroom and was extremely sick. Afterwards she went back to the kitchen and sat for several minutes almost unaware of where she was. Her head ached, as did the rest of her bruised body after Robert's attack on her. There was no sound from the studio. She would like to have spoken to Robert, to have conducted a sane and rational discussion, but there was very little hope of that with Robert in his present mood and she had no intention of trying to communicate with him through an obdurately locked door.

She opened the mail without interest. An invitation to a private view from the Gallerie Aubin in Paris, a note from Milan to say that one of her paintings on exhibition there had sold to a Swiss collector, and sundry brown envelopes, mostly bills. There was one addressed to Robert in his mother's familiar minuscule hand. The last envelope was bright yellow and bore her address written blackly in idiosyncratic italic so sprawling that it scarcely left room for the stamp. Inside was a postcard from Ezra. On the front, funny little plump Bathsheba, on the back a facetious message. 'Discovered this old guy, Rembrandt, seems he can paint a bit. What d'you think? Let me know when you're coming back to Coombe Ferrers or better still to Rosepound. Welcome anytime. We have some unfinished business, don't you agree? E.'

She even managed a smile. Compared to hers, his life came across as innocent and uncomplicated though she knew that to be an illusion, like watching the serene sailing boats on the river. Could that really have been only three days ago? She yearned to be back in Coombe Ferrers though now it seemed like an escapist fantasy. Here and now was the reality; with Robert violent, sulking and withdrawn; Amy alone, hurt and accusatory; herself isolated, awash with guilt for the way she had mishandled both her husband and her daughter. How could she possibly have thought she could change her life as easily as simply deciding to do so? Suddenly and sharply, she missed Inez. It was ridiculous, she was a middle-aged woman but she longed desperately for her mother's comforting presence, the way she took all life offered in her stride, her capacity as a survivor. She would have known what to do. Like the Red Queen she would surely have impressed upon her that it takes all the running you can do to stay in the same place. If you want to get somewhere else you have to run twice as fast. Hester was only just beginning to discover the truth of this herself.

Her headache was worse. She left the table and rummaged in the dresser drawer for painkillers which she thought she remembered seeing there. She rarely resorted to them and the packet had long since become part of the jumble of string, pencil stubs, paper clips, corks and broken knives. Whose decision had it been to keep all this junk in the first place instead of throwing it away? she thought irritably. There was one tablet left which she swallowed with the dregs of her breakfast coffee. Moving about the kitchen she noticed that the stock of spirits was depleted. Robert on one of his midnight excursions, she supposed grimly. She desperately wished that he had some male friends she could call on besides Eustace but Robert was not the sort of man who looked for male companionship; those with whom he would have been likely to have anything in common he regarded uneasily as rivals. Neither, she was sure, would he be much in the habit of confiding in his girlfriends, for part of their attraction lay in the fact that they could not possibly be thought of as equals.

With leaden limbs she went upstairs to lie on the bed since she was too exhausted to do anything more energetic. Much later she came awake abruptly, hearing the front door close quietly. She hauled herself to the window and looked out. A haggard and unshaven Robert appeared beyond the parapet outside the window. She watched him until he turned the corner of the square, then put on her shoes and went downstairs.

Robert's studio smelled of alcohol, stale tobacco and something else too, the unmistakable reek of urine where he had peed in the sink without bothering to rinse it down, probably deliberately. What had happened to the fastidious Robert she thought she knew? Several empty bottles lay on the floor and in the corner a makeshift bed had been thrown together with old dust sheets and drapes. She sat on the chair that had not so long ago been occupied by Caroline, and waited. The one compelling reason Robert would have for leaving his lair would be to buy cigarettes; she would not have to wait long.

He appeared at the door, ashen and with several days growth of beard. His movements betrayed a slight tremor and she caught the whiff of alcohol on his breath. Ignoring her, he slumped down on his pile of dust sheets and lit a cigarette.

'This can't go on,' she said. 'If you won't talk to me, talk to Eustace.'

'Fuck off. Leave me alone.'

Immoderate language was not typical of Robert either.

'You're acting like a child. How long do you think you can keep this up. If it goes on I shall have to ring Eustace.'

'If you ring Eustace I'll kill you.'

'I suppose you've no idea how worried Amy is? If you won't stop this for my sake, do so for Amy's. Or even for your work's sake.'

'My work! My fucking work! That's a joke.'

'Eustace will be expecting to discuss your new studio soon. He'll surely ring when he doesn't hear from you.'

'Tell him to go to hell. You can go to hell too.' He flung himself off the bed and went to lean against the white emptiness of the wall, the hand unoccupied with his cigarette clenched in the pocket of his jeans in an attempt to control the shakes.

'So what do you want, Robert?' she said softly. 'What would make it all right?'

'You know what I want.'

'Blackmail.'

'Call it what you like. I'm past caring.'

'I'll never agree to it. Never.'

'Then get out. There's nothing more to say.'

'So you're prepared to sit it out until I give in, is that the idea?'

'You can do what you fucking well like, just as long as you know the cost.'

'I never realised before what a ruthless bastard you are.'

He watched her with reddened eyes. 'You call *me* ruthless! Jesus Christ!'

There was a silence filled with hostility. Then she left him abruptly and went next door into her own studio where she paced furiously up and down. The black dogs of despair and depression leapt on her again and sank their teeth into her familiar flesh.

In a moment of outrage and rebellion she ploughed through the contents of her painting table until she found a Stanley knife; then she attacked the failed paintings that stood against the wall, slashing them with all the expertise of one used to handling tools, until they lay in shreds at her feet.

CHAPTER TWENTY

Caroline had spent the morning to all appearances working but in fact she had not been doing much more than shuffle papers, in between telephoning Robert's Bristol number which she did at hourly intervals. This he had strictly forbidden but anxiety over his unexplained silence had triumphed over discretion. As it happened no harm was done for all she got each time was Hester's recorded voice briskly asking her to leave her number. There had been no answering call from Robert, there hadn't been for several days. She couldn't stand much more of it. A cold foreboding had taken hold, a horrible conviction that he was already bored by her, especially now that Hester was back in Bristol. It wasn't much more comforting to imagine him instead totally absorbed in the new work, for hadn't he said, 'It's essential for my work that I feel completely free and without distracting commitments.'

Perhaps he had been trying to tell her that there would be no more time for their intimate evenings and nights. It could also be that her power over him was not as absolute as she had believed. It was a power based on sex and surely nothing could be stronger than that, even Robert's eccentric variety? Since his wife couldn't or wouldn't meet his needs what other hold could she possibly have over him? Besides, how could Hester hope to control Robert from a studio a hundred or so miles away in the West Country? She doubted in fact if Eustace's claims about such a studio were true. She had a strong suspicion that as a painter Hester was played out, done for, yesterday's news. It was imperative that she found out for certain. A sudden anger at her own powerlessness and lack of information inspired her to dial the Lombards number and to ascertain that the man they called Gozo, Eustace and his partner Bruno Davidson would be elsewhere for the morning.

Then she called a taxi, arriving in Cork Street in a heavy squall of rain. Rather too soon, as it turned out, for she was just in time to see Eustace blunder through the downpour to a waiting taxi. For a few minutes both vehicles were immobilised not only by the confusion caused by the weather but also by strategically placed roadworks. Impatient, Caroline paid the cabby and made her way through a slalom of red and white cones and orange plastic tapes. She pushed open the impressive tinted glass doors with the name Lombards stencilled across them in gold leaf and allowed them to sigh to behind her. Inside, the quiet reverential atmosphere enfolded her; the objects of worship, Robert's paintings, looming dispassionately on all sides. Towards the far end a vestal virgin sat at a desk. She was fairly new to the gallery but not so new that Caroline's face would be unknown to her, which suited Caroline very well. Too established an employee would be a harder nut to crack, too recent and she would be unlikely to know anything worth knowing.

'Hi, Amanda,' Caroline said casually. 'It is Amanda, isn't it?'

'Yes.' Amanda looked up from behind the replenished piles of gleaming catalogues. She smiled a professional smile. 'Can I help?'

Caroline frowned. 'I'm not sure. I need to get hold of Robert . . .'

Amanda looked puzzled.

'Robert Gibb.' Caroline glanced round the gallery.

'Ah yes.'

'We're running a piece on him. I'm Caroline. You do *know* I'm from *Painting Now* don't you?'

'Yes, of course I remember,' Amanda lied.

'I need to check a few points with him before we go to press. Can you tell me how I can get hold of him? It is rather urgent.'

'Have you tried his home number?'

'Several times but I'm only getting the answering machine. I'm wondering if he's actually there or if he's gone back to New York.'

'No, he's not in New York. I'm fairly sure he's at his Bristol studio,' Amanda prevaricated. Mr Tench hadn't confided in her but she had happened to overhear a telephone conversation from which she gathered that there was some sort of emergency going on in connection with Robert Gibb.

'If you'd like to leave your number I'll see what I can do for you,' she said brightly. 'Mr Tench is sure to ring back, I'll pass the message on to him as a matter of urgency.'

'Ring back? Where's he gone? How long is he likely to be?'

'He's gone down to Bristol this morning actually.'

Caroline rested five immaculate fingernails on the desk. 'Is there something wrong?'

'Something wrong? Oh, no, I don't think so.'

'Isn't it unusual for him to see Robert in his studio unless there's work for him to see? Robert's not ill, is he?'

Amanda felt cornered. There was something remorseless about Caroline, something that reminded her of a minor bird of prey.

'Not that I've heard. But I'll pass your message on without fail.'

'Of course I might ring Hester at her new studio.'

'New studio?'

'In Devon, or is it Cornwall. I can never remember.'

Amanda had gone faintly pink. She knew nothing about a new studio.

'Yes, I'll give Hester a call,' Caroline said.

'I believe Miss Eliot is also in Bristol.'

'Of course. I forgot. I wonder if you could let me have the number for the new studio anyway. I seem to have mislaid it. We're hoping to do something on her in the near future.'

Amanda stood up. 'I'll check in the office if you wouldn't mind waiting.'

She was gone for a couple of minutes. Caroline's nails beat an impatient tattoo on the desk top.

'I think this must be it,' Amanda said in a surprised voice as she returned. She handed over a piece of paper. Caroline glanced at it then tucked it away in her Filofax.

'Good,' she said briskly, adding as an afterthought, 'Thank you.'

'No trouble.'

'You won't forget to pass on my message when Eustace rings will you? It is rather urgent.'

She returned the Filofax to the Gucci bag which she slung over one shoulder. She departed in a flurry of long black legs and short flaring raincoat which she wore half on and half off her shoulders. A faint cloud of the scent 'Paloma Picasso' remained in the air for several minutes after she'd gone.

Eustace and Hester faced each other across the table in the dimly lit restaurant. A shaded lamp cast a mock candlelit glow on the lower half of their faces. Hester's plate had been taken away almost untouched and even Eustace paid more attention to his brandy which he considered he both needed and deserved. He felt too enraged to eat. At the same time the situation was far too delicate for him to give full rein to his feelings. He believed that if he kept his head and persuaded Hester to keep hers, something could still be salvaged from the wreckage. Why else would he have cancelled all his engagements and come steaming down to Bristol.

'All I'm asking for is a little discretion,' he said. 'Go to him and tell him it was all a mistake, that you're confused because you've not been well. Treat him gently for a few days, reassure him. He's been badly shaken but he'll come round, I'm sure of it. You see, Hester, he adores you. He can't function without you, you must know that. He needs reassurances and time . . .'

'How much time? Until he's finished this commission, you mean? Two years, three?'

Eustace shifted uneasily in his chair which creaked in protest.

'I'm sure that given your strength of character you'll be able to repair the damage before then.'

'The damage, as you call it, can't be undone.'

'I think you underestimate yourself . . .'

'You misunderstand. I mean the damage has been going on for a long time. It's been a gradual degeneration, not a sudden rift.'

'I can't believe that.'

'I wish you would because it's true.'

Eustace finished his brandy and took Hester's unyielding hand and cradled it in his.

'Listen, Hester, dear girl,' he said coaxingly. 'I've been a good friend, eh?'

'Yes, Eustace, you have.'

'So as your friend and as Robert's friend too, I'm going to ask you to do something for me.'

He fixed his prominent stare on her face in a way that had been known to hypnotise potential buyers but her eyes remained elusively in shadow. All the detail he could make out was a small dangerous reflection.

'It's something that would never be necessary to ask of an ordinary wife or an ordinary woman. Only an extraordinary woman, which you are. The fact is that I want you to put all this upset behind you and stay with Robert. I'm asking you to lay your own interests aside for two, three years before you come to a decision about your marriage. Stick with Robert, encourage him, just as you've done in the past. Give him the sense of security he needs so much. It's worked perfectly well before, what's so hard about going on?'

'Because his work depends on it, you mean?'

'Not only that. When I saw him today I must confess to you that I was shocked.' Eustace shook his head to show his disbelief. 'This shutting himself in his studio, the despair, the self neglect. I don't want to be an alarmist but you know how he's always admired Mark Rothko . . .'

'Are you talking about suicide?'

'It's something we have to consider as a possibility, to guard against . . .'

'No, no, no. Robert would never kill himself.'

'I'm glad you can be so complacent,' Eustace said, allowing one of the barbs of his anger to escape.

Hester hit back. 'Wouldn't it be a good thing from your point of view? Surely his prices would go up.'

Eustace restrained an urge to shake her. After all, she had been under a considerable strain even though it was of her own making.

'It won't help the situation if we fall out, dear girl. I know I'm asking a very great deal of you, asking you to be a sort of unsung heroine . . .'

'What about my own work, Eustace?' Hester said softly, ominously quiescent.

'I don't honestly see why your own work can't go forward as before . . . just as soon as all this is out of the way. You know you can count on my support. I'll give you all the help and encouragement you want and need. You can rely on that absolutely.'

'But I told you, Eustace,' she said patiently. 'I can't work in the old studio. And surely you don't expect me to produce anything worthwhile when I'm acting as nursemaid to Robert . . .'

'Nursemaid! Don't be ridiculous, Hester.'

'Minder, then. How can anything decent come out of unhappiness and frustration?'

'Surely I don't need to tell you that practically every painter one would care to mention lived a life of unhappiness and frustration. As this old guy so wisely said, "There is no profession in which you may expect less felicity and contentment . . ."'

'Spare me the quotes, for God's sake.'

'All right then. Of course I wouldn't want to underestimate the possible difficulties if you accept the challenge. Believe me I wouldn't ask you if I didn't firmly believe that it will enrich your own work.'

'How can you be sure,' she cut in bitterly. 'What if you're wrong. What if it destroys it?'

'I'm sure you are enough of a professional to rise above petty obstacles.'

'Petty obstacles! You call the putting aside of my own wishes, my own freedom of choice, petty?'

'No, of course not. I was hoping that your freedom of choice would be exercised in Robert's favour, that you would one day thank me for begging you to stay together. Together you have always been something special. Apart, well . . . to tell you the truth . . .'

'Yes?'

Eustace wagged his heavy head from side to side. 'I don't know. Who does? I just know that unless you change your mind I foresee that Robert will be irreparably damaged. It's not something I'd like on my conscience.'

'Now who's being ridiculous? Besides, what about the damage to me? Would you like that on *your* conscience?'

'Hester, dearest. I'm ancient enough to have become something of an expert on human nature. One thing I've learned is that women are stronger than men, psychologically speaking, and you are stronger than most; you've not had to be just a wife, but a wife, mother *and* a first-class painter at the same time. Very few make it, as you know. Being an artist of any sort requires a degree of selfishness of which most women are incapable.'

'That has more to do with efficient indoctrination than our innate unselfishness.'

'You do your sex an injustice.' Eustace reached in an inner pocket of his corduroy jacket for a cigar. 'But let's not talk generalities. Let's talk about you. Now what I suggest is that you take a while to think over what I've said. I'm sure that once you've had a chance to weigh up what's involved quite dispassionately you'll see the sense of my arguments. Meanwhile, I was wondering, could Robert's mother come down? I understand she's very supportive"

'Robert's mother! Who told you that? Oh no, God forbid! If anyone could be guaranteed to drive him over the edge it's his mother.'

'Pity. I hoped that would be a short-term solution. Never mind, leave Robert to me for the time being. It wouldn't be the first time I've had to deal with a situation like this.'

'I thought you were going back to London tonight?'

'So I am, dear girl. But before I go I'll have another word with him. I'm sure we can sort something out. Didn't you say that Amy was at home now?'

'I don't want Amy involved.'

'No? Well, never mind. I just thought she might help to take the steam out of the situation. She's a sensible girl.'

'She has her own problems. In any case she's not at home, she's staying with her friend in Bedminster.' Amy had packed up and left the day before, after their quarrel.

Eustace squinted thoughtfully across the table. After rolling the cigar between his fingers for a minute or two Hester was relieved to see him change his mind and return it to his pocket. He had taken to smoking sickly sweet Burmese cheroots which she hated. Eustace had in fact decided that it was a pity to waste a perfectly good cigar on so volatile a situation; as to why Amy was at home instead of at university he decided not to enquire, one can of worms at a time was enough.

'Tell me something, Eustace?' Hester said sweetly.

'Anything, dear girl.'

'If the position was reversed, if I was in Robert's place would you have asked him to give up everything for my sake?'

'You never would be in the same position, I can tell you that!'

'But if . . . if?'

'It wouldn't be the same thing at all,' Eustace blustered.

'That's what I thought,' she said.

The letter from Katherine Gibb had lain unopened for several days. Robert would never look at it now. In the background came the murmur of Eustace and Robert talking in the studio. Hester ripped open the envelope. Although it didn't sound very likely, Robert had apparently suggested his mother wrote instead of telephoning, unless he thought that a letter was more easily ignored. Certainly he never, to her knowledge, replied to letters unless they were to do with his work. His mother was asking for advice about their wills and wanted to discuss it with him. What, Hester thought, could there be to discuss unless this was an oblique reference to an illness that Katherine Gibb could not bring herself to mention outright? Could Charles be worse? She was forever fussing over his cough. In any case there was no chance at all that Robert would be going to Swindon in the foreseeable future; but there was something pathetic about Katherine's dignified plea for attention from her son which Hester found hard not to respond to. She went upstairs, away from the sound of voices, and wrote a reply. Robert was particularly busy with the new commission, she wrote, was there anything she could do?

CHAPTER TWENTY-ONE

The Golf GTI swung into the car park next to the Victorian Wesleyan chapel and slid to an abrupt halt beside a Land Rover and a battered Triumph. It had seemed a long drive in spite of several hours of illegal speeds on the M5. An elderly man got into the Triumph and backed it out of its parking place and into the hedge on the far side. He drove off with several large twigs attached to the rear bumper. Caroline dismissed the incompetent driver as being unfit to be on the road and locked her car.

Coombe Ferrers was more attractive than she had expected though obviously not a tourist trap. For a small place it also appeared to have more than its fair share of pubs, which made her job less easy. She selected The Cutter as the most promising, pushed open the door of the public bar and found herself in a darkly timbered interior. There was a fair-sized crowd of lunchtime drinkers, mostly men.

They treated her with studied indifference but she was quite aware of being very thoroughly appraised and commented on all the same. Having paid for her drink she did some sizing up of her own, made a decision and moved in on the unprepossessing individual who sat by himself in a corner. She made an excuse to strike up a conversation.

'Just yer for the day then?' The speaker wore a greasy waxed jacket and his scalp gleamed through strands of hair.

Caroline repressed a shudder.

'That's right,' she said. 'Just looking round, you know.'

'Tis a daicent ol' place, Coombe Ferrers. You thinking of biding yer?'

'Biding? Oh, I see. Yes, it's a possibility.'

'I could tell ee a few things,' he said darkly, gazing into his empty glass.

'What are you drinking?' Caroline asked. 'Let me fill you up.'

She furnished him with another pint of the local cider before asking her next question.

'I'm looking for studio space locally,' she said.

'Any suggestions?'

'For painting pitchers and that ol' caper?'

'Do you know of anything suitable?'

He looked at her sideways. 'Well now, funny you should'av axed that. It seems to be all th' rage.'

'Why's that?'

'That Miss Ruddick who runs the Anchorage an' er friend be up to something up at th' ol' Zider Press . . .'

'What's her friend's name?'

'Blest if I can remember. You'm best be axing Miss Ruddick.'

'Where do I find her?'

'I told ee. Down at th' Anchorage.'

'Yes, of course.' Caroline's telephone call to the number supplied by Amanda had at least produced that piece of information.

'And this Cider Press. Where did you say that was?' she said.

Reg Gammon regarded the remains of his pint with a rheumy eye.

'Ah, now . . .' he said thoughtfully.

The price of a refill bought the remaining pieces of the jigsaw. Caroline left in a rush, leaving Reg gazing blearily into his cider while she hurried up the hill, following as best she could his somewhat befuddled directions.

She arrived at the Press out of breath after the innumerable steps.

A builder's van was parked outside and she heard the sound of hammering coming from somewhere within. She stood at the door of the groundfloor room and peered in. Nothing much appeared to be going on here so she sprinted up the outside staircase where she found a carpenter re-aligning floorboards amidst a rich smell of sawdust. The man looked up.

'Can I help you, Miss?'

'I'm just looking round. I understood this place was for sale. Perhaps I've got it wrong.'

'I think you must've. It was to have been a gallery at one time but the owner's changed her mind.'

'The owner being Miss Ruddick?'

The man nodded.

'So no one's using it as a studio?'

The man looked round the displaced boards and the gaping hole in the floor and grinned. 'Doesn't look like it, does it?' Avoiding the hole, she moved swiftly to the arched window.

'But it would make a super one, wouldn't it. Super view. Wonderful light.' She turned to face him.

'I don't think you should be here, Miss,' he said. 'The boss wouldn't like it. The insurance, you know.'

'I'm just going as a matter of fact.' She hesitated at the door. 'Do you know Miss Eliot?' she asked.

He shook his head. 'I don't know many folks in Coombe Ferrers. I'm from Tidemouth myself, just filling in with some subcontracting.' Wasting no more time Caroline left him to his hammering and went to search for The Anchorage Gallery.

As she stepped inside a bell tinkled, summoning a plump woman with a shock of fuzzy fairish hair and a round face. The woman moved with a limp and was rubbing inky fingers on a rag.

'Can I help or do you want to browse?' she said.

'Miss Ruddick? My name is Caroline Childs. You may recollect we had a bit of a chat at Robert Gibb's private view.'

'Oh, yes. I remember.' Alice did indeed remember. This was the character who had tried to pump her about Hester and Robert's marriage. 'How are you? I won't shake hands.' She waggled her black-smeared fingers.

'I've come down because I understand Hester Eliot is staying in Coombe Ferrers. I wanted to see her rather urgently.'

Alice gave Caroline a shrewd glance, then placidly busied herself with the rag. 'You should have phoned,' she said. 'Hester isn't here. She's in Bristol.'

Caroline was unruffled. 'But I did! I telephoned Lombards and they told me she was here!'

She sat down on the only chair and delved into her capacious bag. She brought out a Filofax and riffled impatiently through it. 'Let me see . . . today is Thursday, isn't it? Yes, the girl definitely said that Hester would be here. I'm sorry about this. Not your fault. I suppose I better shoot on back to Bristol and try to catch her there. What a fearful balls-up.'

She got up and fastened her bag. 'I had a look round Coombe Ferrers,' she said, 'And I must say I don't blame Hester for wanting a studio here. It's charming.'

'Is that what she told you?' Alice said, putting the rag down abruptly.

'Have I got it wrong then? I was under the impression that she was hard at work already. A whole new direction, I was told.'

'Perhaps. We shall have to see, won't we?'

'I was disappointed not to see work in progress all the same. I took the liberty of slipping up to the Cider Press myself and frankly I was surprised to see workmen there instead . . .'

'How do you know about the Cider Press?'

Caroline lifted her pale eyebrows. 'Eustace told me,' she lied. 'I understand she doesn't want everyone to know and I'm not surprised. Poor Hester.'

'What do you mean, poor Hester?' Alice snapped.

'Drying up like this just when Robert is really getting going. But then, however much we like her as a person we have to admit that she never was quite in the same league, was she? Don't you agree?'

Alice's face had gone deep pink. 'I most certainly do not. I think Hester has potentially twice his talent if you must know . . .'

She went painfully to the street door and opened it. 'Now if there's nothing I can do for you perhaps you wouldn't mind if I get on with inking up this plate. I don't mind you wasting your own time on fool's errands, but I'm not prepared for you to waste mine.'

Caroline left. She smiled to herself. A defensive friend simply confirmed that her suspicions about Hester had been right on the nail. In fact the idea of commissioning an article forecasting the possible successes and failures of the next five years was already forming in her head. It was the sort of thing that Kurt Sagar would be interested in doing and would do splendidly. Besides, he was the only critic she knew who was arrogant enough to stick his neck out to that extent. He had never actually ruined an artistic reputation but it could be said that he'd caused the prices of certain painters work to fall off rather markedly.

She had nothing against Hester as an artist, in fact she thought Hester's work was very good indeed. It was just that while Robert still held his wife in almost superstitious esteem he would never respect her, Caroline, a mere journalist and part-time mistress. It was good news about the studio however. It really did look as if she had been right about Hester.

Dark clouds, wind and rain rolled over the landscape as she joined the M5 and she put her foot down. Lousy weather she could do without. She had already wasted more time than she should have done on Robert's wife; now she must get to Bristol and find out, if she could, what lay behind Robert's total silence. She wondered if there was any significance in Eustace's Bristol visit other than that of seeing to the special arrangements necessary for Robert's removal to New York. His imminent departure set her mind racing with plans of her own which occupied her until the motorway bridge at Avonmouth loomed into view.

Alice had been having a bad day at the shop, which Caroline's visit had not improved, in spite of selling a pair of Paul's more up-market watercolours, one with Hay Tor, storm clouds, sheep and bracken and another of Yes Tor, violet rocks and foreground gorse. The transaction had been an excellent one for April but the obligatory smiles and chat with the customer had been trying. Ever since she had got up that morning, pain had nagged her without let up, probably brought on by the threat of foul weather, but aggravated by a worry she could not yet admit to herself.

But Paul was coming home, he had rung to tell her to expect him. She would make an effort with the meal and submerge her anxieties. Paul was always hungry and he adored her cooking; having come from a household where microwaved pizzas were considered to be a culinary high water mark, he never ceased to be astonished at anything more ambitious. If she refrained from questioning him she was unlikely to hear any lies; the small niggling voice of doubt would simply have to be ignored.

The minute window of the room behind the shop afforded a small depressing glimpse of churned up river, lashing rain and boats straining at their moorings. The high-pitched clattering of rigging on aluminium masts got on her nerves and, as if to supply the finishing touch to her mood, when she went back into the shop she saw Reg Gammon on the other side of the street ostensibly chatting to one of his drinking chums in the shelter of a doorway but in fact keeping a constant eye on the Anchorage Gallery for a sighting of its owner. At least he never went so far as to come in; art in any form being apparently quite outside his comprehension, there could be no possible reason for him to enter the shop except the real one which naturally couldn't be acknowledged. Alice sincerely hoped the rain would drive him away before closing time.

She took two co-proxamols, reneging on her intentions to postpone them until the evening, and reached for her mackintosh and her stick. She turned the sign on the door to CLOSED as soon as Reg disappeared up the High Street.

Paul was already back. He enfolded her in a bear-like hug and she felt immediately better. Holding her close he glanced at her face.

'Bad day?'

'Lousy. I sold a couple of your landscapes though. How was yours?'

'So-so. There isn't the money around that there was. They're saying the holiday bookings are down this year.' He pushed her gently into one of the ladder-back kitchen chairs. 'You look all in.

I'll make you a cup of tea, then I'll cook you something nice. I've lit the fire. You go and flake out while I grapple with the groceries. Have you got your painkillers?'

'I'm afraid I already took two.'

'Never mind. Not long to wait now.'

Alice went into the other room and found beside her chair a small gift-wrapped parcel. In it was a pair of blown-glass earrings in silver mounts. She held them up to the light; they were like two perfect drops of dew. Paul came in and put a cup of tea down beside her.

'You don't have to buy me presents, sweetie,' she said.

'I like to.'

'They're beautiful. I adore them.'

'Good. You deserve them.' He paused on his way out. 'By the way, there was a weird phone call earlier on. Some flaky female asking for Hester.'

'Hester?' Alice glanced up from putting the earrings back in their box. 'What did she want?'

'I never found out. I told her Hester was back in Bristol but she seemed to want to chat about the new studio. I didn't think it was public knowledge. She wouldn't give her name. Dead peculiar.'

'I hope you didn't tell her too much?'

'I didn't tell her anything she didn't know already as far as I remember.'

Alice was uneasy. They had yet to hear from the planning office and she doubted that the Cider Press would be a practical proposition for Hester without the requisite planning permission. Far too soon for the attention of unreliable snoopers such as Caroline Childs.

They ate by the fire, their plates on their laps. Paul turned on the television as if to forestall too many questions about his absence. They watched a programme about albatrosses. Albatrosses, they learned, mate for life. A hen bird waited anxiously for her mate to return from halfway round the globe to the usual nest site which, barring accidents he assuredly would. Watching, Alice also felt anxious but in addition envious and not a little sad.

Paul turned off the television.

'You're falling asleep. You should get to bed,' he said.

'No, I bloody wasn't,' she said. Nodding off in front of the television was something you did when you were old. 'All the same I think I'll turn in now.'

'I'll help you.'

'I don't need help. Just time.' She got out of her chair with difficulty. 'I'll say goodnight, sweetie.'

'I'll look in later.'

She put a hand on his arm. 'Better not,' she said.

'I didn't mean that.' He grinned then kissed her. He listened to her slow progress up the stairs and was glad that nothing was expected of him tonight. The two last evenings and nights had been spent in bed with Amy in the flat of her accommodating friend Gina. He was desperately in need of sleep. He and Amy were well matched in energy, desire and appetite for sexual exploration, the only constraints the same as those imposed on all their HIV-threatened generation. He felt no guilt towards Alice. He believed that his feelings for her were unaffected, making justification the easiest thing in the world. He was unable to make the leap of imagination necessary to understand how Alice's feelings would be affected had she known about Amy; in any case he did not intend that she should. Alice was Alice; gruff but sweet natured, rock steady, nurturing, familiar. Amy was Amy; exciting, slightly wild, beautiful and unfamiliar. Appreciating either, it seemed to him, involved quite different sets of responses; therefore it followed that neither should have any reason to resent the other.

Satisfied with his logic he went to his own bed and was asleep immediately.

Alice, on the other hand was still awake, tired as she was. Tears of frustration, unhappiness and pain squeezed out of her eyes and ran down into her hair. Paul's manner to her had almost imperceptibly changed. The fact that she fully expected that her luck would some day run out had tuned her perceptions so finely that the smallest changes became highly significant. They made love slightly less often and his attitude toward her on occasions was almost like that of a nephew towards a favourite aunt. Then there were the absences on ill-defined errands. Last year, the first year he had stayed with her and the first year of their love affair, he had not left Coombe Ferrers the whole of the summer. The sense of loss was already haunting her days and disturbing her nights.

PART TWO

CHAPTER TWENTY-TWO

There was no doubt that if Hester had never seen the Cider Press she would have envied Robert his TriBeCa studio. It provided twice the floor area he had in Bristol and nearly twice the height, most of the ceiling consisted of shaded glass and the double doors that led out on to the fire escape had windows which allowed a glimpse of New York's soaring perpendiculars. It was early morning when she first saw it and light filled it to the brim after being bounced off the river and reflected again from tall glass-clad buildings.

The studio and the small apartment that went with it were not in a glass-clad building but in an old warehouse that had at some time been painted duck-egg blue on the outside with a rust-red fire escape. Inside, the studio was painted white.

'What d'you think?' Robert asked her. He leaned against the wall, the perpetual cigarette clamped between his fingers.

'Naturally I'm impressed. That's not the point though. Will *you* be able to work here?'

Robert ground the cigarette stub out underfoot. He looked at her speculatively. 'All things being equal, yes.'

'You realise that I'm not actually prepared to stay with you in New York indefinitely. That I've promised Alice I'd look after her shop while she's in hospital?'

'I still don't see why it has to be you who looks after the shop, anyone could do that, for God's sake!'

'I also want to visit her in hospital. I promised I would.'

Both spoke in low unemphatic voices, treading round each other warily, unwilling to provoke or betray emotion.

'Just as long as I know that I can count on you to come back when I need you. I'm not suggesting we live in each other's pockets, we've never done that anyway. I need to be sure that I can rely on your promise to be there for me and to drop absolutely any idea of going your own way.' He was watching her very attentively for any sign of indecision.

'I've told you once. That should be enough.'

'Tell me again.'

'Robert, I promise that as long as you need me I will try to support and encourage you.'

'Only try?'

'I am not superhuman. That's as far as I go. Take it or leave it.' She turned away from him and looked down at the traffic from her high vantage point. Last night, as soon as they had settled into the somewhat cramped apartment that led directly off the studio, Robert had taken her out and treated her to the Mexican food he knew she loved, a partiality that had to do with her tenuous Mexican origins, she always thought. They had softshell crab tacos which in any other set of circumstances might have persuaded her to stay in New York, as Robert well knew. Yet in spite of experiencing again the city's noise, its characters and its energy Hester never forgot that she was here against her will, under extreme emotional duress. For the first time New York was an alien place and Robert was an alien being. The only way to exist was to put all thoughts of another life out of her mind.

Robert began to move about the vast room, speaking in disjointed bursts.

'You must agree that there's something inevitable about us. To try to break it up was never really on, you know. Apart, neither of us could have survived as artists . . . or as individuals. You would have discovered this if you'd tried to push it to its conclusion . . . once you've settled back into your old routine and you're working again you'll see that Eustace and I were right . . .'

It wasn't like Robert to talk of feelings or to discuss their relationship but since she had made the promise to give it another try he had been uncharacteristically communicative. And he had never been more keen to make love. From the depths of her despair and self-loathing for what she regarded as her capitulation to blackmail, she had acquiesced but had gained neither satisfaction, nor comfort nor any feeling of being closer to him; what she felt was contempt and a disinclination bordering on disgust. After a week or two she put a stop to his physical demands altogether. Robert appeared to accept her eventual promise to give their marriage another try as axiomatic, once it had been extracted. Almost immediately he had stopped drinking, had begun to eat, had shaved himself and when he was strong enough, for there was no doubt that he had deteriorated after his punishing self immolation, he had begun to work. A month passed like a year.

Eustace continued to be wary, though he was fulsome in his gratitude for what he called her 'sensible' attitude. Amy had said very little. She had stopped giving Hester reproachful looks but there were now other constraints between them that had nothing to do with Robert. Hester had apologised for her loss of control but not for her criticism of Amy's conduct. For everyone else it was business as usual. For Hester it was an uneasy truce achieved through unscrupulous trading. Robert had won, at least for the present and the foreseeable future. She dared not look further ahead. She had seen the extremes to which Robert was prepared to go and the thought of having to live through another nightmare like those few terrible weeks caused such a draining away of energy and courage that she had effectively denied herself the only option that would have made any sense of her life. She hated herself for it as much as she hated Robert, yet in spite of everything part of her cared very much what happened to him, felt both responsible for him and desperately compassionate. How easy the solution would have been without any such responses. Yet it might not turn out as badly as she feared; perhaps, as Eustace kept saying, she would be able to paint again eventually, perhaps, as Robert had once dared to hint, it was merely hormonal disturbance.

Below her in the narrow street a chauffeur-driven limo drew up. A vaguely familiar figure in red shot out of it almost before it had stopped. Robert ceased to pace and came over to her. He put his hands under her elbows and drew her close.

'Listen to me, Hester,' he said very tenderly, 'I have this conviction that everything is going to be all right, that this is just the beginning for us. Do you feel it too?'

'Just don't push it, Robert. I'm sure that this is the start of something very important for you, yes. Let's just leave it at that, shall we?'

'For us both. I know it.'

He kissed her. It was unusual for him to touch her first, in all their years together he'd normally left the initiative to her. This had become almost a convention between them. All at once she felt an irrational and unbearable regret that it wasn't Ezra's mouth on hers, Ezra's arms round her. Spontaneously she remembered Ezra's strong comforting hands and how beautiful she'd thought them.

The door swung open and Betty Hirsch sailed in on a wave of scent. Behind her was Hirsch himself, wearing a red track suit over immaculate trainers and a red and white sweatband. Betty Hirsch was in sapphire blue, blazer and pleats, with a large red structured bow at the back of her head.

Robert stepped away from Hester as Hirsch strode towards them, hand outstretched.

'Glad you found the studio. What d'you think, Robert? Large enough, would you say?'

'Absolutely. It's ideal.'

'Got the right vibes, eh? Betty tells me these things are important to an artist. Glad you came, Hester. You know there's another studio a block away just waiting for you.'

'Unfortunately I won't be staying. I'm going back soon after Robert's settled in.'

'I can't believe this! You can't mean you're serious about turning it down. She can't, can she, Betty?'

'Surely not,' Betty said sweetly. 'Waldo and I will be desolate.'

'Robert, you can't let your beautiful wife go just like that.' Waldo moved in circles where wives were, first and foremost, required to be decorative appendages.

'Believe me,' Robert said. 'I would be the first to try to prevail upon her to stay.'

Hester flashed them a smile that felt to her more like a grimace.

'I very much appreciate the thought but I'm afraid I have my own commitments in the UK. Otherwise I would have taken it like a shot, believe me.'

'As you like,' Hirsch said with the air of one too busy to pursue lost causes. 'But let me know soon if you change your mind.' He looked at his hefty gold watch. 'You won't forget dinner tonight at eight? Lafayette, Fifty-six Street East.'

'We're so looking forward to it,' Betty said.

Hirsch subjected Hester to a deliberately lingering scrutiny before vanishing abruptly. Betty smiled indulgently.

'He has to do his set number of circuits round Central Park reservoir,' she said.

Shadowed no doubt, Hester thought, by his chauffeur cum minder who waited in the limo below.

Betty lingered, moving round the space gracefully on her incredibly long legs. She kept glancing at Robert until at last she said, 'Robert, are you all right? You don't look quite as fit as you did when we last saw you. Have you been ill or have you been working too hard?'

Robert shook his head. 'No, I'm never ill.' He leavened his curt response at the last minute with a rare smile. Hester remembered how hard she had worked once, long ago, for one of Robert's smiles. They had seemed worth it then. Evidently they seemed worth it now to Betty Hirsch. The effect was unmistakeable. Betty laid a slim hand on Robert's arm.

'Well, just take care, will you! You're too precious.' She turned to Hester. 'Isn't that so?'

'Of course,' Hester said, searching Robert's face for a trace of irony. When she failed to find it she knew that an even wider gulf than she'd supposed now separated them.

Katherine Gibb followed Hester into the kitchen and sat stiffly on one of the stripped-wood chairs, her handbag held rigidly on her lap.

'Coffee?' Hester asked. 'or tea.'

'Tea, if it's not too much trouble,' Katherine said. She wore a pale-blue Marks and Spencer blouse under a good charcoal-grey suit. At her throat was a necklace of seed pearls. Her restrained make-up and newly crimped hair could not disguise the similarity to her son, except that Katherine was more ungainly in her movements and had a less refined bone structure; in fact she seemed thinner and gaunter than ever. For her to ring up and announce that she was intending to come to Bristol for the day was unheard of, particularly when Robert himself was away from home.

The remainder of April and most of May had, one way and another, been spent with Robert. Hester had been in Bristol while he worked with absorbed intensity on the preparations for the commission, followed by two weeks in New York while he settled into the TriBeCa studio. With some reluctance he agreed to her returning to the UK and Coombe Ferrers. Now she faced his mother across the kitchen, puzzled that Katherine had actually wanted to see her, for she was quite aware of Katherine's dissatisfaction with her as a daughter-in-law.

'I'll put these on a tray and we'll go into the other room,' Hester said, rummaging in a cupboard for a seldom-used teapot.

'Don't trouble on my account,' Katherine said, then as if realising belatedly that this sounded ungracious added, 'I would rather remain here in the kitchen, if you don't mind. It will make it easier.'

Hester poured boiling water into the teapot and rinsed it out over the sink. She glanced at Katherine.

'That sounds like trouble,' she said. 'Is it Charles?' Charles and his cough were Katherine's perennial worry. Hester made the tea and put two cups on a tray which she set on the table between them.

'Charles's cough is no better, I'm afraid,' Katherine said, watching Hester pour the tea. 'Very little milk for me. But there's something else . . .'

Hester waited, sipping hot tea and feeling jet lagged, hoping Katherine would get on with it and then leave her in peace. Yesterday she had arrived back from New York, tomorrow she would be driving down to Coombe Ferrers. Alice's operation was due to take place before the end of the week.

'I liked your letter,' Katherine said suddenly. 'I realise that I might have misjudged you, thought you unsympathetic . . . not that I'm looking for sympathy naturally . . . I just thought you should know the facts.' She leaned forward and picked up her teacup. Her hands were workworn and angular but otherwise very much like Robert's. She looked at Hester meaningfully.

'I must insist that what I have to tell you doesn't go any further. Most particularly I don't want Robert told. I thought at first that he should know, but when I heard about this important new work I realised that it might upset him and that's the last thing I want.'

She sipped her tea and replaced the cup in the saucer. 'Last year,' she said matter-of-factly, 'I had an operation for the removal of a melanoma . . .'

'We never knew that,' Hester said sharply.

'No. I didn't tell anyone because the doctors said it may well have been cleared up completely. They took quite a lot away.'

Hester waited in silence for what she knew was coming.

'Unfortunately they were not successful,' Katherine said without emotion. 'There are quite a few secondaries.'

Hester put down her cup. 'Katherine, I'm so sorry.'

'Well, there we are. It can't be helped.'

'Is there nothing they can do?'

'Certainly. But I've decided not to proceed with treatment. I'm afraid the outcome is not in doubt. The point is that in view of this there are urgent arrangements to be made for Charles which I would very much like to talk over with you. He's not very handy about the house; he's never had to be, you see. Would you mind if we discussed it?'

With a sickening feeling of inevitability Hester prepared herself to be asked to have Charles to stay. She forced her thoughts back into the present and asked Katherine how long the doctors had given her. She had never particularly liked her but there was no doubt that the woman had courage and dignity. She found in herself an admiration for her mother-in-law that was something quite new.

'They say that it will be months rather than years.' Katherine said. Hester passed her hand briefly across her eyes as if to disguise her immediate response. She nodded.

'Yes, I think perhaps we should talk about it. Are you sure you don't want Robert to know. I think he should.'

But Katherine was adamant. Robert was not to be told. Neither was Amy, though Hester was quite sure that Amy would be able to summon up very few feelings in the matter. She hardly knew her paternal grandmother.

They talked about Charles and Hester was so relieved that she was not going to be expected to have him under her roof that she found herself promising freely to keep an eye on him in a less immediate way. Katherine herself would organise such things as home helps and meals on wheels, Hester would help him to make alternative arrangements when he could no longer cope even with this assistance.

Katherine spoke prosaically of a time when she would not be alive to see to things. The house, she suggested, should eventually be sold to pay for a nursing home for Charles, for she already saw the pattern of his future life and death. It seemed to give her a relief of sorts to talk to someone who was prepared to listen. So Hester listened and agreed to do as Katherine asked.

Katherine reached out and laid a hand lightly on Hester's arm. She was not normally one for touching or outward displays of affection.

'I feel as if I've never really known you. You must forgive me for having been hard on you.'

'I never noticed that you were anything other than considerate,' Hester lied.

'Considerate!' Katherine scoffed. She put the third finger of her right hand against her temple. 'In here I was extremely critical.'

Hester shrugged. 'It doesn't matter now. You were probably right anyway. More tea?'

Katherine accepted another cup. 'No, in this I believe I was wrong.'

They spoke of her illness and of Charles, then of Robert and his New York commission. Hester picked her words carefully to avoid any hint of the trouble between her and Robert. Katherine asked after Amy.

'Amy is working, at least for the present. She gave up her Modern Arabic and has a place on the foundation course at Bristol.'

'Art, you mean? Like her father?' Her thin lips produced a smile. 'And like her mother, of course.'

'Yes,' Hester said. 'Like one of her parents, certainly.'

* * *

Hester had at least been able to discuss with Amy what was to be done about looking after The Anchorage while Alice was in hospital and found they were of the same opinion about Amy's earlier suggestion to step in. It was out of the question, even Amy saw that. Hester and April Moffat, one Alice's friends in Coombe Ferrers, would share the responsibility between them.

Amy was back in the Salisbury Square house and such were the remaining constraints between them that Hester was relieved to be able to throw some things into a suitcase and head for Devon again.

Cruising down the M5 the distant blue hills seemed both to beckon and to mock and when the sky widened out with the promise of sea, the ache of longing which she had managed to suppress more or less successfully for weeks turned on her and became an actual pain. Her throat felt harsh with unshed tears.

Alice at least was glad to see her.

'You don't know how much this means to me, sweetie. I hope you really can spare the time. I was quite prepared to trust Amy with the shop, you know. She did offer.'

'I insisted,' Hester said lightly. 'She seemed quite happy market researching. After all you did come to my rescue and since I would otherwise be doing absolutely nothing, why not? Besides I wanted an excuse to get away from New York and see how the work on the Cider Press was going.'

Alice filled the kettle. 'I could murder a G and T but I won't. I'm being very good. It's a touch early in any case. Earl Grey suit you?'

'Yes please.'

'Then let's go and sit in the garden. This weather is too good to waste. There's something very reassuring about a fine day in May. You can almost kid yourself that the world and everything in it is perfect.'

In the weeks that had passed since Hester had last seen the view from the terrace, the light had changed yet again; underneath the verandah the dense young foliage of the vine turned it chartreuse, further off the winter greys and greens of the sea had given way to jade and amethyst. Although it was early evening the sun was still high and a hundred well-stocked cottage gardens tempered the sea air with the fragrance of flowers. The memory of Hester's entrapment in cities fell away. It was as if she had never left. Bristol, London and New York didn't exist.

Alice put the tea things on the table, the familiar handmade teacups with their bird-like decoration in blue and a matching plate holding sandwiches were set on a yellow and white cloth. They drank in silence watching a small flotilla of yachts swarming at the river's mouth as they had done before. This time there were more.

'I heard from Susan Orchard this morning,' Alice said at last. 'They've granted outline planning permission.'

'Alice, I'm so pleased. That's very good. Did she say if she thought it safe to go ahead with the living quarters or do we still have to wait?'

Alice toyed with the long string of ceramic beads she wore. They had been made in earth colours and cornflower blue by a potter friend.

'We didn't talk about going ahead at all. I suggested she spoke with you about it tomorrow. I said I wasn't sure now if you wanted to.'

Hester put down her cup. 'I most certainly do. Of course I do!'

'So time and distance don't seem to have drummed any sense into your head. Sorry, I don't get it. Why do you still want the place when you don't intend to live there?'

'I may need it even more. As an escape.'

'A second home cum studio you mean?' Alice phrased the words in such a way as to imply something discreditable.

'If you like.'

'But Hester, the cost! Especially when you won't see the inside of it more than a couple of times a year. Naturally I'd be the first to go along with the scheme in the normal way but since you've changed your mind about leaving Robert I frankly don't see the point. It would be nothing but a millstone round your neck.'

'I'm not saying it will be easy because it won't. It just seems very important at the moment to know I have a place of my own. One way and another I'll raise most of the capital. While I was in Bristol I spoke to my accountant. Naturally he was horrified but after I'd twisted his arm he did get round to suggesting ways and means; apart, that is, from selling the Bristol house which I can't see Robert doing.'

'What I think is that you should give it a great deal more thought before committing yourself. Have a sandwich.'

Alice offered the plate to Hester. Green light filtered through the vine casting a dappled pattern on the tablecloth. Hester took a small triangle of wholemeal bread generously filled with some exotic concoction of Alice's: cream cheese with a hint of garlic and herbs.

'Giving it a great deal of thought is exactly what I have been doing while I've been away. My offer stands. All very businesslike and so on. I don't want any favours. A private transaction but with all the proper legal safeguards.'

'I think you're bloody mad.'

'But you agree, yes?' Hester persisted. 'I'd like to get it all wrapped up before I leave.'

Alice made a helpless gesture. When Hester was in one of her hustling moods it was useless to argue. The only way to change her mind was to do what Robert had done and play on her other equally powerful instincts of compassion and loyalty. She slid her plump hand into Hester's strong, brown one.

'I still think you're slightly out of whack but yes, I agree. I'll give my solicitor a ring tomorrow and tell him it's on after all.'

'I reckon by the time you're out of hospital our solicitors should have it all sewn up.'

'Nothing like being optimistic, I always say, though I can't say I'm too happy about it, just as I'm not too happy about anything you're doing at the moment. How long do you think you can keep up this charade with Robert?'

Hester watched the sailing boats arrive at the marker buoy one by one and come about with a brisk snap of canvas.

'Until he's finished this commission in America. I think he hopes that by then all this will have blown over.'

'And will it?'

'No.'

Alice put a hand to her head as if she had a pain. 'I don't believe this. If anyone had told me years ago that the Hester I knew would go in for compromise and pious self-sacrifice, I would have told them they couldn't be more wrong.'

'It may be a compromise but it's not self-sacrifice,' Hester said. 'Compromise is part of life, you must know that.' She nearly said, you of all people, but that would have been an unkindness of which she was not capable.

'You know, don't you,' Alice said bitterly. 'That he could go on blackmailing you like this indefinitely. After this commission there will be others.'

'I made a mess of explaining myself this time. I went at it like a bull in a china shop. I should have tried to soften the blow somehow.'

'You mean there are ways of telling someone nicely that you're leaving them?' Alice scoffed.

'Not really, no. I suppose not. In any case I haven't left him, I've done what he asked. I just hope that eventually he'll find that he can do without me after all. I suppose I hope that he'll find someone else. At the moment I just can't forget how awful he looked, it haunts me.' Her voice shook. She omitted to tell Alice of Robert's physical attack on her and how afraid she had been. 'I'm not sure how far he would have taken it but at one time it seemed to me that he was prepared to die rather than face life unable to paint.'

'Come on now, Hester!' Alice scoffed. 'What you really mean is that he was quite prepared to die rather than not get his own way! In any case we neither of us have any proof of how far he would have taken it if you hadn't given in.'

Hester shook her head as if troubled by gnats. 'I know that. The truth is that I still care what happens to him. I suppose I always will even though I no longer love him.'

'The good old self-destruct instinct again,' Alice said picking up her cup. 'We women seem to have it built in to our bloody genes.'

'I do not intend to self destruct, Alice,' Hester said evenly. 'I intend to survive. And while I've been away I've made a decision. I intend to paint again.'

Paul came whistling through the gate, the bag containing his sketching materials over his shoulder. In one hand he balanced a tray of young lettuce plants which he dumped at Alice's feet.

'These were outside the gate,' he said. 'Your secret lover, I presume.'

'Oh, bugger the man,' Alice said heatedly. 'How can I stop him doing this! Do you suppose there's a law against it?'

'You could take out an injunction,' Hester said drily.

'True love!' Paul grinned. 'Nothing like it.'

Suddenly it didn't seem funny any more. Hester noticed that this time Alice too did not smile. She herself could hardly choke back a venomous reply to Paul's attempt at humour. How she was going to share the house with him she couldn't imagine. His cocksureness, his absolute reliance on the unlikelihood of her saying anything to Alice made her fume silently. It wasn't Amy she should have struck, it was Paul. Or both of them.

To Hester's surprise Alice showed signs of preferring to be driven to the hospital by her rather than Paul. She noticed that Alice was less free with him, though not noticeably less affectionate.

'I've arranged for April Moffat to do the shop today,' Alice said to Paul. 'You've had to spend too much time away from your work as it is.'

Hester was silently outraged by Paul's unruffled agreement that this was so.

'Whatever you say,' he said goodhumouredly, knocking back a breakfast of eggs, bacon, toast and marmalade.

Hester drank coffee and ate half a slice of toast. Alice had half a grapefruit.

'Should you be eating?' Hester said.

'They won't be operating today. I've been told that there are to be yet more X-rays, then I have to see the physiotherapist and the anaesthetist. It'll be tomorrow at the very earliest.'

Before they left, Alice rang her solicitor who promised to go ahead with arrangements for the sale.

During the drive Alice was quiet, remarking only on the bronze young foliage of the oak and the incandescent green of the larch. Hester could not bring herself to indulge in reassuring clichés, the sort of thing she would have hated herself. After all this was supposed to be very much a routine operation, wasn't it?

At the hospital she saw Alice into the ward, waiting while she undressed and repacked the suitcase ready for Hester to take back with her. Alice sat beside her bed wearing an outrageously exotic caftan, her face like a pale moon above it. She looked about her at the other patients, all in various degrees of physical discomfort.

'How I detest all this,' she said gruffly. 'Hospitals never were quite my thing, you know. They're always full of ill people. You will come and see me, won't you?'

'Of course I will.'

'Only ring on the day of the op. No good trailing over here if I'm not compos mentis.'

'I expect Paul will want to come.'

'Yes,' Alice said without expression. 'I expect he will.'

'You want him to?'

'Yes. No. Mixed feelings. You know how it is. One is never at one's best sitting in bed wearing a pink fluffy bed jacket.'

'You haven't got one, have you!'

'I was speaking metaphorically. Look, you'd better go. No point in hanging about. I'll expect they'll start doing disgusting things to me any minute now.'

Hester kissed Alice's cheek. 'Well, good luck, darling.'

She picked up the suitcase and left the ward. When she got back she found a note on the kitchen table. It was from Paul to say he had had to go to London to see to the sub-letting of his part of the flat he shared in Islington. He must be running out of excuses, she thought. In an impotent fury at his blatant lie she tore the note into small pieces which she threw into the waste bin.

All the same it was quite a relief not to have to share the house with him after all.

CHAPTER TWENTY-THREE

'I wouldn't mind the run of a place like this,' Paul said, looking into Robert's empty studio. 'Isn't he going to let it while he's away?'

'No, he isn't,' Amy said shortly. 'He doesn't like other people in his studio. Now if you don't mind . . .' She closed the door which Paul, nosing around, had opened. He moved on to Hester's studio and gazed into it.

'Why isn't your ma working these days?'

'She's been ill.'

'She's not ill now.'

'So what?' Amy said bristling. 'It's not like painting by numbers, you know. Not like . . .'

'Not like my stuff, you mean. Speaking of which, I have a new toy to show you. It's going to revolutionise my work. I might even try a new direction altogether.'

'What is it. A photocopier?'

'Oh, witty! Come and see.'

In the kitchen he unzipped his overnight bag and took out a box.

'I bought it this morning.'

'Ugh! It's an airbrush. What the fuck are you going to use that for?'

'For my work, bird-brain. Speed is of the essence.'

'Untouched by human hand, eh! I thought you said your clients liked the personal touch.'

'They won't know the difference. The personal touch will be in the finishing.'

'If you're going to spend the summer coming up to Bristol all the time you're going to need one of these damned things.' She picked it up distastefully and turned it over in her hands. 'Have you used one before?'

'Once. At college.'

'Then you should know better. I think it's a shit of an idea.'

Paul took it from her and put it back in its box. 'What d'you know about the nitty gritty of earning the dosh. It's always come easy to you.'

'I wouldn't call what I'm doing easy. It's sodding hard work if you must know.'

Paul yanked her to him and nuzzled her ear. 'You're just playing at it. Come on, Amy baby, let's go to bed.'

Amy elbowed him in the ribs. Her spite over the airbrush was an outward display of her disquiet over Alice which she had so far pushed to the back of her mind. Now, under pressure she turned on Paul.

'Never mind that! What are you going to do about Alice?'

'How d'you know about Alice?'

'Are you still sleeping with her?'

'Listen, Alice has absolutely nothing to do with us. We're something quite different. In any case, things change. People change. Look how Steve dumped you for that other . . .'

Amy turned on him furiously. 'Just shut up about that, will you! You're a perfect shit. I wish I'd never told you.'

'It's Steve who's the perfect shit.'

Amy's colour rose. 'Shut up! Shut up! I detest you!' She caught up the box that contained the airbrush, opened the rubbish bin, stuffed the box inside and slammed down the lid.

Paul swung round the table, retrieved the box and grabbed her. She took hold of the hank of his hair that today he'd tied back in a pigtail and yanked it until he let go of her and then bolted for the door, across the hall and flung herself behind the giant wooden Buddha. Paul crept softly through the hall and up the stairs, pursuing her. His single gold earring glinted in the light filtering down from a high window. He looked like a pirate on the prowl. Amy came out of her hiding place whooping like a banshee. Paul sailed downstairs on the banisters but Amy dodged at the last minute and tore up the stairs two at a time. He roared after her and felled her with a rugger tackle on the landing. After a noisy struggle involving an expensive North African kelim he succeeded in removing her oversize jersey; he kneaded her breasts, lunging at them wildly with his mouth. Amy seethed, giggled helplessly and finally began to drag his tee shirt out of his jeans. She pressed her hands urgently over the hard muscles of his back while he tore at her short tube of a skirt, then at his zip.

'No, no,' she panted. 'Not without a thingy.'

Cursing, he fumbled in his back pocket for a condom and was finally inside her. The climax for both of them was swift, violent, noisy and complete. Afterwards they lay on the kelim in a tangle of limbs and discarded garments, damp and sticky.

The telephone rang. Paul groaned.

'The bloody phone,' he said, not moving.

'Hmmm.'

The ringing stopped and the Answerphone took over. Amy sat up slowly pulling her jersey over her bare breasts. She gathered up the rest of her clothes and trailed sleepily up the next flight of stairs to her room, leaving Paul laying naked on a bold pattern of red and blue, looking like a felled gladiator.

CHAPTER TWENTY-FOUR

Alice was laying on her back, wedged into position with pillows and connected up to various plastic tubes, but in spite of all these apparent discomforts she was grinning broadly.

'You look positively triumphant!' Hester said. 'What's the secret?'

'The secret is, darling, no pain! I can't believe it. *No pain . . .*'

'I didn't think it would be as immediate as that.' Hester pulled up a metal hospital chair and put a pile of new paperbacks into Alice's hands.

'Hmm. Plenty to read. Thank you, sweetie. Maybe it isn't always instantaneous but, apart from not being allowed to turn over, I haven't felt as good as this for years.'

'I can't tell you how pleased I am.' Hester cast her eyes over Alice's bedside table. It was smothered in cards and flowers.

Alice chuckled. 'There were enough flowers from the Coombe Ferrers Trading Association to supply the whole ward,' she said.

'I noticed the similarity to a florist's when I came in.' Hester smiled, full of relief. 'So you have a shiny new hip at last.'

'They showed it to me,' Alice demonstrated with a cupped hand and a fist. 'The cup is made of polyethylene plastic and the ball of some kind of stainless alloy with a long name which I've forgotten. I just remember cobalt and chromium because of the colours. I'm burbling, aren't I?'

'You're happy, that's all.'

'Too right.'

There was a moment of silence and then Alice said, 'When will Paul be coming?'

'I think in a day or two. He had to go to London. Something to do with sub-letting his flat, bed-sit, whatever it is.'

Alice glanced through the paperbacks that Hester had brought. 'Oh, lovely! You've got me *Possession*.' She concentrated on the cover illustration. 'I expect he'll send a card. I'd rather he didn't see me until I'm back on my pins again.'

'How long will that be.'

'Three or four days, they say. How are things in the shop?'

'Business hasn't been too bad. April Moffat is taking over for the day tomorrow so I'll come to see you in the afternoon. Is there anything you want? Soap, talc, squishy cake?'

'Temptress.' Alice was smiling again, the crisis over Paul's defection for the moment over. 'What I should really like is elderflower cordial to mix with this rather foul-tasting water.'

'I'll bring you both elderflower cordial *and* bottled water.' Hester said.

'And have a celebratory drink on me when you get back, to launch my new hip, will you?'

Hester took Alice at her word and dropped in on the Cutter before heading for home to put together the ingredients of the salad she'd bought from the greengrocer next door to the Anchorage.

The Cutter was full of the usual crowd. Reg Gammon eyed her blearily from his usual seat in the corner. Perhaps he was wondering where Alice was, or perhaps he already knew. Nothing stayed unknown for long in Coombe Ferrers. She turned away, looking round for a seat near the window when a heavy arm was laid across her shoulders.

'Drinking alone then, my old mate?'

She had never thought she would be so glad to see Ezra's beaming bearded face. After weeks of Bristol, London and New York and all that had happened in them it was like coming home.

'Ezra!'

They sat at their old table by the window. The evening sun gilded the river and turned passing sails to translucent gold.

'What are you doing back in Coombe Ferrers?' she asked.

'Aha. The fair Alice told me you were to do some shop sitting for her so I thought I'd drop over for a day or two. Has the deed been done? Is she in possession of a brand new coxa?'

'If you mean the operation, yes. It seems to have been highly successful.'

'Is she well enough for visitors? Perhaps I could pop in and cheer her up.'

'I don't think she needs cheering up. I haven't seen her so relaxed for ages.'

He turned speculative eyes on her, chips of sapphire in a network of sun-induced creases. 'And what about you. Do you need cheering up? You don't look quite as chipper as you might in view of your friend's good prospects.'

'I'm perfectly all right.'

'So the bit of business you had to sort out in Bristol went well, did it? According to plan? All buttoned up?'

'I don't want to talk about it.'

Ezra made an appeasing gesture. He raised his glass to her in salute and swallowed half of its contents in one swig.

'Richard must be getting used to having you around,' Hester said. She took some crisps from the packet Ezra had put on the table and nibbled them.

'Anyone would think I'd been here the entire time since we last met on that disastrous evening. Have you forgiven me yet?'

'Worse things have happened since then.'

'Of which you will not speak.'

'Of which the less said the better.'

'As I was saying, or was I? Richard is still shacked up with his bird in Totnes and is delighted for me to keep an eye on his place.'

'So the car's going?'

Ezra groaned. 'Don't tempt Providence! It's going after its fashion, at least for the moment. What are you doing for the rest of this evening? Have you eaten?'

'I've bought something for later.'

'Forget it. Do you like salmon?'

'Yes, I like salmon. Don't tell me! A trip on the river?'

Ezra jerked his head conspiratorially towards Reg Gammon.

'You see that joker over in the corner? He sold me an extremely fine specimen this morning. What would you say to it poached in butter and parsley and served with a Hollandaise sauce?'

Hester grinned. 'Since Reg Gammon sold it to you I think you can safely assume that it was poached to start with.'

Ezra roared with laughter and heads turned. There were indulgent smiles. He appeared, Hester thought, to have got in with the locals in a surprisingly short space of time.

'So you cook?' she said.

'Have to, my old mate. Learn to cook or starve were the options, and since I like my food too much for the latter I have to admit that over the years I've become a dab hand at the former. Slapdash but sound, I've been told. What about it then?'

'What about what?'

'Sharing this incredible fish.'

'You cooking and me watching?'

'Me cooking and you doing whatever you like.'

Hester scrutinised him narrowly. He was wearing a black cotton waistcoat over a blue denim shirt with its sleeves rolled to the elbows and open at the neck. She smiled. 'Just at the moment I can't think of anything I'd like better.'

'Is that so!' he said, his eyes lighting up in surprise and delight. He finished his drink and glanced across to make sure that she had finished hers. He got up. 'Then let's burn rubber, as they say.'

'I don't think you should speak of things burning in connection with your car. Now that *is* tempting Providence.'

'I thought you wouldn't let me forget that little episode.'

The Deux Chevaux managed the few miles to Richard's barn without mishap. Ezra turned into the gateway beside it and parked the car in a small cobbled yard.

The barn was on the extreme edge of a village, set apart, its footings deep in nettles and foxgloves, the air about it full of the whistling and rush of wings of swifts and house martins. The roof was overhung by a vast chestnut heavy with tall white blossoms. They entered by a low door, dark and cracked with age. Inside it was apparent that only a minimal attempt had been made to make it habitable; at first sight, Hester guessed, simply by moving out the animals and the hay and whitewashing the walls. The effect was rough but pleasing, the space being divided into its various functions by strategically placed furniture. There was a sprawling rug-covered sofa, a dresser that looked as if it had recently been vacated by chickens, more oriental rugs on the floor, a double bed pressed against the wall at one end and a squat black stove with a stove pipe that teetered above it, passing through the wall some fifteen feet up. Otherwise Hester had an impression of some kitchen essentials occupying one corner, shelves of untidy books and a large space at one end mostly taken up by an easel. On the easel was a huge unfinished painting of a nude.

'Richard's bird.' Ezra explained. 'Make yourself at home.' He waved a hand at the general green gloom cast by the chestnut tree outside. 'I'll get you a drink.'

He took glasses from the dresser, gave them a cursory wipe with a towel and sloshed in wine from a bottle he took from the ancient fridge that stood in the corner. He handed her a glass, then bent to the stove, piling paper and wood into its open maw. He lit it and shut the doors; flames licked behind the glass.

'You're surely not going to cook on that?' Hester said, sipping a wine that was cool, slightly sparkling and surprisingly pleasant.

'No fear. But I'm getting it going all the same. It'll be a bit fresh in here later.'

The cooker turned out to be the sort used by students and

designed to sit on a table, in this case a long, battered refectory table that looked as if it had a similar history to the dresser.

'Sit down, make yourself comfortable,' Ezra said. 'Soon get things going here.' On another part of the table he set out a chopping board and the huge fish. He dashed outside and returned with a fistful of mint and practically an armful of parsley; at the sink with its single cold tap, he scraped potatoes into an old-fashioned black saucepan which he placed on the stove. After various preparations, the fish together with most of the parsley disappeared into the minuscule oven. He encouraged the stove with extra logs.

Hester watched him, fascinated. She had never seen a man dealing easily, if in a rough and ready manner, with domesticity. Robert became vague and aloof when it came to even the simplest of chores. All he could safely cope with was the electric kettle and the coffee percolator.

Sitting with her drink on the untidy sofa she idly turned the pages of the latest copy of *Painting Now*, realising it was the issue in which the interview with Robert appeared. There was an atmospheric photograph of Robert in his studio wreathed and half obscured by cigarette smoke and a fairly predictable question and answer piece in which Robert successfully sidestepped any probing questions. She turned the page and skimmed through an article by Kurt Sagar. He was indulging in some comparatively safe prognostications as to which painters were increasing in stature, whose work was being collected and by whom. Robert, though already well-known, was quoted as having recently made a move to America and therefore new heights. She caught sight of her own name. It was amongst those whom Sagar expected, sadly he said, not to make it through the nineties. If she had cared, if she had valued his opinion, the article would have thrown her into the depths of despair. She thought nothing of Sagar, he was a pompous prick; yet for some reason that escaped her he was thought to be 'sound'. He was frequently roped in for arts programmes on radio and television and was never afraid to write the most pretentious crap without apparent fear of ridicule. Why indeed should she care what he wrote about her, especially now? In fact, surely she agreed with him? Her recent work displeased her too, she thought it empty of meaning, but not more so than the paintings of very many others whose work he admired.

She glanced up at Ezra, busy mixing a sauce, stirring and tasting with gusto.

'Have you read this article by Sagar?' she asked him.

'That old windbag! Why should I want to do that?'

'He writes here that he doesn't expect that Hester Eliot will last through the nineties.'

'Corporeally or artistically?'

'Artistically of course.'

'That's cause for celebration, old mate. It means that you have a better chance than most of doing some good stuff after all. Don't tell me you mind!'

'You can't shut your eyes to the fact he's very influential. The Hirschs are buying Robert on his advice.'

Ezra stuck a finger in his sauce, then put it in his mouth thoughtfully. 'More lemon I think. *Do* you mind?'

'I might have done a few months ago. Now I don't think I do.'

He brought the pan over to her. 'Of course you don't. Taste this. What d'you think.' He offered her the wooden spoon. She tasted.

'That is truly impressive,' she said.

'Yes, I thought so too. Right, we'll eat at this low table. Sweep all that gubbins on to the floor. I think there are even some candles somewhere.'

He rummaged in a cardboard box that appeared to contain only a motley collection of rags and old clothes and actually produced four white candles which he stuck in jam jars and put on the dresser. He gave her a plate on which lay the salmon deluged in buttery parsley and sauce together with new potatoes flavoured with a lavish sprinkling of mint. Hester thought she had never tasted anything so delicious.

He grinned at her, seeing her eat with enthusiasm. His beard and his wild hair had been turned into an aureole in the light from the stove and the candles, for the green light of day had faded. Later he made coffee, black because there was no milk left.

'Would you be missed if you chose to stay the night,' he asked.

'Since Paul is away from home, no I wouldn't. If, that is, I chose to stay the night.'

'Paul away from home at a time like this. What's he up to?'

'I told you how things are between him and Alice, yet he goes chasing off up to Bristol after Amy. If he had to cheat on Alice why the hell did he have to choose my daughter and why the hell did she go along with it.'

'That's a sod.'

'Well, I've had my say. I don't know what else I can do.'

'As I see it, very little. Perhaps it'll work itself out without too much damage. I'm an optimist.'

'I noticed.'

'When you said "if" a moment ago, do I take it that you would actually be prepared to consider staying the night. You wouldn't reject the idea out of hand?'

'No, I wouldn't. I'd like to stay the night, Ezra . . .'

'Because, late though it is, I'm quite prepared to trundle you back to your virginal little attic in Coombe . . . what did you say?'

'I said I'd like to stay the night.'

He broke into beaming smiles. 'My God,' he said. 'You're an unpredictable woman. I adore you. But I'm glad we've got that out of the way. A little uncertainty is a great fillip to passion but to tell you the truth I don't think I would be up to coping with the disappointment if you said no later.'

'I won't say no later. Not, that is, unless you plan to treat me rather badly.'

'Treat you badly!' he said choking over his coffee. 'My darling, gorgeous woman! My reputation as regards women is not good, I grant you that, but my faults generally lie in the direction of everyday fidelity and shaky fiscal policies, not assault and battery.'

'That's what I thought.'

'In which case . . .' He crossed to the stove and stuffed more logs into its burning heart. It was already sending waves of heat into the cool spaces of the barn.

'That's better,' he said. He refilled her glass and then sat beside her again. 'Now, shall I begin by telling you the story of my life or shall I just kiss you.'

'Kiss me, I think,' Hester said.

So he did. Gently and with practised dexterity he removed her expensive shirt and laid it carefully on the back of the sofa, then with obvious delight he unplaited her hair and draped it round her shoulders, pushing his fingers through the heavy mass.

'I can't believe this is happening yet,' he said, kissing her neck. He held her head in both his huge hands and moved them to her shoulders with a gentleness that was more erotic than Robert's most intimate caress. Soon they were lying naked on the rug-strewn sofa, the orange light from the stove staining their skin. Ezra no longer had the body of a young man but it was a body that had long ago learnt to give and receive pleasure. Hester had no need to make the kind of effort that was necessary to arouse Robert; it was all happening as naturally and inevitably as breathing, releasing in her a tide of passion that nothing could stop. She held Ezra's large and sturdy body to her, feeling as if she had at last reached a safe and welcoming refuge. That she knew this to be an illusion no longer mattered.

Ezra spoke to her in gruff broken snatches. 'You have a beautiful body, like a Red Indian, like a marvellous cat. Like a young girl.'

She kissed the inside of his elbow, his chest where the hair sprouted, caressed him across the stomach, holding the hardness of his erection against her own flat stomach until it was time for him to come in. In the end she closed her eyes and cried out; Ezra gave a great shout of exaltation that carried her with it; it sounded eerie, primitive and absolutely wonderful.

CHAPTER TWENTY-FIVE

Eustace balanced his great weight on the canvas and metal chair, lit a cheroot and gazed round the TriBeCa studio with the utmost satisfaction. He had abandoned his thick corduroy suit for one of mustard linen which was already slightly crumpled from the increasing heat outside. Inside the studio it was much cooler since it possessed antiquated but reasonably reliable air conditioning. White blinds covered the windows, creating a vast, shadowless space, a light that was particularly flattering to the uncannily wrinkle-free complexion of Betty Hirsch.

Stretched out before them on a sheet of polythene lay a blank canvas twelve metres square, not yet on its stretchers. On the walls were a series of small paintings, forerunners of the versions that would soon take shape on a larger and more monumental scale.

'I don't know how you ever have the courage to make the first mark,' Betty said, her voice a carrying whisper. 'I would find it absolutely terrifying. But that's the difference between us ordinary mortals and great painters, I guess.'

She had on a pink suit with a cleavage that suggested she was wearing nothing much beneath it. There was a white bow in her maize-coloured hair and pink high-heeled sandals on her feet.

Robert, in his white tee shirt and washed out jeans stood smoking moodily beside his almost monochrome paintings.

'It's what makes my job so much more interesting than most.' Eustace puffed away. 'Seeing things appear apparently out of nowhere. But we know, don't we, dear boy, that that's an illusion? They cost, don't they, dear boy?'

Robert lowered his head modestly in assent. Eustace noticed that since the moment that Betty Hirsch had walked through the door, Robert had been watching her covertly. It wasn't sex, Eustace was fairly sure of that, she wasn't his type and thank God for that! Robert must know that cuckolding his patron's wife would be a sure path to self-destruction. On the other hand he suspected that Betty saw herself as a modern Madame de Stael, a Gertrude Stein or a Peggy Guggenheim; Peggy Guggenheim had gone so far as to marry one of her protégés but he couldn't somehow see Betty abandoning Waldo for a painter, however successful.

Betty went to Robert and laid a hand on his arm, leading him to the first of the painted sketches.

'Tell me about this one,' she said. 'I'm intrigued as to how you arrived at this particular motif. I saw that you tried several others . . .'

Eustace chomped at his cigar. He knew that Robert hated 'explaining' his paintings, he left that to experts like Sagar; but on this occasion he appeared to be not too reluctant. Reminded of Sagar, Eustace drew his spikey eyebrows together in vexation, aware of the rolled-up magazine that was even now distorting the pocket of his suit. Robert's voice murmured in the background; this was new indeed. As far as he knew the only person with whom he ever discussed his work before it was finished was Hester. He was almost garrulous. 'You see this, the layer that lies above the background as it were? Up to now it has always been minutely incised or frayed, do you see that now it is more significantly ruptured, almost to the point that it is in danger of becoming two distinct areas rather than one. In danger of becoming a dichotomy, which is what lends it tension.'

'That *is* a radical new departure,' Betty nodded thoughtfully. Eustace noticed that, away from Waldo, she changed. She dropped the little-girl lisp and revealed an altogether tougher, more determined nature. As he listened to her exchanges with Robert, though he winced inwardly, he had to hand it to her, she was a remarkable women and a remarkable listener. She really attended to what was being said and asked reasonably intelligent questions; though not intelligent enough to undermine the self-esteem of her confidant. Eustace had seen Betty Hirsch or her equivalent at work many times. They smoothed ruffled egos, encouraged the shy, flattered the egotist and generally oiled the social wheels with all the ease and graciousness of the complete professional. Robert was not the first to be disarmed by it and wouldn't be the last. Eustace left them to it. For Robert to be taken under Betty Hirsch's wing was no bad thing, he had seen it work wonders for more recalcitrant artists than Robert. Perhaps it wouldn't be as vital to nag Hester into paying another confidence-boosting visit to New York after all.

Without even appearing to detach herself from Robert, Betty turned her attention to Eustace. 'I wanted to ask you how the new gallery was going? Do you know when you'll make the move yet?'

'I'm having to leave most of the arrangements to Gozo. I have to admit that he's better at dealing with these things. Architects and builders and so on. But you'll be the first to know when we have a positive date . . . in fact I was hoping that you would do the opening ceremony for us, cut the ribbon as it were . . .'

'It's so sweet of you to ask! I should be quite thrilled!'

'I'm determined on late August or early September.'

'How exciting. I'm sure it will be a great success. So much more room.'

Besides being one-twelfth the rent, Eustace thought with some satisfaction. 'Much more practical for today's large works,' he said aloud. 'And today's artists. "Reduce him to narrow limits and you cut off half his resources", Huxley.'

'Yes, I do see,' Betty glanced round the studio where no easel was in sight. 'I'm sure you can't wait to move in. I do hope you have the very best people to do the renovations. I never think it pays to try to cut corners. Is Bruno pleased?'

'You know Bruno, cautious to the last.'

'He's well, I hope.'

Eustace assured her that he was, though Bruno was giving him some grounds for concern; not over his health, but over his increasing reluctance to take an interest in the new Lombards. But if he was having second thoughts it was too late now. The thing was as good as accomplished. About Robert he was more than satisfied. Hester had stayed with him for two weeks before leaving again for England but he knew that she and Robert had kept in touch by telephone and that she had promised to return to New York soon. Since the deal had been agreed upon and Robert had moved, if temporarily, to the new studio, Waldo had dropped out of the picture somewhat and Betty had taken over, appearing at the studio at regular intervals to see how the work was progressing. At first Eustace had been worried at what Robert would normally have labelled intolerable interference, but on today's showing he evidently found her visits encouraging, stimulating even.

'Darlings, I must leave you,' Betty said, 'My hairdresser will be cross with me for keeping him waiting . . . but Robert, I adore what you're doing already. Just flat out adore it.'

She dropped a kiss on the cheek of each man in turn and left them alone. After she had gone, Eustace made a move to follow her. He wasn't in New York for long and had a busy schedule to keep but he lingered for as long as he dared, it would be tactless to suggest to Robert that he had other fish to fry, other artists' interests to promote. He was quite sure that Robert liked to think he was his only concern.

'You're becoming quite at home here,' Eustace said. 'I believe you must be a New Yorker at heart.'

Robert lit a cigarette before answering.

'You may be right,' he said, shaking out a match. 'In fact I'm seriously considering making the arrangement permanent if I can.'

Eustace's eyes bulged. He wasn't altogether sure if this was good news.

'How would Hester take that?' he asked.

Robert turned to study an area of one of his trial paintings. He rubbed it with his thumb and stood back to look at it again.

'I'm sure Hester will fall in with whatever will most help the work. As you know she has been somewhat unsettled lately but she'll come round.'

'A bit unsettled,' Eustace repeated hollowly. He had been a little surprised, no, he had been astonished, at the ease with which Robert had shrugged off his extremes of conduct. But there, that was artists!

'Did she tell you when she was coming over again?' Robert asked.

'I haven't seen her just lately but I'll get on to her as soon as I get back.'

'Do that, will you. I rang Bristol the other day and Devon last night but there was no answer. She was probably at the hospital.'

'Hospital!' Eustace looked alarmed.

'The friend. You remember perhaps?'

'Of course.' Eustace nodded several times. All the same he noticed that Robert was not panicking at Hester's temporary unavailability as he would have done just weeks ago.

'Right then, dear boy. I'm off.' He slapped the pocket containing the magazine in which Sagar's article lurked. No point in letting Robert see it if he hadn't already. He didn't want him sidetracked at this delicate stage. All the same, he had prepared a few choice words for Sagar on the subject of Hester which he intended to deliver as soon as he returned, with possibly a follow-up letter to *Painting Now.* He just hoped the wretched man was right about Robert but wrong about Hester's longterm prospects; all the same, Eustace had good reason to believe that in the short term he would be wasting valuable time promoting her. A telephone call from Caroline had confirmed his worst fears.

'Remember the studio in Devon you told me about?' Caroline had sounded almost triumphant.

'Ah, yes.' He had not had time to get down to see it, his priorities having undergone a change since they had last spoken of it.

'You've seen it, of course.'

Damn the woman and her persistence, he thought. He allowed a certain coldness to creep into his voice. 'It seems to interest you unduly, doesn't it?' he said.

'You didn't tell me the place was semi-derelict.'

'Nonsense.'

'It needs six months' work on it at the very least, and there's certainly no painting going on there . . .'

After that he'd been too busy to attend to it or even to take an interest in what Hester was doing except where it affected Robert. If she wasn't working he no longer felt responsible. Anyway, André Veck was taking up a great deal of his time and he had great hopes of André Veck . . .

Just as Caroline paid off the cab, Eustace burst out of the building waving his arms to summon it before it drove off. So intent was he on his mission that he did not appear to notice her standing on the sidewalk. He would hardly be expecting to see her in this setting anyway. She could have been any blonde New Yorker. It reminded her of a similar incident in Cork Street a few weeks before, though then it had been a rainy English day, not a warm New York one. A great deal had happened since then.

She had broken her journey from Devon to London in Bristol, boldly ringing the bell of the Salisbury Square house, with an excuse ready on her lips. (The possibility of another interview, this time with Hester. No need to follow it up.) But there had been no answer to her rings and knocks. The house could have been deserted. She had finally extracted a version of the truth from Amanda several days later. She had taken her out to lunch, flattered her and primed her with wine. Robert, it appeared, had had some kind of minor breakdown but was now recovering and had gone to New York as planned. She did not quite believe it.

The entrance to the building didn't look too prepossessing and the elevator creaked and rattled precariously. It smelled of Eustace Tench's disgusting cigars with the faintest admixture of a half-remembered but very expensive scent. The door to the studio stood open and the smell of Robert's Marlboros took over. As she walked in Robert was standing with his back to her in characteristic attitude as he closely studied the series of small paintings on the wall. He hadn't heard her.

'It's not like you to leave the door open when you're working,' she said.

Robert turned round slowly. She thought for a moment that he wasn't pleased to see her. She thought Amanda must have been mistaken. Robert looked all right to her.

'Aren't you going to say hello?' she said.

'Caroline! What in hell's name are you doing here?'

She walked round the large piece of canvas that was spread out on the floor, put her arms round his neck and kissed him on the mouth.

'I'm glad to see you too,' she whispered against his skin. After a moment or two he responded, pressing his mouth on hers almost too fiercely. She broke away.

'You never even said goodbye,' she said with a slight pout.

'I'm sorry about that but there wasn't time. I was going to get in touch.'

'Promises!' She wandered round looking at everything. 'So this is the great new studio,' she said. 'Robert, it's fantastic. Are you pleased?'

'Certainly I am.' He allowed a pause before he repeated his question.

'Caroline, what *are* you doing here?'

'I've been transferred.'

'Transferred. What do you mean transferred?'

'P.N. has transferred me to the New York office. Aren't I a lucky girl!'

Again she wasn't sure how to interpret Robert's expression.

'How on earth did you wangle that?' he said.

'Never mind. I did. Now I'm here so you'd better appreciate me before the rush.' She gave a little twisted smile at her own joke, a glint in her pale eyes.

'Where are you staying?'

She spread out her hands. 'Darling, nowhere. I'm at your mercy.'

'You can't stay with me,' he said flatly.

She made the smallest moue. 'Not just for a few days until I find somewhere else?'

He moved towards her and put his hands on her shoulders, becoming aware of her narrow body under them. Beneath her eyes were the faintest blue smudges of fatigue, reminding him of a tired child. Suddenly he desired her. His desire did not come frequently, it was too easily swamped by his work, but now he realised that it had been weeks since he had even phoned her and longer again since those spare hips had contained his need. He held her more urgently to him.

'I've missed you,' Caroline murmured against his neck.

'I've missed you too.'

'Liar!' She broke away and kicked off her shoes. Then she walked to the middle of the huge canvas and began to take off her jacket.

'Why don't you fuck me here?' she said. 'Right in the middle of your nice new canvas. Don't you think it would add an extra *je ne sais quoi* to the finished painting? Then when it's hanging in M.O.M.A. you can look at it and laugh.'

Robert felt momentarily shocked. Then he smiled tentatively. He went to the door, closed it, then locked it.

'Why don't you leave it open?' she challenged him but that he was not prepared to do. She might thrive on the frisson of possible discovery but he did not. She was pulling off the rest of her clothes and scattering them about on the surface of the canvas. In its very centre she lay down and stretched herself out with a murmur of contentment. Her bracelets slid down her arm with a tiny clash as she beckoned him.

He looked at her with something like awe as she lay there; he admired her audacity. Her scrawniness reminded him of a nude by Schiele, all projecting hip bones and almost skeletal flanks which had the effect of thrusting her silky mount into prominence.

Carefully, without taking his eyes off her, he removed his tee shirt and jeans, hanging them over the chair lately vacated by Eustace. His canvas boots he tucked underneath.

Then he went naked to join her.

CHAPTER TWENTY-SIX

The young nurse helped Alice out of the wheelchair and on to the lavatory.

'You're doing ever so well considering. You'll be on to a walking frame tomorrow at this rate.'

Alice grunted. Perhaps she had done well but right now she felt depressed and very, very angry. The card from Paul had not only confirmed her suspicions but revealed something else that she had never even dreamed about. She knew she wasn't wrong, it just couldn't be coincidence. She had a pain in her chest and began to cough.

'Damn it all. Now I've got some sort of bug,' she said bitterly. She caught her breath, she really did not feel at all well.

'You're doing fine,' the little nurse said encouragingly.

'No, I'm bloody not,' Alice gasped and lunged for the wheelchair. Then she passed out.

Alice was in intensive care for twenty-four hours. Now she was back in the ward, this time in a bed nearer the door. Hester sat beside her and took her hand. It was bare of its usual battery of rings, pale and slightly clammy. Alice withdrew it almost at once and Hester detected a coolness in her manner that she did not quite understand. Perhaps it was the aftereffect of the pulmonary embolism or the drugs Alice was having to take.

'I'm sorry about this,' Alice said in a hoarse whisper. 'They said I was doing so well too.'

'So you were, and are. Sister said you've made a good recovery.'

'They can't understand why it happened. It's a perfect sod.' She looked at Hester almost fiercely. 'D'you know what? Just before I passed out I really thought I was about to drop off the twig. It's a bloody peculiar feeling, you've no idea.'

'Poor Alice. Were you very frightened?'

'Not exactly frightened. More surprised. I remember thinking, is this it then, is this all we have? And now I realise how much precious time I wasted on stupid and unimportant things. If I'm spared, never again.' She stirred, attempting to get comfortable, but she was once again pinned to the bed with a tube in her arm.

'Anti-coagulants,' she said. 'They're taking it out later today and I'm going on to tablets. Look, Hester, it's going to take longer than I thought. Will you and April be able to manage the shop?'

'Of course we can manage the shop. Sales are picking up just in the last few days.' Hester meant to be encouraging but to her dismay she saw tears squeezing out of Alice's eyes.

'What is it?' she asked. 'Do you feel awful?'

Alice nodded towards the beside table. 'Have a look at the envelope on the top, the one with the card inside.'

It was one of two, both still in their envelopes. Hester withdrew the first card. On the front was an artistic and trendy design, on the other side it was signed by Paul.

'From Paul,' she said, puzzled. 'What . . .'

'Look at the postmark.'

It had been posted not in London but in Bristol. Hester gazed at it dumbly.

'You knew it was Amy, didn't you?' Alice said.

Hester nodded. 'I tried very hard to stop it, believe me, Alice. I can't tell you how sorry I am. Why her, of all people!'

'Not your fault,' Alice said gruffly. 'At my age, what can I expect.'

'Oh don't, Alice!'

'I'm sure that's the opinion of the sender of the card in the other envelope.'

The second card was large, with a sentimental picture of rabbits on the front. Inside there was a message, ill-written and misspelt. 'Get well soon,' it said. 'Remember that while the cat's away, the mice will play so watch out for that yung un of yours!' It was not signed.

'Who on earth . . . ?' Hester began.

'Reg Gammon, naturally.'

'The evil old bugger! Oh, Alice, this is all too awful. What can I say?'

Abruptly Alice raised her head from the pillow. She grabbed Hester's hand almost convulsively. 'Listen to me, Hester,' she said urgently. 'There's nothing you can do for me, but there's something you can do for yourself. You have *got* to stop wasting your life. Up to now I've waited patiently on the sidelines and kept my mouth shut watching you make a complete balls-up of things, but I can't do that any longer. For all I know I might snuff it tomorrow without ever having said my say. You have got to make your mind up:

either you spend the rest of your time on earth as Robert Gibb's creature or you come to your senses and live your own life! Just stop farting about doing neither one thing nor the other. Life's too short and I can now say that with absolute authority. Never mind Robert, never mind Amy and Paul, if it comes to it, never mind me. Just do it, will you!'

She sank back on her pillows exhausted, her eyes closed.

'Alice, are you all right?' Hester leaned over her anxiously, wondering if she should call a nurse. Alice opened her eyes briefly.

'Promise me,' she said.

'All right. I promise.'

'Good. You can go now. I have to get some sleep before they start buggering me about again.' After Hester had left, Alice lay thinking. The shock of the twenty-four hours in intensive care had made a difference to her outlook. She realised that she had loved Paul but always provisionally, keeping part of herself detached, knowing that sooner or later this moment would come. It made it, marginally, easier.

Hester and Ezra were sitting on the old silvered tree trunk on the beach where Hester and Alice had rested not so long ago, comparing their lives. It was warm, now almost midsummer, with only the merest breeze off the river.

'She's only in her mid forties, for goodness' sake,' Hester said. 'She's not old. She can't die.'

'Alice is not going to die,' Ezra said firmly. 'Just concentrate on that. This is just a temporary setback, that's all.'

'But if there was another clot and if it reached her heart it would kill her!'

'Don't think about that. Think about it dispersing. Your Alice has got more fight in her than that. She is not going to peg out, I'd put money on it. You've practically got her in her box already, for God's sake.'

With an effort Hester took command of herself. 'I seem to be obsessed by the idea that death comes in threes. Ridiculous, I know.'

'Threes? Who died besides your mother?'

'I had a miscarriage last year,' she said shortly. 'I suppose you would count that as a death, wouldn't you?'

'Ah.' He covered her hand with his. 'Did you want it very much?'

'At my age! You must be joking.'

'What has age got to do with whether you wanted it or not?'

'I accept that. No. I suppose I didn't actually want it but that's absolutely no comfort at all. That's why I felt so bad. The poor little sod never had a chance.'

Ezra put his arm round her shoulders. 'Life is very precarious, isn't it, old mate? That's why we should live it to the limits, not waste time in speculation or remorse. At least that's my simple homespun philosophy.' His laugh rumbled through his robust frame. 'Or,' he paused and looked at her, 'in self martyrdom unless it's for an impeccable cause.'

'Don't you start! Have you been talking to Alice?'

'I don't need to talk to Alice. It's blatantly bloody obvious that you planned to leave the sainted Robert and he, by some means or other, is holding you to ransom. What's he got on you anyway?'

'Nothing. He's a very vulnerable, highly strung person. It seemed to be just the wrong moment, that's all. You wouldn't understand. You're completely different.'

'What makes you think I'm not vulnerable too. Or that you're as tough as you seem to think you are?' Ezra said roughly. 'Tell me honestly, Hester, and look at me when you answer, do you still love him?'

Hester looked away without speaking.

''Nough said,' Ezra said triumphantly. 'Then I think you're bloody mad. Haven't we just been talking about brief lives, for Christ's sake? Just how much of it do you think you have to squander?'

Hester put her hands over her ears abruptly. 'Be quiet,' she cried desperately. 'Just . . . be quiet, will you!'

Gently he took her hands from her ears and put them in her lap. He put his arm back round her shoulders. Together they watched a boat chugging up the river, as it had done weeks before. Now, as then, Reg Gammon was sitting at the bow. Hester hoped the boat would sink.

'What I think is this,' Ezra said. 'I think you should leave Robert and live with me. We could even get married if you like.'

'Be serious, Ezra.'

'I am. Deadly.'

'Look, Alice is ill. I can't think about anything else, nothing else seems important just at present.'

'What I'm rather failing to understand is why the young lodger has chosen this moment to go AWOL. Does he really want Alice to find out that he's getting his oats elsewhere?'

Hester told him about the cards and about Reg Gammon.

'I've come to the conclusion,' she concluded acidly, 'That Paul couldn't face several weeks without sex. In fact I'm wondering if he can even survive a day without it.'

'A man after my own heart.'

'Don't be so bloody crass!'

Ezra stood up and stretched. He reached out a hand to help her up. 'All the same, he's a bit of a young turk, isn't he? Never mind, the difference between our young friend and myself should be only too obvious. One gets philosophical in one's decrepid old age.'

'I hadn't noticed you being all that philosophical.' Hester said as they crunched back over the pebbles.

'How kind,' he said, his bearded face dissolving into a thousand creases.

Alice awoke to see Paul sitting beside her. She had left instructions with Hester for him not to come to the hospital but he must have called in on the way back from Bristol before going home.

'Hi,' he said softly.

'Hello, Paul,' she said.

'I came as soon as I could,' he said. 'How do you feel now?'

'Lousy. Better than I did.'

'Poor darling. But you'll soon be back to normal. I'm sorry I wasn't able to come earlier but I had to sort that flat business out. Did you get my card?'

'The one you sent from Bristol, you mean?'

'I stopped off on the way.'

Alice closed her eyes tiredly. 'You need not bother to keep up the pretence. I know you've been in Bristol with Amy.'

'That's absolute bullshit! Who told you that?'

Alice lifted a hand weakly in protest. 'Please, Paul! I'm not a fool. At least if I'm a fool, I'm not stupid. I realised, you see, that the situation was beyond redemption as soon as the date for surgery was set. An indeterminate period of celibacy was never really on for you, let's face it. In fact *any* period of celibacy was out of the question, wasn't it?' At one time she had thought she would be well prepared for this moment but she had not expected it to happen when she was at her lowest ebb. But, she thought, she ought to have known that it would be that way, it's in the nature of disasters to happen just when you can't cope. She ought to have been prepared for that too.

'Alice, darling! If you must know it means absolutely nothing. It's quite a different sort of relationship. It won't, it can't affect us at all. You must know that!'

'I'm afraid it already has affected us,' Alice said. It was an effort to speak but certain things had to be said. 'This is what I want you to do for me . . .'

'Whatever you like, Alice . . .'

'When you get back to Coombe Ferrers I want you to pack up all your belongings and find somewhere else to live. I'm afraid the two of us under one roof is not going to work any more . . .'

'But Alice, darling . . .!'

'Be a good boy,' Alice whispered. 'And do as I say.'

Amy was in a bad mood. She was, as she had told Gina on the phone, absolutely teed off with the job but the prospect of finding something else was even more of a bore. She and the other researchers had been told that they wouldn't be needed after next week which meant that she would have to trudge off down to the job centre again. Not that there was likely to be anything on offer. She wasn't exactly short of money, she had her allowance and Hester had sent her more in response to her reluctant telephone call, a stilted affair with Hester asking if she was all right and she telling her mother not to fuss. Her pay didn't seem to go anywhere, it hardly seemed to cover even her everyday expenses, which she found deeply humiliating after her proud boast to her father.

She rather missed not having Paul around but in some ways it was a relief not to be jumped on when she was tired after a day of asking people stupid questions and as often as not getting stupid answers. Paul had an insatiable sex drive which she was beginning to think would get to be a bit of a bore after a while.

She opened the front door and slammed it behind her.

'What the fuck . . . !'

Two men in suits were standing in the hall apparently joined umbilically by a tape measure. They looked as astonished as she was.

'Sorry, but we don't need new carpets,' she said. 'Who the hell are you?'

One of the men produced a card from his waistcoat. A waistcoat in this weather! she thought inconsequentially.

'I'm sorry, Miss . . . but we were told the property would be empty.'

Amy looked at the card. It belonged to a local firm of estate agents.

'Well, it's not empty. You must have the wrong address. And what exactly is going on? Are you doing us over?'

The first man blenched a little and allowed the tape measure to zip back into its housing. 'This *is* number twelve, isn't it? Mr Gibb sent us the key himself, but if it's not convenient we'll come back another time.'

'Too right it's not convenient, but don't bother to come back. The house is not for sale.'

'Excuse me,' said the younger man, speaking for the first time. A smoothy, full of his own importance, was her verdict. 'Would you be Miss Gibb?'

'I not only would be, I was and I am. Now I'm tired and I want a shower . . .' She opened the front door. 'I think you'd better go before I change my mind and call the cops.'

The older man spoke again, not to be so easily fobbed off.

'I'm very sorry about this, Miss Gibb. There's probably been a slight misunderstanding but Mr Gibb did specifically ring us from New York with a view to putting the house on the market. We shall obviously have to ring back and confirm.'

'Don't bother. It's all a mistake.'

'I'm sure we can sort it out,' Waistcoat said as they departed. Amy was left fuming in the hall. What the fuck was Robert up to? she thought, then abruptly she whirled over to the telephone and dialled the international code followed by Robert's New York number. A recorded message advised her to leave her name and number and Mr Gibb would get back to her. He was probably calmly painting while she was getting mad as apeshit with frustration.

All the same she set the Answerphone and went and took her shower. There was still no call by the time she was dressed again so she dialled the number once more before she went to cook herself something. This time Robert himself answered.

'What the hell's going on, Robert?' Amy shouted down the phone without preamble.

'Hallo, Amy.' Her father's voice was slow, quiet and faintly ironical. 'How nice of you to call. How are you?'

'Don't faff about. There have been two creeps here who say you want to sell the house.'

'That's right. I instructed them. I thought you were staying with Gina.'

'You instructed them!' she yelped. 'Then it's a good job I wasn't staying with Gina. Have you gone completely bananas?'

'Try not to be hysterical, Amy. It's a perfectly logical thing to do since I shall be in America for some time. I may even decide to stay here indefinitely.'

'Does Hester know about this?'

'If she's going to be living here too there won't be much point in keeping that great house going in Clifton. Even you must see that.'

'And does she know she's going to be living in New York?'

'She will come round to the idea in due course, naturally.'

'I see,' Amy said with heavy sarcasm. 'There's something else too actually. I wouldn't mention it at all but . . . where do I fit into these fascinating plans?'

'Naturally we shall make arrangements for you while you're at college, though the estate agents don't expect the house to sell quickly, the way things are.'

'Well, thank you,' she said, enunciating precisely. 'That cheers me up no end, I can tell you. Hester agrees to all this, does she?'

'I shall be ringing her. I want her to get over here as soon as possible so that we can discuss it.'

Amy heard a female voice speaking in the background.

'Who's that with you?'

'No one you know. A journalist.'

'Not another interview!' Amy said caustically. She was beginning to suspect that her father had an affair on the go. She wondered if it was his first affair and, if it was, why he was having it now when Hester was so important to him.

'How is the job going?' Robert asked. 'Are you finding time to do some work for next term?'

'Don't change the subject. I shall be ringing Hester tonight, shall I tell her about the house or did you say you already had?'

'No, leave it to me. I'll try to get hold of her again. Unfortunately she never seems to be there.'

'She's either at the shop or the hospital. Alice has been extremely ill.'

'Don't exaggerate, Amy. A hip replacement is routine surgery these days.'

Amy's temper boiled up. 'You're a shit. I hate you!'

She slammed down the receiver and stood trembling beside it. Her familiar world that she spoke of to friends with such cheerful scorn was breaking up under her feet like spring ice. There were no reliable footholds left. Her eyes were full of childish tears which she rubbed impatiently away with her sleeve. She would have to speak to Hester and soon.

Since it was Sunday and the shop closed, Hester found she had time to herself. Keeping The Anchorage going, even with the help of April Moffatt, the hospital visits and evenings and nights with

Ezra had filled her time completely. Now she found she had a whole morning free, time to walk and think.

She strode out along the beach, the air sparkled about her and swallows skimmed low over the river. There was practically no wind; the small open ferryboat on the way to Tidemouth left a silky wake and the sound of its engine and the church bells clangour grew fainter as she passed the coastguard cottages and the last of the beached craft.

The red cliffs loomed as she rounded the first spur and the sights and sounds of the town dropped away altogether. It now seemed months instead of weeks since she had first come to this place but it had lost none of its power. Today the red stacks stood in a mirror of deep water, the arch and its still, reflected image formed an almost complete D. The tide, on its way out, left her only the narrowest of margins on which to walk and she picked her way between a maze of pools and rocks.

Each time she came here more images and fresh meanings crowded in to furnish her inner world. There they would undergo a mysterious transformation that would sooner or later demand expression. She recognised that there was already a pressure building up, not to be interpreted by mere sleight of hand but to be wrestled with as if it were a matter of life and death. An inner journey in which there could be no turning back.

Eustace was leaving her in peace, in fact she was faintly puzzled by his lack of communication. He had not shown any further interest in the new studio, which was perhaps a blessing. He had offered to support her in her decision to stand by Robert but she had heard nothing since she had last seen him in New York, but being human and an agent into the bargain he would promise anything just to avert a crisis. Robert's work was going well, he even hinted at new departures, and since Betty Hirsch seemed to be taking a personal interest, perhaps after all she need not hurry back to New York.

From where she stood, her back pressed against the red, gritty surface of the cliff, the arch soared above her in a leaping perspective. Cornelian on lapis lazuli. It seemed that the pressure in her brain increased. The necessity to prepare for its eventual release drove her back, not by the shore, but up the rugged and vertiginous path that led to the cliff top, then from there across the field to the Cider Press. She assumed that as it was Sunday the place would be locked, but as it turned out the carpenter was there putting in some overtime.

'Why don't you take a look upstairs?' he suggested.

'Is it finished?' she said surprised.

'All done,' he said, before the howl of the power saw interrupted.

She hurried up the outside stairs, which had been stripped of their brown paint and varnished. Inside she saw that all was indeed finished, the smell of wood, varnish and paint still fresh in the air. The floor had been relaid but it still retained its uneven aged look. The new window lights were in the roof and had blinds that could be pulled down, for sunlight now flooded the place. Through the huge window in the end wall the view seemed to go on forever. It was already more than she could ever have hoped for. Even though planning permission on the detailed design of the living quarters had not yet been granted, Susan had been of the opinion that there would be no problems getting it. After that, work on the ground floor could go ahead and should be finished by the end of the summer. It would be hers, yet it would be as much out of reach as ever, for if she kept her promise to Robert for how many weeks in the year could she ever hope to use it? By the time she had paid Alice and begun to repay the loan she'd raised for the rebuilding she would be as poor as she had been when she first left college. It was a very sobering thought. When she returned to the house the telephone was ringing. It was Amy.

Amy came down on the afternoon train from Bristol on her student railcard. She insisted that she had something important to tell Hester that she couldn't possibly discuss over the telephone.

Hester picked her up from Exeter St David on the way back from visiting Alice in the hospital. Although Paul had moved out the day before, Amy said she had no intention of staying the night but would go back later that evening. Her job had another week to run.

'What will you do after that?' Hester asked as she negotiated the outskirts of Exeter.

'Join the queue at the job centre, I suppose.'

'So coming down here couldn't wait until you finished next week?'

Amy bit the corner of a finger nail. 'I thought I'd better come at once. Dad hasn't rung you, has he?'

'Not lately. I've been rather busy. Why, has he tried?'

'Not as hard as I think he should have done, no. Considering what he's up to.'

'Can you stop being so mysterious, Amy?'

'Right. Well, here's the bottom line. He's put the house on the market.'

'That's ridiculous. You must be mistaken.' Hester said calmly.

'That's what I thought, so I rang him up. He confirmed it, he's selling the house.'

'He can't be. Not without discussing it first. I expect he meant that he wanted to talk round the idea.'

'In that case why did he send the men from the estate agents to measure the place up. I came home to find two comedians going over the house with a tape measure. Listen, Mum, he's set on it! He says you're both thinking of living in New York so you won't need the Bristol house any more. Is that true?'

Hester's hands tightened on the steering wheel. She slowed down behind a tractor. 'No, it's not true. I have no intention of living in New York. What did you say to the men from the estate agents?'

'I turfed them out.'

'Good. I think I shall have to ring Robert tonight and clear this thing up. It's too crazy for words.'

'As a matter of fact I'm beginning to think that everything Robert does lately is a bit crazy.' Amy said quietly. Hester glanced at her. She looked strained and unhappy, her loyalties to both parents under stress. Hester took the final turning towards Coombe Ferrers.

When they got to the house Amy plucked up the courage to ask after Alice. Hester said that Alice was making progress.

'Is Paul with her this afternoon?' Amy asked. She sat on the verandah seat. Hester was watering some of Alice's plants that stood outside in pots.

'No,' Hester said. 'Paul has moved out. Alice knows about his visits to Bristol.' She spoke without looking up from her task.

Amy went very quiet, then she said, 'She knows about me?'

'Yes.'

'Oh, God.'

Hester hardened her heart, 'Not from me however. It was a slip of Paul's which I can't help feeling was intentional. I think Alice already had her suspicions that Paul had someone else but the card from Bristol confirmed them.' She spoke briskly and without emotion.

'The bloody idiot!'

'Well, as you said yourself, she couldn't expect to hang on to Paul indefinitely.'

Amy's eyes filled, her face was very red. 'Please don't,' she said. 'Listen, was this before she had the embolism or after?'

'Before, if you must know.'

Amy got up and began pacing up and down. 'Shit! Shit!' She

stopped suddenly. 'I think I'm going off Paul,' she said bitterly.

'It's a bit late unfortunately.'

'Yes,' Amy said humbly. Hester looked at her daughter. Humility was not one of Amy's characteristics.

Amy slumped down on the seat again. 'Do you think it would be any good if I went to see Alice and told her that I think Paul's a complete shit?'

'For God's sake, Amy! Use your head!'

'No, I suppose not.' She spread out her hands in a gesture of impotence. 'But what *can* I do?'

'Will you see Paul again?'

Amy hesitated. 'I don't know. I can't say. It's true he's a shit but . . .' Amy shifted and felt uncomfortable. How could she tell Hester about the hot excitement of being chased, pelting round the Bristol house with Paul yelping in pursuit?

'Then I don't think you should see Alice,' Hester said. 'At least not until you've decided what you're going to do. If you insist on continuing to see Paul then you must realise that I can't support you in it. I can't approve of what you're doing, you must see that.'

'All the same, why should I be blamed especially. People cheat on each other all the time.' She thought of Steve and Kate and the sexy female voice she heard in Robert's New York studio. 'Even people we know well,' she added significantly.

'I'm perfectly aware of that,' Hester said. 'But I don't particularly like being made an accomplice when it concerns two people I love.'

Amy relapsed again into tears and she groped for a packet of tissues. Blowing and crying at the same time, she said. 'Oh, Christ, what a mess. Alice *is* going to be all right, isn't she?'

'I sincerely hope she will.'

Amy finished wiping and blowing. 'What about the house and so on?' she sniffed.

'Leave it to me. I'll sort it out. Why don't you go and stay with Gina for a few days, or have her to stay with you?'

'Yes, I think I will.' She put the tissues back in her purse.

'Do you think we could eat now. I'm absolutely ravenous.'

Hester made a vegetarian meal for them both and later that evening drove Amy back to the station to catch the Bristol train. After she had seen her off she motored through the quiet countryside back to Coombe Ferrers, thinking over Amy's bewildering piece of news about the house. She could not imagine what had precipitated Robert's extraordinary decision to put it on the market and to put it on the market without consulting her. They had lived there a long time, having bought it before house prices in Clifton had begun to soar and at a time when both of them had their first successful exhibitions and when they were both teaching. She could distinctly recall how excited they had been to have a place of their own with more space than they'd ever had before and how later, as they prospered, they'd built the two studios at the back. Now she came to think of it she couldn't remember if the house was in their joint names or in Robert's only, if the latter then she would have to act quickly, though she couldn't believe that Robert was serious about selling. In fact the more she thought about it, the more it seemed to be one of Robert's ploys to make sure he had her full attention or even to bring her back across the Atlantic with all speed. As soon as she got back she telephoned his New York number.

After a few preliminaries she got to the purpose of her call.

'Amy says you want to sell the house,' she said.

'Yes, I did get Sturmers to give me a price,' Robert said, evidently unruffled by her challenge. 'I'm glad you phoned, I've been trying to get hold of you.'

'Don't you think it would have been a good idea to let me know before you sent the estate agents round to the house. Amy was extremely upset.'

'Amy gets upset very easily as you must have discovered by now.'

Hester bit back a sharp reply.

'You've surely no objection have you, darling?' Robert said. 'Since it looks as if we'll both be living here eventually as soon as you can get away from Devon. It does seem the most sensible idea, don't you agree? You see, now that I've worked in a large space like this I don't think I could go back to a small studio again. In fact, I've been seriously considering the idea of us moving to New York in perpetuity, especially if this commission goes well. I also remembered you mentioning your own reservations about working in the Bristol studio. '

Hester began to pace up and down the hall, clutching the telephone to her chest. 'Robert, you take my breath away,' she said. 'This is not just studios you're talking about, it's our home and Amy's home. Didn't it occur to you to ask us what we thought? Or don't you actually care?'

'Of course I care, Hester. Naturally I care. But I honestly thought that you would, like me, think that this must be the next logical step. Surely you can see the soundness of the move. It would be ridiculous to live in New York and still keep on our liabilities in Bristol. We need to be free of all that, don't you see?'

'If you think you can use this to force me to commit myself to living in New York, you're making a mistake, Robert? I absolutely forbid you to sell the house. If we'd discussed it before I might have agreed that to sell it sooner or later would be a good idea but I'm damned if I'll consider it now! Besides, don't you think you're being just a bit presumptuous and that there's a slight whiff of burning bridges in the air!'

'I think I can safely say that the Hirschs are absolutely to be relied on in the foreseeable future, even without them I shall be doing a damned sight better in America than I ever did in the UK. You can rely on that.'

'This doesn't sound like you, this new-found optimism.'

'If you could tear yourself away from Devon and Alice Ruddick and get back here I think you would see what the position is.'

'Certainly I will, as soon as I can leave Alice. Until then I shall ring Sturmers and tell them to cancel the whole thing.'

'As a matter of fact you can't do that, Hester.'

'Watch me!'

'Sturmers tell me they already have a provisional offer, sight unseen.'

'Too bad.'

'I think you're forgetting that the house is in my name; I shall do what I like with it.'

CHAPTER TWENTY-SEVEN

Betty Hirsch sat in a canvas chair at the side of the studio, her endless legs in sheer black. The lapels of her white suit were trimmed with black and gold gleamed in the plunging neckline. There was absolutely nothing about her appearance that could be put down to chance, except perhaps her height. Otherwise it was all maintained at the cost of time, money and a vigorous programme of diet, exercise and the occasional attentions of a plastic surgeon.

Robert, of course, knew nothing of this and would have cared even less. The final appearance, however achieved, pleased him. He had been working without a break for five hours and did not in the least mind her presence in the studio. Her visits were regular and expected, events he anticipated with pleasure. She came at mutually agreed times and just often enough to see progress.

The two assistants who had been helping him at this stage of the project had knocked off for the day. Robert's feet were bare and he was sweating only slightly in spite of his exertions, the results now evident in the changes to the once-white canvas.

He stepped back and lit a cigarette. Naturally Betty Hirsch did not smoke but seemed to have no objection to him doing so. They were contemplating the day's work.

'That is the most amazingly subtle grey, with, I'm sure I'm not wrong, a touch of maroon; I can't imagine how you achieved that,' Betty said, her voice as always when she was away from Waldo, stronger and more decisive. 'Tell me what you do before you start on an area this size? It intrigues me.'

Robert smiled, his eyes more veiled than usual. He could hardly say that he had begun by having sex with Caroline in the centre of the canvas. In fact, the memory of it slightly appalled him though he had no doubt he would allow the same thing to happen again. So he edited the version he gave his patroness.

'I sit for one, maybe two hours without doing a thing, before I even touch it. It's important to conceptualise the space I'm intending to create first, I like to call it an energy field. You see there's an ambiguity to be resolved because edges in the real world are mostly perceived rather than actual and so I see my task as setting up and then dissolving both the pictorial limits and the frontal plane of the canvas . . .'

Betty nodded. 'And the superimposed rectangle?'

'Another ambiguity. It is attached to the first colour field but it also has to float free.'

'What about the way the rectangle appears to be torn or cut.'

Robert smoked in silence for perhaps half a minute. There was a barely detectable tremor in the hand that held the cigarette; he was more agitated when he was working, the cool exterior less apparent.

'That's the point at which these canvases will be different from anything I've done before . . .'

'Yes, I remember what you said about the danger of creating a dichotomy by increasing the split.' Betty leaned forward to study the canvas that lay on the floor, draping a long, elegant hand over one knee. 'But all the same I see it as the only way forward. A complete rift. A separation.'

'As I said, there are risks . . .'

'All the same I'm sure you'll handle the resolution beautifully,' she said. 'I shall be absolutely fascinated, not just as a bystander either. I feel involved.'

'Do you, Betty?' Robert said looking at her. He sat crosslegged on the floor near her chair. 'Well, I'm glad. I feel as if your involvement gives me energy.'

'Good, I like that. I see for the first time the amount of sheer energy painting demands. Will you be able to take a break this evening and dine with us. Nothing formal, just the three of us?'

'I'd appreciate that, Betty.'

'Then you must tell us more about your idea of selling your house in England.'

'That's already well under way as it happens. In fact there's a possible buyer.'

'I'm very glad to hear that, Robert. I don't think it's good for an artist to be worried by material responsibilities. All that should be taken care of by others to leave him free to work, I always feel. Waldo and I would be delighted to help if you're thinking of looking at real estate over here. And I'm sure you can leave the disposal of your property back home in Hester's hands, especially as she's not under pressure at the moment.'

Robert smoked thoughtfully, gazing at the vast area of colour that he and his two assistants had spent the morning creating.

'I'm afraid she's still not reconciled to the idea of moving. It's a matter of some concern to me.'

Betty stood up and smoothed down her skirt. She paced, then spoke.

'Robert, would you mind if I gave you a piece of advice?'

He looked up expectantly.

'First I want to ask you a personal question. I'm afraid you'll think me impertinent but I'll ask it anyway. Do you still love Hester very much?'

Very deliberately Robert crushed out his cigarette in a paint lid. 'I have difficulty with the concept of love in the sense in which I believe you are using it . . .'

'Okay. You don't love her, not perhaps in any sense?'

'I've always relied on her to be there when I needed her, and I'm sure she would say the same for me.'

'But you need her now and she's not here, Robert.'

'No.'

'In fact, to be blunt, she doesn't give me the impression of being much of a wife at all if you don't mind me saying so . . . why are you smiling?'

'I'm smiling because that's exactly what my mother's always said. I could never explain to her that Hester was a painter in her own right.'

'But she's not, Robert. At least not at the moment and, if I read the signs correctly, I think the time will come when she will no longer be considered seriously as a top-class painter. In fact I think you should consider your position very carefully.'

Robert rested his chin on his hand, like Rodin's Thinker.

Betty crouched elegantly beside him, the crisp white linen of her suit stretched tightly over her long thighs.

'Do you know what Waldo would do if I could no longer come up to scratch as a wife?'

At close quarters Robert looked into her sapphire coloured eyes.

'I think I can guess.'

'Too right. He'd ditch me. Top men can't afford a wife who can't cope. Look, Robert my dear. It's all the more true for men like you. I know it sounds tough but you have to remember that you're an artist and your responsibility is to your work like any artist worth his salt. I'm touched by your concern for Hester but I also care very much about art. And I very much care at the moment about yours.'

'I see what you mean.'

Betty stood up and went across to her chair where she retrieved her bag, a small black leather envelope depending from a fine gilt chain. She turned to face him again. 'After all, Robert, you're not some two-bit painter, you have a terrific career in front of you, so don't let anyone screw it up. The artist owes it to society and to his patrons, if I may say so, to be somewhat self-centred. So you want support and encouragement? What d'you think I'm here for?'

He stood up as she prepared to leave. He was still pensive. Briefly she held her hand against his cheek. 'Think about it,' she commanded. 'Tell me what you decide to do when you come tonight.'

'Tonight!'

She smiled. 'You Brits!' she said, without explanation, and was gone.

For minutes afterwards he prowled round the studio agitatedly, sometimes stopping to examine the area of paint that had been applied that morning, sometimes standing at the narrow window and gazing out at the roofs of the building opposite and the maze of fire escapes below it. Then he stood looking blankly at nothing at all although his brain seethed with entirely new vistas.

His original motive for putting the Clifton house on the market had been only half serious, a stratagem to smoke Hester out and bring her to New York, to remind her of her duty towards him and her promise of moral support. She had been too long in Devon, at least ten days, and he didn't like it. Now he saw that he had inadvertently provided himself with a positive course of action, which would at the same time guarantee him enough capital to remain in New York even beyond the two years to which he was already committed. Previously he had seen only his status as an artist as being important, not necessarily the possession of money. Here he mixed with the very rich in a way he had never done before and he was beginning to see that he would not get far without at least some financial security. The Clifton house would fetch nearly half a million, even in the current recession. It was a start. Money had never been important to Hester but if she insisted on sharing the proceeds she knew where to come. If she dragged her feet about New York as she had been doing so far then she would only have herself to blame for her comparative poverty.

Much later, as she lay naked by his side, Caroline noticed his preoccupation. She also detected the lingering suggestion of Betty Hirsch's scent about him. A sexual connection was, she knew, hardly credible, but as her knowledge of Robert deepened she was beginning to believe that sex, even the very specific variety that she had to offer, was not enough, even when backed up by the publication of flattering articles in glossy periodicals. Betty Hirsch had influence and money, a great deal of money, and although she was barely aware of Caroline's existence she would be a new and formidable rival. Robert's dependence on Hester was almost visibly diminishing but at the same time his reliance on La Hirsch was increasing daily. Her guess that Hester's failing reputation as a painter would lower her standing in Robert's eyes had been right; he was already showing signs of uneasiness, as if he might be tainted by the association. But what to do about Betty Hirsch was even now giving her anxious moments.

Robert turned to her. 'Let's do that again,' he said, putting his hand on her silky pubic hair. This at least was a good sign – twice running had never before been possible – but tonight there was something decisive about him, something almost like elation.

CHAPTER TWENTY-EIGHT

Alice was up sitting beside her bed, looking candle pale. Ezra was ebullient, not artificially assumed for the occasion, Hester thought gloomily, but his usual self. He had brought Alice a huge bag of cherries, which he dumped on her lap as he kissed her extravagantly on both cheeks.

'Now look, Alice my old friend,' he said cheerfully. 'You can't come the old soldier like this, you know. Anyone can see you're as fit as a butcher's dog.'

Alice didn't seem to mind this exaggerated approach, in fact she seemed more pleased to see Ezra than she did Hester. Hester couldn't blame her, the issue of Amy and Paul stood between them, poisoning their friendship.

She gave Alice a pile of letters and cards (she'd removed the bills and anything that looked remotely like a communication from either Paul or Reg Gammon).

'And I've brought a copy of *Painting Now* which arrived for me,' Hester said. 'I don't know why, I certainly didn't order it.'

Alice pulled a face. 'I'll look at the pretty pictures.'

'There's the article about Robert in it which should amuse you. And my name is mentioned in a derogatory kind of way.' She grinned. 'But I shouldn't waste your energy on it.'

'She's joining the Ishmaelites,' Ezra said, helping himself to cherries out of the bag.

'I don't like the sound of it at all. I don't think I'll read it,' Alice said. 'What's the news of the Cider Press? Have you been up there recently?'

'I have, and it's progressing very well. Everything's done that can be done until we get the go-ahead for the living accommodation. Susan's still waiting for that.'

Alice looked at Hester gravely. 'And you're still sure you want to go through with this?'

'More sure than ever.'

'Ezra, I think you should take her away and give her a serious talk about fools rushing in and all that kind of thing.'

'I'll leave that to the accountants,' he said. 'I think any enticement that will lure her away from Cork Street has a lot to recommend it. What shall I do with these cherry stones?'

'That's your problem,' Alice said unsympathetically. 'You shouldn't have eaten so many.'

The interior of the barn in late June was, if anything, darker and greener than it had been just a short time ago. The roof was now half submerged in a Niagara of leaves that pressed against the windows.

Hester gazed disconsolately at the painted image of Richard's well-endowed girlfriend which had acquired more than a hint of pea-green since she had last seen it; perhaps Richard had been influenced by the viridescence of the light. In the background he had added a patchwork of one-armed bandits and fruit machines.

'Is there some significance there that I'm failing to pick up?' she remarked.

'There is to Richard, whether he realises it or not,' Ezra said. He stood behind her and wrapped his arms round her shoulders. 'Alice is definitely improving so why the long face?'

'Oh, you know, things.'

'No, I don't know because you don't tell me. Why don't we sit down, have a drink and discuss the whole thing. I'd really like to know what I'm supposed to be worrying about on your behalf.'

He went to the fridge and poured two beers; then they sat on the rug-strewn sofa and Hester told him most, if not all, of what had happened in Bristol in the preceding weeks. She spoke hesitantly, the pain and hopelessness of the situation raw in her voice.

'And now he's selling the house. It's his, he says, so he can sell it if he likes,' she said bleakly.

'I think that sounds like the best idea he's had yet.' Ezra said. 'It will surely help you to buy the Cider Press, won't it?'

'I think he's doing it to bring me back to New York. Then there's Amy to consider . . .'

'Amy's young. She'll settle down in some flat with a bunch of other students. It will be a whole lot better than rattling around in the Clifton house all on her own.' He took a swig of his beer. 'Now, how I see it is this, speaking as a rank outsider of course . . . Whether he knows it or not, Robert is trying to tell you in the only way he seems to know how, that the marriage is over, finished, kaput.' He sliced the side of his hand down on his knee. 'End of problem. You can pay off your overdraft with the proceeds of the sale and settle down in your little eyrie at the top of the town. Only one drawback, as I see it.'

'Which is?'

'You'll be alone.'

'That's the idea.'

'Not a very good one, my friend. What you should do is divorce Robert and marry me.'

She threw him an amused glance but it appeared that he was quite serious.

'Oh, yes? And how long d'you think that would last?'

'Indefinitely. Why not?'

'Because you're you and because I don't actually think I want to be married to anyone anymore.'

'If you could get used to the idea that I might *occasionally* stray from the straight and narrow but would always come back with my tail between my legs, I think I can guarantee that it would be one hell of a lot of fun.'

'How about keeping me in the style to which I am accustomed?' she said, smiling.

'I don't get the impression that you're all that much attached to it,' he said with dignity. 'And since I'm not after your loot, let's keep money out of it.'

She put a hand on one of his that was resting on his knee. 'Look, Ezra,' she said. 'I'm seriously fond of you, really I am, but it wouldn't work. Let's just keep it as it is, shall we?'

He turned to her, pulling her to him until her face rested against his rough textured shirt. 'Why so bloody independent?' he grumbled.

'That's just it. I thought I was but I'm not. Perhaps now is the time to give it a try.'

'I'd let you have all the independence you wanted,' he argued.

'When you consider how you worded that, you'll understand what I'm talking about,' she said.

Bewildered, he shook his head. Then he kissed her. 'Time to put a stop to all this brain work and get down to the purely physical.' Gently he removed her loose cotton shirt and then his own, pulling her head on to his broad chest. She felt his hands on her back and her breasts, and his lips and beard on her mouth.

He was physically very unlike Robert but it was a difference she found seductive, mostly, she realised because she associated it with the only things in her present existence that represented peace, stability and tenderness.

* * *

The following day it all started again. Leaving the shop to April she drove to Bristol, found with difficulty a parking place and went straight to the offices of the estate agents, Sturmers. They were scrupulously courteous, sympathetic even.

'But you see,' said the man with the waistcoat, 'We are bound to respect the wishes of the owner in this and I'm afraid he's intent on selling.'

'But over our heads?'

'I agree this is extremely unfortunate and I can assure you we don't like it any more than you do but . . .' He made a gesture that suggested that there was nothing he could do about it.

'But as the market is at the moment you can't turn down the possible sale of nearly half a million's worth of house,' she said acidly. She felt rather than saw that the other employees of Sturmers were now covertly listening.

'We can only act as we are instructed,' he said stiffly.

'And if we won't let you in.'

'We have our own keys,' he said.

'There are ways round that.'

'Mrs Gibb,' he said. 'Far be it from me to advise you on this but I think that perhaps you should raise your objections with your husband at the first possible opportunity. It is not in our remit to do anything other than what we are instructed to do by the bona fide owner. As it happens we already have a possible buyer. We showed him over the property this morning and I have to say that he was very favourably impressed. I do assure you that given the present downturn in the market you will be getting an extremely fair price. Perhaps you should reconsider your objections . . .'

'Thank you but I don't want to be told by you what I should be considering. I would just like some say in something as important as the sale of my house . . .'

The man shook his head sorrowfully and since there was nothing more she could do or say, beyond making even more of a fool of herself, she turned and left, aware of the murmur of general comment behind her.

Back at the house there were signs that both Amy and Gina were in residence but both were out, Amy doing her last few days of market research and Gina at the polytechnic.

She tried Robert's number and got only a recorded message. He had left a message of his own asking that the rest of his summer clothes be sent on to him in New York. This request she ignored, wondering that he could ask any favours at all when he was acting with such unpardonable high-handedness. There was, it seemed, nothing else she could do except to telephone her solicitor who told her that legally Robert was within his rights but if she wanted to take further action perhaps she would like to discuss it? She would, whatever happened, be entitled to half the proceeds of the sale of the house. Fuming with frustration and humiliation she left a note on the kitchen table for Amy and drove back to Coombe Ferrers. By the time she got as far as the turn-off for Taunton she was beginning to come to the conclusion that perhaps she shouldn't resist the inevitable. If Robert was serious, and it really seemed that he was, perhaps she should let it happen. Ezra could be right after all; despite evidence to the contrary this might well be Robert's way of telling her he had at last accepted that the marriage was over.

Amy received both Robert's recorded message and Hester's note. There didn't seem much more she could do about the sale of the house except to resolve to be as obstructive as possible about viewing, but since there were no more visits from either estate agents or potential buyers there was no opportunity to put these tactics into practice; she and Gina were left in peace. She had a telephone call from Hester on the evening of her mother's visit suggesting that she allowed Sturmers in if she happened to be home when they called. Amy thought Hester was giving in too easily and said so.

'Please do as I say, Amy,' Hester said. 'My quarrel is with Robert, not with Sturmers.'

'If that's what you want,' Amy said, acquiescing reluctantly.

It was not until the weekend that she had time to attend to her father's request for his clothes to be sent on. She made enquiries with a local international carrier and then returned home and went up to her father's room. There she took all his Louis Vuitton suitcases from the built-in cupboard in his bedroom and emptied his wardrobe of his summer clothes, casting them all on his bed in a heap. Then she opened his drawers and placed his underclothes, shirts, socks and shoes in piles on the floor. She packed everything with far more attention to detail than she ever lavished on her own belongings. Her father was meticulous about his clothes, she knew that, but she had never before realised that he had quite so *many*; and these were just the ones he'd left behind.

The shoes in cloth bags went in at the bottom, followed by neatly folded socks, underclothes, trousers and jackets. On the top went jerseys and shirts, but in each suitcase she left a small nest-like space.

After that she struggled downstairs with them each in turn, glad that Gina was not there to ask questions. Gina had gone with her boyfriend to help launch a hot-air balloon, but wasn't sure if she was to go up in it or not.

Amy took all the suitcases into Robert's studio and threw back the lids. She took her time selecting the last item for inclusion. There was a choice of black, white, umber, grey and a dark red, like old blood. She liked the red. Robert frequently used both matt and gloss house paints and some of these had already been partly used. She attacked the lids with a screwdriver, prising them up to make quite sure that they were loose, then she tucked them down into their ready-made nests, one to each suitcase. With the suitcase flat on the floor she made quite sure that the tins were bedded down in an upright position, and when she moved them into the hall to await the carrier and attached their labels, she saw to it that they remained that way. She couldn't be responsible for what happened after that, could she? she thought bitterly.

As she finished her afternoon's work the doorbell rang and, suspecting it was Sturmers wanting to view, she opened the door cautiously. It was Paul. He was in shorts and a tee shirt and he was very brown.

'Hi, there!' he said cheerfully.

'What are you doing up here?'

'Just felt like paying you a flying visit. Aren't you going to let me in?'

She opened the door grudgingly.

'What's the matter?' he said. He reached out and drew her to him by her belt. He kissed her but she turned away grimacing.

'What's up. Have you got your period?'

'No, I haven't got my period.'

'PMT then?'

'Shut up, dumbo,'

'Aren't you going to offer me a cup of coffee?'

She stumped off towards the kitchen. 'Come on then.'

'I do like enthusiastic welcomes,' he said equably. 'Who's going away?'

'No one. Why?'

'All those suitcases.'

'They're Robert's.'

'Is he staying in New York indefinitely then?'

'Looks like it. He's selling the house.'

'This house!' Paul's sun-bleached eyebrows shot up. He sat himself on a kitchen chair turned the wrong way round. 'That was sudden, wasn't it?'

'It's his house. He can sell it if he wants to.'

'Sure he can. What will you do?'

'Me? Oh, I can doss down anywhere, you don't have to worry about me.'

He looked at her suspiciously. 'Don't tell me you'll have to join the grown-ups!'

Her hand hesitated over her own Capricorn mug and Hester's Aries but she finally chose an anonymous one with a blue border. She put instant coffee into it.

'Very funny. *Trés amusant*.'

'Aren't you having coffee?'

'No. I don't feel like it.' She poured boiling water into the mug and handed it to him.

'Where will Hester live?'

'I don't know. New York, Coombe Ferrers. You tell me.'

'If she comes to live down our way I suppose I shall have to get the hell outa Dodge City. That town ain't big enough for the both of us.'

'Why? Yes, of course.' She looked away.

He did not tell her that he had been forced to find alternative accommodation over the Coombe Ferrers newsagent's. He put sugar in the coffee and drank. When he set the mug down again he reached across and stroked her bare arm. 'Let's do it,' he said softly.

'If you like.'

He got up and went round the table to her. She put up no resistance to his urgent caresses and let him lead her upstairs. There was no chasing, no hiding and no laughter. Afterwards she got up straightaway. Paul slept for half an hour. When he woke he saw that Amy was gone so he rolled lazily out of bed and put on his tee shirt and shorts. The body hair that had been exposed to the sun was like platinum dust on his brown skin. He knew he looked good and couldn't understand her less than enthusiastic response to his lovemaking.

He found her on the landing wrapping her Egyptian goddesses in layers of newspaper and bubblewrap, after which she placed them carefully in a tea chest. It wasn't until then that he realised that her bedroom had looked empty of its usual clutter. He crouched beside her.

'If you didn't want to go to bed why didn't you say so? I don't get it.' he said kindly.

She didn't answer.

'Come on, for God's sake stop messing about with that and tell me what's up?' He grabbed her hands, busy with newspaper and held them. She remained inert.

'If you must know,' she said. 'I think it's over.'

'You mean us! You're not serious, you can't be. It's hardly begun.'

'It began. It finished. That's all there is to it.'

'But we're great together. It's been terrific fun.'

'Fun? Yes, I suppose so. But as you said just now, I've joined the grown-ups.'

'You won't find many guys who can give you such a good time in bed.'

She regarded him broodingly. 'That could well be true, but sex isn't everything and besides I seem to have gone off men for the moment.'

'Amy, for God's sake! Join the grown-ups by all means but not the bloody feminists.'

'Look, do you mind going now. I've rather a lot to do.'

Paul stood up abruptly and looked down at where she crouched on the floor. 'You sodding little cow!'

'Please?'

'Look, if I go I don't come back. When I walk out of the door, that's it, see.'

She stood up slowly, looking at him. She wondered if what she was doing was complete madness. He was young, goodlooking, fun and they were sexually compatible. If he left now she could look forward to a lonely summer just when she most needed something or someone to distract her.

'I'm sorry,' she said.

He went towards the stairs. His hand on the newel, he said, 'I'm off then.'

'Goodbye, Paul.' She smiled wanly. 'It was good while it lasted, really it was.'

'Women!' he said. 'I'm buggered if I can understand what goes on in your heads half the time. I thought we had it made.'

She held out her hand politely. 'It was nice knowing you.'

He took her hand, looking bemused.

'Christ!' he said. 'Well then . . . goodbye.'

He went downstairs shaking his head, let himself out of the front door and drove back to Coombe Ferrers.

Amy went back to packing her belongings which she did meticulously using many layers of newspaper and bubble wrap. Now and again a tear ran off her nose and fell into the tea chest. She had never felt so desolate in her life.

CHAPTER TWENTY-NINE

Gozo had everything well in hand: the publicity, the caterers, the last-minute cleaners, the electricians putting the finishing touches to the lighting; yet in spite of this Eustace whirled anxiously about the newly waxed floor, getting in everybody's way. He was unusually spruce in a new linen suit of susceptibly pale cream which he wore with a pink shirt and a coffee coloured bow tie. He bore a passing resemblance to a Neapolitan ice cream which before the evening was out would show distinct signs of melting.

He had been lavish with the invitations but lately had been waking up at three or four in the morning in his enormous bed after nightmares in which on the evening of the Great Opening *no one had come*. It had taken all Gozo's powers of persuasion to convince him that all would be well. Before that the substance of Eustace's nightmares had been simply that, come the day, the new gallery would not be ready. However, neither mishap was destined to occur. The doors had been opened with a flourish and a thin trickle of less important guests was already arriving. All Eustace had to worry about now was the eventual appearance of his guests of honour, the Hirschs.

Gozo was at his side, his hair slicked back in twenties style. He had on a sludge-coloured suit and a green and white striped shirt which for him was restrained.

'This is it then,' he said cheerfully. 'Thank God it's fine.' Eustace looked round the gallery. 'You've done a splendid job, dear boy. Absolutely splendid.'

That it was splendid seemed to be the general consensus. The old bottle factory had taken on a completely new lease of life. The pink brick exterior had been cleaned and the window frames painted, the bay where lorries once delivered or loaded made an imposing entrance; large glass doors with the name Lombards across them in black now took up most of the space. Inside, the top two of the four storeys had been used to house the gallery, linked in the centre by an open staircase. At intervals over the huge area of each floor were the supporting brick pillars, like punctuation marks. On three sides new inner walls had been built ten feet inside the outer shell which preserved the windows in their original state and provided more exhibition space.

On the side next to the Regent's Canal windows had been put in that extended between both floors, and doors led out on to a roof garden where large sculptures could be shown. On this fine August evening the doors had been thrown open, and a good thing too, Eustace thought, surreptitiously dabbing at his neck with his handkerchief, it was almost too hot.

'Where's Bruno?' he asked Gozo in between greeting new arrivals. 'He should be here.'

'You know Bruno. Not the extrovert type, is he?'

'I think he's getting worse lately.' Eustace stopped to pounce on André Veck who had just slouched in. 'André, dear boy!'

André grunted and made for the crate of Fosters which had been brought in specially for him and secreted behind the drinks table.

'A man of few words, our André,' Eustace said. Gozo only snorted.

'I'm particularly pleased with the lighting,' Eustace went on imperturbably. ' "Lighting is the first of painters." Emerson.'

'Decent lighting has made all the difference to Hester's "FourSquare",' Gozo said slyly. 'I love it.'

Eustace grunted. He'd had a tussle with Gozo over the siting of that particular painting and Gozo had won.

'Yes, well,' he temporised. 'I had to include one of Hester's paintings.'

'You sound as if you begrudge her the space. Come on now, she's one of our best.'

'Was one of our best. Lately not pulling her weight, I regret to say.'

'She *is* coming tonight, isn't she?'

Eustace shrugged.

'I do believe you're still sore about Sagar's article,' Gozo hissed. 'You've taken it seriously!'

'Sagar is influential. I'd be a B.F. not to.'

'Talk of the devil,' Gozo breathed.

Kurt Sagar approached, holding out his hand, his thin brownish lips pursed into the approximation of a smile. Eustace grabbed the hand, holding on to it a second too long. Sagar glanced round the gallery with eyes that missed nothing.

'Congratulations,' he said in the characteristic, breathy voice so well known on arts programmes. 'This looks extremely promising.

Quite a change of ambience. I do like the idea of the division of space. And such space! Still quintessentially Lombards however.'

'The idea, you see, is to be able to have one show running and one in preparation,' Eustace gushed. 'Besides having the actual physical height to show even the largest work. That André Vèck on the end wall, for instance. *That's* what I wanted you to see. Impressive, eh?'

He flapped his hand at the painting which was lit dramatically by several spots. It appeared to be a barn door on to which had been nailed a number of sawn-up lorry tyres, subsequently pelted with red paint. Sagar half closed his eyes and nodded in slow motion as if his neck was on a spring. Otherwise he offered no comment except to repeat his compliments about the gallery as a whole. Then he drifted off for a closer appraisal.

Eustace looked after him, his eyebrows oscillating like antennae. 'He seems to approve,' he said.

'Let's wait for the reviews,' Gozo said.

Caroline had taken trouble over her appearance. Jet lag had never had any appreciable effect on her, she was of a type and generation that was tailor made to traverse the globe as casually as they might cross the road.

She travelled light when she could; the outfit she was wearing that evening, bought in New York, had come rolled in an overnight bag and consisted of a short white coat that twinkled with bead embroidery worn over a minimal black tube that scintillated darkly underneath.

Robert had arrived on the same flight but without the same equanimity; there were purple smudges under his eyes which, when Caroline came to think of it, might have been there before though less marked.

They arrived together, an eventuality carefully planned by Caroline though its significance was entirely lost on Robert, if not, she was pleased to see, on some others of those present. She glanced quickly round to check whether or not Hester was one of them and was faintly disappointed to see that she was not.

Eustace waylaid them with open arms.

'You're looking like a million dollars, my dears,' he roared in welcome. Now that the success of the evening looked almost assured his effervescence was increasing by the minute. 'The New World seems to agree with you.'

'Or perhaps it's just the First New World and Union Bank,' Gozo murmured at their side.

'Don't be dreary, Gozo,' Eustace said. 'Go away and be sociable.'

Gozo drifted off and Eustace took another, more searching look at Robert. In spite of what he'd said he thought Robert looked fatigued; not that he necessarily disapproved so long as it was brought on by overwork. If the boy was screwing Caroline too, so be it, since she was his type. It probably meant that he was settling down very well in New York without Hester, for Hester's visits to New York had been curtailed recently. Fortunately Robert seemed not to mind as he once did. Eustace believed that Hester was currently still in Devon. He had been too busy to keep in touch.

'How goes everything?' he asked. Everything being a euphemism for work.

Robert nodded. 'All right. Yes.'

'Did you see our piece about him?' Caroline asked.

'Very good, my dear young lady. Glad you took my advice about the photographs.'

Caroline grimaced at the 'dear young lady' bit. '*And* mentioned in Kurt's article,' she said. 'Not bad, I thought.'

Eustace gave her a shrewd look. He wasn't sure if 'not bad' meant her own efforts or Robert's.

None of them remarked on Sagar's disparaging comments about Hester, or her non-appearance on an occasion at which her absence would once have been considered unthinkable; all that concerned Eustace at the moment was the arrival of the Hirschs. They could justifiably have cancelled at the last minute because of the trouble in the Middle East. If so, they would not be the only Yanks to do so, Eustace thought grimly.

'There they are!' he almost screamed with relief and delight. It would have been hard to miss two such towering individuals. Waldo, tanned and exquisitely tailored, Betty in pale apricot pink with a scattering of diamanté embroidery on one shoulder. There were real diamonds in her hair which tonight was heaped into a sculptural confection. She had paid them the compliment of treating the occasion as a major event.

Eustace left Robert and Caroline and rushed forward to greet the new arrivals.

'Absolutely delighted,' he cried. 'Especially in view of the situation. So brave!' Betty bent to kiss the air beside both Eustace's pink ears in turn. Waldo shook hands heartily.

'This is literally a flying visit,' he said. 'We've had to change our plans and leave early tomorrow,'

'I understand absolutely,' Eustace said.

Waldo looked round. 'Now this is a whole new ball game,' he said. 'The showcase you could have done with several years ago. Better late than never. Not so convenient for the West End though; we had some trouble finding it, didn't we, Bee?'

'It was *worth* a little extra trouble, Waldo! Look at it, after all. And just look at Robert's 'Fracture', now isn't that just breathtaking? What a gift!'

'It surely is,' Waldo nodded. 'Yes, I think you made absolutely the right decision moving here, Eustace. I really think you did.'

Now that he had the Hirschs safely in tow, Eustace took a silent inventory of the cosmopolitan sea of guests. Museum curators, critics, collectors, celebrities and showbiz people, bankers and of course the Press, had turned out in satisfyingly large numbers. Bruno had been all for an unobtrusive opening since the market was so quiet, not helped by talk of war; but unobtrusiveness was not Eustace's style.

'I'm a showman, not an undertaker,' he had grumbled.

Word must have got round that this was the place to be seen in, perhaps because any glitzy distraction was welcome, for the place was filling up. The noise grew.

Then he saw Hester. Her sudden appearance startled him, not solely because he had not seriously expected her to come, but more particularly because of the way she looked. He had believed that if she turned up at all she would at least have done so inconspicuously and modestly as befitted her new status; though what that status was, he wasn't absolutely sure.

For a start he had never seen her wearing her hair loose, let alone in a cloud round her head and decorated with two narrow beaded plaits. Otherwise compared to Betty Hirsch and some of the celebrities she was dressed simply, but it may have been that this in itself attracted attention. Her dress was very dark green, the green of forests and deep pools, which hung in sculpted folds that stirred gently when she moved. With it she wore silver on her hands and in her ears. Certainly she did not look inconspicuous; neither did she look in the least apologetic, so his first instinct which had been one of pity was nipped in the bud. She had done as he'd asked, she had promised to stick with Robert but paradoxically he found himself unable to approve of her. No, he could not pity her and he could not patronise her. One would just as soon pity and patronise the Medusa.

He watched Gozo approach her and give her a spontaneous and

emotional embrace. In the circumstances he guessed that only Gozo could have got away with that.

'Darling! You look gorgeous. Like the hair.' Gozo herded her into a quiet spot beside a pillar. 'So glad you came. Eustace thought you might not.'

'Did he? I wonder why?'

'Because he's being annoyingly prima donna-ish lately, that's why. I'm really not sure about Eustace at the moment. He's also showing signs of inconstancy and disloyalty as I expect you've noticed. I really hate that. One likes to know where one is. Trust is so important, don't you think? I suppose you know who's turning his crank now, do you?'

Hester shook her head, the little plaits swung. Gozo touched them.

'Love these,' he said.

'Do you mean professionally or emotionally?' Hester asked.

'Professionally, I think. But who knows?' He half turned and pointed to the painting made from lorry tyres. 'What d'you think of that?'

'Can't say I'm enthusiastic.'

'Don't you like it, duckie? Listen, my trick to make up my mind as to whether a thing comes up to scratch is to imagine it amongst the clobber and muddle of some dusty old studio or attic. If I think it would look good in spite of that, then it's passed the test.'

'What you're saying is that the rubber tyres failed the attic test?'

'Too right.'

'What's this got to do with Eustace? Are you saying he's lusting after André as well as promoting him like mad?'

Gozo narrowed his eyes and smiled. 'Perhaps he fancies a bit of rough for a change.' He stirred himself into attentiveness.

'What am I thinking of! You haven't got a drink. Now stay exactly where you are, I'll get one.'

Hester put a restraining hand on his arm. 'No. Don't. Tell me, have you seen Robert?'

'Arrived about half an hour ago. What exactly is up between you two?'

'I'd have thought Eustace would have told you.'

'Yes, all right, I've heard the gospel according to Eustace. You know, you don't have to worry about Caroline Childs.' He flicked her a crafty look. He was attempting a tone of confidentiality which was difficult because of the noise of several hundred people all speaking at once.

'Caroline Childs?' Hester repeated.

'The blonde exocet.'

'The current girl?'

'You didn't know?'

'It's not important. Look, Gozo. You see Betty Hirsch standing over there beside Bruno?'

'One can hardly miss her.'

'Now, *she* is the woman to be reckoned with.'

'I think you're wrong there. She's not generally known to have affairs with her artists, duckie. Or if she does she must keep them very, very discreet.'

'Not that either. But if my gut feeling is correct she is going to be my salvation.'

'She's interested in your work?'

'No. Not that I know of.'

'You're being maddeningly obscure. Tell me.'

'Not now, Gozo. I have to find Robert.'

'You do that, darling. See off that blonde cow!'

Hester had approached the evening as an occasion on which she had several distinct pieces of business to attend to and they were her sole purpose for being there. After that there was no reason for her to have any further dealings with Eustace, Robert or the Hirschs. She would get it over with and leave. She was neither apprehensive nor nervous, in fact what she felt was detached, they could all have been perfect strangers.

She made her way through the crowd. The smell of expensive scent, newly waxed floors and the lingering and powerfully evocative hint of oil paint filled the high gallery. The guests radiated the kind of wellbeing that money could buy and sparkled like a starry night.

The exhibition was intended as a showcase for Lombards' brightest talents and there was no doubt that the work looked spectacular on the lofty white walls; all the same, she thought, almost anything would look good there, even André's terrible old tyres.

She felt a vice-like grip on her arm.

'Hi! Some gig, eh?' Melanie Sofford was without her knitted hat and grubby lace. Instead she wore a dusty black dress with part of the back missing. It had a bright yellow snake embroidered on it, starting at her left bosom and finishing on her right buttock. She was fairly drunk, but short of an undignified and unfriendly tussle there was no chance of escape. 'Hallo, Melanie. Glad you could come.'

Melanie waved her glass about. 'Wotcha doing lately? Saw the bit in that rag about you. Sagar's some ratarsed piece of shit, in't he?' Her black-ringed eyes brightened suddenly and she let go of Hester's arm and put out a beringed claw to waylay Sagar himself who was not quite quick enough to take avoiding action.

'Just talking about you,' she cried.

Sagar made an attempt at a dignified response.

'I'm full of admiration for Eustace,' he said speaking rapidly. 'What a courageous venture this is!'

'And you'd know all about courage, wouldn't you, Mr Sagar?' Melanie put the emphasis on the Mr, then added in an ordinary tone of voice. 'What I was actually saying was that I thought you were some rat arsed piece of shit. Isn't that what I said, Hester?'

'Melanie, I think perhaps . . .'

Sagar compressed his lips. Fury burned in his gaunt cheeks. 'If you're referring to my article I can only say that I'm in the business of writing what I consider to be the truth. I don't set out to demolish reputations, as I'm sure Miss Eliot knows.'

'Thank you for trying to put in a word for me, Melanie,' Hester said. 'But it's absolutely immaterial what Mr Sagar writes about me now.'

Melanie shook her head at Hester, 'Who pulled your chain, Hes? Just shut up, will you. This old fairy thinks he can predict the future, in't that so?' She shook his arm, which she had not yet released, none too gently. 'Know someone once who claimed they could do that. Got run over by a milk float!' She shrieked with laughter. Hester saw Eustace through the crowd. He was looking in their direction and though he could not possibly have heard what was said he nevertheless wore a faintly horrified expression. He would blame her for asking Melanie, naturally.

'Well, that's your reputation taken care of,' she said.

'My reputation never did owe anything to the frigging male establishment anyway,' Melanie scoffed.

Sagar repossessed his arm and, with a look of pure venom said. 'One wonders, Miss Sofford, what will be left of your *art*,' He put deliberate and scornful emphasis on the word, 'when you have finished menstruating?'

Melanie giggled helplessly. 'I'll frame my sodding corn plasters and support hose, won't I?'

Hester detached herself in a hurry. Any minute now someone

was going to have to carry Melanie out and she had no intention of staying to see it.

Eustace gave the impression that he was attempting to conceal himself from her behind the gigantic Hirschs but when he saw that she was intent on seeking him out he emerged, pink as a prawn, to greet her.

'Hester!' he cried. 'For a moment there I thought you were going to desert us.'

'Why ever should I do that?' she said sweetly. He kissed her on both cheeks.

'I thought in fact it might be the other way round,' she said and while Eustace blustered she shook hands with the Hirschs. 'Mrs Hirsch, I believe I have you to thank for being so supportive of Robert?'

'Call me Betty,' Betty pleaded. She smiled dazzlingly. It was quite impossible to read her eyes. 'And please don't mention it. I'm renowned for being a complete pussycat where artists are concerned. I'm just so fascinated by the whole process. I hope I haven't been a nuisance to him.' Her eyes widened in a kind of innocent dismay.

'Far from it,' Hester said. 'He's told me how much he appreciates your interest.'

'Robert's so patient with me!' She tossed a little-girl look of complicity to her husband who stood by smiling. He was well aware that his wife's association with Gibb was both innocent and comparatively transitory. He made it his business to know these things; any suggestion of infidelity on his wife's part would be severely dealt with.

'In fact I think he rather depends on your encouragement,' Hester said.

'Is that a fact!' Betty breathed huskily. 'You mean like a Muse?'

A waiter appeared with more champagne. This time Hester took a glass. 'That's right,' she said with a straight face. 'A Muse. The work is going to take at least another two years; do you think you can stick being a Muse for that length of time?' She smiled as if it was a joke but there was a serious question in her eyes. Betty appeared puzzled for perhaps five seconds and then came a dawning light of understanding.

'Oh, I see,' she said. 'Yes, of course. Of *course*. That's if he can put up with *me*,' she laughed gaily. Hester nodded, satisfied.

Eustace and Waldo were vaguely aware that a transaction had taken place but neither was sure what it had been.

'And what goodies do you have in store for us, Hester?' Waldo asked.

Eustace answered for her. 'Hester's taking a sort of extended sabbatical, aren't you, dear girl?' But it was clear to Hester, if barely to the Hirschs, that he was no longer concerned. In his mind, if not in fact, he had already replaced her. André Veck was now the up and coming star of Lombards and indeed in the next breath Eustace trotted out more praise of his new find.

'Socially a bit rough round the edges at the moment,' he said in what passed for a whisper, 'but it's amazing what a few years of success will do.'

'That's right,' Betty said. She wasn't particularly interested in André and was scanning the gallery for Robert.

'I'll say this for André,' Eustace ploughed on. 'He doesn't suffer fools gladly.'

That sounded so much better, Hester thought, than admitting that André was a surly bastard.

Eustace caught sight of the man himself drinking lager out of a can and beckoned him furiously. André slumped over, the laces of his Doc Martens trailing.

'André, dear boy. Let me introduce you to Mr and Mrs Hirsch,' Eustace gushed.

Hester watched sadly, seeing a man dominated by the superficial, the latest fad. Betty caught her look and lifted her glittering shoulders prettily. The gesture seemed to say that while she was prepared to go along with it, she all the same recognised the situation for what it was. But perhaps, Hester thought, she was reading too much into that minimal gesture. She nodded at Betty and turned away. Eustace didn't notice her leave.

Bruno was standing in front of Hester's painting, the only one in this mixed exhibition. Robert had three and even André had two, but very few people were actually looking at the paintings anyway. He liked this one. The shapes were geometric but on a subtle sea of grey-green that suggested movement suppressed and at times almost obliterated by order and restriction. It seemed to sum up what he had always thought of Hester; that there was more there than met the eye, an unfulfilled potential.

'I hate the damn thing.' Hester put her hand through his arm. He turned to her with affection and concern. Obscurely he sensed that she'd had a raw deal though he knew no details.

'Hester. Good. I'm glad you came. You may hate it but it is

actually a very interesting painting.'

'Why do you say that?'

'It tells me, indeed all your paintings tell me, that you are holding something back. As if you were reluctant to let us know who you really were.'

'Are you accusing me of insincerity, Bruno?'

He patted the hand that lay securely against his jacket and felt rather proud to have such a striking woman on his arm.

'Not at all,' he said. 'I just feel as if you had yet to grasp the nettle, as it were. My dear, you're not drinking!'

'I seem to have mislaid the drink I had just now.'

Bruno signalled to a girl with a tray and obtained two more glasses of champagne, or what passed for it.

Hester sipped hers. 'Bruno,' she said. 'You are a very perceptive individual, do you know that?'

'I've always been very interested in your work for the reasons I've just put forward. Besides,' he said with a self-deprecating smile. 'I must confess to having always been just a little in love with you.'

She teased him for having had too much champagne but suddenly realised that he was probably speaking the truth.

'I understand you've taken a studio somewhere in the West Country?' he said.

'Yes, that's right.'

He nodded approvingly. 'Sounds like a very good move.' He looked at her searchingly. 'And what of you and Robert?'

Hester looked into her drink as if into a crystal ball. 'I'm leaving Robert. We're going our separate ways. '

'I'm very sorry.' Though he made the conventional reply, it occurred to Bruno quite forcibly that leaving Robert was the only way Hester was going to be able to develop her full powers as a painter.

He pressed her arm. 'I'm glad you'll be working again. Eustace will be relieved.'

Hester shook her head. 'I'm sorry, Bruno, but I won't be staying with Lombards. I just can't submit myself to this kind of thing anymore.' She indicated their surroundings with a slight movement of her glass. 'I can't believe that it's not possible to survive as a painter without Eustace's brand of hype.'

'It won't be easy but I daresay it's possible.' Bruno turned to face her, looking serious. 'Look, Hester. Since you've been honest with me it behoves me to return the compliment. You and Robert are not the only ones who have come to a parting of the ways. I have to tell you that I too am leaving Lombards . . .'

'But you *are* Lombards! How can you leave?'

'I'm starting again in a small way. The way I've always preferred in my heart of hearts. I like this new gallery, of course I do, but as partners, Eustace and I can hardly run it efficiently when there's such a divergence of taste.'

'But where will you go?'

'I don't know yet. It won't be the West End. Somewhere I can show some very high-quality work to really discerning buyers, I hope. That's why I want to get in first and ask you to think of me when you have something new.'

Hester smiled. 'I didn't think you were interested in living artists?'

'I'm interested in *good* artists and just so long as you're not thinking of working to this scale,' he glanced at the paintings round them, 'perhaps we can do a little business. I backed Eustace as much as possible in this venture but these are not really my thing, you know.'

'I realise that. I think, possibly, they're not mine.'

'I'm sure you'll give it some thought. Unless you're set on hiding your light under a bushel?'

She laughed. 'Probably not. Artists are natural show-offs, I'm afraid.'

'And what a good job they are!' Bruno turned to look through the great crush of bodies. Now that the evening had really got going, flashbulbs were popping for photographs that would eventually appear in some of the glossier magazines. They noticed André posing in front of his second painting, which consisted mostly of motorcycle parts, with his arm rather drunkenly round the shoulders of a very pretty actress.

'You see what I mean by show-offs,' Hester said, smiling.

'There are, after all, degrees.' Bruno admitted. 'And talking of showing off, will you be staying for the fireworks?'

'Are there to be fireworks?'

'Oh, yes. Eustace is going the whole hog. After Betty Hirsch, metaphorically speaking, cuts the tape we are to be treated to a display of pyrotechnics, I understand.'

'Good heavens! Eustace doesn't care about any recession, does he.'

Bruno chuckled.

'Look, Bruno dear, I have to find Robert. Meanwhile, thank you for your offer. I shall certainly bear it in mind.'

'Please do,' He released her hand which he had unconsciously grasped a moment before. 'And, by the way, I'd love to see the new studio some time.'

'Of course you shall. Join me later upstairs on the terrace. We'll watch the fireworks together.'

He watched her go, sensing a perceptible change in her. As if at last she had a purpose and a direction. It inspired him, making him feel full of hope about the course he himself was about to embark upon.

Very large glass doors had been flung open on to the terrace, which was in fact the roof of the smaller building next door. A few people had strayed on to it, either in expectation of the fireworks or merely in search of air.

The night was close and humid and the last of the daylight was draining away behind the distant roofs of Kilburn and further south the Post Office tower stood like an illuminated exclamation mark against the sky. Heaped up against the north and west were the dark trees and glimmering lights of Hampstead. Below the terrace the Regents Canal snaked surreptitiously through the modern city carrying on its back the painted barges of another era. Hester could hardly fail to be impressed. Eustace had chosen his site well.

It was here that she came across Robert who had sought refuge on the terrace to smoke. With him, in a posture that suggested a closer acquaintance than interviewer and interviewed, was Caroline Childs. That there should be something more between them came as no surprise, since Gozo had enlightened her. She should have guessed before: Caroline was so completely his type of woman, she was almost a caricature. Something else also occurred to her that she would have tumbled to long since if her mind had not been on other things; Caroline's visit to Coombe Ferrers and her remarks to Alice were not solely the result of journalistic curiosity, nor was the appearance of Sagar's article in *Painting Now* with the slighting mention of her name, merely coincidental. She did not have to look further for the reason why it was so important to Caroline to damage her; and it was all for nothing. She laid no further claim to Robert, and for this deliverance she was, if anything, grateful, had Caroline only known it.

Robert noticed her first and froze as if he hadn't expected to see her here. Caroline went on talking until Robert's expression caused her to turn round.

'Hallo, Robert.' Hester ignored Caroline.

Robert made no move to kiss her or embrace her. He simply said. 'Hallo, Hester.'

'I think we have something to discuss.'

'Have we?'

'Do you mind leaving us, Miss Childs. It's rather private.'

'Robert doesn't have any secrets from me.'

'I'm sure he doesn't. But I have. Would you mind?'

'If it's about Robert's and my relationship, yes it's true. You had to know sometime.'

Robert looked as if he was going to be sick.

Hester said. 'I couldn't care less what you and Robert get up to.'

'You couldn't? But Robert said . . .'

'No. Now perhaps you'd like to leave us alone. Perhaps you could go and drop some more of your special brand of poison about some other poor sod into Sagar's receptive ear?'

Caroline was caught momentarily off guard. Then she collected herself. 'I don't know what the fuck you mean by that!' she said; but she went.

'That was uncalled for, if I may say so,' Robert said. 'There's absolutely nothing between us, you know. Nothing important.' He picked up his glass from the parapet wall and drank.

'She seems to think there is. Anyway that's not what I came to talk to you about. I most certainly don't care what you do with either Caroline Childs or Betty Hirsch.'

'Betty Hirsch! Now that *is* absurd.' Robert put down his glass. 'In any case I don't believe that this is either the time or the place for discussions of a personal nature.'

'I couldn't care less what time or place it is. Since this is the last time we shall meet it will have to do.'

'What in heaven's name are you talking about, Hester?' He glanced round. The terrace was filling up. Betty Hirsch would soon declare the gallery open and press the button to set off the first of the fireworks. Robert saw that Caroline had not gone far, in the hope of overhearing what passed between himself and Hester.

'First of all,' Hester said unemotionally. 'It must be quite clear to even you that we have to separate. I want a divorce.'

Robert said nothing. He reached for a fresh cigarette.

'And there's something else. I rang the estate agents today and they say the house is finally sold. It would have been nice to have been told.'

'I had to do it. I've explained about that. I needed the money. It's not cheap living in New York.'

'Presumably you've given some thought as to what is to happen to Amy?'

'You'll find something for Amy. Kids of that age don't mind where they live. Besides, Amy has a side to her that you're too soft to see. She can be inordinately vindictive.'

'That's ridiculous. But of course I shall find somewhere for her to live just as I've found somewhere to live myself.'

'I presume you'll be with me in New York. Because the proceeds of the Salisbury Square house won't stretch to keeping two establishments.

'I shall be living in Devon.'

Robert tapped ash from his cigarette thoughtfully. In that moment Hester knew that she was no longer important to him; she saw with enormous relief that her role as provider of emotional and moral support had already been filled by someone else.

'In that case, if you insist on living elsewhere,' Robert said. 'You will have to make your own financial arrangements.'

'I guessed you had something like this in mind. Live with you in New York or forfeit my share of the money? Except that you *don't* want me there after all, do you?'

'You must do as you like, but I wish you'd try to understand about the money. If you choose to sell the contents of the house I'd have no objections to you keeping the proceeds.'

'That is most generous of you.' Hester discovered that she was still holding the drink supplied by Bruno. She took a sip. Then she said, 'And I want to talk to you about your mother.'

'My *mother*? For God's sake!'

'You remember her then? The woman who encouraged you and who still worships the ground you walk on in spite of being ignored and despised?'

'You're being overemotional as usual. In any case, what the hell has my mother to do with anything? Why bring her into the discussion? You don't even like my mother.'

'Your mother wrote to me. I think she'd appreciate a visit while you're here.'

'You know I haven't time for that.'

'Have it your own way, Robert,' Hester said quietly.

She was aware that there were more people on the terrace now and that some were eavesdropping on their discussion. There was a stir as Betty Hirsch mounted a small rostrum and spoke into a microphone. She began a pretty little speech about Lombards.

Hester went to stand next to Robert by the parapet.

'I'm only just beginning to discover how devious and self-centred you are,' she said.

'For God's sake leave it, will you. I'm trying to hear what Betty has to say.' Betty's voice sailed lightly above the popping of flashbulbs and the crackling of the microphone.

'Your mother will be loyal to the last, Robert,' Hester spoke loudly enough for Robert to hear distinctly what she said in spite of the general racket. She couldn't help it if one or two of those nearest to them also heard. 'Even if you hurt her. Like you've hurt Amy. As it happens she loves you and all you've done is ignore her, treat her as if she didn't exist. You had the chance lately of winning her sympathy and good opinion indefinitely, yet you managed to balls it up.'

'Amy's a spoilt brat, but presumably she'll grow up eventually.'

'And then there's me.'

'You can't say that you have cause for complaint . . .'

'I think you started to lose me when I realised how utterly unconcerned you were about the miscarriage.'

'Don't for God's sake try *that* line on me. You didn't want the kid yourself.' He lowered his voice though his anger was visibly building. At that moment the first firework shot into the night sky and burst in a coloured waterfall of stars. There was a cheer and applause.

'No, and I hated myself for it. I wanted you to feel the same but you didn't. You rejoiced that your cosy, self-absorbed little world was not going to be disturbed after all . . .'

'In any case, how did I know that the kid was mine anyway?'

'What did you say?'

Some of those near them who had been following snatches of the conversation all along and who had been only momentarily distracted by the speeches and fireworks now covertly turned their attention back to what promised to be a more interesting sideshow.

Robert spoke in a rough whisper. 'The way you've been acting lately gives me some grounds for doubting that the kid was mine. That's what I said.'

'Hester.' She was aware of Bruno at her side. 'Hester, please . . .'

Another firework whooshed into the air, exploding with a loud bang and showering light.

'*You're* accusing *me*?'

'I don't want to discuss it. And most particularly I don't want to discuss it here.' Robert picked up his drink from the parapet and turned his back on her. Caroline stepped forward and stood beside him.

'Robert, come with me. There's someone I want you . . .' she began.

Hester grabbed Robert's arm and spun him round. 'Don't you dare turn your back on me, Robert. I want an answer.'

'Go to hell!'

'Hester!' Bruno repeated. Hester looked down at the glass in her hand which was still almost full.

'Yes, Bruno,' Robert said fatally. 'For God's sake get her out of here.'

The champagne hit his face and the front of his loose Armani jacket at the precise moment that several fireworks at once shot up, burst and rained a thousand stars. There was a shocked silence from most of the onlookers but one or two of the drunker guests, mostly other artists who for a number of reasons heartily disliked Robert Gibb, gave a small cheer.

Robert instantly reached for a clean folded handkerchief and dabbed at his face and jacket, white with suppressed fury. Caroline, who had not entirely escaped Hester's champagne, flapped at herself with a paper napkin, swearing audibly.

Hester turned away.

'Bully for you!' Melanie hissed in her ear and for the first time Hester realised she must have been there all along.

She turned to Bruno. 'Now, Bruno. Let's watch the fireworks, shall we?' She put her hand back on his arm.

'That was quite a night's work,' he said smiling. 'But I'm afraid that what Eustace has laid on can't quite compete.'

Behind them Robert and Caroline pushed their way out of the throng and made for the stairs.

CHAPTER THIRTY

It was Gina who suggested carrot cake and it had immediately seemed precisely the right thing. Flowers were unoriginal and Amy knew that Alice tried hard not to eat chocolates; in any case Amy was of the opinion that an offering that required some effort on her part would at least go some way to demonstrate that she was in earnest.

That was how she and Gina came to spend an afternoon in Gina's shared flat, baking. It turned out to be more fun than Amy expected. Gina grated the carrots and Amy beat the sugar and eggs and chopped the walnuts. When the cake was in the oven she rushed out to the shops before they closed since she had suddenly decided that it wouldn't be complete without butter icing and marzipan decoration.

That night she was up late helping Hester to pack last-minute items for the carriers on Monday. There wasn't very much, mostly rugs and books, the rest having been sold. The following day Hester drove to Swindon to see Granny Gibb. Amy had not told her mother what her own plans were; now that her mind was made up she didn't think she could bear it if Hester tried to dissuade her.

She took the train to Exeter St David and, discovering the bus for Coombe Ferrers had left half an hour before, she hitched the rest of the way.

It would be the first time she had seen Alice since before the operation and she silently rehearsed what she had to say as she made her way up the lane. By the time she pushed open the garden gate she had a pain in her stomach from anxiety. The idea of the cake suddenly seemed paltry and insulting after what had happened, it must surely be one of her crasser ideas. She would leave the thing by the gate, perhaps then Alice would think it had been left by the old man who was always hanging about. She would go back without seeing Alice at all. She was about to put her thought into practice when she remembered that sooner or later she would have to face Alice again and then probably with other people present; better to get a painful situation over with now, in private.

She gathered what remained of her courage and went into the garden. Grapes hung in great clusters from the vine over the verandah, small in size but ripening to the translucence of wine. Her hand was trembling and her palm sweaty as she knocked on the kitchen door and when Alice answered it she felt her cheeks go hot with embarrassment.

'Amy! What a lovely surprise. Come in, sweetie, come in.'

Alice kissed and hugged her as if everything was normal; she was without a stick and moved easily about the kitchen.

'I was just going to make lunch,' she said. 'What would you say to a mushroom omelette?'

'Oh, God. I'd forgotten it was lunchtime,' Amy tripped over her words awkwardly. 'I'm sorry, I didn't mean . . . Yes, I would love an omelette.'

'Not like you to forget lunch,' Alice gave her a shrewd look. 'But we'll have a drink first, shall we? Let's go in the other room, it's a bit breezy to sit outside.' She led the way into the sitting room and poured two glasses of dry sherry. They sat in the high-backed armchairs, Amy stiff and on edge.

'I don't think I've ever had sherry before,' she said.

'That doesn't surprise me.'

'You're walking terribly well. Are you pleased with your new hip? Does it hurt anymore?'

'I'm not quite back to normal yet but they say I'm doing very well. The best thing of all is that it doesn't hurt. I'm a new woman. No more pain, it's like being in heaven.'

'I'm really very, very glad . . . You can't imagine . . .' Amy heard her voice trail into silence, remembering Alice's life hovering in the balance. Then she thought of the cake and delved into her bag to lift out the large tin which she had been so careful to carry upright. She had wrapped it in paper with a design of shells on it. She handed it to Alice, almost dropping it in her confusion. 'This is for you,' she said.

Alice put down her sherry and did battle with the wrapping.

'A present! How gorgeous.' She opened the tin and revealed the cake. Amy had made Matisse cut-outs of marzipan and coloured them in bright primaries.

'I knew it was your birthday in a day or two,' Amy said. 'It's a sort of birthday present.'

'It looks absolutely scrumptious. You surely didn't make this yourself, did you?'

'Yes, I hope it's all right. I never actually made one before but I thought that as long as I followed the recipe exactly nothing too horrendous could go wrong . . .' Now that she had started she rushed on, the words tumbling out. 'Only I wanted to do something different to say that I was sorry about . . . what happened. I really am. I expect you know I'm not seeing him anymore, only after Steve and I broke up I was feeling like shit and then there were the rows between Mum and Dad about the house and the separation. It was all so perfectly bloody . . .' She stopped for breath. 'Oh, God. I'm going O.T.T. again, aren't I.' Scalding water ran into her eyes and began to spill over. She scrabbled for a tissue. 'Sorry about this. Crying a lot is one of my many weak points . . .'

Alice got up, which she did now almost with ease, and went to Amy. She perched beside her and put an arm round the hunched, despondent shoulders.

'It doesn't matter, Amy. It honestly doesn't matter,' she said. 'A lot's changed since I had that little hiccup after surgery. Believe me, if it hadn't been you, it would have been someone else.'

'D'you think so?' Amy said through a layer of wet tissue.

'I know so. I confess that at first I was very angry and hurt but that's over now. I've had time to come to my senses and to accept the fact that Paul is as he is. It's not necessarily because he's young. I daresay that if I'd had the sense to choose a steadier young man it could have lasted indefinitely despite the age difference, but you need only ask your mother to know that I was temperamentally incapable of choosing anyone like that.'

'You said was. *Was* temperamentally incapable?'

'Yes, I did, didn't I? Perhaps I've changed.'

'Because of nearly dying?'

'I don't think I nearly died. That's a bit dramatic, but it may have made a difference, yes.'

'I feel terribly guilty about that. I thought Paul and I may have killed you . . . I wasn't thinking straight, everything seemed to be going down the tubes, so it didn't seem to matter. What a complete idiot.'

'If anything nearly killed me,' Alice said. 'It was my own anger. You can get angry about anything, you know.'

Alice actually sounded amused and Amy glanced up at her.

'I think you're a tremendously nice person,' she said. 'No wonder my mother likes you and always keeps in touch. You are her oldest and closest friend, did you know that?'

'I'm not too happy about the "old" but I should say she is also mine, make no mistake.'

'You've helped her a lot this year. D'you know, before all this happened . . .' Amy paused while she returned the ball of wet tissue to her pocket. 'Before this happened she was like two quite different people. One was the tremendously successful painter, doing terribly well in public life, very gregarious and self confident. And the other . . .' She paused again. Alice went back to sitting in her own chair so that she could study Amy's face. In it she read puzzlement and a dawning sense of discovery.

'The other was someone quite ordinary, yet not ordinary because of taking responsibility for everything and being worried by things. Most people didn't know that person at all. Do you know where she is now?'

Alice shook her head.

'She's belted off to Swindon. Apparently Granny Gibb, who she's never got on with, has had to go into hospital so she calls on Hester to help her with things. And do you know why I think she went?'

Again Alice shook her head, her eyes round with the fascination of watching a more grown-up Amy emerge.

'Because of Inez. She always felt very bad about Inez dying so suddenly when she was busy and didn't have time. You see Robert won't go to see Granny. He hates things like that, illness and so on. He says it makes him physically ill himself and then he can't work.'

'I think you've got something there,' Alice said. 'About Hester and Inez, at least. I can't comment on Robert.'

'You see,' Amy said. 'Her dashing off to Swindon is another example of how she feels she has to take responsibility for absolutely everything. No wonder she nearly had a nervous breakdown.'

'But she's very much better now?'

'There's no comparison. She's suddenly looking ten years younger.'

'So you're not too upset about your father moving to America?'

Amy shook her head. 'Not after what he did.' She snapped off the words briskly.

Alice picked up her glass, sipped thoughtfully and waited.

'Do you know what I did?' Amy went on. 'I mean, I see it now as terribly childish behaviour but I'm not really sorry all the same. He wanted his clothes sent on so I did as he asked and packed them up very carefully and had the carriers call for them . . . all his lovely suitcases . . .'

Alice put her head on one side attentively.

'But in each one I put a pot of paint with the lid off.'

'You mean, with his clothes?' Alice said.

'It was an awful thing to do, wasn't it? All those lovely clothes and those beautiful cases. I don't regret it but I am sorry I spoiled all those nice things . . .'

'So, if you had the chance again, you wouldn't do it?' Alice said, beginning to smile.

'No, I wouldn't. I'd send them to Oxfam.'

Alice choked slightly over her sherry and had to put her glass down. She got out her handkerchief and tried to catch her laughter in it but it was too late. It escaped and her eyes squeezed up with mirth and the tears ran out of the corners.

'Poor Robert,' she gasped. 'Poor Robert. Oh, God.'

Amy's worried expression turned to a glimmering of a smile before she too, laughed.

'So you don't think it was too dreadful?'

Alice shook her head wordlessly. When she could speak again she said, 'Well, if he hadn't before, I'm sure he finally got the message about how you felt.'

'Yes, that's what it was, wasn't it. It's very difficult to get through to my father. He doesn't listen to other people, you know. I sometimes wonder if they exist for him in any real way. I expect Hester's told you that she's having trouble getting her share of the money from the proceeds of the sale. He says she can only have it if she comes to New York and that he needs it all just to stay there . . .'

Amy sipped the sherry, which she was not sure if she liked. On the other hand it seemed to be quite potent stuff since she was chattering away like a budgie on speed.

'To tell you the truth,' she continued. 'I don't think he really wants her in America anymore, though he did at first; it's just an excuse for keeping the money. He knows very well that their marriage's over and that she's absolutely set on living in Coombe Ferrers. I thought at one time she might want to live in Mexico, go back to her roots as it were. She went there for a working holiday once but when she came back she said that they might have been Inez's roots but they weren't hers. After all she did spend most of her childhood here, in Devon.'

'And what about you. Where do you want to live?'

'Oh, it's arranged that I shall stay with Gina in term time and I hope here during the holidays. At least for part of the time. If I get a job in Bristol I shall stay there, but there aren't many jobs around. Firms don't like employing students if they can help it because they leave when term starts. I'm just finding that out. It's a sod.'

'So it will be a whole new start for you. Are you looking forward to it?'

'Actually I am.' Amy toned down her exhilaration, her impatience to start the course, but the light in her eyes was not lost on Alice. 'You won't tell Hester what I did, will you?' Amy said seriously. 'She'd think it was incredibly juvenile and spiteful.'

Alice said, 'I can't believe that Robert won't have something to say about it to her. Unless that is, he thinks it too humiliating.'

Amy got up and started pacing about the room examining Alice's collection of sculpture and paintings.

'All the same, I shall miss my father,' she said, stopping in front of a watercolour by Paul. 'If only because I shan't have anyone to fight with.'

'I'm sure he'd like you to visit him in New York,' Alice said. 'He is your father after all.'

'Yes, I could do that, couldn't I?' Amy looked more closely at the watercolour. 'You still have Paul's paintings?'

'By all means. Whatever my feelings are for him now doesn't change the fact that, at his best, he was a very able artist.'

'Hm, he wasn't bad, was he. Not as good as you or Hester, though. No soul.'

It was to be a modest house-warming. Unlike Eustace, Hester had no desire to make grand gestures. As her new home it offered longed-for tranquillity, as a place of work it was everything she could hope for, but she had yet to discover if the work she produced would measure up to the promise of a new direction in her creative life. She had not put it to the test.

The final stage of the planning permission had come through at the end of June, the sale was completed and the builders had started on the last part of the conversion, the living quarters. It was only in the last few days that the workmen had moved out and that she had been able to move in. It was all new and untouched and she felt almost superstitiously jealous of everything that happened within its substantial walls; not least the party that would launch it as a home, as a studio and as the chrysalis that contained the beginnings of her new life.

She had not done any serious cooking for a very long time and she embarked on a day's baking with apprehension. Amy had some arrangements to complete with Gina and was travelling down later that afternoon; Alice, busy picking up the reins of business once again, was in the shop. She made the preparations for the party alone, which she thought was fitting.

The *pièce de résistance* was to be chicken in herbs and white sauce with mushrooms and asparagus, covered in a pastry crust, and to go with it she cut wands of carrots which she planned to simmer at the last minute in olive oil with a spoonful of orange juice and sugar. Then there would be local runner beans, helpfully uncomplicated to cook. For pudding she made a cheesecake which at least could be made early and left in the fridge; she picked over some raspberries to go with it. If she hadn't been so nervous of both her own rusty powers as a cook and of the new and untried oven she might have enjoyed herself a great deal more; but as the slate worktops began to fill with the results of her endeavours she experienced the first stirrings of a sense of achievement, as if she'd just completed a particularly successful piece of painting.

The materials that had been used in the new living quarters of the Cider Press were slate on the floors, worktops and the sills of the deep window embrasures, whitewash on the rough stone walls and wood (from renewable sources, Susan assured her) for the doors. Hester had been into the paddock and picked great bowers of leaves and berries which she stood in earthenware pots on the floor. She was hurriedly counting glasses when there was an impatient knock on the door; she went to answer it. Amy was looking round the paddock, an unwieldy bag slung over her shoulder.

'Someone tidied up out here then?' she said, grinning broadly.

'Just enough to allow the wild flowers equal chance with the dock and nettles,' Hester said. 'As you see we found an apple tree under the old man's beard.' She hugged Amy. 'Hallo, darling. Did you have a good journey? Come in and see it all in its finished state.'

Amy returned the hug. The ice was thawing slowly. She examined every part of the Cider Press with cries of 'wow' and 'shit' by which Hester gathered that she approved. Eventually she sat herself on a cushion in the window seat.

'You can see right along the coast from here, I'd no idea. I am going to be allowed to stay here out of term time, aren't I? I mean I would try not to get in your way and so on.'

Hester had been pouring them both a cup of tea. She looked at her daughter in dismay. 'Of course you can stay here. This is your home too. What an idiotic question.'

'Well, you know, I just wondered.'

'I'm appalled that you should doubt it.' She handed Amy her

tea. Amy drank some as fast as its heat allowed.

'Just lately we haven't been hitting it off too brilliantly, have we. By the way, I love those old rugs on this slate floor. They look much better here. I never really noticed them in the Clifton house.'

'These old rugs, as you call them, came from Turkestan and Morocco and are actually quite valuable.' Hester stood at the window gazing out, sipping her tea at intervals. 'We were both trying to survive in the best way we could, it doesn't always bring out our most attractive qualities, whatever they say. There's a lot I'm not proud of.'

'Me too,' Amy said quietly. They exchanged slight ironic smiles which seemed to be enough.

'So you think you'll like living here?' Hester said.

'I'll adore it. Shall I tell you something?'

Hester looked at her daughter questioningly.

'I never really liked the Bristol house. It was . . . well, it was empty. Like a great hollow shell.'

'Yes, I see what you mean. I think you're right. It was.'

Amy got up to fetch herself more tea. 'So, who's coming tonight?'

Hester went into the kitchen to check on the preparations.

'There's Alice, of course. And Bruno Davidson, you remember him?'

'Eustace's partner.' Amy sounded surprised.

'Eustace's ex-partner. He's setting up on his own all over again.'

'Good. I never liked Eustace much. He was a patronising old git.'

Hester smiled to herself. 'And a man called Ezra.'

'Is he someone important?'

'In a way. I met him here in Coombe Ferrers.'

'You're looking enigmatic. We're not by any chance talking stepfathers here, are we?'

'No, we are not,' Hester said, then she laughed. 'Look I think everything's ready here. I'm going to change. Then perhaps you'll light the candles.'

Half an hour later, Amy got busy with matches and the cell-like rooms glowed with light.

'It looks monastic and festive at the same time,' she said. 'Come to think of it, that's a good description of how you look too.'

Hester had on the same dark green dress she had worn at the Lombards' opening but instead of having her hair lose and untamed as on that occasion she had tied it back with a ribbon. On her finger the large silver ring remained but the silver wedding ring had gone, put away in a drawer, not to be resurrected. In her ears were earrings made for her by a jeweller friend in silver and malachite.

When he arrived, bringing Alice, Ezra crushed her to him and held her as if they had been apart for years.

'You look practically edible, my old mate,' he said. 'And like a giant refreshed.' His cherry-red shirt, which was inexpertly ironed though clean, was worn under a waistcoat of quilted velvet in some dark paisley design. He had made an effort; his beard was newly trimmed and he was even wearing a tie of sorts.

'This is Amy,' Hester said, hoping that Amy's first reaction would not be as condemnatory as hers had been.

Apparently not, for they shook hands amiably enough while Hester turned her attention to Alice. Alice gazed round her.

'I never in my life imagined the old place could look like this,' she said. 'It's absolutely magical.' She went to the window and looked out. Across the water the lights of Tidemouth were embedded like diamanté in the dark hill, itself set against the last soft flush of daylight.

Alice thrust a flat package into Hester's hands. 'I found the original amongst my old junk and I thought this was by far the best place for it,' she said.

It was a newly-framed blown up photograph of the Cider Press which must have been taken nearly a century before. In front of it was a cart overflowing with apples, a patient horse and a line-up of sturdy looking characters in shirt sleeves and braces, except for one who wore a coat and bowler hat.

'My great grandfather,' Alice explained.

'This is perfect. I love it.' Hester kissed her friend.

Later, when there was a calmer moment, she would give Alice the hand-made pottery bowl that she had ordered weeks before and which she had only recently had time to collect. It was to be not only a late birthday present but an expression of her feelings towards a friend who'd helped her at a dark time in her life.

The other guests were arriving and she and Amy became busy taking coats and offering drinks. Susan came in her Land Rover and Bruno turned up in a taxi, he was rather reserved and reflective at first but thawed out in the warmth of the welcome.

They all trooped up the outside staircase (which Hester had specifically asked not to be moved to the inside) and admired the new studio. She found herself shy and anxious, as if the slightest false response or grudging mood might in itself change the atmosphere that she felt so strongly; but she need not have worried, the sense of warmth and rightness stayed intact. Susan answered questions about the renovations, she had enjoyed this particular contract, it had been a labour of love, she said.

Downstairs the table was set in front of the window and lit with candles. The chicken pie was after all a great success – Amy having her own version of it with the asparagus and mushrooms only – the carrots gleamed in a mantle of caramelised orange sauce, a satisfactory colour contrast to the runner beans, Hester thought. Ezra, sitting next to her, tucked in with enthusiasm.

'You've been holding out on me. You didn't say you could cook.'

'I wasn't sure I could.'

'Are you absolutely certain you still want to turn down my offer?' he said quietly, below the level of the general conversation. 'Our joint talents would be something to be reckoned with.' He glanced round the spare furnishings of the room. 'This place is like a god-damned anchorite's cell . . . is that what you want?'

'If you insist on a religious label, I'd prefer to call it contemplative.'

'Same bloody thing . . .'

'And yes, it's what I want at the moment. What I need.'

'After the hurly-burly of life at the top, I suppose. That reminds me, how did the great opening go?'

'It went very well. I'm sure Eustace will make a lot of money in spite of how things are at the moment.'

'Was the sainted Robert there?'

'Naturally.'

'So it really is over?'

'It really is.'

'I don't want to lose touch,' he said dolefully.

Hester put a hand briefly on his. 'You've been a wonderful friend and a tremendous encouragement and you've made me laugh . . .'

'Is that all?' Miniature candles were reflected in his pupils and in hers too, she supposed. They held each other's gaze for a few seconds. She lowered her voice to a whisper. 'And a really wild lover.'

He laughed out loud and said, 'What more could you want?'

The others turned to them and smiled. Bruno, who hadn't laid eyes on Amy since she was a baby in a carry-cot, asked her how she would like her new home. 'It will seem somewhat spartan after what you're used to, won't it?' Hester had told her that he had been dark-haired in the early days. Now that he was completely white it was difficult to imagine.

'Of course I shan't be here all that much.' Amy felt that she had to impress on him that she was now grown up with her own life to lead. 'But yes, I think it's great. I don't like being cluttered up with possessions. I think the rich nations consume far too much anyway. I'm glad we sold most of our stuff.'

'You're right. We've all been far too greedy. I myself am coming to the conclusion that small is beautiful.'

'My mother says you're opening a new gallery of your own. Have you decided where it's going to be?'

'I'm afraid it will have to be in London but not Mayfair, you know.'

'Because of the rents?' Amy offered him more cheesecake but he shook his head, wiping the corner of his mouth delicately with his napkin. 'It was absolutely delicious but, no. As I was saying it's partly because of the rents but also because I hope to run an establishment with an un-Mayfairish atmosphere. The sort of gallery where your mother's new work would sit comfortably . . .'

Amy smiled. 'She hasn't done any yet.'

'But of course she will. And you will too, before long, I understand?'

'I don't know. Perhaps.'

Bruno turned to Ezra and asked him politely about his painting.

'I'm not in the swim, you know,' Ezra warned him. 'Unless it's against the tide.' He roared with laughter and lifted his glass.

'You'll be in good company then, Hester.'

'Not quite,' Ezra said, leaning back so that Amy could serve him with more cheesecake. 'I'm an old reactionary. I imagine Hester's reaching out for something quite different. Thank you, Amy. I can't resist it.' He took up his spoon.

'You could bring some of your work up for me to see.' Bruno suggested. He turned his glass so that the wine shot out sparks of candlelight.

'Kind of you to offer but I'm strictly a local bird. Not one of your high-flyers. Thanks all the same.'

Bruno smiled and shrugged. 'Let me know if you change your mind.'

There was a lull in the conversation and their eyes turned automatically towards the window. Down on the river the dark passing shape of a yacht coming up to its moorings under power sliced through the spangled reflections and scattered them. The faint hum of its engine cut out and the distant pipe of a curlew took over.

Hester got up to make coffee. Ezra made a move to clear the

plates but Alice forestalled him, pleased with her new-found mobility.

Bruno spoke quietly to Susan. 'I like the way you've done this place very much, Miss Orchard. It demonstrates a great sensitivity to materials. I think you should give me your telephone number? Hester may have told you that I'm opening a new gallery. Now, I believe I've found exactly the right premises. Perhaps you could come up and cast your expert eye over them?

'Of course. I'd love to.' Susan said.

The conversation became more general and Ezra murmured in Hester's ear, 'I think I shall have to move to Devon.'

'That would be a great mistake. Cornwall's your place. But I want you to promise that you'll stay here often.'

'You never did come to Rosepound, did you?'

'I will. I promise.'

Bruno and Susan left first. Susan offered him the novel experience of a lift in her Land Rover where they talked more about the proposed new gallery.

Alice and Ezra lingered. Hester made more coffee and placed a large and awkward parcel in Alice's lap.

'The bowl!' Alice cried when she'd torn off the wrappings. 'I never meant . . . it's absolutely magnificent.'

It was one o'clock before Alice and Ezra reluctantly left. In the lane the Deux Chevaux, true to form, refused to start. Amy and Hester, almost helpless with laughter, pushed until the slope took over, Ezra put it into gear and the engine coughed into life and its tail lights disappeared down the hill.

CHAPTER THIRTY-ONE

Very early in the morning she walked over the springy turf on top of the cliff. The summer sun had turned the grass to the colour of sage and the gorse to swarthy patches of dry scrub, though it was still dusted with bright, cadmium yellow. Beyond, the sea was the blue of Bristol glass, stunning and unexpected, and the red cliffs rolled back into the clear distance. Their tops were shades of blond and tawny, stands of trees on their flanks, soot black.

The walk had taken her as usual along the shore, passing the stacks, under the Belstead Arch and finally up the cliff path.

It was September and she was alone at the Cider Press; Amy had gone back to Gina's to get ready for the new start at the art college; Ezra had returned to Rosepound; Alice, since she was now able to pay April Moffat for help in the shop, was easing herself back into routine gradually; her mobility was very much improved but there was no doubt that the embolism had set her back. All the same she was enthusiastically planning a holiday in Egypt later on. They heard through the never-failing Coombe Ferrers' grapevine that Paul had left the town and, with relief, that Reg Gammon had switched allegiance and was presently laying seige to the woman who ran the Riverside Tea Rooms.

Hester had seen Robert just once since the Lombards' opening. His mother had died a fortnight ago and she had gone up to the funeral. It was, she realised, the third death that she had superstitiously feared. Not Alice but Katherine. Robert appeared to be more relaxed and they had even had short, not unfriendly, discussions about what was to be done about Charles. But Katherine had planned with her usual efficiency and there was nothing, at least immediately, for either of them to do. They had parted on reasonably amicable terms.

For the first time for what now seemed years, she felt herself free from both a perpetual sense of urgency and the vague dread of failure, of not being able to come up to expectations; and not least for not having in addition to bear this anxiety on Robert's behalf.

Her mind, her emotions and her perceptions were as clear and untrammelled as they were ever likely to be; she owed nothing to and need not satisfy any other criteria than her own, but over these last months she had reached the conclusion that these criteria were actually more stringent and precise than those of any dealer, critic or artistic guru. The one overwhelming virtue was that until her own expectations were met there was no compulsion to show her work. True, she still had the overdraft to pay off, since she had neither the time nor the emotional energy to fight Robert for her share of the proceeds from the sale of the house, but she couldn't and wouldn't worry about it. It was a small price to pay for a life she could now truly call her own.

She was starting again from the beginning with no money and indeed no work. The studio was neatly stacked with everything that was required to produce it, there were even some newly primed canvases laid out on the floor, their scale smaller and more intimate than anything she had done for Lombards. Though they were blank, the process of creation had already begun; in fact it had begun months ago.

She went through the iron gate now cleared of some of its brambles and up the outside staircase of the Cider Press, shutting the door behind her.

On the trestles were a number of oil sketches on paper and board, the work of several weeks. She set them out and looked through them, all at once aware of their affinity to cave paintings, which had been quite unconscious at the time she had done them. The colours were of red sandstone, tawny rocks and blood; the faded yellows of harvested fields; the olive greens, the metallic greys and cornflower blues of the sea in all its moods. The shapes were those of buried fossils, shells, lost babies, upheavals and erosions of rocks, the surge of tides. Not seen with a distant analytical eye but entered into, experienced from within.

She laid out her colours, and rejecting the tasteful greys and blacks and cautious reticence of her former imprisoned self, she requisitioned the entire spectrum, orchestrating it, making it her own.

She picked up a one-inch flat, its long flexible fibres having just the right amount of resistance, and began to paint.